JUST DEX

LES'S BAR
BOOK 1

JODI PAYNE
BA TORTUGA

This is a work of fiction. Names, characters, places, and incidents either are the product of the author's imagination or are used fictitiously. Any resemblance to actual events, locales, organizations, or persons, living or dead, is entirely coincidental and beyond the intent of either the author or the publisher.

Just Dex, Les's Bar Book One

Edited by LC Hinson

Cover illustration by AJ Corza
http://www.seeingstatic.com/
Cover content is for illustrative purposes only and any person depicted on the cover is a model.

ISBN: 978-1-951011-39-0

Published by Tygerseye Publishing, LLC, January, 2021
Printed in the USA

JUST DEX

Les's Bar, Book 1
By Jodi Payne & BA Tortuga

Dexter is rudderless and headed down a dark path. Cyrus knows the young man has great potential, but will Dex let him prove it before it's too late? Just Dex is an opposites attract, D/s romance featuring a young hobby baker and a Dom who's made his lifestyle his career.

When Dexter Appleton's best friend Huck commits suicide, it damn near kills Dex too. Huck was a bull rider with a crazy life, and leaves behind a big house, and a ton of unanswered questions. But Dex is just a simple guy, just a Texas redneck trying to scrape together a life, and he can't handle much more before he breaks.

Cyrus Hughes is a therapist whose patients have very particular needs. He's shocked to learn that Huck is gone after meeting with him twice a month for years, and he didn't expect to miss a client so much. When he heads to Texas to pay his respects, he instinctively feels protective of Huck's anxious and unlikely best friend, Dexter.

The attraction between them grows, even long distance, until Cyrus insists he needs Dex with him in New York. Clinging to his last bit of hope, Dex takes a leap of faith and moves what little he still owns in with Cyrus, hoping to find his place in the world.

Their path is full of trial and error, triumphs and misunderstandings. Cyrus and Dex will have to adjust their expectations to create a life together...one where Dex understands that he is not "just" anything.

LES'S BAR SERIES

Just Dex

Hide Bound

Wholly Trinity

New Tricks

Lost Boy

These are all stand-alone novels with some crossover characters.

To our wives.

1

Dex let himself into Huck's house, his hand shaking so bad that he missed the lock twice.

Twice.

Huh, you'd think he was a drunk on a three-day binge.

Maybe he would be soon. Who knew? Maybe he'd run away from Salado, drive down to Galveston, up to Beaver's Bend, away. Maybe he'd just go home and have a long nap. Maybe he'd head to Sixth Street and play with the college kids.

Maybe.

He could hear the alarm deal when he opened the door, distantly, and he wandered to the keypad, turned it off. Huck could do it from his phone—got a kick out of turning it on when he was house sitting, in fact.

Dex stood there in the foyer, the sun pouring into the house, lighting all the wood up, the dust making patterns in the air.

There was an alligator.

A tulip.

A longhorn.

A leaf.

A noose.

His knees buckled and he hit the floor, hands slapping down so hard it hurt.

Suddenly it was like he was Huck, hanging from his bullrope in a hotel bathroom, throat closed, body going heavy and swollen, nasty with gas and bacteria and flies and…

"No."

The scream that wanted out was just a tiny squeak, but it proved he was here. Here in Huck's house. Here, waiting for somebody—anybody—to tell him what the fuck to do.

His best friend in all the world—the face he'd known from the nursery at First Baptist, the first guy he'd ever kissed, the person who quit the baseball team when he got thrown out. Huck.

Huck was dead.

Jesus Christ, Huck McNamara was dead, and Dexter was…not.

Tuesdays were quiet enough that Cyrus could sit at the bar. He hauled himself through the front door out of the rain and stomped the water off his boots, shivering for a second as the air conditioning hit him. His iPad was stuffed under his jacket to stay dry and had been tucked against his side so hard he thought maybe he'd bruised something.

Ironic. He'd managed not to pick up any new bruises all day despite his client being particularly needy.

The bartender gave him a wave, and he waved back before hanging up his coat on the pegs by the door.

Tuesdays should be Greg behind the bar, but Greg

finally got cast in some new off-Broadway show Cyrus couldn't remember the name of and might be at rehearsal.

He set his iPad down on the bar at his usual spot with a good view of both the TV and the door.

"Mr. Hughes. Always good to see you." A mug of hot coffee landed on the bar along with a bowl of pretzels.

Not Greg. Good for him. "Oh, perfect. Thanks, Perry."

"It's a fresh pot. I'm mainlining it tonight. I pulled a double yesterday and picked up Greg's shift tonight. I'm toast." Perry leaned against the bar, blue eyes shining in the lights. Such a lovely young man.

"Well, I won't bother you much. I have a little work to do."

"Bother me when you're ready for a break. This place is dead with the weather." Perry winked at him.

"Okay." Sounded like Perry wanted some company. He'd just get the pressing stuff done, then he could chat awhile.

He took a sip of his coffee and hummed as the warmth chased the last of the damp summer rain away. Then opened up his iPad. His calendar was full. He'd had inquiries from two potential new clients, but fitting them in would be a challenge. He looked his week over and shook his head. The rest of this week was impossible but maybe—

Well, maybe next Thursday if Huck didn't answer his phone soon. Cyrus had been calling him since he no-showed last week. It was the first time in nearly two years that Huck had missed an appointment; the cowboy was as regular as the sunrise. Twice a month on a Thursday since the very first time they'd met. It was more than a little worrisome.

He pulled out his cell phone and found Huck's number, trying it one more time.

"McNamara's phone. What can I do you for?"

Damn, that was...odd. Now he was definitely worried. And curious.

Okay. Discretion. He found his professional voice. He'd done this lots of times. "Hello. I'm looking for Huck. Is he available?"

"Oh hell's bells, am I talking to his therapist? That's what comes up on the phone." So, another Texan—lover? Family?

Therapist was pretty common. He found the different ways people referred to him so interesting. "Yes, it's Cyrus Hughes. Who am I speaking with?"

"Dex. Dexter Appleton. I—" There was a shaky breath, a pause. "Damn, Sam. This never gets easier. Never. I'm sorry, buddy. Huck hung himself in Nashville. He's gone."

"He what?" *What?* He knew something was wrong, but he was thinking rodeo accident or that Huck was in a wreck. Cy covered his other ear and listened. "I—I'm...sorry for your loss." Hung himself. Cyrus would never have—he had no idea Huck was— "Shit."

"Yessir. The funeral's planned here for Monday. I mean, if you want to come out. You in Austin or Dallas?"

"New York," he said absently. "I'm in New York." *Huck. Why didn't you call me?*

"New—What? Did you say New York?" The shock on the other end of the line was...huge. Like he'd said he was from the moon.

"Where are you? What was he doing in Nashville? How could he have hung himself?" Right. He needed to stop talking before this Dexter guy hung up on him.

"I'm at Huck's house. We're outside Salado. He was at a bull riding, and he used his motherfucking bull rope." The guy's voice started to crack, and he heard Dexter take a deep breath. "Sorry. Sorry. You need to know where to send flowers?"

"I think—" *I think I need to be there.* "When... When did you say the service was? Is it in...you said Salado?"

Perry glanced at him and he shook his head sadly, which made Perry come over and give his shoulder a squeeze. That was kind, but he really had no idea what he was feeling right now. He was in shock, obviously, as Dexter probably was as well. It definitely felt like real grief though.

"Monday afternoon at one. No viewing. Broecker here in town. I'm burying him next to his momma. Hold up." There was a pause, and then, "Goddamn it, y'all! I am trying to deal with shit. Take that beer outside!"

He typed the date and time right into his calendar and the name of the town and the place into the notes. "Got it. I'm sorry, I won't keep you. My condolences, I'm really very sorry." He started to say that Huck was a good man, but what did he know really? He'd learned better than to assume. You'd think after all this time he'd know, but he didn't.

"Thank you. I'm sure he, uh, he...liked you?" A soft chuckle sounded. "I'm sorry. I don't know how that works—therapists."

"He did. He trusted me." In his world, that was the highest compliment Huck could have given him. "Thank you. Have a good night."

He hung up and set his phone carefully on the bar.

Perry looked at him seriously. "You okay, Cy?"

Cyrus shrugged reflexively. "I lost a...a client." It was really strange to think that a man with as much fight in him as Huck would hang himself. Sure, Huck was obviously frustrated, maybe angry, but suicidal? Wouldn't Cy have seen that?

Should he have?

"Shit. I'm sorry, man."

He tossed a twenty on bar and pushed off his stool. "I'm going to head home."

"I get it. Safe home, Cy."

He scooped up his iPad, tucked it under his arm and stepped out into the rain.

He was nearly home before he realized he'd forgotten his coat.

Fuck.

He'd go back for it tomorrow.

2

Dex stood next to the coffin. They'd had to put a tent up, because the rain was pouring down. He was guessing they were going to have to wait for the things to dry out a little before they put Huck in the ground, but one way or the other, it was done.

Everyone was heading to the Salado House to eat, thank God, and he was standing here like an idiot.

"You suck, man. I mean, I swear to God. You and me been together for damn near thirty years, and you don't leave a note? You don't call? You got everything in the whole damn world, and what? It wasn't enough? Fuck you and the horse you rode in on. I hope you regret it now. I so do." He looked at Huck's folks, took his hat off and nodded to them. "Mama M., Pops. I hope he finds you. Someone needs to beat his ass, pardon my French."

"I can promise you that wouldn't have stopped him."

A deep-voiced guy in a black raincoat stepped up next to him. Dark hair, dark expression. Nobody he recognized.

"Sorry. Sorry, mister. That was inappropriate." And he

thought he was alone, dammit. Now he had to figure out—funeral director, cowboy, reporter.

Man wasn't all in his face trying to move him on and that voice didn't drawl, so not funeral home. Wearing pussy shoes and no hat, so not cowboy. Must be a reporter, which meant he needed to just go.

The guy looked at him, eyes deep, dark pools. "Are you Mr. Appleton?"

"Yes, sir. I got no statement, though, except Huck was a good man and his family loved him." He'd said that over and over—to magazines and TV people, the rep from the rodeo, everyone.

Huck was a good man, and his family loved him.

"He told me he didn't have any family." The guy stuck out his hand. "I'm Cyrus Hughes. Huck's therapist. We spoke on the phone."

"I'm sorta family." Therapist. Great. And he was talking to the dead guy. They couldn't put you in the funny farm for that, right? Right. He took Mr. Hughes hand and shook. "It was awful nice of you to come."

"I'll miss him. I wanted to pay my respects, see where he was from. Get some context. You're a close friend, I guess?"

"Knew him since we were two years old." Close? No. How could he have been close and not see this coming? How could he not have known?

"I'm sorry but can I ask you a couple of questions? And then I'll leave you be, I promise. I just—" Mr. Hughes ran a hand through damp hair, looking uncomfortable. "Do you know if he left a note or talked to anyone before..."

"You don't?" Oh, that wasn't fair. "You mean you didn't know?"

"That Huck was suicidal? No. He didn't ever give me any—we didn't—" Mr. Hughes looked away, took a deep breath and puffed it out heavily. "I had no idea. I keep wondering if I should have."

"You motherfucker!" He turned to the coffin, blind with a rush of hurt and rage. "You had help? You had help, and you did this and didn't tell no one?"

He bellered with everything he had, one fist slamming into the casket.

Oh. Ow.

"Hey." Huck's therapist reached for his fist and held it between soft, warm hands, and the man's voice was gentle. "Sometimes help is just that. It's help. It doesn't fix the problem. Sometimes it can't."

Well shit.

Come on, Dex. Breathe. In and out.

"I guess me and Huck got some shit to work out." He tried to grin, tried not to just freak out, because God, he wanted to. He'd never been so alone and scared in his entire fucking life, and didn't that piss him off? He was deep in his thoughts when thunder clapped, and the wind went from blowing to I will skullfuck you with a 2x4. "You got questions you said? You want to come to the house? Storm's fixin' to let loose."

Because he had questions too.

Mr. Hughes dropped his hand and turned a collar up against the wind. "If you don't mind, that's kind of you. Do you need a ride? I have a rental."

"Yeah. Thanks. Folks picked me up at the house."

Old Nate and Scotty were waiting to take down the tent and all, and he waved to them.

"You need a ride home, Dex?"

"No, sir. I'm catching one with Mr. Hughes here. Y'all feel free to go eat with all them, iff'n you want."

"No. There's probably eighty folks at Huck's place, waiting on you."

Oh, for fuck's sake. "They'll just have to go."

They jogged through the rain to a gray sedan. Mr. Hughes ran around and opened the passenger door for him, closed it after him and then ran back and sank into the driver's seat. "All I do is get rained on anymore."

"I'm sorry. That sucks." Did it rain a lot in New York? He wouldn't have thought so, but he didn't know.

"Call me Cyrus, by the way. Mr. Hughes is way too formal." They stopped at the end of the driveway. "Which way?"

"North." He pointed the way. "We're about ten miles out." Huck's big old fancy custom house and his shipping container in the back past the barns.

Cyrus turned onto the road and started driving, and somehow he resisted reminding the man which one was the gas pedal. City drivers.

"So, you have a few guests at the house it sounds like."

"They won't go away. Every goddamn busybody in town wants to find some bit of gossip to share."

"I'm a New Yorker. I can give them lots to talk about." Cyrus's laugh was rich and easy. Genuine. "I can also... encourage them to go home. I've got nothing to lose. Just say the word."

"God, that would be nice. I've been—" What? Tired? Down? Worried? Overwhelmed? Scared? "—busy."

Damn busy.

"Watch me." It was quiet in the car for a bit except for the rhythm of the wipers and the swoosh of the water under the tires. Silence like that could be awkward, but for some reason it wasn't. Cyrus was just a calm, solid presence behind the wheel.

He started feeling heavy, the stress of the last few days pulling him down into sleep. He blinked, the motion getting longer and slower.

When he opened his eyes again, they were still driving, but the rain had let up. Cyrus had the radio on quietly and was sipping a Coke from a McDonald's cup.

"Oh Jesus. What did I do? Fuck, man, I swear to God, I'm not usually so rude." He'd fallen asleep. What the fuck?

"No worries, you were out, and I didn't know where I was going so I just kept driving. I got you some fries, they're in the cupholder." Cyrus switched the cup to the other hand and turned up the radio. "I got as far as Waco, then I turned around and headed back."

Cyrus wasn't making fun of him or anything. Just 'eh, drove forty-five minutes to Waco and got lunch, want some fries?' Like this was totally normal.

"I found this great satellite station that's all George Strait, which is pretty much all the country music I know. Are you feeling better?"

"I'm feeling like a shitheel for putting you in a weird-assed position. You're a good guy. Thank you." For fuck's sake. Seriously? Fall asleep in a car of a man you don't know? You must have scared this poor man to death.

"You're welcome. But please don't feel badly. It's not weird. Grief is exhausting. I have nothing to do until my flight home the day after tomorrow. I wanted to see a little of where Huck lived, and this counts."

"It does. Now I'll show you Huck's house. It's nice. Huck worked hard on it." He actually stole one of the fries. He was empty as a worm.

"I'm looking forward to that." Cyrus lifted the container of fries out of the cupholder and handed it to him. "Hopefully your visitors have given up on you and gone home."

"Hopefully folks aren't stealing everything in the whole damn house." That was possible, but unlikely. There were enough of the good old cowboys there to watch. Damn. He should turn on the alarm deal and scare them all.

"Such a strange custom that people just show up and let themselves in without you being there. That wouldn't happen in New York. We don't trust anybody." Cyrus laughed.

"No? Everybody knows Huck. Knew. You know what I mean." He looked at the guy, who was surprisingly pretty for a man that was so studly. "Did Huck go to New York a lot?"

"I really don't know. I saw him twice a month, typically on Thursdays. How long he stayed in the city or if he was there other times… I have no idea. I only know what he told me."

"Twice a month is a lot." He'd never gone anywhere—Austin sure, Dallas. He'd driven to the beach twice, but just to go to New York like it was nothing? No.

"Then I guess I saw him a lot." Cyrus shrugged. "This is starting to look familiar. Are we close?"

"Observant. We're going to take the next get-off and make the second left. Huck's ranch is a few miles down."

"The next get-off." Cyrus smiled. "So, tell me something about growing up with Huck."

"He loved baseball. He wanted to be a pitcher, but he couldn't throw worth a shit." Dex grinned and shook his head. "When we were in high school, I got kicked off the team, and he told the coach off and quit."

Cyrus looked over at him. "That sounds like the man I knew. Loyal."

"Yes. Turn here. He was a good man. He never once said he wanted to die."

"No. He didn't. Every time I saw him it was almost exactly the same as the time before. Minor things would vary, sometimes he'd want to talk more than others, but he never let on. I've been over it a hundred times. I've looked at my notes. I've thought about the things that seemed to work and the things that didn't...if it was there it wasn't in any recognizable way."

Dammit.

"There's the house." It was pretty—rose granite with a huge porch that wrapped all the way around. There were still four or five trucks there, including his. It wasn't too bad.

"I like it." Cyrus pulled in and parked next to the line of trucks. "So, it's yours now?"

"I guess. That's what the will says. My house is back there." He pointed to the bright yellow metal container by the barns.

"That's...a shipping container."

"Yeah. Cool, huh? Huck let me use the land since I dealt with the critters." It was more than a fair deal.

"Do you have electricity and water and everything in there? Is there a bathroom?" Cyrus seemed as interested in his crate as in the house.

"I do. I have electricity run in, and I'm on the septic and I have my own water meter." It was simple and open, but his.

Cyrus climbed out of the car. "That's pretty cool. I've never seen that before. Good color too. Can you see it from space?"

"It's possible." He chuckled softly, tickled as all get out. "If I ever meet an astronaut, I'll make sure to ask. Come on in. I'll get you a cup of coffee and something to eat while I see what's what."

He needed to feed. He needed to see who all was still here. He needed a beer.

"Sounds good to me." Cyrus followed him to the house, and the front door opened wide before they even got there.

"Dex! You okay, man? Where have you been? All the church ladies were worried about you." Hoover Vance stood there, the bullfighter three sheets to the wind.

"I was taking care of some stuff, honey. You okay?"

"That's what you do, huh?" Hoover's man, Chris, popped up under Hoover's arm. "I'm driving. Don't worry. Who's this?"

"Friend of Huck's from out of town." No one needed to know a damn thing more. "Y'all heading out?"

"If you don't need us no more," Chris said. "I'd like to get him home."

"You need some help getting him in your truck?" Cyrus offered easily.

"Nah. He's a sweet drunk. He takes it hard when he loses one of his own. Thanks, though. See you, Dex. You call if you need us."

Like he would do that. He was going to call this biggie-wow bullfighter. Shit. "Thanks, buddy. Y'all take care."

"I'm very sorry for your loss." Cyrus watched them go. "Sounds like this happens too often."

"Yeah. It's not a friendly sport, huh? I guess you know all about that." He couldn't imagine what all Huck had told him.

Cyrus just shook his head and followed him into the house. "Oh, wow. It's nice in here. Who are the rest of these guys? More bull riders?"

He looked and sighed. “One ex, one former English teacher, and the sheriff.”

Goodie. That meant that Paul the Prick had caused trouble, and Mrs. Feezel’d called Big Jim.

“Your ex or his?” Cyrus sounded amused.

“His. Let me take care of this.” He took a deep breath and waded in. “Mrs. Feezel, ma’am. Thank you for coming.”

“Of course, son. We found this young man up in Huck’s bedroom. The sheriff would like to know if you want to file obscenity charges.”

“Ob—Are you fucking kidding me? What the actual fuck?” Dex did not need this shit right now.

“When was the last time you talked to him, Paul?”

He looked at Cyrus, who’d just waded into a pile of shit. He hoped the guy had his boots on.

“Who the fuck are you?” Paul snapped, and the response from Mrs. Feezel, Big Jim, and Dex was swift and immediate.

“Watch your mouth!”

Cyrus watched Paul so calmly, head tilting like he was studying the asshole. Cyrus didn’t even raise his voice. “Did he tell you he was going to do this? Did you know?”

Everything in Dex went white-hot and icy cold all at once. Oh Jesus. If Paul knew and didn’t say, didn’t get Huck help? He would take the bastard out back and beat him to death, swear to God. His hands curled into fists, and he could hear his knuckles creak.

Mrs. Feezel reached out and took his arm, her fingers cool against him, steadying him like she had when he was a kid, the woman a rock.

“Fuck no! It’s a lie. There’s no way he killed himself.”

Dex only wished. He’d seen the body. He’d read the

police report, the ME's report. Huck hung himself in the fucking bathroom. Lying didn't fix it.

"We didn't see it coming either. But he did, Paul. Every report that exists says so. We all miss him. What were you doing in his room?"

Paul rolled his shoulders like maybe it would be easier to hit Cyrus than answer that question, and Cyrus reached out and put a hand on Paul's arm. "You don't have to answer that. Not with all these people around. Let me walk you to your truck. I have something to tell you."

Paul let Cyrus just walk him out, and Dex stood there, afraid to even move.

"Dexter? Dexter, son? What do you need?"

Huck to be okay.

That was what he wanted to say, but that was mean. He was stupid, not real ambitious, and a bit of a turd, but he wasn't mean, so he didn't.

"Thank y'all for coming. Seriously. I think I'm just going to sit with myself a second."

Please go away.

Mrs. Feezel was cleaning up the kitchen, and Big Jim was finishing a cup of coffee when Cyrus finally came back inside.

"You don't have a black eye." Jim laughed into his cup.

Cyrus shrugged. "He's fine, Sheriff. He's headed home. You should too, it's been a long day." Cyrus walked past Dex toward the kitchen, patting his shoulder on the way by. "He won't be back."

"Thank you, sir." He shook his head, trying to make himself move, do something. Anything.

Mrs. Feezel kissed his cheek. "Call me, son, if you need to talk. Jim's going to follow me home."

"Yes, ma'am."

"Safe home." Cyrus got the door for her and closed it after Big Jim. The house was finally quiet. "Well, that was interesting. You look like you need to sit down, Dex."

"Sorry for all that." He couldn't move. If he moved, he would start screaming. If he started screaming, he might cry. He'd already done that. "You want a beer?"

Cyrus put an arm around his shoulders. "No, thank you. Do you? I'll get you one. How about we go sit? There's a lot of food too. You said you were hungry." Cyrus put a little pressure on his shoulders, making him lean enough he really had no choice but to move his feet.

"Did I?" He didn't remember being hungry, but that didn't mean shit.

"You inhaled the rest of my fries. I don't think you even chewed them. Comfortable?" Okay, Cyrus had him on the couch. Good. And he didn't even scream. "You want to lie down?"

"No thank you." Dex swallowed hard, opening his fists, not at all surprised to see the blood-filled crescents in his palms. "Sorry about all this. You must think we're a band of fools."

"What makes you say that?" Cyrus hopped up and grabbed a damp dishtowel, a long stride bringing Cyrus back quickly. "Here."

"Thanks." The towel was cold and felt good. "Please, have a seat. Relax. This is Huck's place."

It was sort of a shrine to bull riding—the art, photography, geegaws, they were all about rodeoing. Everything not wood was leather, and everything was classy.

"Grief is a strange thing. Nobody knows how to behave, how to feel. You, me, all those cowboys. Even Paul. None of it is wrong."

Dex nodded like he understood, and he guessed he did,

he just didn't care. He wanted normal back. He wanted to sleep in his little bed, check his email to see if someone needed him to work, see if he'd sold any cookies, drink a beer, jack off, and rest.

Cyrus sat beside him. "Huck had good taste, didn't he? The house seems well thought out. What would you be doing right now if Huck were here?"

"Whatever Huck needed, I guess. If he didn't want something, I'd be sitting and watching the rain. That or fishing."

"What did you do when Huck wasn't around?"

"If someone needed me, I'd work. If not, I'd be sitting and watching the rain." He grinned at himself. He was the boring redneck riding the coattails of his best buddy.

His grin faded. What if he was part of what was wrong with Huck? What if Huck wanted him gone and couldn't just say? What if Huck hated the yellow building? *Jesus fuck.*

Maybe if he started drinking now and just kept on, he'd stop asking questions.

"That simple." Cyrus put a hand on his knee. "He took care of you, leaving you the house. He loved you."

You don't do this to someone you love. Hell, you didn't do it to someone you liked. He didn't say it though, because again, meanness. This guy wanted to make it better, and he couldn't. Dex didn't even know how to start getting better.

Cyrus just sat quietly with him, the two of them watching the rain together for a long while. The sky was getting dark when Cyrus finally spoke. "I think I'll dig in the fridge and find us some dinner." It wasn't until then he realized they hadn't just been sitting there. Cyrus had an arm around him, and he was leaning hard.

Oh God. What was wrong with him? What the fuck was

he doing? "Let me fix you something. There's lots of dishes. You said you had questions?"

He was a worthless son of a bitch today. Damn.

"Not as many now." Cyrus lifted his arm away without a word about it. "Let's go find some food."

"Yeah." The kitchen was this huge thing. He used it a lot, for his cookies, but now the counters were filled with casserole dishes, buckets of fried chicken, and dishes.

"I guess you're not going to go hungry for a while." Cyrus lifted a piece of chicken right out of a bucket and took a bite, chewing while he spoke. "You want to wrap some of this up and freeze it or something?"

He looked around and all the food, all the shit, and he knew he wouldn't eat it. "I think I'll put it in the fridge and tomorrow run out to the Walmart. I'll get me some disposable pans and fix up a bunch of dinners. God knows there's folks that need it more than me." That way he could wash the dishes and deliver them back.

"Sounds great. Can I help?" Cyrus moved on from the chicken and dropped a scoop of one of the casseroles onto a paper plate. The man could eat.

"Sure. Fill yourself up first, though. This is the best folks can do. You'll not find better. What do you drink? I got tea, Red Bull, Shiner, Coors Light, orange juice, and cranberry juice." He wandered toward the fridge. He knew where everything was. He did Huck's shopping.

"Iced tea sounds good. Thanks. You need to eat too. I don't know what this casserole is, but it's really good. Sorry if I'm a little bit of a pig. I have a crazy metabolism, and I get low sugars sometimes. I need to eat."

"Have all you want. That's what it's here for." He got a glass, ice, the tea. "If you need sugar, there's Sweet N Low on the counter."

"Sweet'N Low isn't sugar. But I like my tea straight up." Cyrus was on to something else now. Looked like meatballs maybe. "Dex. Look at me."

He glanced up as he was told, and into those strangely deep, dark eyes.

"Eat something." Cyrus didn't even twitch after giving the order.

I don't remember how. He looked away from Cyrus, glanced over the vast amount of food that was here, and, for a second, things looked like they were breathing. Just eat a bite of something, and he'll stop worrying. He reached out, hand landing on a kolache. He grabbed it, nibbling on the edge of the pastry. "You want one?"

"Dex." Cyrus put down his plate and went to him, taking him by the shoulders, sitting him at the kitchen table. "When did you sleep last? And I don't mean in the car today."

"Wednesday. He died Monday. They found him Wednesday. The league called Wednesday."

"Okay." Cyrus crouched down in front of him, which was great, so much easier than trying to look way up there. "And where do you sleep best? Your bed? Huck's?"

"Home." But he had so much to do. So much. "Feels like forever since I walked back there."

"I want to see it. Will you show me?" Cyrus offered him a hand and pulled him up out of the chair.

"Sure. Sure. I got to make sure someone fed for me. Huck likes it when they're on a schedule. You want you an umbrella?"

Cyrus shook his head. "I can pull my raincoat back on. It has a hood. Thanks. I'll follow you."

They headed out into one hellacious storm, and by the

time he reached his house, he was soaked to the bone and breathless from trying to keep his feet. He'd grabbed Cyrus, determined to make sure the man didn't fall.

He got the door open, shoved Cyrus in, and ran to get them towels, doing fine until he slipped and skidded across the concrete floor, slamming into the kitchen island.

"Whoa." Cyrus was right there, catching him this time. "Are you okay?"

"Yeah. Please. Come sit. This storm. It's like the whole of Texas is crying for him. I'll get you a towel and some coffee." Dex felt like he was talking through oatmeal. "I love your coat. I'd look like a fool in it, but you look good."

Towels. Towels and coffee.

"Thank you. It's soaked. I haven't been out in a storm like that in a long time." Cyrus took it off and hung it by the door. "It's wild out there."

"It's crazy." He found the towels and handed them over, then stripped off his shirt, goosebumps popping up all over. "You dry or do you need a robe?"

"Top is dry, bottoms...are not. And forget the shoes, I might just be trashing those." Cyrus chuckled and slid out of his dress pants, the long tails of a button-down shirt just barely covering the waistband of blue plaid boxers.

"Hrm. Okay. You're built like a brick shithouse, but I got a pair of sweats somewhere, maybe..." There was no fucking way. A blanket. That will help. "Right. That's a fab idea. Here's my blanket, wrap up."

"Don't like my boxers? Keep your blanket. I'll just use the towel." Cyrus wrapped a dry one around his waist and used the other to dry off his short, dark hair. It looked even darker when it was wet.

"They're plaid. That's cool. Mine aren't. You're not cold?"

Dex was cold, so cold his nuts ached because wet jeans were evil. "Coffee?"

"Water will be fine. It's eighty degrees out, Dex." Cyrus reached out and pressed a hand to his forehead.

"Is it?" He blinked, because no one had done that to him since his momma died.

"Get out of those wet jeans, please." Cyrus stepped past him and after a couple of tries, found a glass and filled it with cold water. "And then into bed. Do you have any Tylenol?"

"I guess so. Yeah. I sleep here on the futon and—" Thunder clapped, and the lights went out with a click. "Seriously?"

He started laughing, because he was wet with a half-naked therapist that was weirdly lovely, and God hated him.

There was a long pause and finally Cyrus turned on the flashlight on his phone, dimly lighting up most of the crate. "It's dark in here without windows."

"Yes. Hold up." *You have to start coping, man. You have to. They'll take you away if you don't.* The thought sobered him, like ice water in his veins. He found the blackout curtains and eased them open to expose a tiny window. The sky was dark as all get out, but there was some light there, and that let him light a candle or two. "Okay, that's better. I'll call the co-op and find out how big this is. Come have a sit. You're safer here until the storm passes. I'll get you a bottle of water real quick." He eased over to the fridge, grabbed a bottle for Cyrus and took the glass for himself. "What a great story you are going to take home with you."

"Take the Tylenol and get in bed, Dex. You're not well. You're exhausted. I don't know how you're even on your feet right now. I'd like the story I take home to be about the lights going out, not about you ending up in the ER."

Damn. Cyrus really sounded worried.

"I had to put Huck to rest, you know? He was my friend and…" He sat on his futon. "I worry that he's floating around lost and scared. Do you believe he'll be at peace?"

Cyrus's face was in shadow, but his tone was clear enough. "Dex, Huck is dead. You don't have to worry about him. He's not in pain anymore. Wherever he is now has got to be better than the hell he lived in here."

It wasn't hell. This place wasn't hell. Huck had built this house just like he wanted. Huck had done everything he wanted. Huck had traveled and ridden, had been a hero and famous, and any time he wanted to come home, Dex had been here, making it decent.

But Cyrus was the therapist and maybe he knew secrets Dex didn't. Maybe Huck had been in hell, and Dex was just too damned stupid to know.

"I hope he's happy." And that was a bit of a lie, but that could be between him and God because God would forgive him where no one else would.

"I hope he understands what he's done to you."

"He doesn't." Dex knew that, but what did it matter? It didn't. He was going to have to figure things out, deal with a thousand stupid details, but…not today.

He grabbed his blanket and wrapped it around him, staring at Cyrus. What was he supposed to ask now? His small talk gene was tired, melted, shattered. Did genes shatter? Split? *Christ.*

Ask the man something.

"Lie down, Dex. You're running on empty." Cyrus put a hand on his shoulder and tipped him right over.

"I want to go home." He knew when he said it that it made no sense, but it didn't matter. It was true. Everything was wrong. Everything.

"For now, just go to sleep." Cyrus rubbed his back, a large, warm hand moving in wide, slow circles.

"Don't drive in this storm. It's..." He yawned, his eyes refusing to open.

He wasn't sure whether the 'bad' came out.

3

Cyrus sat on the end of the futon watching Dex sleep, mostly because he didn't have anything better to do.

He was trapped in this industrial container surrounded by mud in the middle of nowhere Texas in the pouring rain without electricity. Cell service was nearly hopeless, his laptop was in the car, he'd already played two hours of poker against the stupid robot in his phone, and he'd done two full crossword puzzles.

It took a great deal to try his patience; Cyrus had a lot of it. But even he was starting to crack a little around the edges.

He'd tried to sleep, but it just didn't happen. He found another bottle of water and drank it, he found peanut butter and jelly and made himself a sandwich. He'd done pushups and crunches.

The one good thing he had going was that Dexter was sleeping hard. He hoped the guy slept a long, long time so when Dex woke up they might be able to have a rational conversation. As it was, Dex was one second shy of hysterical and probably dehydrated enough to consider medical attention.

He wouldn't be here except he felt so damn guilty, and he needed answers to put that feeling to bed.

If he was honest, he knew this trip was self-indulgent and stupid. Even if he'd seen that Huck was capable of something like this, what the hell could he have done about it? He wasn't equipped for that; Huck never gave him names or an emergency contact or anything. It might have been worse if he had known because he would have felt completely hamstrung, incapable of helping.

Okay. Yeah. He was getting near the end of his rope now.

God, he wanted a beer. Just one. Dex had one in the fridge, he'd seen it. No one would ever know, right?

Except him. He'd know. He pulled out his phone and hunted around for a signal finding a weak one near that silly, tiny window. He fired off a text to Les. Now Les would know.

CYRUS

tell me not to have a beer

It took a while, but he got a response.

LES

Don't have a beer, asshole. In two weeks it'll be four years.

Right. Good old coping skills. Now someone knew. Didn't stop him from wanting that beer though.

Cyrus looked back at the dark lump on the futon, wondering how long Huck had been dicking the guy around. Dex was a sweetheart. Strange, but a sweetheart. And Huck...wasn't.

There was nothing about Huck that suggested that he would have a little wild guy in the back of his property. Not a thing. But then how well did he know Huck, really? All he really knew was that Huck needed to be put in his place every two weeks and had paid him well to do it.

Mostly it was just the rodeo and whatever buckle Huck had recently won or lost that came up. This house never came up. Dexter's name never came up.

It didn't surprise him. Often the services he provided didn't involve the partner at home at all.

The lights flickered on for a second, and Dexter sat up, eyes wide, staring at him with the panic that came from living in a state of constant stress. "Fuck. Hey. Still raining?"

"Yep. Go back to sleep, Dex. Everything is fine." *As long as this crate doesn't decide to sink in the mud.*

"Don't worry. She's stood during the flood a few years ago and through three tornados. She's solid. The noise is wild though, huh? The first storm I sat here sure that it was going to come apart. Took everything I had to stay."

That's what was making him itchy, the noise! Hours of it, and he hadn't figured that out for himself. But how did Dex know he was— "What makes you think I was worried?"

"Want lines. You got them deep. Maybe we ought to run back to the main house. At least there's chicken and the pool table."

The want lines were probably not about the crate, but Dex wasn't wrong about him. He wouldn't argue with chicken and a pool table. "How do you feel? Are you still cold?"

"No. Not like I was. Let me grab a pair of sweats and socks. I know Huck had Peter's spare stuff, and it would fit you." Dex stood up, a skinny man with huge hazel eyes, sharp cheekbones, and this frenetic energy. "Lord, this storm would make Huck happy, wouldn't it?"

"I think it probably would." He didn't know, but Huck had seemed to be attracted to power, and there wasn't much that was more powerful than thunder. "Who's Peter?"

"Three lovers back? Four? Big old boy. Trucker. It was a crazy ride—he just got into the semi with Peter and rode. I had to wire him money to fly home." Dex stopped for a second, before shooting him a wicked smile. "I told him, after Peter and Paul, he ought to find him a boy named Mary."

"Or Dexter, if he wanted a musician." Cyrus pointed to a mandolin hanging over the futon. He hadn't noticed it before the lights went out.

"Ha! Me and Huck tried once when we were teenagers, but we weren't lovers."

That was interesting. He'd assumed they were. Dex certainly made it sound like love. But if it wasn't then... "Sorry. But the way you talk about him I thought—well, I misunderstood."

"He and I have been friends since we were babies. Is it weird, that we're both gay? Maybe." Dex sighed. "It doesn't matter one way or the other. You want to risk the run to the main house?"

"Let me get dressed." He dropped the towel he was still wearing on the futon and reached for his still-damp trousers. "I didn't mean to be disrespectful, Dexter. I'm sorry. I know a lot less about him than you'd think. Less than I should."

"No worries. I never would have thought that I didn't know him too, and you have way less time in."

Cyrus pulled on the pants and his damp shoes. "We should probably put all that food away. Maybe I can throw my stuff in the dryer."

"Yessir, sounds like a plan. So, is it like the TV, where you live?" Dex pulled out a pair of sweats and a shirt and rolled them up in a ball and then shoved them and a pair of ancient flip flops in a bag.

"New York? I suppose some of it is. Times Square and Broadway, the view from the top of the Empire State Building, those things are iconic. I don't really live a TV life though. Most people don't. I've got a decent apartment and a neighborhood bar I like to hang out in, friends, work. It's just normal stuff."

"Cool. This isn't like Texas on TV, so I wondered." Dex went to the door and sighed. "Good thing I'm not made of sugar. You ready?"

"Sure." Sure. It was dark and pouring rain and he couldn't see a damn thing, but sure. He was ready.

To go back to New York.

"Go for it."

"Right on." Dex rolled his eyes and headed out into the rain, soaked immediately. Another flash of lightning cracked, so close Cyrus could smell the ozone, and a wild hooting laugh sounded, sudden and sharp on the air. "I hear you, you fucking asshole."

Cyrus wondered what exactly Huck was trying to say.

He caught Dex's shoulder as his shoe got stuck in mud, but he managed to rescue it. His coat, which was already damp from the last slog through the rain, was basically useless by the time they made it to the house, and he was soaked to the skin.

"Lord have mercy. Come on, honey. Let's get this taken care of." The little nap seemed to have perked Dex up, and suddenly Cyrus had towels, sweats, a t-shirt, socks. "Now, tea, right? I'll let you make your plate before I put the food up. Leave your clothes there, and I'll see what I can do."

Sleep deprivation was a real thing. If he'd ever doubted that, Dex was proof.

Respecting Dex's earlier call for modesty, he stepped into the powder room to change. He took off everything, including his boxers that were now soaked through, and pulled on the dry clothing. He'd just go commando under the sweats. No problem.

He toweled off his hair and combed it through with his fingers, then gathered up all his wet stuff in the towel and left it where Dex had told him to.

"Ah. Dry is good." He took the plate that Dex handed him and went grazing, filling it up with things he knew he'd never get like this in New York. Maybe not so good for his waistline, but oh, so good for his soul.

Dex disappeared for a few minutes before popping back in. "Do you need it warmed up? Are you a table person or a sit with the TV on person? Either way, I can set you up."

"I can put it in the microwave. Thanks. And I'll sit wherever is easiest, how about you?"

"This table is nice. It was my mom's." Dex cleared him a spot. "Do you like music?"

"I do, and I have broad taste, so pick whatever you like."

He was determined to figure this guy out, and a man's choice of music was telling. A lot about what Dex was doing at the moment was telling and seemed like more than just being a good host.

"Rock on." Dex went to his phone, and suddenly the sounds of bluegrass filled the air. Dex turned it down to a level where talking would be easy and started puttering around the kitchen, cleaning and sorting food.

"Oh, good choice. Aren't you going to join me and eat something? I feel like a glutton. Come sit and tell me about this table. And then I'll help you with the food."

"Sure. Uh..." Dex looked at the smorgasbord. "God, there's too much to choose from."

"Right? The casserole in the blue Tupperware is spicy and yummy, um..." He looked over the counters from his seat. "Oh. The mac and cheese... Oh my god." Really, he was going to gain five pounds just looking at it all.

Dex began to chuckle, the sound bubbling out of him, making Cyrus smile. That was a joyous noise.

He laughed for a second, but then started to wonder if there was a story behind the mac and cheese he ought to know. "Wait. Did someone spit in it?"

"What? God no. No. I swear to God. Oh you looked like you were fixin' to co—Uh. Get happy. Oh fuck. Never mind." Dex turned as red as an apple.

He laughed softly. "I'm gay, and I'm from New York, Dex. You can say 'come' around me. Try some and join me." He took another bite. It was better than his mother's. Damn.

"I can do that." Dex grinned, so sheepish. "I try to be good, you know." Dex grabbed a spoonful of mac and cheese and a roll and came to sit.

"I'm sure you're a very good boy." He blinked. *Whoops.*

Dex chuckled softly. "Okay, *Huck.*"

Well, that was interesting. "Huck, huh?"

"He used to say that to me. It just reminded me of him, is all. It was a good memory." Dex shrugged and grinned, the look sad and fond and warm, all at once. "So, how did y'all meet? He never ever said he was going to New York City."

The answer to that question was simple but the implications were complicated. The issue was how much he should say about the private life of a man who was now gone. How much did Huck's people have the right to know? How much did Dex have a right to know, if Huck hadn't shared anything at all before his death?

If Huck hadn't told Dex he was going to New York at all, then Dex certainly had no idea what Huck was seeing him for. Would Dex judge? What possible good would it do to reveal what Huck had obviously kept secret for a reason?

"He was referred to me by a therapist friend of mine in Denver. I'm...a specialist."

A full half of his clients were referred to him by therapists who knew him personally or had patients who could vouch for him. He didn't have a medical degree, but he had legitimate success stories, and a spotless reputation in his field.

"So you knew he was sick? I feel like shit, thinking he didn't think he could tell me. I'm not all 'depressed people suck' or anything."

"He wasn't depressed that I could tell." The man had specific needs; that didn't make him sick. The fact that he had other issues...well, that was between Huck and his therapist, assuming he'd been seeing one. He didn't consider that his business.

"Oh." Dex obviously didn't know what to say, and the silence set between them, heavy like a blanket of snow.

"I know. It's difficult for me to know what to say. Out of respect for his privacy, I don't think I ought to give you details. I'm sorry." He wasn't bound by any kind of confidentiality, but he felt like Huck had rights, even still.

"Of course not. That's creepy, and you could get in trouble. I was just...well, no one expected it, but... I guess it doesn't matter, does it? All sorts of shit happens, and you just do your best to clean up the mess after." Dex pushed the mac and cheese around the plate, and his lips trembled, but only for a second. Then they firmed, turning into a wry smile.

Cyrus watched Dex and gave the guy a minute to breathe, then he reached over and rested his fingers on the back of Dex's hand. "How can I help?"

"Oh honey, you are dear." Dex moved his thumb, to press his fingers in a strange motion that felt like a hug. "I haven't even figured out how to help myself yet, much less ask it from someone else. You got to be hurting too, I know, or you wouldn't have come all the way out here."

In truth, Cyrus was here because he didn't know how he felt, how he was supposed to feel. "I don't know. I'm shocked. I feel like I should have known, like I let him down."

He was going to miss their sessions too. He'd be lying if he didn't admit that he enjoyed them, that there was a part of him that needed what Huck gave him. Maybe that was true with all of his clients, but Huck's truth was raw and dangerous and beautiful.

"Me too. I thought they were lying, playing a sick joke. I yelled."

"I knew when he missed our session last week that something was wrong. He hasn't missed one in nearly two years. I called and he didn't answer, which was normal, he often didn't want to in company. But he would text back, always. I knew. And then you answered his phone..."

Huck was a client. He'd paid his respects; it was time to go home and get back to his own life. "I've never lost a client before like this. I'm not sure how to put it in perspective."

"I can tell you that it gets better. I've dealt with it some. The hurt—confusion for you, maybe—it sorta backs away. I don't think brains can hurt forever. Eventually they just start looking for something else, you know?"

"Self-preservation." It was ironic, how close Dex was to understanding Huck's needs. To let go, to get out of his head, to think about something—someone else. "Thank you. I know it will get better, but it's good to hear."

"You're welcome." Dex smiled at him—not in his

direction, but at him, seeing him, eyes clear and focused. "I'm glad to have met you. I mean, even with the craziness, the storm, all the shit. I'm glad that I got to meet someone so important to him. That's a blessing."

He returned the smile. "I feel the same way, Dexter. And I'm going to have a good story to tell my friends up north, right? Plus...this mac and cheese...my god." He laughed and took another bite.

"There you go. Good food, crazy rednecks, and wild storms. Sounds like Texas to me."

"I'm not sure I understood what you do for work. You were a little wonky earlier. I know you said that you took care of this place for Huck...and did you say day work?"

"I take care of the place for Huck, I play down in Austin when they need me, I paint houses, make a lot of cookies. Whatever people need, that's what I do, and sometimes I get paid for it."

"You play mandolin, right? I saw it hanging on your wall. That's cool. Blues I guess?" And cookies? *What*? There really was no straight line to an answer with Dex, was there?

"Blues, country, bluegrass—I'm easy. I just like to play and watch the people dance. It's like being hypnotized. You ever been hypnotized?"

He laughed loud. "Oh, Dex. If you knew me better you would know how amusing that question is. No. No, I have not, and I doubt it's even possible."

Dex didn't seem the least bit offended. In fact, all he got was a grin. "I have, couple times. It's rocking cool. Like from real-life hypnotists. They can't make you do anything you won't do, though. It's not really, like, mind control. More like just seeing things from a distance."

"I'm a bit of a control freak." *Understatement of the century.* "I don't even like letting other people drive. I can't imagine allowing that." He was having a hard time even having the conversation. Possibly there was something to explore there, but he had no interest in doing so.

"You didn't tell me why your mother's lovely table is in Huck's house. Are there other things that are yours as well?"

"Yeah. The hutch and Huck's bedroom suite were my momma's."

Huck slept in Dex's mother's bed, and Dex slept in a shipping container in the backyard. He let that thought sink in for a minute.

"When did you lose your mom?"

"When I was almost seventeen. My dad shot her and then shot himself. Huck was eighteen and had a little place and let me come. That was my half of the rent for the time it took me to get a job." Just like it was something that happened every day.

"I'm...sorry about your mom." *Jesus, Huck.* Maybe he should stop asking questions.

He never stopped asking questions.

"Seventeen, and you're what? Twenty-five now?" Dex looked young, but he was guessing.

"Twenty-seven, no, I turned twenty-eight, end of May." Dex looked at his hands for a second. "Hell of thing, ain't it? Mrs. Feezel was at both funerals."

And that was how Dex knew it got better. It didn't help to feel sorry for people, but he hurt a little for Dex and how losing Huck had to feel now. "I'll admit I don't know what to say. But I imagine this is that much more difficult even ten years later."

"You don't have to say a thing, honey. My dad was a fuck, and one day he lost it. Game over. I'm a big boy; I survived it. Rumor is I'll survive Huck too, even though he wasn't a fuck. I'm not sure what to call what was wrong with him.

Obviously, he was miserable here, with me." There was a raw moment where there was a mixture of guilt, horror, and crushing sorrow in Dex's eyes, then it disappeared, that wry smile covering it like a set of blinds. "Maybe if he'd moved up north he would have been better, who knows."

"Not a lot of rodeo in New York." If Dex were a sub, Cyrus would have the boy on his knees right now, and they'd let that emotion out. It was difficult to resist giving the order. Sadly, he wasn't very good at other ways of getting people to open up. He just knew what Dex needed and he—

You're not here for Dex.

Dammit. Right. Not that he was sure yet why he was there. It definitely wasn't to get rained on.

"No, I reckon not. Have you ever seen the parade? The Thanksgiving one? I think one day I'd like to see it for real."

"I have. It's a long, chilly morning full of loud marching bands playing frozen brass instruments, a lot of lip-synching, and the chippie pop singer of the week, but in my opinion, it's completely worth it."

He went every year. Every. Year.

"The balloons rock. That's so fucking cool, man. How exciting! I'll look for you on the TV now."

"The balloons are the real reason to go. And the Rockettes. And if you actually saw me, I'd be surprised." He picked up his empty plate and Dex's and tossed them in the trash. It was late, he should get out of Dex's hair, get back to his hotel, take a shower. "Let me help you put this food away."

"It's okay, honey. I need things to do. Just leave it." Dex stood up, and Cyrus noticed that Dex hadn't changed out of his wet jeans, still. "Let me grab your clothes for you. Wear that stuff home. You can leave it for housekeeping, if you want. Huck won't mind."

Dex disappeared into what had to be a laundry room, then reappeared with his clothes neatly folded, clean and still warm from the dryer before he could even process that he hadn't said he wanted to leave. "I didn't mess with your coat, because it's fancy."

"Thank you. It'll dry. It's made to." He took the clothes and went back into the bathroom to change.

He had all day tomorrow. Originally, he'd thought about spending it in Austin, seeing the city, but he felt like he wanted to spend it with Dex instead, make sure the boy was ready to take care of things before he left town.

All he could do was shake his head at himself because he couldn't leave it be, even when he knew he should. He could pretend all he wanted to that Dex would be fine if he just made sure everything was okay before he left town, but he knew better. He also knew that wouldn't stop him from trying.

"Thanks again for the dry clothes," he said as he came back from the bathroom. "I appreciate it."

"Sure. Can you find your way back? You're okay driving in this mess?" The kindness in Dex was something special. The man didn't know him from Adam, and yet was honestly worried about him.

How about that? They were worried about each other.

"I...uh." If he'd met Dex at the bar, or on the street, or at a party, he'd ask to stay. He would. He tried to cover his hesitation while he talked himself out of even thinking about asking.

Because you didn't do that to a vulnerable guy after an emotional day on the heels of his best friend's funeral.

"I have GPS." *There you go.* "It's only like...it's a short drive." He was staying near Austin. It wasn't a short drive, but he wasn't about to say so. "Maybe I—why don't I give you my number in case you need anything."

What? Why don't you give him your number? Sure. For all the good it will do him. You'll be hundreds of miles away the day after tomorrow.

"Honey, why don't you stay? There are two guest rooms, plenty of food, and you can rest. There's a whole media room deal, a pool table—you can have company, or I can disappear, but I hate to think of you out in the storm."

"Two guest rooms, huh?" He grinned a little sheepishly. "My hotel is actually down by Austin so..." Dark, rural highway in the rain for what, an hour? That sounded like his idea of hell. He hadn't driven on a dark road at night in maybe ten years.

"Please stay. Hey, your clothes are clean, huh? You're golden. There's plenty of food after all."

"I'll make you a deal. You change into those dry clothes you brought over with you and let me help you with this mess, and I'll stay. There's nothing worse than a helpless house guest."

Dex looked down at himself like he had no idea he hadn't changed. "Fair enough. I'll even share dessert with you. There's an apple pie in the fridge already."

"Oh. Say it isn't so. I love apple pie. What's your favorite movie?" He started hunting, finding covers for the containers that had them.

"Anything about Robin Hood. I love that story. Be right back. I'll change."

Well, here he was. Staying the night. He'd better keep his hands busy.

Cyrus kept closing up food until he couldn't find any more lids, and then he started searching drawers for foil or cling wrap to cover things with. It actually felt good having something to do instead of being at loose ends in Huck's house. He thought he understood what Dex meant.

"Sorry. I washed up real quick. I felt like I smelled bad." Dex started working, moving quickly to help. It was amazing to watch the quick, efficient movements. "Do you have a favorite movie?"

"Not really. I just like movies. Which version of Robin Hood? There are at least a handful. I like the old Errol Flynn version. The black and white one."

"That one is totally great. I like the one with Kevin Costner too, for all people make fun."

"I like that one too mostly. But I've been known to make fun. He just...talks funny." He opened the fridge and moved the few things already in there to the top shelves. "Getting all of that in here is going to be like Tetris with casseroles. Or...do people still play Tetris?"

"I don't think so, but people don't dial phones and we still say it. Can you grab the pie, please, sir, and I'll work this out."

"That's true, we do." He grinned. "Hold on, boy, and I'll get this pie out of your way." He pulled it out of the fridge and ducked around Dex with it.

"Mmm... It smells good, even cold." It was the first thing Dex seemed interested in eating.

"What's not to like about pie? Do you want to nuke it, or should I warm up the oven?"

"Let me see it real quick..." Dex leaned over him, looking the pie over. "I'd say oven at 250. The crust can take it."

Oh, right. Cookies. Dex was a baker. "I can do that. Are any of these your cookies?" He checked the oven to make sure he wasn't going to set anything on fire, then turned it on.

"No. No, I—Okay, you have to promise not to tease, okay?"

Cyrus turned back from the stove and looked at Dex. "I promise." Teasing wasn't in his DNA.

"Okay. I make designer cookies. Miss Sugarsparkles is my Etsy store. I mean, like this..." Dex opened his phone and showed the pictures—portraits and flowers, baby showers, weddings, monsters, pumpkins. Amazing, wild art on cookies.

"Wait. What?" He took Dex's phone and adjusted his glasses to get a good look. "This is you? Dex, you're talented. These are incredible. Ha! I love the purple monsters."

Not a single thing—with the possible exception of the monsters—was at all his personal taste, but he knew talent when he saw it.

"Thanks. I make quite a few. I know they're silly, but I can do them, and people love them, so..."

"A man's gotta make a living." He grinned and handed the phone back. "I can see why people would love them. How did you...do you just like to bake? What got you started with this?"

Cookies. Of all the crazy things. Still, that kind of work would sell anywhere.

"I saw it on the TV at a doctor's appointment and thought, I can do that. So, I came home and tried it a couple times, and I learned how."

"Oh, you're one of those people. I used to hate those people when I was younger. The I can do anything people." Okay, so maybe there was a little teasing in his DNA after all. It fit with Dex's personality though—a little of this and little of that. Cookies. Mandolin. Day work. Those people were always much more capable than they gave themselves credit for.

"Jack of all trades; Master of none. That's me." Dex took his phone back and pocketed it. "Huck used to say I was like a chihuahua. Running with the big dogs and trying to keep up."

"I can't imagine you have to try that hard. You seem quite capable to me." *When you're not sleep deprived and staring at the rain.*

He put the pie in the oven and helped out, handing Dex dish after dish until they'd managed to get every last one in.

"Tomorrow I'll run out to the Walmart and deal with getting this to folks." Dex nodded to himself. "That'll be better than keeping it here."

Someone was used to talking to himself, Cyrus thought. He decided to answer.

"Sounds good. Just let me know what you need, and I'll help."

"Hmm? Oh. Oh, that's sweet to offer. I was in my own little world." Dex came back to him, full-focus. "Would you like to watch a movie or something?"

"Did we not just decide on Robin Hood? Or was I inferring? We can pick on Costner and eat pie. I don't guess you have ice cream...or a hunk of cheddar?"

Dex blinked. "Like cheese?"

"Cheddar cheese. Yes." He looked at Dex. "This isn't a Texas thing, I take it. Apple pie and cheddar cheese? Don't knock it 'til you've tried it."

"Huh. Why not? Just because it sounds weird don't mean it's bad, honey. I try all sorts of shit. Let me see whether the good stuff's in here. I like my cheddar so sharp it dries out your tongue." Dex went to the fridge and bent down, sweats pulling tight over a tiny little ass.

His lips twitched. "That's...perfect. The cheese, I mean. Sharp cheese. Delicious." He shook his head at himself.

What else would he think you'd mean, you perv?

"Do you like the white or yellow?"

If Dex was going to keep bending like that, he was going to keep looking. "White if you have it, but the sharper the better."

"I got it!" Dex crowed, butt wiggling as he stood. "I buy Huck's groceries; I knew it was in there."

"Excellent."

So, was Dex Huck's sub? Did Huck just treat Dex like one? Did Huck even treat Dex that well? It didn't seem like Dex got anything from their...friendship? Relationship? Whatever it was.

Dex did Huck's shopping, laundry, looked after the place, fed the animals; what did Huck actually do other than rodeo? Date, apparently, though the choice of lovers was questionable at best. Travel a bit, spend money? Cyrus wasn't all that impressed with the picture Dex was painting of his client. And what made a man with money and devoted friends and his pick of lovers kill himself?

The answers to all of those questions were right in front of him he was sure. He could look harder, but he wasn't certain he wanted to.

"So...when you say slab, honey, what does that mean?" Dex shook his head. "I wonder what Huck would say—you and me sitting here fixin' to have pie and cheese."

"By slab, I mean..." He knew just what he meant but he couldn't explain it. "Kind of cut it like this. Like a triangle so you can pick it up with your fingers and bite it, you know?"

At this point, he had no doubt that Huck would throw him out. None. He left that question alone.

"I can do that." Dex cut two pieces of cheese, holding one up for inspection. "This do for you?"

He plucked the hunk of cheese out of Dex's fingers and

set it on one of the paper plates. "Perfect. Thank you. I'll check on the pie."

"Did you want milk or coffee to drink?" This time Dex didn't offer beer. Interesting.

"Is the coffee easy? I don't want you making a whole pot on my account."

"It's one of them Keurig deals. You got a preference to type?"

"Dark, if you've got it. No flavors." Flavors were for sippers. He drank his coffee.

"Yes, sir. I'm on it." Dex whistled along with the music, pulling out two K-cups, two mugs like he'd done it a thousand times.

"Mitts are...?" He opened a drawer next to the stove. "Right here. Cool." He grabbed a couple, pulled the pie out of the oven, and set it on the range.

Dessert plates appeared like magic, along with forks, and soon his coffee was at his hand too.

Dex was vaguely like an elf, making things happen without being asked.

"Thank you, boy. Where are we watching? Living room? This pie smells amazing." He was a bottomless pit today. He could only imagine what Dex was thinking. Not that he looked like he ate anywhere near as much as he did.

"Huck's got himself a media room, but there's a DVR player and a couch in the family room. That work for you okay?" Didn't that 'media room' come with an amazing eye roll?

"Couch it is." Well, this wasn't bad at all. Coffee in one hand, pie in the other, evening movie company...it was like vacation. "Do you have a side you like?"

"No, sir. Just have a sit. I'll set the movie up." Dex put his stuff down on the long, low coffee table, then went to the television, chuckling softly as he slid open a drawer on the entertainment center.

Jesus, the thing was vast—three lines of drawers, shelves, cabinets. There were tons of strange knickknacks—toys and games, carved wood and puzzles, a rifle, a samurai sword. It was like a young man's fantasy, barring the pinup girls.

"Is all that stuff his or yours?" He sat on the couch, set his coffee down and dug into his pie. Bite of pie, bite of cheese. "Mmm. Good."

"I guess it's his? This is from before. This is the part the people worth money couldn't see." Dex didn't look up from the drawer. "He grew up, but he didn't want to get rid of everything, so it came to live in here. He teased all the time about locking me up in here and pulling me out when he needed me, but we all know I'm just in my container." A soft laugh hit the air. "God, he loved that joke."

"It's not funny."

He blinked. Damn. This whole thing was none of his business, he needed to keep his nose out of it. Maybe Dex hadn't heard him.

"Maybe not, but it sure made him laugh." Dex pulled out a DVD. "Found it. It wasn't in order."

He just watched, slightly horrified at how Dex had just brushed that off. "Well, pop it in and come sit then. Your pie is getting cold."

Dex got the movie in and settled on the sofa and started things going before grabbing his plate. "It smells amazing. Donna brought this. She owns the bookstore."

"I've been known to enjoy a bookstore." He wondered why all those people came to the house. Some of them were for Huck for sure, the cowboys. Some were nosy, that was the nature of the beast. But he wondered how many came for Dex. How many people got to see what he was seeing, and knew how devoted Dex was to Huck?

"Yeah? Me too. What do you like to read?" Dex watched him, not the movie, and the curiosity, the focus, was a bit heady.

"Anything that scares me. Horror, mysteries, psycho-dramas, forensic novels, whatever. If it can set me on edge, I'll read it." His life was much too comfortable. He needed a good scare. "You?"

"I'll read anything. I think my favorite is history—Westerns and medieval stuff, even novels like *Shogun*. My grandpa loved that book."

"*Shogun*. I remember that one." Cyrus took another bite of his pie. "Do you have any other family? I mean, siblings? Cousins?" *Anyone that cares about you?*

"Not any more. This is—I don't know if you know anybody with a murder/suicide, but everyone disappears. Especially when you're a teenager, because what if what's wrong with them is wrong with you? You don't go to anymore parties, you don't go to prom, and you absolutely don't go to graduation." Dex reached out and patted his hand. "But don't you worry, honey. I'm a survivor. I'll deal with all the fall-out from this and see where I end up."

"The funny thing about worry is you don't get to tell people whether or not they should. It's an empathetic emotion, so people can't really just decide not to. If you're a worrier, you're a worrier." He winked at Dex. "I'm not a worrier. I'm concerned. But I see how capable you are. Resourceful. I believe you when you say you'll deal with this. I'm interested in what happens when the dust settles."

"The dust settles? I'm not sure that's a thing, but that's neither here nor there. Are you saying it's rude to tell someone not to worry? That's being nice."

"No, boy. I'm telling you that—"

What? He's not your boy. Had he just said that?

"Um. Sorry. You can say that to be polite, but you can't control whether or not they do. And most of the time, they can't either."

Cyrus couldn't be sure he hadn't done that before. That was disconcerting.

He was tired. That was all. Long day.

"Well, I don't think... Huh. I sure don't want to hurt anyone's feelings. And you don't worry, so I can say that to you. I'll always be thinking about that now, though." Dex tilted his head. "Am I bothering you? All of the sudden you look pinched."

"You're not bothering me at all. I've enjoyed your company all day, in fact. I was just thinking. I got off on a tangent. Apologies."

"No worries." Dex blinked, then began to laugh, just wholeheartedly cackling.

Cyrus had to grin because the laugh was so genuine, but he had no idea what could possibly be so suddenly funny. "I missed something." He laughed lightly. "What did I miss?"

"I made it a whole fucking sentence, man. Maybe two without telling you not to worry."

"Oh." He grinned wider, laughed a little more earnestly too. "Well. Don't you worry, I won't."

That laugh rang out again, warm and happy. "I hear you. Yes, sir."

Christ, Dex was lovely. Genuinely.

"So what was with Huck and that Paul guy? I let him off easy just to get him out of your hair." Cyrus had been surprised how easy it was actually. People carried weird guilt. All Cyrus had to do was tell Paul it wasn't his fault.

"Paul thought he was special, but they weren't that into

each other. I think he probably left something up in Huck's bedroom, or maybe Huck was, like, Casanova or something. I don't like him, regardless."

"The obscenity charge the Sheriff suggested was... interesting. I guess Paul's not liked by many."

"Sucks to be queer in Texas. This ain't Austin. They probably caught him crying in the bedroom with his dick in his hand."

He nodded. He felt bad for Paul if that was the case, because he believed Dex. It probably did suck to be queer in Texas. "I've heard crazier things. He was definitely broken up."

"I get that. I did my screaming, might try it again in a few days, you never know."

"Go for it. It's good for you." Cyrus set his empty plate down. "That was some pie."

"You want the rest of mine?" Dex hadn't eaten two whole bites, if that. "I'll share."

"Believe it or not, I'm full." He put a hand on Dex's thigh, giving it a pat. "I'd like to see you eat. You need it."

"Full is good. Not eating is like, how I deal with stress, I guess. I'm never hungry."

"That means you need to eat. The less you eat, the less hungry you feel. Your body stops sending signals." He put his feet up on an ottoman and stretched out. "Ah, that feels good."

"It's a comfy couch. Seriously." Dex picked up the pie, playing more than eating, but a few more bites got in there.

Cyrus propped up with a throw pillow and, finally, looked at the TV. "Okay, what's going on in this movie now?"

4

Cyrus had a couple of interested, potential clients but he found he couldn't bring himself to fill the Thursday appointment time that Huck had held for so long. Not yet. He needed to give it another week, maybe two, until he stopped thinking about it as Huck's spot.

He wasn't going to sit and stare at the wall though; that wasn't healthy or constructive. He'd already made a plan, and as the hour approached, he found himself a snack, poured a cup of coffee, and settled in his living room to call Dex.

This was just a social call. A well-being check. At least that's what he'd told himself it had to be, no matter how much the b—how much *Dex* had been on his mind since he'd flown back from Texas. Dex was kind and needed a friend right now. Dex had confided in him that everyone he'd known had disappeared. Well, Cyrus didn't intend to be one of those people.

He found Dex's number and dialed, having no idea what to expect from Dex, answering a call out of the blue.

"Hey, Mr. Cyrus. How goes?" Dex sounded...tired, maybe a bit frazzled, but not at all unhappy to hear from him.

"Hello, Dex. I'm fine, settled right back into work when I got home. I was thinking about you and thought I'd call." He didn't trust his first impression over the phone, though. Dex seemed adept at covering anything he didn't want someone to know. Cy had decided to leave some open air, not ask too many questions, see what Dex wanted to tell him.

"Well, isn't that kind of you. It's good to hear your voice. I thought...well, I guess I reckoned you just forgot about us out here."

Small talk. He hated small talk. "I couldn't possibly forget you, Dex. That was a fairly intense couple of days. We're friends now, wouldn't you say?"

"Yessir. I so would. Is—is it weird, not having Huck visit?" That was tentative, a little shaky.

Perceptive though. Dex was uncanny that way. "As a matter of fact, this is our usual meeting time, and because he isn't here to work with today, I called you. Is it weird? I'd say it's more disappointing. And I do miss him being here, more than I anticipated. I know you miss him too."

"I do. I pretend sometimes that he's just out of town, just on the road. It's real quiet otherwise." Dex chuckled softly. "Hold on, I'm going to grab a drink. I have a powerful thirst."

"All right." He didn't point out to Dex that it was a cell phone and could go with him. He just waited and pretended that Dex was getting a lemonade and not a beer.

"Got you on speaker. I mean, it don't matter. Ain't no one here. Just me. So, you've seen where I live. Tell me about yours." He heard a bottle opening, the hiss of carbonation.

He would, but he was curious. "Are you in your yellow... box? Or Huck's house?"

"I'm in my house. Huck's house is...well... Huck's, you know?"

"I understand." He wouldn't want to knock around alone in Huck's house if he were Dex, either. "So, I have an apartment in a high-rise in Manhattan. It's got three bedrooms, a living and dining room and a decent kitchen. I don't have much of a view, but I'm high enough up to get lots of light. One of the bedrooms is my office, one is a guest room."

Dex hummed, the sound sweet as pie. "Oh wow, that's cool. I worked for a day doing security in a high-rise in Austin. It was wild. Super neat places."

"A whole day, huh?" He had to laugh, the idea of Dex as a security guard was just too strange. "Did you quit or get fired?"

"Nah, I quit. The uniform was itchy. I don't like that."

He grinned, glad that Dex couldn't see it. He learned more about Dex from comments like that than from some of his deeper questions. "A boy who needs to be comfortable," he observed, though he hadn't meant to say it out loud.

"Yeah, you know, if you're thinking about your thighs itching, you can't be thinking about working." Just as straightforward and practical as anything.

He imagined Dex had a hard enough time finding focus without the itchy clothing.

There were too many miles between them. Dex had plenty to keep him busy. Cyrus shouldn't be thinking about how he'd like to help Dex find that focused space and stay there. But he worried about the—

Dammit.

"What are you having for dinner?" *You have to eat. You don't eat enough. You're skin and bones.*

"I got some tater tots and a limeade from the Sonic this

morning when I went to the feed store. Oh, and I got me a Three Musketeers for later."

He sighed. "Dex. The chocolate may soothe your soul, I know it certainly can mine, but none of that is going to nourish your body. You have to do better."

"Oh." There was a soft little sound, and then— "It's no fun to cook for one person. I love to cook. I love the whole process, but there's no reason to mess shit up for me."

"I know. I also live alone. Promise me you'll have something good for you today. If you won't want to cook, go out and get something. Chicken. A salad. Real food."

"What are you going to have? Do you like salad? I make a really nice Chinese chicken salad." Dex went on to tell him about the salad, about how it was probably not Chinese, about how he loved little mandarin oranges.

Cyrus happened to love them too. But he didn't let Dex distract him. "Is that what you're going to make yourself tonight, then?"

"No. No, I'll probably have an egg. I got eggs." When Dex said eggs, it came out 'aigs' and had way more syllables than he was used to.

"I approve of an egg. Perhaps a glass of milk? I'm sure you have milk." The temptation to simply make it an order was nearly undeniable. But Dex might not understand him. Not yet.

Not yet. He shook his head at himself. It would take more than a disagreement over dinner for him to make the kind of overture he'd really like to.

Dex chuckled, and Cyrus swore he could see the boy's nod. "Okay, an egg and milk. Your turn, what are you having?"

"I have no idea. Take out, I suppose. Sushi maybe." He didn't have a boy there to cook for him today. Not that all of them cooked, but some did, and he ate well on those nights.

"What's your favorite? I like the spicy salmon one that Huck brings home."

Huck had never brought him sushi. "I love the spicy tuna. That's my favorite. Cucumber roll, eel, and avocado roll. I'll probably have tuna tonight. And seaweed salad. And edamame." He was hungry.

Well, he was always hungry.

"Do you have cookie orders to work on?"

"Yeah. A bridal shower. She wants her bouquet recreated in cookies, because that's not hellish."

He laughed. "Better you than me. It sounds like it will take forever."

"I have about thirty daisies done. I have to do the blue button looking ones and then the roses."

"Oh, daisies are my favorite flower. Will you send me pictures when it's done?" Dex was a true artist, if his website was to be believed.

"Sure. Sure, I'd love to. I—I'm so glad you called. I like talking to you. A lot. Sometimes I feel like I'm the only person alive in the world."

"You're not." He let his tone grow more serious, he wanted Dex to hear him. "You're not alone, Dex. I know we only just met, but I think about you often. You can call me, text if you'd rather, any time. Any time, I mean that."

"Yeah? Okay. Okay, cool." Dex took a deep breath and let it out. "Same for you. If you get lonely, bored, you want a friend or to watch a movie, I'm here."

"I appreciate that." The offer was so sweet, so genuine. "You'll hear from me again soon."

"Ditto. Let me know how your supper was, and I'll send pictures of cookies."

"I will do that. You will keep your promise to me and have a good dinner?"

"Eggs and milk. I promise. I'll text pictures. You too." A beep sounded. "Time to make the cookies, Mr. Cyrus."

He had to respect the boy's time, as much as he'd like to keep Dex talking. "Have fun. Don't work too hard. Take care, Dex."

"You too. Night, you!" Dex's laughter filled the air, cut off as he hung up the phone.

Who could say what set Dex laughing. It could have been anything. It could have been that he'd told the boy not to work too hard.

Cyrus was glad he'd made that call though. It was good to hear Dex's voice, to know he was okay. It was the right way to fill the empty time left by Huck's absence.

He thought maybe he'd take some of his own advice and not work too hard. He didn't have a client, so he decided he'd have a nap.

5

Dex sat in the middle of a world of chaos. Everything was fucked up.

Everything.

He didn't know how to fix any of it, either and that, somehow, made it worse.

The lawyer guy had explained things. First, that everything was his. Second, that everything had this huge tax on it. Third, that everything that didn't have this huge tax on it was owed on or mortgaged or owned by a bank.

In other words, Dex was fucked.

Up the ass.

Sideways.

With a rusty chainsaw.

So here he was, in this house with a for sale sign in the front, everything tagged for a huge estate sale, including his yellow container and the livestock.

Thank God Mrs. Feezel's son wanted the dogs.

It was weird and horrible and wrong, so he texted the guy that was the only right thing left—and if it was because Cyr was in New York City and didn't know any of this and

Dex could pretend every night when they called and texted that shit was normal? So be it.

DEX

Hey you. Good day?

His had been miserable.

CYRUS

Pretty good. It's raining hard here, so all I'm seeing out my windows is fog and water, but work was rewarding.

Cyr just didn't know how to text without using full sentences and long words.

DEX

Cool.

No rain here. Lots of work, but it sucked. There was no reason to say that, though. That was just mean.

DEX

Stay dry.

CYRUS

Planning on it. How are you?

The million-dollar question.

DEX

Been busy.

Miserable. Hurting. Mad. Lonely. Soul hurt. Shit, he was a lot of things, mostly scared right now, but Cyr didn't need that sort of bellyaching. He didn't need to lose any more friends.

CYRUS

Busy isn't how you are, it's what you're doing. Did you eat today?

He wondered if beer counted. It had calories, right?

DEX

Yep. How about you? Did you have something amazing?

CYRUS

Not yet. I've got a lovely butternut squash soup someone made for me today, I'm looking forward to that with a nice sturdy bread. So, how are you?

Sturdy bread. Lord, the word sturdy sure looked weird. Stur-dy. Stu-rdy.

DEX

I'm a little wore around the edges. Fixin' to take a shower.

CYRUS

Do you sing in the shower?

He swore he could see the teasing grin on Cyr's face.

CYRUS

Rock? Country? Opera? I'm a fan of Broadway myself. I do a mean Jean Valjean.

He didn't know who she was, but he thought Cyr's voice was a little low to sing like a girl...

DEX

I sing backup harmony mostly.

CYRUS

Ah. Because that's what you do when you play your mandolin? I'd love to hear you play. Maybe you can send a video.

DEX

I'll see if I have 1.

He was going to sell everything that wasn't important. He needed to keep his mandolin though.

DEX

Do you have fun plans tonite?

CYRUS

I'll go down to the bar to hang out. Talk to some people. Watch whatever is on the TV. Drink coffee. You?

He was fixin' to have a shower and get drunk. Like totally fucked up, forget how fucked he was drunk. Then he was going to puke a lot.

DEX

I got no plans. TV maybe?

CYRUS

A busy man with no plans.

There was a little pause while he decided what he ought to say to that, but then Cyr followed up with another text.

CYRUS

I want you to come visit. I know you have things to do, I know the cookie business is busy. But sometime soon. I'll show you around.

DEX

I'd love that.

It wouldn't happen, and he wasn't stupid enough to believe in it, but it was a nice gooey dream in the center of a hard-crack nightmare.

DEX

I really could.

CYRUS

Good. Look at your calendar and let me know what works. I am an excellent tour guide, and I know all kinds of good places to eat.

DEX

I will.

He sat there for a second, right there in the middle of the floor and let himself cry, good and hard, because no one would see, no one would know, and when it was over, the hurt wouldn't have anything to hold onto for a few minutes.

"Why did you do this to me, Huck? Why did you leave me like this? I wasn't mean to you, I wasn't. I took care of you."

There wasn't an answer, and there never would be. That wasn't how the good Lord worked.

The answer was probably, suck it up, Buttercup.

When he looked back at his phone there were a couple of texts waiting.

CYRUS

We'll have sushi.

Did I lose you to your shower?

Get some rest. Eat dinner.

Talk soon. Goodnight, Dex.

DEX

Night you. TTY2morrow.

Dex stood up, lips tight, and he headed for the fridge. He needed to have a beer and make a plan. He needed a place to live. He needed a real job. He just needed to do something right for once.

Something smart.

6

Dex looked at the truck. Just looked at it.

Damn.

"I fucking wish you were here, you bastard. I wish you were here, because I would tear you apart with my bare fucking hands."

Huck had left him the house, the land, the truck, the animals, the loans, the credit card bills, the twelve-thousand-dollar bill to bury him. Everything.

Life insurance didn't pay out for suicide.

The estate sale had gone well enough to pay off a lot of the bills, and he'd bought out the good truck with what he had in savings, then emptied out his container.

Now he was sitting here on the front porch, drinking a beer, and pondering his drive north. Salado wasn't Austin, but it was pricey. Tyler had a studio apartment for five hundred and change a month, a Walmart that needed a stocker, and...

And that was that.

If he stopped drinking, he might freak out, but he didn't

intend to do that for a few more days. Never enough to be drunk, but enough to coat the hurt that he wore like a coat.

Dex finally pulled the keys off his keyring and tossed them in the house and locked the door behind him.

He had to go.

He would stop at the post office, drop off the box that had all of Huck's personal papers to Cyr, and then head to Tyler and find a hotel so he could sign his lease in the morning. Three hours, one hundred and eighty miles, and a whole world away.

Lord help him.

Dex made it to Waco before he needed to pull over, piss, and grab a Route 44 Dr Pepper with cherries. Then he got on the road again and looked at the time. Six. Eight Cyr's time. He hit the man's name and hoped Cyr answered.

Dex did his dead-level best to keep his shit out of Cyrus's worries. None of this belonged to Cyr, but somehow, they'd become friends. Buddies. So they had a couple texts a day, a phone call every so often. Today could be one of them days.

"Hello, Dex."

Cyrus sounded downright cheerful. Maybe it would do him some good.

"How's business? I might have another customer for you."

"Do you now?" He was on hiatus for a few days, but the apartment had a wee baby kitchen.

"I'll text you the info. A client's daughter is getting married. How are you?"

I want to go home. "Been busy as all get out."

"That's good, right? You don't like idle hands. Are you eating?" Why did Cyr always ask him that?

"I don't like to be lazy, true. I'm getting my calories."

Shiners had one hundred and forty-two calories a piece. "You doing anything fun this weekend?"

"Well, it's June in New York so that means it's Pride everything. Some friends of mine, a couple I've known forever, are throwing a party Saturday night, so I'll drop in at some point, and I'm sure I'll get up to some other mischief if I decide to go looking." Cyr laughed. It was a good sound, relaxed and easy. "How about you?"

"Just more of the same, I guess?" Just moving to east Texas to an apartment with a truck bed of stuff. No big deal. "Pride isn't a thing where I am."

"Austin doesn't have a parade? Really? If you have any time off you should come up. I'll take you around. It's the next best thing to the Macy's Parade. You'd love it."

"Austin does, yeah, but that's gonna be a ways. I mailed you a package today. You should get it mid-week."

"Austin's less than an hour, right? Did you send me pie?" Cyr laughed again.

"No, sir. I sent you a bunch of Huck's journals and shit." Plus a couple of little doolies from the house—nothing serious, but all fun. "I thought you might want them."

"Journals?" Cyr sighed. "That's, uh. Okay, thanks. Why are you sending—did you read them?"

"I thought..." *I thought maybe you would be able to figure it out. I thought you'd want them. I thought you'd be interested in them, when I just wanted to set them on fire. But obviously I was wrong because I'm so goddamn mad at him. That's what I get for thinking.* "Just toss the box in the trash or return to sender. My mistake."

"No. No, I'm not going to do that, Dex. I'll look at them for you." There was a pause and then Cyr asked, "What's going on? Are you okay?"

He shook his head. Nope. Not even a little bit. "It's been

a hell of a day, honey, and I just wanted—" A friend. "—to talk."

"So talk. I'm listening. Where are you?"

"Uh, somewhere between Waco and Trinidad, I guess. I'm not real sure."

"Where is... Trinidad... Trinidad? What are you doing up there?"

"I'm moving. I'm moving." He hadn't said during all this time, right? Now he could tell.

"You're moving? Why are you—Dex. Why are you moving?"

"Well, you remember when I told you he left everything to me? That means everything. The credit cards, the loans, the funeral bill, the mortgage, everything. So, I been dealing with all the stuff. Had a big sale. Sold everything. There's a job for me at the Walmart in Tyler and a tiny apartment I can afford." And if he thought about it too long, he'd lose it, and he couldn't until he found a hotel.

Cyrus sighed and then cleared his throat. "Tyler, huh? You like Tyler?"

"It's a town. They're famous for their roses." It was the place with a job and a cheap apartment.

"Have you ever worked in a bar?"

"Yessir, but Walmart ain't a bar. It's a Walmart." Silly man.

"It is." Cyr chuckled in his ear. "But I have a friend who owns a bar, and he's hiring. He just had someone quit last weekend. It's not Tyler, of course. And it's not Walmart either, but..."

"Oh honey, you're sweet, but you told me all about those apartments. I got three thousand dollars, a truck, and my momma's table to my name." Three thousand dollars was pennies there, and he knew it. "Thank you, though. I didn't call to be a burden. I just wanted to say hi, and I'm a little drunk and a little stressed out."

"Oh. No, no. I have a room for you. It's just...empty. If you want it. Or if that's weird. Maybe that's weird? If that's weird a handful of Les's guys live in a place right over the bar. Les owns the building. That would be a lot of roommates but cheap. But I do have a room." There was a pause. "Fifteen an hour."

"I—I can't think right now. I'm fucked up and tired, and I fucking hate him for doing this!" The last bit came out in a roar and he slapped at the phone, fishtailing off the road to scream and rail, slamming his fists against the steering wheel. His heart hurt, his soul hurt, and his head was fixin' to explode.

He finally ran out of voice, ran out of energy, and leaned back against the headrest, raking in breath and letting it out in harsh pants.

"Dex? Dex! Are you there? Pick up the phone! Dex!"

No.

No. God. He cleared his throat, took a deep breath. "S-sorry. I'm sorry. Hold up." Okay. See him. See him suck it up. "Hey. Sorry. I'm cool."

The relief in Cyrus's sigh was genuine and clear. "Thank god."

He drank some of his Coke, got the truck moving again. "Sorry. I just... You shouldn't have to hear that shit. I just had a rough few days."

Cyrus cleared his throat again. "I apologize for adding stress. That was misguided on my part."

"Don't feel bad. That wasn't cool, losing my shit. You were being nice, and I—I'm so sorry. I'm so embarrassed. I—Yeah." His cheeks were so hot they had to be glowing.

"Anyone in your position would be finding it hard to

cope, Dex. You're fine. I'm just glad you're all right." He could hear Cyrus shifting around on the other end of the line. "So what's your plan then? You'll get to Tyler tonight? Have you signed your lease?"

"No. No, tomorrow. I can't move in for a few days. Everything I brought is in the truck."

"Where are you staying? When does work start?"

"I don't know. And I train next Monday. I'll get a cheap hotel tonight and look for a campground tomorrow. Everything happened so fast. I think I'm never going to get my feet under me." He sighed and shook his head. "I'm not a bad man. I didn't expect Huck to take care of me, but I didn't expect this."

"Do you want me to—I could come. There. To...keep you company for a couple of days."

He nodded but managed to say. "I'd never ask you for that. You have a neat weekend planned. I'm just going to drink until it stops hurting."

"You didn't ask. I offered. Text me the address of whatever hotel you find and stay there until I find you. Okay?" Cyrus didn't sound panicked or stressed, the man's voice was calm. Deep and gentle. "Text me."

"My soul hurts, honey. I'm trying so hard." He was crying and nodding and driving even though he couldn't hardly see the road.

"I know. You've lost a lot more than Huck in this deal, Dex. You're doing fine, you hear me? You're okay. You need to drive carefully, find a place to stay as soon as possible even if you don't make it all the way to Tyler, okay? Text me when you do, and then rest. Just rest until I get there. Sleep. You can do that. Right?"

"Yes, sir. I can. I'll text. Promise." He could do that. He could let Cyrus know when he lit safe.

“Good. I knew you could.” Cyrus hummed into the phone thoughtfully. “There aren’t any flights left to Dallas tonight, so I’m booking one for early in the morning. I’ll be there by lunchtime. We’ll figure the rest out after I get there. I want you to rest tonight, Dex. I’ll help tomorrow.”

“I’m sorry. I wouldn’t have called, but I needed to talk to…you.”

“Please don’t apologize. I’m glad you called. Honestly, Dex. We’re friends, right? This is what friends do. If I were in a bind, you’d do the same for me, you know you would.”

“Yessir. I would. Thank you. I’m gonna drive. I’ll holler when I find a hotel, ’kay?” He said his goodbyes and hung up, telling himself that he’d tell Cyr not to come when he texted.

7

Cyrus's flight to Dallas was easy. Early—really, really early—but easy, and he was in a rental car by ten o'clock. He had Dex's texts. The one saying you're a nice guy but please don't come, and the one Dex sent after he insisted Dex send the hotel address anyway.

Honestly. He might be losing his mind, but at least he understood why he was in Texas this time.

His GPS had been pretty good so far, so when it told him to leave the highway, he did, passing a sign for Tyler right before he hit the off-ramp.

Or...what had Dex called it? The get-off. He loved that.

The hotel was...less than spectacular, but it seemed clean, and he knew right where Dex's truck was. The entire cab was crammed with trash bags of clothes and bedding, the bed covered in a huge tarp.

Christ, Huck, what have you done?

He parked next to the truck, took a breath and pulled out his phone. He didn't want to surprise Dex so he texted that he was there and sat in the car another minute to give

Dex a second to wake up in case Dex had actually slept as he'd suggested.

Cyrus had no idea what to expect. Dex had a Masterful poker face, and while he wasn't exactly in denial, Dex managed pretty well just telling himself it was going to be okay.

Last night on the phone though, Dex had definitely not been okay, and that truck was proof that things leaned far closer to disaster than Dex wanted to admit. But Dex had reached out, and that was the reason Cyrus was there. It had to have been difficult for Dex to look for support, and he wanted to—well, he wanted to reward that.

He understood what that sounded like, as clearly as he knew it was ridiculous. Even Les just laughed, shook his head, and reminded him to text.

All right. Time to go in. Cyrus left his bag in the car, walked over to Dex's motel room door, and knocked on it firmly.

A rumpled, hollow-eyed Dex opened the door, but Cyrus got half a grin and a nod. "Hey, honey. I told you—It's good to see a friendly face."

The door closed, and they stood there, staring at each other.

What at the funeral had been lean was now gaunt, stress and worry literally eating at Dex.

"I didn't listen." Long experience had taught him to be wary of a starving dog, but he couldn't help himself. He reached for Dex anyway, fingers sliding behind the boy's neck. "It's good to see you too."

Dex dropped his head forward with a sigh. "I'm trying, honey. So hard."

"I know." He stepped closer until Dex's head pressed into his chest. "You're doing fine."

Dex's hands were warm where they came to rest on his waist. "Liar. I'm cracked down the middle, and I know it."

"Mm. Maybe. Maybe a crack. But you haven't totally fallen apart. I'm here to make sure that doesn't happen." He pulled Dex in and wrapped an arm around the boy's back. "I've got you. You're going to be fine."

"I'm so glad to see you." Dex leaned hard. "I tried... I swear to God, I tried to do this and keep it together."

His heart was breaking for the boy. Dex had done everything right for Huck while Huck was alive, done everything right after Huck left him with a mess that could easily have buried anyone. And the reward for doing everything right, for all that devotion, was sitting in a pickup truck outside a motel.

"You have done everything possible. Now you should let it go and just let me catch you. I promise you I will."

He didn't know why Dex would believe that his promise was worth any more than Huck's, but he offered it all the same.

"You're a good man." Dex sighed, the sound defeated, weirdly like a last huff of air from a deflated balloon.

He hoped he was. He tried to be.

If you were mine I would just order you into that truck and drive you north.

Simple. Forget this—because what was it really?—and just start over. But Dex had earned the right to make that decision for himself and proven capable enough to fend for himself.

And Dex wasn't his. Not by a mile.

Not...yet.

He held Dex for a bit until the boy was leaning so hard it felt unwise, and then he helped the boy to sit on the edge of the bed.

"So...you have a job?"

"Stocking at the Walmart. I put my shop on vacation right now until I have the apartment. That's today. See the studio, make sure there a real oven. Pay the first and last month's rent and deposit. There's no KOA, so I'll stay here until I can move in." Dex stopped himself, took a long, slow breath. "I've been trying to make a plan that isn't run away from home and jibber like an idiot."

Cyrus wondered if running away might not be a bad idea though. "Where's home, Dex? You said that on the phone too, that you wanted to go home? Where is that?"

Dex closed his eyes, the expression there totally gutted, absolutely devastated, and the grin he got when those eyes opened was a total crocodile. "I guess I don't get to have one anymore."

Jesus Christ. Hitting bottom is ugly and mean, and hard to watch.

"Nonsense." He took Dex's hand, wondering how many people that grin had actually put off. He wasn't one of them. "You get to make a new one. One you want. One you like. You can't run away from nowhere. You can only run *to*."

Dex nodded, eyes on their hands. "I'll figure it. I got enough to pay a deposit, a truck, and a job. Lots don't. I know I was a big titty baby last night. I was drinking."

"Stop that." He turned and looked at Dex, square on, a little weary of the apologies and the self-criticism. "Stop acting like you're not allowed to be upset about all of this. Like you're not entitled to lose it once in a while. I appreciate that you called me. I'm honored that you trust me that much. Everyone needs help. Not everyone knows when to accept it." Or how. Dex still didn't know how.

"You're my friend. Maybe the best one I got." Dex

shrugged and shook his head. “That’s a little embarrassing, isn’t it? I lived here my whole life, and met you once and…”

He squeezed Dex’s hand firmly. Nodding. “And.” He’d already learned that reeling Dex in was tricky. It was more of a spiral than a line, needed a twist instead of a tug. “And you can spit it out, boy.”

Dex rolled his eyes. “I feel like we hear each other. I know it’s stupid, and it’s your job to make people feel that way, so you must be really good at your job. But I do, even if it’s stupid.”

“In fact, that’s not my job. It’s really more my job to make sure people hear themselves. The mutual understanding isn’t necessary at all.” That was all true, without all the details that might make Dex have to think about how friendly they should be.

“I hear myself a lot. It’s a skill. Shit, that’s why I drink.”

He blinked at Dex. It was possible the boy already knew him too well. “Doesn’t work. I thought that was why I did too.”

“No? That sucks. I believe it though. If you want to function, you gotta stop. If you want to just make things quiet, you gotta fuck shit up.”

“No.” He knew what he was talking about, and he wanted Dex to hear him. “No, you don’t. You find something that demands your focus. That gives you no choice. Something big enough to push everything else out.”

“Wouldn’t that be something?” Jesus, the look of pure hunger in Dex’s eyes threatened to knock him back on his heels, but it faded. “I envy that, that focus. I’m a mayfly. I know that.”

A mayfly that had stayed with Huck for almost fifteen years, taking care of the man’s whole world.

"I can help you make it happen." Why did words have a way of bypassing his brain and leaving his mouth when it came to Dex? "If you ever decide to come to New York, I will help you. This is what I do for people, Dex. I can do it for you."

"New York?" Dex sounded like he'd suggested they fly to the moon. "Shit, I've never even left Texas. And afford you too? I seen how you dress. You're fancy. But I appreciate the offer. I believe you could do it."

Never left Texas? With his best friend traveling constantly? Hell, Huck had airline miles to take Dex somewhere, right?

Dex stood, taking a deep, shaky breath and stood at the window. "One day, I'll come visit you, you wait and see. One day when I save enough pennies, I'll come see you and you can show me around. I bet you're hungry, huh? I can feed you. Show us both around here."

Cyrus stood as well and moved slowly over to Dex. "I don't understand why Huck used you so terribly, but I'm a different man."

He stepped up behind Dex, close—too close—and slid his hands over Dex's shoulders. "Come to New York with me, on my dime, stay with me for a few days, and if it's not what you need, if you don't want to stay, I'll fly you home in time for your training on Monday."

He didn't know what he thought he was doing. Three or four days wasn't nearly enough to gentle someone like Dex into the kind of lifestyle Cyrus imagined Dex needed. It wasn't even enough to properly explain it. It wasn't like him to take risks, to be so impulsive, but Dex was right to say they understood each other.

Dex knew him somehow. And he knew he was what the boy needed.

"Is it weird to want to say yes, so bad?" Dex's heart was beating so fast it felt like a hummingbird under his fingers.

"Maybe what you're feeling is how much I want you to say yes."

Dex nodded, took a long, slow breath and leaned toward him. "I need to find a safe place to store my truck and stuff. I bet there's a storage place. I kept my momma's table."

"I saw that. You'll be glad you did." He pulled Dex against him. If Dex were to stay in New York, he'd find a place in his apartment for it.

"I feel things about you I didn't feel for Huck." Dex whispered and leaned back toward him.

"Huck didn't deserve you." He nuzzled Dex's hair, inhaling the bright scent of shampoo and the musky scent of hard work.

"Huck doesn't belong here." Oh. Oh, smart boy.

"Quite right." Feeling a little disoriented by Dex, Cyrus took one more breath of the boy's hair and then stepped back. He wasn't avoiding what was clearly happening, but he didn't feel the time was right yet, either. "Do you want to go sign your lease? Is it a month-to-month?"

"No. I'll call them and tell them I'll come in when I can. If they rent it, this is Tyler, there's another one." Dex nodded like he'd made a decision. "I just need a driver's license to fly, right?"

"That's all. Maybe some clean underwear." He grinned at Dex. "And a ticket. Let me get on that." There was a tiny table in one corner of the room, and he sat in the only chair to arrange travel on his phone.

Dex perched on the edge of the bed, fingers flying, taking notes on the little hotel pad.

He booked them flights in the morning. There was one they might have reasonably been able to catch tonight but adding stress didn't make any sense. Tonight he'd make sure Dex ate and slept.

Then his stomach growled loudly, and he remembered it was well past lunchtime, getting closer to dinner, and he hadn't eaten all day.

"Making a list?"

"Yes, sir. I got a place to park the truck, emailed the apartments, found me a place to feed you, and reserved a little storage room for the table."

There you go. Give the boy a purpose, and Dex was good to go.

"Can we start with food? And then we can get down to business." Cyrus was starting to feel a little off. He needed to eat.

"I figured. We'll go to Stanley's. You won't have to wait, you can get a lot, and we can stop at the Brookshires for snacks after."

"That sounds perfect." He wasn't picky, he just liked food. A lot sounded like just what he needed. "What's your favorite thing to eat there?" *Because you're going to eat more than three bites of something.*

"They got decent brisket sandwiches, Frito pies, ribs. Everything."

That sounded so good he almost moaned. "Bring it on." He stood up, stretching out the kinks of travel. "We're on a morning flight, so we'll have to leave here early. Have you ever been on a plane?"

Dex said he hadn't left Texas, but Texas was big enough to fly across, wasn't it?

"No, sir, but I'm not scared. I'll just follow your lead." Dex pulled on his boots, unfastened his belt to tuck in his shirt, exposing how his boy was skin and bones. "Let's get you fed."

"It will be an adventure." Cyrus pulled his keys out of his pocket and opened the door. "I'll drive."

"Works for me, Cyr. I'm tired of driving."

Oh, how lovely was that? He opened the passenger door for Dex. *Not to worry, boy. I've got the wheel now.*

8

Dex sat on the shuttle bus to the airport, watching the lights in the early morning start to flicker off. His truck was in a gated parking, his stuff was in the storage building. His clothes were in Huck's old suitcase, and his chargers and shit were in his backpack.

Lord have mercy.

He was going to New York City to...to what? Seriously. To what? He looked over to Cyrus, eyes dragging over the man's face, a little low buzz burning him.

He was going to see whether this thing he felt for Cyrus was something that was going to mean something.

Cyrus was a solid presence beside him, still and quiet. It wasn't the hour, or the drive from Tyler. Cyr wasn't tired, it was just the way the man was. Still.

He chuckled softly, looking down at his feet that were tapping restlessly. Christ. There wasn't anything still inside him, not even when he was sleeping.

"I'd never been to DFW before yesterday. In fact, I'd never been in Texas before I came down for Huck's funeral. It's exciting, going to a new place, don't you think?"

"Yes, sir. I like having an adventure." Most of his adventures were small, but he was all in for having a big one.

"If you could do one thing in New York while you're there, what would it be? Is there anything you're curious about?"

Cyr wanted to touch him. He could tell by the way the man leaned in his direction, and the way Cyr's fingers moved.

"One thing..." He understood. He wanted to hold Cyr's hand. "I want to take a picture of the Statue of Liberty."

"Then that's what we'll do tomorrow. The weather should be great for a visit to Lady Liberty." The bus stopped at their terminal and they grabbed their carry-ons and climbed off. "Have you ever been on a ferry?"

"Nope. I been on a bass boat, a canoe, and a kayak." He liked being on the water and... "Oh! And a party barge. Those are fun."

"A party barge? That sounds like a bad idea."

"Oh, they're cool. Pontoon boats only for partying on the lake—coolers, swim platform. It's fun as hell. Got the worst sunburn of my life on one of those." And it had been worth it.

"Like I said. Bad idea. Skin Cancer. Alcohol. Drowning. I'm not really one for taking those sorts of risk." Cyrus sounded so serious but gave him a wink and a grin. "Let's see...we are this station."

They headed in, and it made him stop and stare some. This place was like a city all on his own. Damn.

Cyrus shepherded him through a line where everything including him got x-rayed. They made him take off his damn boots. But after that Cyrus got some food, and they got in line to board the plane.

"The seats aren't fancy but they're in front of the wing, at least."

"It's so loud in here, huh?" The noise just never stopped. He held the coffee Cyrus got him in one hand, his little backpack in the other, and told himself that he was not going to embarrass himself or Cyr by panicking.

Cyrus took his backpack and stuffed it under the seat by his feet. "It is, loud is part of the deal unfortunately. Does it bother you? I usually get used to it after takeoff." He could feel Cyr watching him.

"No, sir. I'm cool." He was, right? Yes. He so was. He wasn't scared, just a little...nervous. "So do you just sleep?"

"No. I'm terrible about that. I can't sleep on planes very well. But lots of people do, if you can, please go ahead. It would make the flight go faster at least. I usually read or watch a movie."

"Can we talk? Or is that not cool."

"Of course." Cyr laughed. "I'm so used to travelling alone I don't usually do a lot of that unless I get lucky with a good seat partner. That's pretty rare."

"Good. Because I'm awake-awake." And nervous. And trusting in Cyrus a lot.

Cyrus glanced at him, then reached over and took his hand, letting their tangled fingers rest in his thigh as the flight attendants started talking. "How did you learn to play mandolin?"

"One of my teachers promised to teach me if I made all As in the third grade. I'm way better at getting things if there's a reason, you know? If this, then that." He turned part way so he could see Cyrus. "I like to learn shit. I'm not, like, a great musician, but I do well enough."

They talked for whole flight, and not just him. Cyrus made him laugh, caught his attention and kept it.

"Hey. That's New York." Cyrus pointed out the window at a hazy view of tall buildings crowded together.

"Wow." That was the biggest thing he'd ever seen, and he just couldn't fathom what his eyes were telling his brain.

"We'll be landing soon, and then we'll go to my place and drop our stuff. What do you want to have for dinner? We could literally have anything. What can't you get easily in Texas? Anything?" Cyrus gave his seatbelt a tug and took his hand again.

How would he know? He was interested in learning about Cyr, more than anything. "Take me to your favorite everyday sort of place."

"Okay," Cyrus agreed readily. "Burgers and beer."

"Works for me." Huh. He'd sorta got the impression Cyr was a teetotaler, but he'd just watch and see. Lord knew he could drink a beer or two. Or ten, if he stayed up all night.

The plane banked around so they couldn't see the skyline anymore, but he could tell they were losing altitude. The engine hummed and the plane shook a little...the noise was kind of awful, but Cyr looked totally relaxed.

He squeezed his fingers, refusing to be scared. If Cyr could do this without screaming, so could he.

As the wheels touched down the pilot put on the brakes hard, which made sense but was startling all the same. Cyrus looked over at him and smiled, not looking at all concerned. Just happy. "We're here."

He nodded, clearing his throat. "Cool. Rock on."

Okay. He'd done his first flight. He wasn't in Texas. Okay. Go him.

They got off the plane, and Newark airport was crowded and busy and under construction. They marched with a sea of people through the airport to the light rail and got onto a crowded car. Cyrus didn't say much, just steered him through and stood close as the narrow transport took them to the train station.

Everybody just wandered around like this was normal, like no one understood how someone's world could just be...different. Boom.

At least you're used to that now, he told himself.

The train was better, they got seats, but a lot of people ended up standing in the aisles. He got a longer view of the city this time, before the train went into a long, pitch-black tunnel.

Cyrus gave his knee a squeeze. "We're almost there. Are you okay? You're doing fine."

He nodded, smiled. When you don't know what to say, shut the fuck up, right? It was cool and wild and weird and overwhelming all at once.

He hadn't understood how underground they were until they took stairs up to a main level and then a long escalator up to the street. "We'll take a cab. I'm not going to put you on the subway after all of that."

It wasn't until they got in the cab that Cyrus cracked a little. "That was crazy."

And this wasn't? There were cars everywhere. Like Houston at rush hour where you knew to just find a bar and wait for a few hours.

He told himself to breathe.

First cab ride. Check. First train ride. Check.

He might have to take one of Huck's muscle relaxants tonight, but right now, he was going to let all the firsts just pour in.

"I should have just gotten us a car at the airport, but I thought this hour on a weekday wouldn't be so crazy. I was rather spectacularly wrong. Sorry about that."

"No worries. It's...something else. You live somewhere

amazing." And huge. And he felt so tiny. Still, it was something no one would believe he'd seen.

He felt small in the cab, but Cyrus's apartment made him feel even smaller. The furniture was leather and metal and very modern, the floors were wood, the walls were mostly bare except for a carefully placed and large piece of art here and there.

"The bed in the guest room isn't made up but you can put your bag in there for now. It's the open door there, after my room." The door to the room at the end of the hall was closed.

"Thanks." God, this looked like one of those movies that you didn't know were science fiction until the robot showed up. No wonder Cyr had gawked at his little house. Thank God Dex hadn't taken Cyrus to look at the apartments. At least Huck's place was nice. Maybe that was what Cyr would remember.

He poked his nose into the guest room. It was just big enough for a double bed and an upright dresser that took up one corner by a window that got some light, but the view was of a brick wall about ten feet away. With all that open space and light and sparseness out there, this room felt cozy. The bed had a heavy and handmade looking quilt on it, the floor was carpeted, the walls were a nice sage green.

Cyrus rested a hand on his back. "Take your time. The bathroom is right across the hall there, see it? I'll be in the kitchen when you're ready. Through the living room. Really, take all the time you need." Cyrus drew the hand down his side, then walked across the living room to the sound of shoes echoing against the high ceiling.

Dex sat on the edge of the bed, careful not to move anything. Okay, breathing. Breathing was good.

He did that for a few minutes, and shit, that was boring,

so he plugged in his phone and his tablet, then went to wash his face.

All right, he didn't come all this way to hide in a room. He was here to be with Cyr. Also, beer and burgers.

Time to find Cyrus and...well, whatever happened would happen.

The big room, which was both dining room and living room he supposed, actually felt pretty cheerful as he walked through it. Less intimidating to be in than to look at. He found Cyrus in the kitchen as promised but stopped short of going in so he could get a good look.

It was amazing.

Long countertops, double oven, big fridge, butcher block island, storage everywhere, and windows that looked onto the street.

Oh, and Cyrus, looking as relaxed as ever, reading the newspaper in a chair at the little round kitchen table.

"Wow." He could make a shit ton of cookies in a setup like that.

"Like it? I thought you might. I'm hoping we can cook while you're here. It would be fun." Cyrus closed his paper. "How do you feel? Are you hungry?"

"I don't know. Can I have something to drink, please? A glass of water?" He was dry as a bone, and he needed a hug.

Cyrus looked at him a second longer than seemed reasonable for a yes or no, but finally smiled and answered. "Of course. The glasses are in the cabinet next to the fridge. I keep filtered water in the fridge as well in a pitcher, you'll see it. Keep it full, please, boy."

"Yes, sir. You want one?"

"I would. I like a little ice in mine."

"Good deal." That was something he could do. He liked to do for people.

He found the glasses—not one of them had Pac-Man or Bugs Bunny on them—and figured a quarter of the glass was a little ice. He poured out, refilled the pitcher, and put it back. Cyrus's fridge was clean, pretty organized. He approved, even if it was a little empty. The state of someone's fridge said a lot.

He brought Cyr his glass. "Here you go. It's a good idea, using the pitcher. I keep bottles in my truck."

"Thank you, boy. New York has clean water, but it tastes a little like chlorine to me. The filter takes the taste out." Cyr sat back in the chair. "Have a seat."

"Thank you." Dex sat and drank deep, feeling the water splash into his belly. The cold hit him, making his abs draw up in a barely there cramp.

"I want you to know what I've planned so you don't get overwhelmed and you can be prepared. Today we're going to take it easy, have some burgers, take a walk. I might take you to meet my friend Les later at his bar if he's there." Cyr sipped his water and then went on. "Tomorrow we'll have fun. We'll take the ferry out to the Statue of Liberty, then shop on the way home and have dinner here. The next day... well, I have some surprises for you. All of that sound okay?"

"Yes, sir, it sounds like a hell of a good time. What all would you like for supper tomorrow, or do you want to see what trips your trigger at the grocery?" Either way worked for him and he didn't reckon it would take twenty minutes to drive to a store.

Cyrus laughed and finished his water, then got up. "Well, let's wait and see how we feel tomorrow. We could make dinner and dessert, with your baking skills. I can cook, but I'm hopeless with baking anything that involves more than putting something in the oven."

"Works for me. I do okay with damn near any recipe. Let

me rinse these out and then I'm yours for the duration." He held out his hand for Cyr's glass.

He didn't get a glass. Instead, Cyrus set the glass down on the table, took his hand and stepped close. Really...close. "Mine. I do like the sound of that, boy."

God, Cyr smelled so good. He leaned, fascinated, drawn right in. There was something about Cyr's eyes, something that made him feel like Cyrus really saw him. "You do?"

Cyr cupped his cheek, studied his face, drew a thumb along his bottom lip. "Do you?"

"Yes, sir." Why lie? They were both grown-ups and weren't either one of them innocent. He kissed the pad of Cyr's thumb. "I do."

"Mmm. Good boy." Cyrus bent to kiss him and for all it was respectful and sweet, he could feel the carefully contained heat underneath it. Nothing else tasted like desire. He sighed, letting Cyrus drive, tell him what all Cyr needed. All the while neither one of them closed their eyes.

Cyrus ended the kiss gently, leaned back enough let him breathe and took his glass from his hand, then set it down on the table too. As their lips met again, Cyr was more demanding, one arm tucking tight around his waist while a hungry tongue tested him.

Oh damn. He gave it up, arms lifting to wrap around Cyr's neck. He opened to Cyrus, leaning hard and letting their bodies touch, all the way down. Damn. Damn, he wanted a piece of that.

Hell, he wanted every goddamn inch.

Cyrus backed him into the kitchen wall and grunted as they hit it, breaking the kiss and staring into him. Whatever Cyr saw must have been enough. "Dex, this is... I didn't bring you here to—"

This sure felt like Cyr wanted to. But he got it. Cyrus had

flown him out here, he was the biggest fish out of water ever, and he'd acted a little crazy. It was dear as fuck, but no one was taking advantage of him. He had money in the bank, a phone, and the ability to Google. All was well. "I know that. I don't mind. I want you, all of you. I'm not a kid or a virgin. I like sex, and I'm betting that sex with you is going to be hot as hell, but if you don't want to, all you got to do is say."

"I do. We have takeout in New York, and it's looking like a good option." Cyr winked at him. "I want all of you, Dex. More than you might understand yet. I just don't want you to think I'm cornering you."

"I know. That's sweet as all get out." He didn't say *but*, because there wasn't one. That was the dearest damn thing he'd ever heard, still... "I'm here because I want to be here."

"I'm not planning on wearing a towel." Cyrus teased, pressing him back again, those dark eyes smoldering.

"It'd be hard to suck you dry through terry cloth, you know." Goddamn Cyrus was pretty.

That rumble in Cyr's chest was something too. "Damn right." Cyr grinned and scooped him right off his feet. The man could move fast on those long legs.

He blinked but got to chuckling. It was hot as hell and made him a little stupid. "You're fucking amazing."

Cyrus didn't say much to that, but he got tossed, literally tossed onto, an enormous bed. The thing didn't even creak.

"I want to see you bare, boy."

He nodded and rolled up, grabbing one of his boots and yanking it off. He put it and his other at the foot of the bed before he stood up and pulled his shirt off. It didn't take him much longer before all he had on was a wristwatch and his gold necklace.

"You're beautiful." Cyrus smiled and reached for his wrist, gently removing his watch, then set it on the nightstand. Cyr touched a finger to his necklace. "Tell me about this."

"Huck gave it to me a few years ago on my birthday. It's nice and heavy, huh? Can you unhook it for me?" The clasp was weird, and he had the devil's own time unfastening it. He'd had it on forever.

"Happily."

Oh. That tone was telling, to say nothing about the growl that followed. Cyr futzed with the clasp for a second before managing to get it off, but it didn't end up on the nightstand, Cyrus walked it all the way across the room and put in in a dish on the dresser.

Damn.

"Thank you, sir." He wasn't sure what all was wrong, but he was pretty sure he wasn't part of it. He walked over to Cyrus, hand sliding over his side. "Can I see you too, please?"

Dex got a kiss in answer as Cyrus tugged the soft shirt out of the waistband of his jeans and let Dex work on the buttons while he kicked off his shoes.

"Mmm...pretty." Oh, He shivered and reached out, moaning as he ran his fingers through the dark curls on Cyr's chest.

"Thank you." Cyrus's chest filled with a deep breath, nipples going hard under his fingers.

"You holler if you don't like something, 'kay?" He stroked in a lazy circle, getting closer and closer to the very tip. So fucking hot.

"You're joking, right?" Cyrus slid hot fingers along his hips to his back, lips finding his again with a low moan.

He pushed up, fingers closing on Cyr's nipple as they devoured each other, things going from heated to blistering.

Cyrus backed him toward the bed, hands, hips, eyes all

laser-focused on him. “Get my jeans,” Cyr ordered, voice thick and rough.

“Yes, sir.” He got the buckle undone, fingers quick as a bunny. He wanted that cock, and he was fixin’ to get his eyes on it.

He could feel Cyrus’s eyes on him as he pushed the denim away, the leather belt dragging the jeans to the floor, and Cyr’s thick cock landed heavy and hot in his hand.

A deep, raw damn sound escaped him, and he measured, root to tip, and right back down. His mouth went dry, and Dex licked his lips as he glanced down.

Cyrus caught him under the chin and lifted his face into another kiss, sensual and deep, stealing his breath until he swayed. Cyrus broke it off catching him with one arm. “Now you can.”

He slid down to sit on the edge of the bed, one hand gliding down to weigh Cyr’s heavy balls. His other hand brought that fine prick to his lips so he could slide his tongue over the tip. Damn.

He worked the slit until he could get a taste of what he needed, and when the salt hit his tongue, he took Cyrus in.

A firm hand landed on the back of his head, and Cyrus sighed for him, the long breath tinged with need. Cyr’s grip in his hair was a clear but patient demand. “That’s right, boy.”

Okay, that was fucking blistering—both the words and the touch—and he moaned in response, spreading his legs to make room for his aching cock. Then he got to the happy business of learning every hot spot from balls to slit.

Every time he glanced up, Cyrus’s eyes were on him, watching him with interest, letting him explore, tease, whatever he wanted. His only real feedback, apart from the heat in Cyr's eyes, were the rich sounds, hisses and grunts, soft moans.

He took the noises and used them as rhythm—up and down, slowing the tempo to linger when there was a noise he liked.

Cyrus rocked toward him, hips thrusting just slightly as a second hand joined the first and tangled in his hair. Cyrus had been holding back, he knew, and this was his real reward; that hot little crack in Cyr's self-control.

The rush of excitement flooded him, and he slipped one finger back behind Cyr's balls, dragging it firm as hell along that little strip of skin, knowing it lit a man up.

"Damn. Fuck." Cyrus arched over him, hips tugging back and sinking slowly forward again. "Enough, boy." Cyr growled at him, but it was all heat and need, and those fingers stroked through his hair approvingly. "Damn."

He eased up, giving Cyr long, lazy strokes of his tongue, letting the tension back down, so they could build up again.

"That's right. Now, come up here and kiss me." Cyrus tucked a hand under his arm and helped him stand, pulling him into an embrace that lifted him up off his feet.

Damn.

Goddamn.

He felt like he was in the eye of a hurricane, like he might go flying if Cyr let him go, even for a second.

Cyrus laid him out in the big bed and moved right over him, devouring him with a kiss that took his breath and demanded his focus. Dex bent one leg so Cyrus and he could touch, all the way down, and his body moved without a bit of permission from him.

The kisses moved slowly down his chin and across his neck to a collarbone as Cyr explored him, mapping his body with a hot tongue, the trail on his skin cooling as it was left behind. Cyr drew a line right down the middle of his chest, stopping at his navel and circling it, humming to him along the way.

His belly drew up, rippling hard. Cyr's shoulder pushed his bent knee out, stretching him wide. Dex reached up high, hands finding the headboard, making room for all the want inside him.

Long fingers wrapped around his cock and stroked much too gently, lazily, as Cyrus looked him over. "You're something special, Dexter. Beautiful."

Him? He was just a redneck, common as pennies, and he knew it, but it was sweet to hear, true or not. He didn't argue, but he knew better. "Thank you."

"Maybe you'll feel beautiful when I'm done with you." Cyr ducked lower and bathed his cock with a curious tongue, circling the head, shoving the tip into the opening until he could feel it stretch.

"Oh sweet fuck." Everything tightened for a second, leaving him bright and tingling, the world stopping short before it revved.

"Beautiful boy." Cyr stroked him again, firmly for a few strokes and then let him go. "I want to see you fly higher than that airplane."

"Please." He was all in. More than he ever had been.

Cyrus was probably gone for a second, but it felt like a year lying in the big bed exposed and waiting. Dex caught sight of the lube and heard the foil tear and then Cyr was back, pushing his thighs up and settling between them. "You ask so nicely, boy."

He brought his hands down and reached for Cyr, hands sliding up the broad chest. "Mmm...look at you."

"You like?" Cyr smiled and slick fingers pressed up against his ass, teasing, circling.

"I do. You're fine as frog hair."

Damn, that touch, it made him want to beg, to wiggle. To turn over and offer his ass like he was in heat.

"I like that." Cyr's finger slipped inside him and swirled in a circle and another one followed a second later.

He grabbed his knees and pulled, baring himself and his hole to that touch. "You've got smart fingers."

"Thank you, boy." Cyrus slapped his ass cheek, then smoothed a hand over the skin to take the sting out.

Oh, didn't that twist him up a little? He'd had a couple fuckbuddies that were into slap and tickle, but usually that happened right before you shot.

Those fingers slipped away, the thick head of Cyrus's cock pushing slowly inside him, stretching him as Cyrus moved up over him.

"H-hey." Oh fuck him, that burn was... Jesus, that was just right. Nice and slow so he felt every inch. His fingers opened and closed, his neck arching with the stretch.

"You okay?" Cyrus asked through his teeth. "Fuck, you're —you're good?"

"I'm fucking great. Don't stop, man. I need it." Words. Go words. Now fucking.

"Yes." That must have been enough, because Cyrus started to move in long slow strokes at first but building steadily to a heavy rhythm. Cyrus hooked a hand behind one of his knees, bending him even further.

He met each thrust, forcing his eyes to stay open, to watch every second of this. You never got a first again.

Cyrus was watching too, looking down at the way their bodies came together, then back up to find his eyes, holding them for long stretches. "Beautiful." Cyr's long fingers gripped his shaft, working it double time to each strong thrust.

"Fuck. Fuck, honey. Cyr." His belly went taut, and his balls drew up so tight that he might die. *Right there. Just like that. Oh Jesus, thank you for a man that knows what the fuck he's doing.* "Fixin' to..."

And then he did. He shot so hard that he was pretty sure he broke something deep inside, ropes of spunk spraying over Cyr's hand.

"Jesus. Tight. Fuck!" Cyrus forced out through gritted teeth, hips going wild. Cyr turned bright red for a second, veins popping out at his temples, then everything just stopped like a bubble bursting, the look on Cyr's face pure bliss.

Yeah. Fuck yeah. He nodded, trying to remember how to unclench his fingers, his toes. Everything was locked up in pleasure.

That head of thick, dark hair landed on his chest and Cyr's shoulders sagged a little, well tired out. It was the first time he'd ever seen that strong body look vulnerable; even Cyr's usually perfect haircut was rumpled.

That loosened him, and Dex found his hands again. He stroked across Cyr's shoulders, petting for a bit before he began to rub. Cyrus had given him so much; this was the least he could do.

"Mmm." Cyr leaned up and kissed him, slowly, his hum so satisfied. "Pretty when you come."

"You make me blush, honey." He ran his hand through Cyrus's hair. "Thank you."

"Oh. My pleasure." That was an awfully smug grin, wasn't it? Shit, Cyrus deserved it.

"I think it was my pleasure, man. Seriously."

Cyrus laughed gently and stretched out next to him. "Well good. Then we get to do it again soon." Cyr's feet slid right off the end of the bed in a long stretch. "I'll admit, seeing if you were interested was definitely on my agenda, but it wasn't in my plan for tonight. I think I'll blame you."

"Works for me." He'd happily take the blame. No problem.

"Mmm. Perfect." Cyrus tucked an arm over him. It felt... protective? Possessive? Whatever it was, it was clear Cyr didn't want him going anywhere any time soon. "Little nap, boy. And then we'll order something to eat."

Cyrus was all about his appetite.

"Sounds good." Dex wasn't hungry, but he was happy, so he'd just stay put.

Rest.

9

"Mmm."

Cyrus smelled coffee.

He rolled onto his back and stretched, surprised that it was light out until he felt the lovely ache in his thighs. The room smelled like sex, his bed smelled like Dex, and he was feeling decidedly satisfied.

He got out of bed, wanting coffee and a kiss, two of his favorite things on earth. He replayed the bit of their afternoon he'd been coherent enough to remember, grinning like a fool. Dex was lovely; a little tragically lovely at the moment because the boy was so thin and pale, but he was sure that was temporary. Just lovely. Eager. Completely capable of taking what he could dish out.

At least in bed.

That was a bit of a hurdle still, wasn't it? But the boy was up and making coffee and was someone for whom simple service came naturally. Other service too. The way that Dex had gentled him back to earth after his first non-solo orgasm in about six months was kind and caring, and the boy had asked him for little—nothing really—in return.

He looked around his bedroom as he found sweatpants to pull on. Well, he certainly made no effort to hide who he was, did he? The cuffs and tie-downs hanging on the headboard were plain enough to see. At least his tools were all in his dungeon.

Though without a lock on that door, it was possible Dex had already gotten an education.

It would be what it would be. He couldn't change who he was, or what he needed. In the end, Dex would take him or leave him.

"I smell coffee," he called as he made his way through the living room to the kitchen. The clock above the fireplace read ten after six. Thai delivery sounded good.

"You do. I hope you don't mind I dug for a coffee cup. I needed some. Would you like a cup?" Dex smiled at him, the look in the boy's eyes warm, easy. "Dark, no flavors. I remember."

He went right to the boy and took a gentle kiss before he answered any questions. "Yes, please."

"Mmm..." Dex squeezed his fingers, the touch warm and sweet. "I'll get you a cup."

"Thank you." Things weren't weird. That was a good sign. Sometimes guys didn't know how to navigate the waking up together moment well. Especially the first time. "Did you manage to sleep at all?" He hadn't slept long, maybe an hour or a little more, but he'd needed it.

"I rested my eyes until the pull of caffeine was too much to bear." Dex handed him his cup, making sure the cabinet was clean after. "You have a neat place—it's like from a magazine."

"It is a little. I like that sort of minimal look for the living areas. The bedrooms are cozier, especially the guest room." He took the coffee, took a sip and tucked his hands around it. "Mm. Good. I'm glad you felt comfortable enough to just make yourself at home. It's nice to see you that relaxed."

"I didn't snoop farther than to find coffee, cups, and a touch of half and half, I promise." Dex winked at him. "I can only imagine what you thought about my place and its insanity."

"I thought your place was a damn good spot to get out of the rain." He leaned against the kitchen counter and sipped his coffee while he watched Dex flit about, fuss over a drop of spilled coffee, wash a spoon they were probably going to use again in five minutes. So busy. "I wasn't accusing you of snooping. I really am glad you know I trust you."

"It was a good place, and thank you so much for bringing me to see. Seriously." Dex took a deep breath and stretched up, swaying side to side.

"You're welcome. I love an adventure." He was hoping Dex would be his next adventure before too long. "Sore?"

He grinned at himself, knowing how that question sounded. He couldn't keep the Dom out of his voice if he tried.

"Only in the best way, honey. That's a sweet kind of sore." That smile was happy, well-satisfied. "I got to admit, you know how to make a man happy."

He nodded his thanks. "You're rather inspirational. And handy." He held up his mug.

The coffee isn't this good when I make it.

Actually, lots of things were better when he was with Dex.

"How do you feel about Thai food?"

Dex blinked and grabbed his phone, scrolling and frowning. "Huh. I don't know that I feel anything. Never seen anything like it. It's like Chinese food without rice or egg rolls, right?"

"It's much tastier than Chinese and has lots of vegetables and noodles. If you haven't had it before then that's definitely what we're ordering." He grabbed his phone and opened the website, placing an order for them online. "Spicy is okay?"

"Yes, sir. You want my card to pay? I'm happy to buy supper." Dex dug out his wallet. "Or I got some cash."

"Thank you. I'll let you buy me a Coke at the bar." He didn't want to be insulting, but Dex was on a kind of limited budget he hadn't been on in years. Cyrus placed the order and put his phone back on the charger on the counter.

"Well, thank you very much. Today's a day of firsts, isn't it?" Dex stared at him for a second, like he was making some momentous decision, then he sighed softly. "I know it's weird to ask and all, but—can I have a hug? Please?"

He smiled at Dex, set his coffee down and opened his arms. "Nothing weird about it."

Dex nodded and came to him, and his boy was shaking, trembling in his arms. He folded them around Dex and held the boy close, holding off on words and just letting the closeness be comfort.

There wasn't much they needed to say. Dex had lost a friend, a home, everything he knew and, apart from Cyrus, he was alone. It would be good if Dex could let some of it go.

Dex muscles jerked as he fought to relax, fought to give in, and finally just Dex leaned away with a soft sigh. "Thank you."

Oh, no. No, no, pet. Don't give up yet, a voice was shouting in his head and he struggled not to pull the boy right back in. But Dex wasn't ready, and it wouldn't help to push.

He knew Dex was watching, paying attention, and whatever Cyrus did do next mattered. The boy had taken a big step, and he didn't want this to feel like a failure.

Make up your mind quick, dammit. The boy is waiting.

He hooked his fingers behind Dex's head and gave the boy a quick kiss, pulling away with a smile. "You're welcome."

"Been a big day, huh? Cool, but big." Dex went back to fluttering—another cup of coffee for both of them, another wipe of the counter. It was exhausting and fascinating at the same time.

"It has." He was dying to give the boy something to do. Dust or polish or clean something. Cook something. Something productive to help with that energy. *Soon*, he told himself. It had been a big day, but it was going to be a bigger weekend. "I love contact, you know. Touch. Holding hands, a snuggle on the couch, spooning. You don't ever have to ask. The answer is yes."

"Oh? Oh, that's—that's sort of wonderful." Dex wandered toward him, moving around to stroke his shoulders. "Really. I kind of want to touch you a lot. It feels right."

"I think I was a cat in another life." He picked up his coffee, paying close attention and relieved that the kiss seemed to have done the trick, and that he was right about the boy craving contact. So far, so good. "Any time. I'll just purr for you."

"Here kitty, kitty." Dex chuckled softly, hands sliding over his back, fingers curious, searching out knots and rubbing them away. "I think I was a bird—something like a grackle or a crow."

Birds were smart; that seemed perfectly appropriate. But he was curious, doubting that was what Dex had hit on. "What makes you think that?"

"I like to learn things, and I'm curious about everything. Also, I like to make a nest wherever I am." Dex chuckled, the sound wicked, surprising him. "And I can be loud when I have to."

"Oh, yes. Or when you want to." He turned his head, hoping he might have made the boy blush. "Those are all good reasons." Also great insight. A nest, hm? He could help with that.

Dex kissed his cheek, hiding behind him.

Bullseye. He laughed softly. "Where do you want to eat? In here at the table? Or we could have a little picnic in the living room and watch a movie or something?" He had a dining room table, but it was huge, and he never sat at it.

"Let's picnic. That sounds like a good way to share supper together. Can you believe you were eating barbecue in Tyler last night? Just last night?"

"Flying is weird like that. It's also earlier there. An hour I think. That was good barbecue though." It was. And it was more food than even he could eat.

"I love watching you eat. It's so—I don't know. Real? Like you feed your hungry for real. That sounds stupid, but it's true."

"Food is love, Dex. Good for your body and your soul." Good thing too, because he was hungry a lot.

"Yeah. I—yeah."

He hadn't figured out this thing with Dex and food, but it was a priority for him, and he would. He reached back and took one of Dex's hands, then turned around to look at the boy. "I can't offer you a beer. But I have some amazing teas."

"I like tea." Dex's head tilted. "You don't drink, huh? I can tell. I'm sorry I offered those first few times. It takes me a little bit to catch on, but I do eventually. I've been drinking a lot lately because...well, you know. I got shit on my brain."

"Please don't apologize. How could you have known?"

He drew a finger along the line of Dex's jaw from ear to chin. "There's nothing wrong with drinking. Just remember it's a short-term fix."

"Everything is but Jesus, right?" Dex leaned into his touch, face relaxing. "No offense, but me and God aren't talking right now. I'm sorta pissed at Him."

"You're not the first, and you won't be the last." He'd never been good at blind trust and just accepting things. He came around eventually, but it was never an easy road. Cyrus bent to give Dex another kiss but the door buzzer went off, so it turned into a quick peck. "Mmm. Dinner's here. Let me show you how to buzz them in."

"Okay. Yes. So, they're downstairs?" Dex followed him, hand warm on his back.

"Yes. The building has a handful of doormen, so that's who is buzzing. They'll tell you who is here, and you can allow them up, or not." He paid a premium for a building with a doorman, but since it was also where he worked, it was handy to have someone screen people. He showed Dex which button to hit, had a quick conversation with Mac, and in another minute they were on their way back to the kitchen with the bags of food.

"My stomach is growling." No shock there.

"You need to eat, then. Let's feed you." Dex breathed in deep. "It doesn't smell like anything I know. So cool."

And that was his plan. He'd ordered the small sizes of a bunch of different things. If he could get Dex to try one bite of everything, that would be four or five more bites than he'd seen Dex eat in the last two days.

"I hope you like it. Adventures are all about new things, right? New York is full of new things to try." He let Dex fuss around, find plates and silverware, while he found a tray to carry the food containers out to the living room.

"What's your very favorite food, like of all time? Also, do you want water, honey? Or do you have tea bags where I can make you some iced tea real quick?"

"You can make iced tea real quick? Must be a Texas trick." Cyrus pointed to a drawer under the coffee maker. "Lots in there. And my favorite food of all time is..." He blinked at Dex. Did he have a favorite? He just liked food. "I don't know. Maybe french fries." He laughed because that sounded so stupid. "I think I could live on french fries."

"Really? Me too. My whole freezer had just frozen fries. You must've known in your heart. You got me french fries that first day." Dex started digging, pulling out six tea bags. "You got a mason jar or a plastic deal with a lid?"

Wow. He had no idea. But who didn't like french fries?

"I do. Um. Above the microwave. Might be a stretch for you, I'll get it." He pulled out a jar and looked at it for a second wondering why he had it. He couldn't remember. "Will this work?"

"Yes, sir. Thanks." Dex kissed the corner of his mouth, the touch unexpectedly erotic. "Give me five minutes, and I'll have you iced tea."

"Magic iced tea. I like it. I'll take the food out." And steal a few bites before his head started to swim. He set the tray down on the coffee table and sat on the couch, then thought better of it and moved to the floor. This was a picnic after all. And his artfully shaggy area rug deserved a little love.

The polite thing to do would be to wait for Dex, but fainting was less fun, so he picked up a fork and dug into the container of Pad Thai, which, despite typically being the most popular dish, was still his favorite.

"You know, I'm going to get the stuff to make you granola bars tomorrow. Just little ones to carry with you all the time. They'll help."

That wasn't a bad idea. He'd never been a snacker really; work made that hard so he mostly ate big meals. "Probably, thanks. Sorry I started but…" He didn't need to explain obviously. Dex had that figured out. "Sit. You need to try this."

"Here's your tea. I did a little orange in it, and you know I don't stand on ceremony. You eat what you need." Dex sat easily, staying close to him.

Cyrus took a sip of his tea and then set it on the table. "Mm. The orange is perfect. I like this miracle five-minute tea. I'll have to keep you around." He held out a bite on his fork. "Try this."

Dex opened up and took the bite, closing his eyes as he chewed, focusing totally and relaxing as he did. Oh that was lovely.

He waited, watching, until Dex swallowed, wondering if this was going to be his future. Feeding his boy off his own fork. Somehow, he didn't think he'd mind. "What do you think? It's not french fries, I know."

"It's so cool—I've never ever had sour noodles and peanuts before. And there's a little bitty kick in the back. Yum. Thank you."

"This one is my favorite. It's called Pad Thai. But I got a bunch of other things we can taste. Don't worry about leftovers, they'll get eaten." He huffed. "By me most likely. Everything is listed on the receipt. Which one do you want to open up next?" He handed the receipt to Dex to read.

"Oh, dude. How cool is this? Okay. Pad ki mao. Let's try that."

He looked around and found the container—wide noodles, pork, garlic, and some real heat. This one was going to make an impact.

He opened the container. The spiciness making his eyes

tear a little. "Oh, they did well by us on this one. Smell that? What do you want? There's pork and these great noodles, these little tiny shrimp, veggies..."

"Whoa. That smells good." Dex leaned into him, looking. "That'll heat you up, huh?"

"It's spicy, no joke." Dex was curious, which was so great, and he wasn't going to argue with sitting close. He forked up a piece of shrimp, a noodle, and a strange little mushroom he didn't know the name of and held it for Dex. "Tasty too."

"It's an Alice of Wonderland mushroom!" That happy laugh was like a drug, and then Dex opened up to him, letting him drive.

He linked arms with Dex and grinned. "So you don't fall down a rabbit hole." He tried a bite of the spicy stuff himself, chewing the noodles happily.

"Oh, I like that." Dex licked his lips. "Spicy. Can I kiss you? I bet it's wild."

"You may." He offered his lips, letting Dex kiss him, giving the boy a chance to steer.

Dex hummed and pressed their mouths together, tongue sliding over his lips, the heat building and burning before Dex pulled away.

He blinked at Dex, eyelids a little heavy after that kiss. "Mmm. Thai is good. That was better."

The last time he had it this bad for someone, it was simple, but he wasn't sober enough to hold onto it. This time even though he was completely dry, it all seemed complicated as hell. So many layers to peel back still. But the pull in that kiss was real, the affinity was real. Dex's intuition was spot on, and Cyrus just had to hope his was too.

"It is. I do like your kisses, and that was a sweet burn." Dex leaned back with a grin. "Eat. It's good for you."

He put the container he was holding down and picked up another. "Let's try the curry." Curry always smelled so good. Warm and cozy like comfort food.

"I've heard about curry. I think I had curry popcorn at a party once. Do you like it?" Dex breathed in deep and smiled. "Oh that's something nice."

"I do. To me, it feels like something mom would make. So Indian curry is usually just the dry spices, which was probably what was on your popcorn. Thai curries have coconut milk and are usually sauces. Here…have a bite." This was fun, and Dex was about to take a third bite of real food.

Dex took the bite from him, eyes going wide, and he heard Dex's stomach rumble.

"Good?" He grinned, offering another bite.

"Super good. You need some too." But Dex took it, snuggling into his side with a happy moan.

He took a big bite, enjoying it thoroughly. "Comfort food, right? Like mac and cheese or chicken soup." Or french fries. God, he could be such a goon. He took another bite and then offered one to Dex.

"Make sure there's enough for you, now. You like it." Dex searched his eyes, checking in with him.

"You're a good boy. Thank you." He held his gaze steady, letting Dex study him as long as the boy needed to. He understood what he was up against; Dex's mind was probably busy trying to remind the boy that there were things to worry about. The best that he could offer was a calm and steady course.

Finally Dex gave him another one of those smiles, and then Dex melted against him. "My favorite is the curry. I like that. I wonder if you can make it at home."

"We should try. I bet we could figure it out. We may have

to go to one of the specialty groceries to find what we need to though." He had no idea how difficult it would be, but he'd try anything, and he felt like cooking was something he and Dex could enjoy together. He knew damn well Dex would do most of the work anyway, the boy just moved so much faster than he did.

He took a big bite and tempted Dex with one more.

Dex hummed as he ate and then his boy looked to him. "What do you want next? Do you want to have more of your Pad Thai one?"

"Sure. Are you wielding the fork now?" He stretched past Dex and grabbed a remote so he could put on some music.

"I am." Dex made him up a bite, making sure to choose a little bit of everything before feeding it to him.

"Mmm. I think it tastes better this way." He reached out to brush some hair off Dex's forehead, then studied the boy, tracing an eyebrow, running his thumb under one eye, resting his fingers against Dex's cheek.

Dex didn't flinch away from his gaze, didn't hide from him, just breathed for him and waited for him to see his fill.

"You have a wise face, Dex. Have you ever heard that before? Keen eyes."

"My mom used to say I was an old soul, but I think that meant that I didn't drive her crazy."

He touched Dex's chest lightly. "It means you have something in here that can't be taught. Something you just know."

"That's a good thought. I do, you know, even though I'm stupid, I know stuff sometimes. And I take good care." Dex swallowed hard, pain written on the sweet face. "Excuse me, huh? I gotta use the facilities."

Damn. Dex pulling away that suddenly left him off-balance.

"I...uh. Of course. Do you know where you're going? There's a half off the kitchen, one in your room, one in mine."

"Sorry. Be right back. I—I got all this... Be right back."

He cleaned up dinner while Dex was gone, needing to do something with his hands so he could think. The boy wasn't stupid. Cyrus was frankly surprised and saddened to hear Dex say that. He had so much more work to do with Dex than he could manage in a few days, and it was so important that the boy felt everything about being here was a good experience. Even if Dex went home. Even if Dex decided not to come back. It was important.

Maybe the pain and the tears in Dex's eyes was a good thing. Maybe some of what was bottled up was finally breaking free. He just wished Dex had allowed him to be there for it.

"I'm so sorry. I got all caught up, and you've been in the middle of that shit too much. I would have cleaned up the food, I swear."

"I needed something to do." He dropped the sponge he was holding in the sink and dried his hands. "Come here."

"I'm sorry." Dex came right to him. "I'm just still mad. You had to come to Texas. I never got a chance to just not be fucked up and know you. And now I want to know about you more than ever, and I'm not worth shit, and it makes me mad."

"Whoa. Hey." He pulled the boy into his arms. "You and I met when we met for a reason. Be angry, be hurt, sad, whatever you're feeling. It's my job to meet you where you are, boy. We'll get to know each other, not to worry. I think right now the reason this is so good is that we're able to be what the other one needs in this moment."

Dex breathed and gave him a nod, cuddling in. "I'll get my shit together. I will. I'm sorry about the drama. It's not usually me. Usually I just...do my job, but I don't have one right now. And I've been stupid busy for not having work for months now. You know how frustrating that is, man?"

Oh, my boy.

Cyrus told himself to breathe in and breathe out for a moment. It was tempting to spill it all right then, all the things he knew he could do for Dex—the purpose, the calm, the guidance—and he was so close, so damn close to that revelation.

Soon, pet. Soon.

"I understand. Meaning is important. That's what keeps you moving forward. It's not enough just to keep busy. You can't be your best self that way." He held Dex protectively against him, wanting the boy to feel secure. Safe. "You don't owe anyone an apology, Dex, least of all me. I knew what I was doing when I offered to help, and I'll listen. I listen to all of it. Your anger, your pain...and I won't judge. That's not my place. I'm here for you because I want to be. Don't ask me to explain why. I don't have words for that yet, but I think you know somehow, in your way. I can...take care of you. You can take care of me. You'll understand it better in time."

That was more than Cyrus meant to say; the poor boy didn't need lectures right now, but it barely scratched the surface of everything he could have said. Everything he would say, eventually.

Dex leaned hard, resting heavy against him. There was trust there, Dex pulling comfort from him. "Thank you for hearing me. You've done it from the start, like you were meant to."

Like he was meant to. That was it exactly. Like they were meant to. Cyrus didn't understand it, but he didn't need to. Life threw stuff in his path all the time, and he was learning to see the opportunities as they came up for what they were. Choices. He chose to roll with this one.

"It's possible." Everyone deserved to be heard.

"What's your favorite color?"

"What?" He shook his head at the sudden change of subject. "I don't know. Green maybe." He thought about it another second, he knew for Dex this was a real question. "Yes. Green."

"Like your sheets and the comforter on the guest bed." Dex nodded like he'd learned something, understood something.

"I love that room. It has a good energy. The quilt on the bed and the little dresser in the corner were my mother's."

"Are y'all close?" Dex's hands moved over him, touching him everywhere, restless, curious boy.

"We were. Now she lives in a cemetery in Pennsylvania with my dad." He'd never found a way to say his parents were gone that wasn't awkward for everybody. "I lost her about a year ago. Little less. It was sad but okay. She didn't remember who I was by then."

"Oh, I'm sorry. That's hard. Miss Maydell next door to us had Alzheimer's, and it was awful for her and her grandbabies. I know for them, it was a blessing." Dex squeezed him gently. "I hope you have great memories of her."

"I do. Many. She was just very young for that kind of diagnosis." Mom had been addled at fifty-five. By sixty-five it had become serious dementia, and his brother had handled most things after that. He got home once a month, not enough to make sure she knew him, but nobody really wanted him there. "I'd call it a blessing. More for her than us, I think. I can't imagine living that way."

"No. No, I hear you. That sucks." Dex held him now, so easy to offer support and care.

"But the point is, she made the quilt in there for me and it happens to be green, so I guess I must have always liked green." He kissed Dex's forehead. "You give wonderful hugs."

"Thank you. I'm glad I'm here with you."

"You're welcome to stay awhile. I'd like it if you did, but I know you have your plans."

"I want to stay, but I'll have to start making cookies soon. I'll keep the store on vacation, but the back-to-school party orders will start soon."

"Have you seen the kitchen?" He laughed.

"I have. It's so fucking cool. I wouldn't need much for supplies, and..." Dex stopped himself, breathed. "Let me think about it for a few hours. All I want while I'm in your arms is to stay here."

"I'm sorry. You haven't even been here a day yet. I didn't mean to push." *Much.* His position wasn't going to change whether Dex was in his arms or in the guest room. "Do you want to get out of here for a while? I can take you out for a beer."

"That sounds good. I'd like to go out and about with you. Do you have a place you like best?"

"I do. I have a regular neighborhood place that is owned by my friend, Les. He's the one with the job opening—"

Shit.

He backpedaled a little. "That's not pressure, so we won't even bring it up, I promise. It's just my favorite place."

Dex chuckled, kissed the corner of his lips again. He was

learning that was Dex's way of saying, 'it's okay'. "I can't wait to see it."

"Good." Cyrus looked around the kitchen and decided it was clean enough. "Ready? Oh. We should probably get dressed."

"What kind of dressed do we need?" Dex was like a fairy or a brownie, zipping around the kitchen with a rag and putting it to right.

He chuckled. "No shirt, no shoes, no service? Otherwise, whatever you want."

"What are you wearing then? I want to just fit in."

"Jeans. T-shirt. Boots." His usual, when he wasn't wearing leather.

"I can do that. Give me five minutes and I'll be ready." Dex shot him a relaxed grin.

Cyrus gave the boy's ass a pat and sent him into the guest room before heading off to find jeans.

Dex was truthful with him, out and dressed by the time Cyrus walked out. Jeans, a dark green T-shirt that had fit ten pounds ago, a longhorn buckle, and shiny cowboy boots made Dex scream Texas.

He had said boots. His were more of the motorcycle variety, but hey, everyone looked good in boots.

And a green T-shirt.

"Look at you." He took Dex's hand, headed for the door. "Those are great boots."

"Thank you, sir. They're comfy as all get out." Dex pulled a cap out of his back pocket and put it on. "Yours look fine too."

Dex was adorable with that cap on. "Thank you. They're solid. I like how they feel." It was warm out on the street. Not summer warm yet, just a nice spring evening, so lots of people were out, even in his off the beaten path Eastside neighborhood.

"Mmm...it's pretty out here. And busy. Lord have mercy." Dex's eyes were wide, looking at everything with a happy shock.

"Both, yes." His neighborhood had a few trees at least, and the street wasn't that wide, so the traffic was light. He kept a good grip on Dex's hand anyway, just so the boy remembered he was right there. "We're not going far. Just a couple of blocks."

"Cool. This is...this is a little like Austin, huh? A little like, but not." The curiosity would serve Dex well. Dex was like a sponge, drawing everything in.

"Cities are funny like that. They're all a little like each other...and not." It had been a long time since he walked down the street hand in hand with anyone, and Dex was getting noticed now and then, which just made him that much more proud to be doing it. "We're going right here." They rounded the corner onto 3rd Avenue, which was a great deal busier.

"Cool." Dex moved closer, right up against him to avoid knocking into other people.

"You'd be surprised how quickly you can get used to this. When you know your way around and have somewhere to be, you become just like everyone else."

"You think? How long have you been here?"

"Oh, I've been here a long time. I moved here as soon as I turned eighteen. I lived in a one-bedroom apartment with five guys and had a handful of jobs. It was crazy."

"You're brave. That's cool. I'm no coward, but I tend to find a place and make a life there, you know?"

"I'd have stayed if I could. I wasn't moving to New York, I was leaving Pennsylvania. I don't know if it was brave. I didn't feel brave at the time. I was terrified." He remembered his first night in the city, sleeping on a friend's couch and listening to all the traffic and the sirens and thinking he might manage to not starve, but he'd never be able to sleep again.

"I hear you. I been there. A few times." Dex shot him a shit-eating grin. "This week."

"True enough, boy." Cyrus laughed, the sound echoing off the tall building they were passing. He stopped Dex before going in. "We're here. I like this place. You don't have to. If it's not your thing, or it's too...anything, you speak up."

Dex blinked at him like he was speaking Swahili. "Okay...it's a bar? Right?"

"It's a bar. A regular neighborhood bar." Possibly crowded, possibly loud, definitely gay.

"Okay. I have been in a number of bars. We're safe."

"You're making fun of me." He pretended to pout. Too bad if Dex thought it was ridiculous. He was doing his job.

"I am not. You're all tense. I'm being comforting. Like patting your butt, but without the potential that someone kicks my ass." It was amazing, that gentle happiness, that soft tease.

He was tense? "I am not tense." Was he? He pulled Dex inside. "Come on."

The bar was fairly busy—men laughing, music playing, the lights not low, but comfortable.

"Nice. Not a bit of a dive. You going to let me buy you a Coke still?"

He wasn't, but that was so sweet. "If you insist." He hooked an arm around Dex and ushered him to the bar. Thursday... Oh. Perry was on.

"Mr. Hughes! Nice to see you." Perry started pouring him a coffee. "Beautiful day out there."

"Gorgeous. Perry, this is Dexter Appleton. Visiting from Texas." Perry would put two and two together and figure out who Dex was. He hadn't used names, but he'd vented a bit when he got back from Huck's funeral.

Sure enough, Perry looked at him, then back at Dex. "Good to meet you, Dexter. What can I get you?"

"I'll have one of whatever he's having, please. And I'm tickled as all get out to meet you, sir." Dex tucked his hat in his back pocket.

He leaned over and spoke softly in Dex's ear. "It's okay if you want a beer. I'm in here nearly every night, people drink around me all the time."

Dex turned and met his gaze, hazel eyes so warm. "I appreciate that, a lot, but that ain't nice, Cyr. I care for you, so I won't drink around you."

"Oh." He held those eyes. Nobody did that. Once he let someone off the hook, they always had their drink. He had no idea what to say. "Thank you."

"No problem." Dex nodded and turned to look at the back of the bar. "This is awful pretty with the lights and the mirrors."

"It's my second office. I sit over there on the end a lot with my iPad and work."

"And drink a lot of coffee." Perry sat a mug down in front of Dex.

"And that," he agreed. "It's better than mine." Maybe not better than Dex's though.

"Excellent. It looks like a good place to hang out and people watch." Dex sipped his coffee, looking around, watching people in the mirrors.

"It is, and I do a lot of that. And I've met a lot of neighborhood people. It's a good spot."

Perry leaned close to Dex. "He sits here and lets people bend his ear all night long."

"I like people." Cyrus shook his head at himself as he realized at some point he'd become a neighborhood fixture. That guy always at the bar drinking coffee.

He watched Dex, who was looking around, taking everything in. Learning the place in that way the boy learned everything—by being curious. There were worse things than being the nice guy at the bar, but part of him was hoping he might be doing less of it in the near future.

"He's damn fine at listening." Dex's focus and smile made Perry flutter. "I bet you are too. Good bartenders have to be."

"I try." Perry patted the bar. "Speaking of which, I don't mean to pry, but Cy told me. I'm sorry to hear about your friend."

"Thank you. I appreciate it." Dex nodded once, the boy giving nothing emotional away, even though Cyrus knew it was still raw. Then Dex turned to him. "So you're a Cy, not a Cyr? You should have said."

"I'm Cyrus, Cy, Mr. Hughes and now, Cyr. I like Cyr. Don't change a thing." He winked over his coffee and took a sip. He was Sir and Master too, but they hadn't had that discussion yet. He'd planned it for Saturday. Statue of Liberty and touristy stuff tomorrow, get Dex more relaxed and then Saturday they'd talk. Of course he hadn't planned on sex until maybe Saturday either, so...well he'd have to see.

I love doing, but I want it to mean something. Those words kept returning to him, over and over.

He couldn't help wondering what it meant to Huck. It had to mean something after all those years of friendship. Huck wasn't looking for a friend, so he knew very little about the sub. Occasionally he'd get Huck to open up about something as part of a session but without real context he wasn't sure he could weave those bits together into anything that would be helpful to him, or to Dex.

There was no question that he knew what it would mean to him. He was wary of putting labels on anything he was feeling yet though.

Dex watched as couples met, greeted each other, kissed. The expression on his face was soft, the smile fond. "Isn't that sweet?"

"It is. I guess you don't see a lot of that where you are. We're privileged to be able to be fully out here." He put a hand on Dex's knee. *Yes, pet. You could have that too.*

"Some places in Austin, but you're right. It's pretty damn rare." Dex covered Cy's hand with his own. "What's your favorite song?"

"You know, I don't think anyone has ever really asked me questions like this." He didn't know. Again. All these details he wasn't paying attention to. "Probably...well, I'm a big Clapton fan so maybe...how do you pick one song? 'Layla', maybe." Or any of a handful of others.

"Mine changes with my mood. 'Layla' is a great one. Did you know it was about how Clapton was in love with George Harrison's wife? At least some?"

"I heard that once. I didn't investigate. Sometimes you just want to enjoy the music. So what's your mood? What's your favorite song right now?"

"'A Little Dive Bar in Dahlonega', before that it was 'Comal County Blues'."

"I don't know those by name, but I like the titles."

Perry dropped by and refilled their mugs, then went to pour someone else a beer.

He looked for some small talk that wasn't too small,

something to keep Dex's mind occupied. "Do you have any siblings? Or are you an only child?"

"I had a sister a long time ago, but I'm really an only." What an odd turn of phrase.

"What happened to your sister?" He had a feeling he'd hit on another tough family question, and he felt badly about that but at the same time, he needed Dex to open up more.

"I don't know. She was taken away from Momma when I was little. There were a few pictures of us together and that was it."

"They took your sister and not you?" Oh. Damn. He squeezed Dex's knee. "Sorry. That just popped out. You don't have to answer that."

"It's no thing. I was living at my granny's back then, or that's the story. Momma didn't tell them there was a little one too."

What a life little Dexter had. "Have you ever looked for her?"

"No. No, she never looked for me, and I never left, so I figure she has a whole life of her own."

That was probably true, but it was also possible she didn't know where he was when she was removed or that she'd forgotten. He was going to leave it alone though.

"So what are you all doing while Dex is in town?" Perry set a bowl of pretzels on the bar in front of him and he dug right in.

"We're going to the Statue of Liberty tomorrow."

"Oh nice. You should have great weather for it." Perry looked at Dex. "Have you ever been to New York before?"

"No, sir, I haven't, but I'm having a ball so far."

"He hasn't even been here a day." It felt like so much longer.

"You'll like it out there. It's nice. And it's not a Saturday, so it won't be as insanely busy either. Go first thing in the morning if you can. What else are you going to see?"

"I need to buy some groceries for him. I want to make him some snacks. Besides that, I'm at Cyr's disposal." Dex beamed at him, just so easy, so relaxed in his skin.

"He catches on quick." Perry winked at him.

"Dex has taken excellent care of me on a several occasions now." He returned Dex's smile. "Did I tell you Dex is an exceptional baker?"

"Like bread and cakes and stuff?" That was utter incredulity.

Dex's laughter made Perry smile. "Mostly fancy cookies, but yeah. I like to cook."

"Cy, you lucked out."

"I know." Although saying that he'd lucked out might be a tad bit premature. He didn't mind Perry's insinuation one bit, though, and was actually hoping Dex heard it. Putting ideas in the boy's mind wasn't necessarily a bad thing. "If he makes cookies while he's here we'll bring some down."

He'd noticed that some of his usual bar buddies were keeping their distance, respecting what must look like, and hopefully was, a date. Kind of them.

"Excellent. If you're taking orders, chocolate chip is my favorite."

"Duly noted." Dex watched Perry leave. "They're real nice here and busy for a weeknight. Is it crazy or dead on the weekends?"

"Crazy. The music gets loud, and Saturday there's a band." He came sometimes on band nights, but he didn't stay long. It was lonely being in a loud room by himself.

"Do you dance?"

Another question, and they weren't diversions, just curiosity.

"I haven't in years. And I wasn't ever good at it. It was fun though." Years. Like...ten? More? A long time. "Do you?"

"I know how. I'm not fancy, but I can two-step just fine." Dex wrinkled his nose. "So do you have any allergies?"

"I don't recall breaking out on the dance floor, no." Cyrus winked at Dex.

"Oh, nicely played!" Dex high-fived him, then gave him a wink. "Okay, you can ask questions now."

"Oh yeah? Okay." Cyrus shifted on his barstool and took Dex's hand. "What's your favorite shark movie?"

"*Deep Blue Sea*."

"What? No. *Jaws*."

Twenty questions went on for a long while and at least another cup of coffee each, and when Dex started to lean on him, Cyrus figured it was time to take the boy home and tuck him in. That didn't mean Dex would sleep, but he could at least get his arms around the boy and see if Dex would try.

He got them up and moving, Dex holding his hand.

"I like your bar, Cyr. It's got a good vibe," Dex said.

"Thank you. It's nice to have a friendly bar so close to home. I wanted you to see that not everything about New York is flashy and loud and crowded. You can always find that, sure, but you can easily get away from it too." *You don't have to be intimidated by the city.*

"That's cool. Seriously. I have to admit, though, I'm ready to rest my bones. With you, if you want."

If? Oh, if you only knew. "I would like that. Truly." He lifted Dex's hand and kissed it.

"Me too. I—Lord, you're fixin' to make me cry. That's...

dear." Dex was ready to be in bed, ready to let himself dream, Cyrus could tell.

"It's just us, boy. I'm not going to tell anyone your secrets." He let go of Dex's fingers, but only so he could put his arm around the boy instead, hold him closer.

"God, you smell good." Dex trusted him so easily, following his lead.

He took Dex back to his apartment quietly. There was value in quiet and he wanted Dex to know that silence was safe too.

"If you need anything from your room, go ahead. You're welcome to join me whenever you're ready." He stepped into his bedroom and sat on the bed to take off his boots.

He heard Dex wandering in the bedroom, turning on the water in the bathroom, then Dex appeared in the doorway in a huge pair of Spiderman boxers and an old t-shirt.

"I wasn't sure what all you wanted for sleeping clothes..."

God, how adorable. And unnecessary. "Do you need clothes? I typically don't sleep in anything." He lived alone. Sometimes he didn't watch TV in anything or read the paper in anything either. He started to undress, dropping his clothes on a high-back chair in the corner of the room.

"Oh thank God. No, sir, I sure don't." Dex stripped down, folding the shirt and shorts up. "Which side do you want me on?"

That he did care about. "I prefer the right, so I hope the left works for you." He reached over and tugged the blankets down. It was summer and he liked the bedroom cool at night, so his AC was usually on. But then, he hadn't had an overnight guest in a long while.

Cyrus climbed in, hunkered down into the pillows and held out a hand to Dex. "Come, boy. Let me hold you."

"Yes, sir." Dex climbed right in, snuggling around him with a soft little sigh. "Thank you. Night, Cyr. Sleep well."

And just like that, Dex was sleeping.

"Goodnight, my boy," Cyrus whispered, knowing he couldn't possibly sleep, not right away at least. He was too elated to even close his eyes. He held Dex and listened to the boy's deep, even breathing, feeling the weight of true relaxation for the first time since they'd met, and he knew this was no small victory.

This was trust. This was surrender.

This was a gift from his boy.

10

Dex felt like he was in a strange dream.

They'd woken up early, had coffee and a bite, and then they were off.

This was the wildest thing he'd ever seen—so many things to see, so many noises, so many people.

And the Statue of Liberty was...wild. And real. And he'd seen it with his own eyes.

They'd eaten pizza, they'd laughed, they'd groceried, and Dex was happier than he'd been in...well, hell, he didn't know when.

He reached for Cyrus's hand on the way back into the door of the apartment. "Thank you."

Cyrus squeezed his fingers. "Oh, Dex. Thank you. I haven't had this much fun in a long while." That was hard to believe; a friendly guy like Cyr had to have more of a social life than he did, but he had to admit Cyr did look happy. That smile was as bright as the sunshine over the bay this morning.

"You sure are fine to me." That was sorta personal, but he'd woken up with his morning wood pressed against Cyr's hip, so personal had been bypassed some.

Cyrus's fingers brushed his cheek, so gentle. "Thank you. You bring out my best side, no question." Cyrus unlocked the door and held it for him. "Are you hungry?"

"I can make you a snack, if you'd like." He'd eaten damn near a whole piece of pizza. He might never be hungry again. "I got cheese and crackers for you at the store."

He'd make granola bars in a bit.

"That sounds great. Thank you." Cyrus set the grocery bags down on the counter and started unpacking them. "So let's see. Lots of firsts today, right? I know you have an amazing list. First ferry ride, first time at Lady Liberty, had you ever been shat on by a seagull before?"

"No, sir. Been shit on by a lot of stuff though, so it's no big thing. I wash off." He set himself to making Cyr a plate —cheese, crackers, some berries to make it pretty. "It's been a great damn day."

"I had some firsts too, you know." Cyr leaned on the counter, still and watching. "First kiss on a ferry, first kiss on Liberty Island, first kiss in Famous Ray's Pizza..."

Dex's cheeks burned, and damn, wasn't that fine to hear? His body tightened, and he leaned over for another of those kisses. "I like our firsts. Like the seconds and thirds, too."

"Mhm." His lips buzzed where Cyr hummed against them. "Me too. I enjoyed my wake-up call this morning."

"Yeah. I'm right with you." He'd started the day off right. "Come sit and eat. I'll put the rest of the groceries away. Do you want tea? Water?"

"I would love some more of that iced tea." Cyr sat and let him put the plate on the table.

"Yes, sir. I'm on it." He hummed and dug around in the teas, deciding to add a bit of hibiscus to today's brew. Five minutes in the microwave gave him a chance to put the rest of the groceries away, get glasses, fill them with ice, wash the morning's coffee mugs. All the while he replayed the morning, finding himself grinning like a monkey.

He had an eye on Cyr, who was reading the paper and munching the crackers he put out. That was a perfectly content man right there. Cyr had a way of sitting quietly and absorbing energy. Dispelling noise. He couldn't figure out what the guy did with it all. He guessed it was nice, because he had plenty of energy just roaming around.

He got two glasses of iced tea made, gave one to Cyr, put the rest of the concentrate away, and pondered granola. Not too crumbly, but not sticky. Nothing that would stain his fingers. Heavy on the nut and fruit, light on the oats.

Damn, he had the perfect pan in that box in his truck. He started hunting through cabinets, opening and closing them—man, there were a lot—looking for something similar.

Cyr didn't even twitch.

Finally he found something that would work and set to work toasting oats and nuts and making his syrup. "So you want coconut? Chocolate chips will make a mess, but I can put M&Ms..."

"Coconut sounds good. I'm not a big chocolate fan, maybe raisins or something?"

"I picked up golden raisins and dried cranberries." A little cinnamon to warm things up then, and a hint of orange peel. "Do you have a zester?"

"A zester... Like a grater? Cabinet next to the range, top shelf."

"That'll do. Thank you, sir." He wished he had that tote from his truck, but he knew better than to make wishes for ridiculous things. His mess and insanity didn't belong here in the middle of Cyrus's calm. He was a visitor, not a resident. Still, he was grateful as hell to be invited in, and he was going to enjoy it. Make sure that any memories he left behind were good ones.

Chimes went off, tinkly and quiet and he looked around for a little antique clock or something, but it turned out to be Cyrus's phone.

"Hello." Cyrus got up from the table. "I may have an opening on Thursday, let me look." He could hear Cyrus's low voice in the living room but couldn't make out the words.

Busy man. He imagined that Cyr would nap this afternoon, and he'd check his emails and stuff. The granola bars made up easy and went to set up in the fridge, and he set to fixing his mess.

He wasn't looking forward to having to go back, but even if Cyrus let him stay, he had to go get his things, his truck, and...and that all was a lot to think about right now. Lord have mercy, what was he thinking? Just come to a huge city and, what? Stay with Huck's therapist? This was a magical few days outside of real life, before he had to deal with learning how to do whatever Walmart needed him to do.

How many people got this? Days outside of real life.

Not many.

So he was just going to love it while it was happening.

"Sorry about that. I rescheduled with my client for today, but my phone is still on business hours. Did you find everything you needed?" Cyrus sat back down and took a sip of tea.

"Yes, sir. You got bars setting up, and I'll cut them up in a bit and wrap them up so you can have one whenever you feel like you need it." He offered over a smile. "Thanks for rescheduling for me. I know you didn't have to. I do appreciate it."

"You think it was for you. Maybe it was for me." Cyr winked at him.

"Fair enough." He wandered closer. Cyr was like a flame, warm and safe. "Thank you for rescheduling for us."

Cyrus calmly watched him, but he could tell something was on Cyr's mind. "I'm looking forward to trying your granola bars."

He didn't think that was what had Cyrus thinking so hard.

He went over to touch, because Cyr had said he could. He ran his hands up over Cyrus's arm—skin warm and smooth until he found cotton, and he missed the skin.

"Us is a big word." Cyr looked up at him. "A very small very big word."

"Yep." What else should he say? They'd had sex—and not random hook up bathroom sex, but real sex where they woke up together and didn't freak out sex—and that sort of meant at least a little us-ness. Hell, Cyr had flown to Texas to help him. It didn't have to be scary us, though. He wasn't a stalker. He knew when to leave. He hadn't stayed with Huck because he was a mooch. He'd stayed because it was his home, and Huck had wanted him there.

Okay. Okay, breathe. Focus.

"Boy." Cyrus's voice cut through the noise and he found himself sitting on Cyr's lap, unsure whether Cyr put him there or he'd gone on his own. "Look at me. It's a good word. I'd like it to be a real word."

"It's a kick-ass word." He met Cyr's eyes, and as hard as it was to just open up, he knew it was harder to wait to hear what you needed to hear. "And I'd like that—to be an us."

Cyr nodded. "I would too. So, I need to tell you about me. About...my work."

"Okay." There was worry in Cyrus's eyes, so he stood up,

drew Cyrus to the sofa so they could sit and be comfortable, together, safe.

Cyrus sat with him. "This is a good spot. I was going to wait for...well tomorrow. I don't know why I drew that arbitrary line but anyway, I think if you want to use words like 'us', you deserve to know all of me first, so you know what you're saying."

Cyr tangled their fingers and met his eyes, not hiding or running, but not entirely comfortable either. "This is a little like coming out, where you worry what the other person's reaction is going to be." Cyr smiled. "But what I haven't told you, Dex, is that I am a Dominant. In my life, and in my work. My clients are submissives, and generally, my lovers are as well."

Dex frowned, running through the words, and he just wasn't sure he understood. He got the words, but not in the order they were coming out, exactly. He'd seen a ton of porn and all, but... "So...that's a job?"

"It's what I do. I don't have a medical degree, I...offer a service. I consider it therapy and many of my clients do as well." Cyrus was as still as ever, watching him and speaking slowly. "You can ask me anything you want; you should understand."

"I don't know what to ask." So, he wasn't sure if he was an idiot or if Cyrus was just too embarrassed to say he had sex for a living. People did what they had to, and Lord knew Cyr was doing okay for himself.

It was a little weird, though, thinking that he was making love with someone Huck had.

"Do you...do you understand what I'm talking about? Do you know what a submissive is?"

"Let's say I don't, because I only know what's on the internet. That's more fair than me imagining, and you assuming my thoughts are your truths." He squeezed Cyrus's fingers. "You're okay. I promise not to freak out."

Cyrus chuckled. "Okay. Thank you. By the internet, I'm going to assume you mean porn, which is horrible representation. Have you heard of BDSM?"

His cheeks went red-hot. "I've pressed the button on Bing when it came up..."

"Okay, no." Cyrus sighed. "So, you've seen people being tied up and fucked. Basically."

"Yeah. I'm sorry." He wasn't sure what he was sorry for, but he felt like he'd messed up.

"No, no. That's fine. That means you get to learn it from me, and I'm perfectly happy with that." Cyrus actually looked a bit more relaxed. "So. D/s, Dominance and submission, is about the exchange of power. Someone is Dominant, in charge, making the rules and someone else is submissive, following rules and serving the Dom as they require."

"Okay, like a boss." That made sense. Sort of.

"Like a boss, on a surface level. It goes much deeper though. It's easier to think about it in terms of the sub. So a sub gives up complete control in service to a Dom, and in return the Dom sees that the sub's deepest needs are met. If you don't mind me using your words, because I keep thinking about them, you said that you don't mind doing things for someone, you just want it to be meaningful. Yes? And this kind of relationship brings meaning to service. Purpose."

He tried to figure this. So, Huck wanted to... Okay. Huck wanted someone to boss him around? And he needed to pay someone to do it? And fly to New York City? How the fuck had Huck found this? Was there a—a classified section in the Salado Village Voice? "And people pay you to do it. Give them purpose."

"If what they are looking for is purpose, yes." Cyrus smiled, shifting their grip, reminding him they were still connected. "If you add in some of the tools of the trade there are other reasons my clients come to me that fall less under submission and more under the masochism umbrella. And literally everything in between."

Huh. Wow. And he thought making cookies was an odd way to make a living.

"Well, I got to say that I'm surprised, and I never met anyone that did that sort of thing, but you got a good life, and you're happy, that's good enough for me." The details would probably haunt him later, but the immediate part was Cyr's worry about his job.

Cyr looked confused. "So… We're good? I mean, I haven't turned you off?"

"Because you got a weird job? That would be shitty of me. Right now I'm fixin' to be working at the Walmart." He squeezed Cyr's hand. Guys dated exotic dancers all the time and didn't get shit for it. If anyone asked, he'd say he was dating a therapist in New York City.

"Right. Walmart." Cyrus gave him a half smile and got up. "I'm just going to get my iced tea."

"Oh I messed up somehow. I'm sorry. I'm just trying to say I'm not going to be evil to you." Dex stood, suddenly flooded with nerves, and his stomach cramped, acid filling his throat. *Oh come on. Just fucking stop it. Please. Let me get through the day.* "I was just trying to be decent. I'm sorry."

Cyrus stopped and turned back to him, took his face in both hands and kissed him gently. "I do appreciate that. Thank you."

He leaned into Cyr's hands, but he knew he'd done

something wrong. He didn't know what, but he knew he had. He wanted to just hug Cyr tight and apologize for being stupid and slow. So he just did what he always had in this situation, and asked, "How can I fix it?"

Those dark eyes just seemed to get darker, but Cyrus found a smile for him. "You can't. Nothing is broken."

"Liar." He kissed the corner of Cyr's mouth, and then murmured an excuse as he hurried to the bathroom, losing his lunch in a rush.

Pizza was way better going down.

11

His iced tea had gotten warm, but Cyrus drank it anyway, and looked out the kitchen windows without seeing.

He'd had no idea what to expect from Dex, and really, as these things went, the fact that Dex was still trying to be kind was one of the better reactions he'd received. The reminder that Dex had a plan in Texas that didn't involve him, as hopeless as that plan seemed, wasn't lost on him, however.

He took a deep breath to force down the sting. That was okay. It was okay. He'd just breathe through it and...do something. Start dinner. Change the subject. Change his train of thought, because dammit, he'd wanted that. He'd really wanted that.

He squeezed his eyes shut like that could banish everything and thought about dinner. Vegetables. Right. He'd start there.

Warm hands landed on his shoulders, rubbing gently. The touch made him tense, and then he felt Dex's forehead on his back. "Please don't be so mad that you want me to go.

Not without letting me make it right. I'm slow, but I *will* get it. I swear to God."

He didn't know what to say, but if they were both going to hurt then they could both at least try to make tonight better. He put down the knife in his fingers and turned around, pulling Dex in close. "I don't want you to go. Not at all. But I can't be anything but what I am. It's okay."

"I don't understand. Did I do that? Ask you to be something? I was saying that I've never met somebody with your job, and I had your back."

There was still a disconnect somewhere. "I appreciate that. I'm a little slow too, I guess." He ran his fingers through Dex's hair and let go. "If you're not leaving then we have some time to figure it out. You want to clean the mushrooms?"

"Yes, sir." Dex nodded and turned to the container of mushrooms, taking a paper towel and wiping them clean. "Do you need them cut or whole?"

"Sliced if you don't mind." He took a breath. "So, what I do doesn't bother you, then?" He went back to cutting the other vegetables for the stir fry.

"It's a little weird, knowing that Huck was here for that, but you're not a bad man, so you wouldn't force someone to do anything they didn't want to do. I believe that."

"No, that wouldn't be very good for business. They come to me. Huck was referred by a friend in Denver, and had very specific needs. He was here twice a month without fail to make sure they were met. It was important to him, that much I do know." Though Cyrus wasn't sure why.

"I'm glad he had you."

The words were quiet, but they weren't shaky; they were well-meant.

He held back the unkind things he'd been thinking

about the way Huck treated Dex and stopped himself from saying that Dex was too good for the guy. Several conversations later he still didn't understand their relationship, or how Dex really felt about Huck.

"It's a shame I couldn't help him enough." But it wasn't his job to fix his clients, and he'd never claimed he could. He'd had this conversation with his brother a couple of times. He couldn't fix himself either, and he didn't really care to try.

"Hell, I'd been his buddy our whole lives, lived with him and took care of him for eleven years, and I wasn't enough. I understand."

He nodded. This was better, reconnecting a little about Huck, maybe the only thing they solidly had in common. "So my work isn't a big deal, but what about me?" That was an easier question to ask without looking at Dex and he kept on chopping. "I'm a Dom whether I'm being paid to be or not."

"You're a big deal to me." Dex looked at him and waited for him to meet those hazel eyes. "You liked me this morning. I like you. Shit, I'm stupid about you. I don't know what you mean, for sure, but were you treating me differently than you would otherwise?"

"No," he answered quickly. Probably too quickly.

Yes...

"Yes. Yes and no." He sighed. "I would treat you just as well. But there would be expectations. Structure. Some of it would be different."

Because you'd be mine. Because I'd have a responsibility to you. Because I would have your devotion.

"Okay. So, I don't know what your expectations are, so you'll have to tell me, or is that something I'm just supposed to know? Do you want me to start the rice for you?"

"Yes, please. In the cabinet to the right of the sink. You can't possibly know. You have to trust that I'll tell you what I want you to know. You have to trust me implicitly. It's a big ask." And if he was right, which he was sure he was, the reward could be greater than the ask.

He couldn't believe that they were even having this conversation. He'd either misunderstood something, or Dex was desperate enough to do anything not to lose him. If that proved to be the issue, he'd deal with it.

Dex had his head down, was washing the rice with violently shaky hands.

"Dex." He put a hand on Dex's shoulder. "What's the matter?"

"You don't understand. You don't know how fucking tired I am. You say shit like that, like 'I'll tell you what I need', and you don't get it. You don't understand how tired I am and how much I just want to take care of somebody and let them take care of me for a minute! You're all 'this is so big'—" The rice slammed into the sink, flying everywhere. "Big is losing fucking everything! Big is taking care of shit for eleven years and figuring out that you're just a fucking loser after all! Big is falling in love with a guy that lives a million goddamn miles away who wouldn't believe me if I told him! Don't you tell me about big. I fucking know big!"

The words cut off like someone had turned a faucet.

The temptation to meet that energy head-on was huge, but he knew better. He wanted to throw his arms around Dex and start making apologies, promises, but he made himself wait. He took a long, deep breath letting the silence between them linger until it was unbearable.

"I will take care of you."

"I—" Dex stood there for a minute, shaking like a leaf. "I'm fixin' to fall down."

"I've got you." Cyrus moved decisively, getting an arm under Dex and half carrying him to a kitchen chair. He pulled the other one up for himself and sat, knees interlocking with Dex's. "Breathe. I'm right here."

"I'm sorry for yelling at you," Dex whispered. "I keep doing that. Losing my shit."

He knew Dex wouldn't understand that outburst was actually a win for him. He needed to think about what Dex had said, but it was out, and that was good. "I don't feel yelled at. I feel…honored that you trust me with those feelings, that you knew it was safe to let them out. You've had it all under a cork for as long as I've known you. It's healthy to finally let it go."

"I dropped the rice for supper."

"Don't worry." He leaned forward and took a gentle kiss. "I'll let you clean it up in a minute."

"Okay. It's mostly in the sink." Dex rested their foreheads together. "I don't know what to do, but I know how to take care of things. It's what I'm good at."

It was, and it gave the boy a sense of purpose.

"You know more than you think, you'll see. And the rest you'll learn as we go. It's not a test. It's a lifestyle. It'll make us even closer, you'll see." They had work to do. He had even more. But he'd already seen reward for his effort. "Do you need some juice? Are you lightheaded?"

"No thank you." Dex looked vaguely terrified. "I don't want anything."

Cyrus ducked a little to catch Dex's eyes. "Hey. This is going to happen. We're going to misunderstand each other, and we're going to lose it sometimes, because we're human. Right? You're okay. We're okay."

"Totally. I can't throw up anymore. I'm tired. Fair?"

Oh, pet. Such simple requests.

"Fair. So you clean up the rice, I'll make myself some veggies and put you in bed."

"Are you sure you don't want me to make them for you? I will. And you need starch." Dex had a tic in his left eyelid, Cyrus could see it.

He gave Dex's knee a pat and stood up, then put his chair back and headed back to his stir fry. "Don't question me, boy. You need sleep more than I need starch. Besides, someone made me some lovely granola bars."

Somehow he'd managed not to pass out in the last few years. He could probably manage tonight.

"I worry." Dex stumbled to the kitchen sink "It's wet. I don't think it's going to be okay tomorrow."

He'd wanted to let Dex 'do' a little before tucking him in, but he wasn't sure now. He stepped up behind his boy and rested his hands on Dex's shoulders. "Leave it. I want to take care of you."

"I tried so hard to do it all. You don't know how hard I tried." It was as if Dex was experiencing emotional muscle failure. He had held himself together as long as possible, but the crack just kept getting bigger.

"You did your best. You always do." He led Dex away from the sink, moving slowly through the living room toward his bedroom. It was too late to wish Dex had asked him to help; he needed the boy to look forward now. Even if forward was only as far as the bedroom.

Dex nodded. "I did. It wasn't enough, but you're right. I tried my best."

"You're enough, Dex. It was all too much for one person, that's all." Cyrus helped Dex undress, touching often, staying close.

Dex watched him, blinking nice and slow, almost asleep on his feet.

"My bed, boy." He pulled back the comforter and got Dex settled, climbing in as well, intending to stay until his boy was fast asleep.

Then he'd clean up and eat. And think.

"You're safe. I'm here. Sleep well, pet."

"I'm sorry." Dex curled around him with a sigh. "You're warm. Thank you for...you."

"You are welcome." There was no point in going into why apologies and thank yous were unnecessary. To rest, Dex just needed to know he'd heard. He kissed his boy's forehead and held on, letting his eyes close too.

12

Dex woke up at five, eyes wide.

What had he done?

He had ruined their suppers. He had screamed at Cyrus. He had confessed that he loved the man. Christ.

He would slip out of bed to shower and wash himself up for the day. He would make sure the kitchen was clean, would make coffee and muffins and then make sure that he was not a psycho all day.

This was a great plan.

But first he'd have to figure out how to break out of Cyr's arms. Cyrus was curled around him, face pressed into his neck and one protective arm over his waist, holding him tight.

The urge to curl in and let Cyrus hold him was too big to deny, at least for a few minutes. He stroked Cyrus's hair, loving on him, touching and taking care of this beautiful man. Cyr's hair was heavy, dark, and obviously trained, because it never looked awful. The strands fascinated him, the way they curled around his fingers.

"Mmm. Morning." Cyr's eyes weren't open but, he got a

sleepy smile anyway, and one warm hand traveled up his back.

"Morning. It's early. Rest." He nuzzled Cyr's temple.

Cyr hummed again. "I had dinner and came to bed early. You were irresistible. Beautiful, sleeping so peacefully."

Irresistible.

No one had ever said that to him before.

"It was amazing to wake up in your arms."

"I'm shocked you're still here and not halfway through cleaning the house or something."

Cyr's smile was teasing now, more of a grin.

"I couldn't figure out how to get up without waking you." Dex kissed the corner of Cyr's lips.

"Good. I much prefer to wake up with you than without you." Cyrus's eyes were finally open, less dark in the morning than they seemed at night.

Dex reached out and started stroking, petting Cyr's eyebrows before holding his face and carefully rubbing under the dark eyes with his thumbs.

Cyr watched him, fingers roaming as well. "Let's stay home today. Rest and watch movies and cook. Your flight is early tomorrow... I wish I could come take the drive back with you, but I've already disrupted things with my clients. I need to catch up."

"You do." He had so much to do. He had to sell a bunch of stuff, get his stuff down to its smallest. Maybe he should drive back to Salado and have a garage sale there. People would know him. If they knew him, they might ask questions, and then what? Maybe Mrs. Feezel would like his momma's table. If he got there, took a bus from the airport to Tyler, he'd get into town six a.m. Monday, pick up the truck, drive to Salado and get there at five-ish. Get some beer and some rest. Deal with shit, cookies, garage sale

Friday and Saturday. Drive out Sunday. It would take either two or three days. Maybe a week, if he wandered, because he might never see some of this shit again.

Then again, two weeks was a long time—to miss Cyrus, to keep his store closed.

He needed to call Mrs. Feezel and ask her for a room. That would be good. Just for a couple of days.

A soft chuckle brought him back to the room. "You have it all worked out now?" Cyrus's eyes crinkled at the corners happily.

"As best as I can. Don't you stress it. I'll figure things." He winked. "Are you sure you want me back?"

"Are you kidding? Think about how organized I'm going to be." Cyrus kissed him, lingering close after the kiss before leaning back enough to look at him. "Bring whatever you want back with you. We'll find places for it. You can put your mom's table in the dining room if you want to."

"I don't know if it will fit in your house. It's old, and this place is new." If he could hide it in the little guest room, he would. He imagined most everything he brought would be in the little guest room.

"This place is mine, and it's going to be ours. Bring it. Bring anything you like, and we'll figure it out. Maybe you'd like to use the guest room as your office for your business and put it in there. We could move the bed out."

He wasn't sure, but he hadn't been sure about anything for months, so he could just be unsure some more. "At least there's a great truck I can offer for us."

"And there's parking under the building. Handy. But you have plenty to offer. I know what you're thinking, but I'll show you. You'll see." Cyrus was still smiling at him, eyes warm.

"I should make you breakfast, hmm?" Dex traced that smile. "I already miss you. It'll be weird, going back to texts."

"But we're good at them. And you won't be that long, right?" Cyr stomach rumbled, right on cue. "Eggs?"

"How do you want them?" He could do Cyrus eggs, bacon, and toast to start before he made muffins.

The way Cyr looked at him, he knew the answer to that question was important. "I like breakfast to be simple. Well done scrambled eggs, just two pieces of crispy bacon, and I have a sprouted grain bread in the freezer I like for toast. Two pieces. Raspberry jam. That's my usual weekday breakfast. Weekends I often go out for brunch in the later morning and just have coffee and something light like cereal when I wake up."

Easy enough. "Butter on the toast and super toasty, barely toasty, golden toasty?"

"Oh, good boy." Cyr looked absolutely delighted. "Super toasty, as you say, and butter."

He kissed Cyr softly. This was part of taking care of someone, learning them. "Let me get you coffee, and then I'll make you some food. Do you like cranberry muffins? I can make them and then you'll have them all week."

"I like muffins. It happens that cranberry is my favorite, especially with a little orange zest in them. Banana is a close second, no nuts." Cyrus let him go and stretched long. "Coffee would be perfect."

"Do you mind if I do some laundry? I won't have a chance to do any on the road, much." He started gathering their dirty clothes.

"Do laundry any time you like. We don't really need to discuss chores. I trust you to handle them however you like." Cyr propped himself up in bed and looked at his phone. "I'll show you my dry cleaner and all of that when you get back."

He nodded and went to start coffee before he grabbed some sweats, his notebook, and his dirty clothes. He had so much to worry about over the next however long, and he needed lists. Lots of lists.

Cyrus hadn't moved a muscle when he brought in the coffee. "Thank you, boy. You can set it there on the nightstand for me. I'll be up in a few minutes."

"You're welcome." He smiled, but he was busy. He had to make breakfast for Cyrus, do laundry, make some muffins—maybe a double batch to freeze some, and get ready to fly home, get a bus ticket, check his emails, figure out what to do about things...

He chuckled at himself. His vacation day was over, and if he'd held his shit together last night, he wouldn't have lost it to sleeping. That was his own fault.

Still, he was made for busy. He lost his shit when he had time to think.

13

DEX

Hey you. Here. Miss you.

Dex didn't have to stop at baggage. He'd left his suitcase. Now he had to decide whether to rent a car or get on the bus. The bus was a twelve-hour ride overnight, and he'd have to wait until six tonight to get on. He'd already be in Tyler. Hell, he could be in Tyler and have the truck loaded...

CYRUS

Miss you. I tracked your flight. I'm glad you're safe. Got you a rental at Enterprise, reserved in your name. Check email for conf.

DEX

??? You didn't need to do that.

Butthead. He needed to hide his notepads.

CYRUS

Ha! I didn't snoop, I just knew. Promise. That's my job. Had a muffin after you left. They're yummy.

DEX

Good. There is another dozen in the freezer and more granola bars in the cookie jar.

He rolled his shoulders and followed the signs to the rental, getting in the long assed line and checking his phone again.

CYRUS

You're good to me. Clients will be cleaning for you this week :D

He'd managed not to think about that—about how Huck had sort of been for Cyrus what he was now. Was that creepy? Did that make him nasty?

No thinking. None. Zero.

DEX

Ha ha ha. Be nice.

CYRUS

They don't pay me to be nice. ;-) Did you get a snack? Don't forget to eat something. Small, okay? But eat.

DEX

I will.

Later. He would grab a thing of fries in Tyler.

DEX

Don't worry ;-)

Saying that made him laugh now, every time.

CYRUS

It's not worry, boy. It's concern.

So serious. That made him laugh more. Really? What was the difference?

DEX

Have a good day, huh? Don't work too hard. Miss you

CYRUS

I will. Be careful. And boy? Come home soon.

He intended to.

14

Day three and Cyrus was already starting to feel lonely and even anxious. That was ridiculous, and he knew it. Dex had things to do, and his boy would be home when they were done. He had nothing to worry about.

But he'd had Dex here and safe and doing better, and now the boy was back in Texas, back among the things that were a source of stress, probably not sleeping well, definitely not eating, and he couldn't do a damn thing about it. There was nothing worse than making a control freak wait.

He had a good session that afternoon though and was able to channel some of his stress into the falls of a long-tailed flogger and that helped. Now he was at the bar with his iPad, Gregory was bartending, and he had coffee. Business as usual. What was wrong with that?

He looked at his phone, but Dex had been mostly quiet today. Busy, he supposed, or driving. Or sleeping. Not training at Walmart. Definitely not that.

CYRUS

Hey. I'm at the bar having a coffee. How was your day?

DEX

Long. It's raining.

CYRUS

Sorry. That sucks. Where are you?

Raining like the day of Huck's funeral. *Are you dry? Did you get things done? When do you head north? Do you miss me still?*

DEX

Uh. Allen Town?

Allentown? His boy was in Pennsylvania?

He googled quickly on his iPad and discovered there was no Allentown in Texas.

CYRUS

You're in PA? When did you leave Texas? Why didn't you tell me? Are you okay?

He should have known his boy was on the road. They were going to have to have a talk.

Oh, shut up, idiot. Your boy is on his way home.

It took more than twenty minutes before his phone rang, Dex's name coming up. By then he was pacing in between Les's office and the stockroom.

He'd started out patient, telling himself that Dex was driving, safety first, all of that. But now?

Goddammit.

He was worried. Cyrus even fumbled the phone as he tried to answer it. "Pet? Are you okay? What's going on?"

"Hey, you. I stopped for more coffee. It's raining hard. How's your day?" Dex sounded blown as hell.

"Better, now that I've heard from you." *Finally*. He left that out because right now he just wanted Dex to get to New York safely, not add to the stress. "So, how long have you been driving?"

"I left yesterday afternoon early. Had to stop at a rest stop and close my eyes about two this morning. I'm about a couple-three hours out now."

Jesus Christ. Okay. So whatever he said next needed to be encouraging. He could lose it later when his boy was home.

"I've missed you. I'm looking forward to seeing you."

"Me too. I'm not looking forward to this last bit, but then it'll be over. I'll be able to sleep with you tonight." Dex yawned. "You having a good day?"

Dex had asked him that three times. "Are you sure you should be on the road? With the rain and everything? Maybe have a nap first."

"Not even a little, but I don't know if this truck stop is the safest place on earth to sleep, so I'll get out and run around the truck a few times and then turn the air on."

He was going to have to fret about his boy for three hours or more? *Dammit*. Someone should have told him taking on a live-in sub was this nerve-wracking. He was going to give Les a piece of his mind.

He took a breath, determined to keep his cool. "I understand. Take your time and be careful. I'd like you in one piece when I see you."

"You and me both." This time he got a warm little laugh. "All right, gorgeous. I'll see you soon. Pray for me that I make it through the traffic."

"Pull the car up out front when you get here, I'll have Chris park it." The doormen didn't usually park cars as far as he knew, but Chris had the night shift, he'd just slip the man some cash. "Drive safe, pet."

"Yes, sir. I got this. I wanted to surprise you, but..." He could see Dex's shrug in his mind's eye.

"I'm surprised." That was the truth. He made himself smile, to send his boy off on a positive note. "And I'll be very happy to see you."

"I can't wait. Bye now." Then the phone went dead. Little shit.

Bye.

He tapped the bar. "I'll have another coffee." He was going to need it. It was going to be a long night.

15

By the time Dex pulled up in front of Cyr's apartment building, he was fixing to lose his shit in a serious, hard-core sort of way. This was traffic like he'd never driven in, and he'd been going without rest for too damn long.

DEX

I'm here.

Thank God. He dropped his phone; his hands were shaking so bad. He was soaked to the bone, having stopped to tighten down the tarp twice.

He saw the screen light up and knew it had to be Cyr's reply, but he couldn't quite make it out. He squinted at it but was startled by a loud knock on the driver's side window.

Oh. That had to be the doorman. The guy gestured at him to get out of the truck.

"Hey. How goes?" He stepped out, grabbing his bag of necessaries. "Good evening."

"Hey, man. I'm Chris, are you Dexter? Shit, you're soaked. Come on inside. Lock the truck." Chris held an umbrella over him until they got out of the rain. “You want me to call Mr. Hughes upstairs for you?”

“Please. Thank you for parking it for me. I been on the road for twenty-six some odd hours, and I’m buzzing.”

“Mr. Hughes did say you’d be tired. Why don’t you sit down, man?” Chris plonked him in a chair by the front desk and called up to Cyrus. He could hear Cyrus’s voice over the speaker, but it was too soft to make out. “You just sit, he says. I’m going to move your truck somewhere safe. Mr. Hughes is coming down to get you. Okay?”

“Yessir.” He sat, just sorta staring, unfocused, letting the lights cross his eyes and make patterns.

“Dex.” Cyrus called his name with a calm authority and came to him in just a few strides on those long legs.

“Hey, stranger. How’s you?” Damn, his man was pretty as all get out.

“You’re soaked, pet. What happened? Come on, let’s get upstairs.” Cyrus got him in the elevator, but he wasn’t sure if he’d walked or been carried. Either way those hands were gentle and sure, handling him like he mattered. “You must be freezing.”

“I had to fix the tarp. It kept me awake, huh? A little bit.”

“Well, you’re here. So we’ll get you warm and dry and fed and then I’m taking you to bed. Chris will look after your truck, and everything else can wait until morning.”

He could sense the little fissure in Cyrus’s still, calm energy. A little stress, a little worry. He hadn’t heard it on the phone, but it was unmistakable now.

He should have surprised Cyrus. He should have. “I am. I didn’t want you to stress, and I…it was the right time.”

Suddenly he’d been sitting at a club in Belton, two beers in, and he’d known. If he’d ordered a third, he’d just be there, drinking Shiners, until the end of time.

"Well." Cyrus sighed as they entered the apartment. "It isn't as if it will happen again so I'll just say I'm glad you're here safely and leave it at that." The door closed and Cyrus locked it, then pulled him in fast and hard with a kiss that stole the last of his breath but gave him so much more.

Dex nodded, pushing back. He'd fought hard to come to Cyrus, harder than he thought, and he needed to be rewarded, dammit. He needed to be loved on.

Cyrus was focused on him, muscling him down the hall as determined fingers worked his buttons open and rid him of his wet clothes, letting them drop where they were.

He wanted to help, but his fingers were clumsy, and Cyrus brushed them aside to strip another thing away. "Missed you."

Dark eyes met his and held them. "I missed you." Cyr's voice was rough and hungry. "Is this... I don't want to... I just want you."

"Please. I came here to be yours."

"Mine." Cyr stripped out of a T-shirt and sweats, eyes never leaving his. They stood there naked together, energy buzzing between them, and Cyr tipped Dex's face up for another kiss. "Good boy," Cyr said before their lips met again, every bit as hungry as it was in the hall.

He opened up, his eyes closing so he could focus on nothing but Cyr, nothing but the energy that built up between them. His skin tingled, and his entire body shuddered.

Cyr lifted him off his feet and lay him out on the bed, easily moving over him, lips finding his jaw and moving down his neck. "Mine." Cyr's soft words were clear but muted against his skin.

"Yes." Oh. Oh hot spot. He arched, his whole body rippling.

"Mm." Cyr teased him, tongue swirling over the area again. "I'll remember that spot."

Dex hoped so. That was like heaven, drawing his balls up, making his nipples hard.

Cyr's lips traveled lower, across his collarbone and down to one nipple, which Cyr pinched between gentle but threatening teeth.

For a second Dex stopped breathing, his eyes focused on Cyr's mouth on his skin. Jesus. He felt wide-awake, lit up.

Cyr moved lower again, lips dropping kisses over his ribs and around his navel and then making a very deliberate and slow trail farther south.

An hour ago he was in hell. Now he was in heaven.

Cyr's tongue ran up the length of his prick without warning. "Do you want my mouth, pet?"

Did anyone say no? Anyone? "Yes, please. I want you."

"Oh, good boy. Asking so nicely. Mmm." Cyr lapped the head of his cock and did something with that tongue that made him see stars before his cock slid past those lips and into Cyr's mouth.

His hands curled into fists, and he spread wide. His hips rolled without a bit of his permission.

Cyr's fingers slipped back to stroke the sensitive skin behind his balls, then rubbed over his hole and back again, making it hard to concentrate.

He wanted Cyr. He needed to be taken and touched and…

Cyr. He needed Cyr.

Cyr sat up and one hand took over, pumping him steadily while the other dug around in the nightstand. "I feel you. I know what you need." It wasn't but a moment later before those fingers were back, slippery and chilly as they firmly pressed inside.

"Oh." He was caught a moment, his entire body working to spread, to give himself over.

"You're beautiful. God, I missed you. Just another second, pet, and you'll have me." Cyr was barely whispering, but that voice was all he could hear. That and a rough exhale.

He nodded, his mouth dry, his ass full of that sure, firm touch. "Missed you. Please. Please."

Dex needed a good, hard fuck, a nap, and possibly a glass of milk.

He was only empty for a second, fingers replaced quickly by Cyr's thick cock nudging him firmly, sinking in torturously slow, as Cyr arched above him.

"Dex. Pet." Cyr started to thrust impatiently, fighting to let it build slow, but he knew this was bigger than either of them. Even Cyr was quick to give in.

"Yes. Hard." He grabbed Cyr's ass and pulled him in deeper. Harder. Demanding what only Cyrus could give him.

"Fuck, yeah." Cyr met his demands and started driving hard and deep, pinning Dex with sheer body weight and brute strength.

Dex could see him work, the effort making Cyr sweat, and his expression shift from pleasure to determination and back again.

He pushed up, offering his lips, bearing down harder on Cyr's prick.

The kiss was graceless and truthful, and neither one of them could get enough of it. Cyr stubbornly fought for that connection in spite of the need for air and the trembling in those strong arms.

Dex was stuck, though, pushed up on his elbows, and he couldn't reach his cock, stroke himself off.

Cyr wrestled him back down and arched, working a hand between them. “Got you.” Cyr eased up, fucking him deep and steady now, both of them focused on getting him off. “Show me, beautiful.”

“Good to me.” He arched hard, his entire body bowing as his balls drew up and he shot, come spraying over his belly. “Cyr!”

“God. So gorgeous.” Cyr’s cock leapt inside him and Cyr groaned, hips rocking hard again, losing their rhythm. Such a sight, watching someone like Cyr lose control, knowing he made that happen. “Dex! I—fuck!”

So hot, the twist of pleasure on Cyr’s face, the involuntary spasms in Cyr’s hips. The trust he’d earned so Cyr could be that real.

He sighed softly, blinking up at the most beautiful thing he’d ever seen. Eventually Cyr looked back, eyes full of wonder, like Cyr had never seen him before.

“Mine,” Cyr whispered and kissed him lightly, lips lingering for a moment. “You worried me. And now I understand... I love you.”

“Oh...” He held Cyr’s face. “I’m home, huh?”

“Yes. You’re home. Thank God. You belong here.” Cyr kissed him and shifted to his side.

Dex had so much to say, so much in his heart, but he was happy, warm, and in Cyr’s arms. Life was good.

16

Cyrus felt like a million bucks. He'd never quite understood that expression until this morning when he'd woken up to coffee and breakfast just like he liked it with plenty of time to enjoy it before his client arrived. A million bucks felt like anything was possible.

Dex should be still sleeping; the boy looked like death warmed over. But Cyrus was learning that all things were not equal with Dex; his boy's needs had to be prioritized differently. Making him breakfast fed Dex's soul in a way that was as important, or even more important, to Dex's overall health than rest. At least for now.

Dex kept touching him, stroking his jaw, hand sliding over his shoulder, the small of his back. He was craving those touches, and he had no doubt that his boy knew it, just as Dex needed them. Little reminders that they were solid and safe couldn't be undervalued.

He needed more coffee and, just as he thought to ask, Dex went for the pot. "The bacon is just perfect. Thank you, pet."

"You're more than welcome." Dex filled Cy's mug, before

filling his own and then going to clean the kitchen. "When is your first appointment today?"

"I only have one a day, and they always start at ten." That was true of his standing appointments. Occasionally there were exceptions and emergencies, but Dex was trying to understand his routine. "I expect you'll be unpacking your truck today. Leave the heavy things and we can move them together before dinner. I mean that. I plan to help you, clear? Do you have any concerns?"

"Concerns?" Dex looked honestly confused, and Cy knew his pet had no idea how adorable that was.

"Questions, then. About your day, about my expectations, about my client being in the apartment? We haven't been through ground rules yet. I'm sure that's a little disorienting, but I have that planned in small chunks for this week." This was step one, formalizing the D/s relationship. He knew Dex had little to no idea, consciously anyway, what he meant, but his boy craved structure, and somewhere in there he knew a piece of Dex was hearing him.

"I thought I'd just sorta disappear and let you work. I don't want to be a bother. I'll be quiet as a mouse."

"No, no. That's neither necessary, nor desirable, pet. This is your home." He'd considered that he might need to find a new location for work in the future, but he wanted to see how things played out first. "Something important you should know—subs have rank. You outrank my clients in every possible way by virtue of being mine. They are not mine; they pay to become mine for a few hours. It's not even remotely the same thing. While I don't encourage a lot of interaction, when it does occur, they will know their place. And you know yours."

"I—I don't think I know what to say. I'm sorry. Not sorry I'm yours. That's good. Sorry I don't know what to say."

"It's okay. We're working this out as we go, right? The important thing is that you understand that this is your home, and that you are my priority." Dex had no idea what he really did for a living, no matter how accepting his boy wanted to be. But all of that would come with time.

"Thank you." Dex eased into his arms, begging a hug. "Did you want lunch at noon? Do you have a plan?"

"I typically eat lunch at one, though you know me, I'll be out for a snack earlier. Hard to say when exactly, of course. Typically I wrap it up around three, though sometimes I've had a client stay in the office as late as five. The way we leave things at the end of a session is important, and sometimes they need time to adjust their headspace before they can get back out there." He grinned. "At five they get shown out if they haven't said goodbye on their own."

Steven, today's client, always had a friend come pick him up in a cab at four o'clock sharp. He needed much more time to recover than Cyrus could offer him.

"Okay. I'll make sure you have something for one." Dex looked at the clock, then snuggled back in for a bit.

The temptation to sit here with his boy for a while was strong, but it took him some time to get dressed and then he had to ready the room. "I have to dress, pet. Would you like to help?"

"Whatever you need." Dex kissed his jaw, then chuckled, the sound soft, a little wicked. "Although dressing you sounds way less fun than undressing you."

He caught Dex's face in one hand and grinned. "That might depend on how much you like what I'm wearing."

That should be interesting. It was entirely possible that Dex could get back in his truck and head home again this afternoon, wasn't it? He took a breath, reminding himself that he was who he was and Dex was going to have to accept all of him or none.

"I like *you*, Cyrus. All the way." He got another of those soft kisses to the corner of his lips. "Let's get you ready for work."

"All the way, hm?" He let Dex pull him out of his chair. A sudden vision of Dex cleaning his leather vest for him made him blink and his balls ache. *Damn*. "Come on."

Cyrus had two closets in the bedroom, both full. One with his regular wardrobe, and one filled with black clothing and leather, harnesses, and all kinds of accessories like hats and belts, sunglasses and gloves. And on the floor were six pairs of boots, ranging from soft to studded.

He went right to that closet and opened the double doors wide, pretending like that wouldn't be the least bit shocking to Dex as he dug through, pulling out what he wanted to wear.

"Eventually, you know where I keep everything in here, and you'll be able to lay things out for me." He loved that idea.

"Wow. That's a lot of black. Love that smell, though." Dex was wide-eyed, but he just accepted it. Just took it in like everything else. It made Cyrus wonder if Dex had lost so much that he was just empty, or if this was just Dex, full stop.

Curiosity, he reminded himself. Dex was all about new experiences. If his boy had lost that much, he would fill it with the things that belonged to him. To them. And this was as good a place to start as any.

Cyrus handed Dex soft leather jeans and a studded harness, and he pulled out his cap and sunglasses and chose heavy-heeled boots. Steven was all about the visual.

"Pants first, then the harness." He was going to let Dex undress him, let his boy do everything.

"Doesn't that pull your hairs, honey?" Dex put the harness aside and buried his face in the jeans, breathing in deep. "Mmm...that's you all over."

Good God. He didn't have time for what he wanted to do to that boy right now and his dick was seriously disappointed.

"Okay, let's lose the sweats." Dex eased them down, hands smoothing over his ass.

They were going to have to start the dressing process earlier in the morning.

So there'd be time for Dex to blow him.

This was sounding better and better the more he thought about it.

"Easy boy," he teased. "I don't have time to fuck you again before work. A shame."

Dex chuckled, shaking his head as he blushed. "Listen to you. You need all your energy for working. Do you just step into these like plain old jeans?"

That blush made every vision he'd had to conjure up in his mind of ice cubes and the Antarctic worth it.

"Yes, but you have to be very careful with the fly. Especially at the moment." He crossed his arms over his chest.

"I promise." Dex knelt down without being asked, looked up at him, and he was saying something, but Cyrus couldn't hear a thing with the blood rushing in his ears.

Goddammit. He was a Dom, right? Steven could kneel five extra minutes. He reached down and tangled his fingers in his boy's hair. "Do it. And don't tease, pet."

"Yes, sir. It's my pleasure." Dex nuzzled his shaft just

once, and then took him in, surrounding his prick with a fierce heat and suction, fingers working his balls.

His eyes crossed and his toes curled, and it was so perfect. Not playful or pretty, just exactly what he needed. He tightened his grip but didn't need to move. Dex was doing just fine. "Fuck, pet."

Dex hummed, sound buzzing all along his prick and into his body. Then Dex took him deep, swallowing hard.

Hum. Swallow. Hum. Swallow.

Cyrus was going to fucking explode.

Soon.

"Close," he warned, followed by a low growl. His boy was damn good at this. And damn happy to do it. That was a combination he could get used to.

His ass cheeks clenched, his balls were on fire, and he couldn't see. He thought for a second he might fucking die.

Dex grabbed his ass and pulled him in, his boy's throat working him convulsively. He looked down, and Dex was watching him, so focused. So pretty.

"Pet." The name floated on a rough breath and he grunted, balls pulsing as he shot seed down his boy's throat.

Dex swallowed, taking him, every inch, then cleaned him off, tongue dragging on his shaft.

He breathed in deep, getting control as quickly as he could manage, which frankly wasn't nearly fast enough for his liking. Damn sub. Making him insane. After a heavy exhale, he looked down and stroked his fingers along his boy's cheek.

"Thank you, boy. Or damn you. I'm not sure which it is yet." He grinned, making sure Dex knew he was joking. "You're magnificent."

Dex let his cock slip free, then kissed the tip. "Thank you. Come on, you're fixin' to be late for work. Pants."

Dex's voice was husky, his boy's cock hard in his shorts.

"Pants." He pulled them over his hips himself and then offered Dex a hand up. Poor boy. He'd just have to deal with that later.

Dex stood and tucked him away, patting his spent prick. "Okay, what next?"

"Boots." He slid his hand along the ridge in his boy's shorts. "Socks are in the top drawer. Tall black ones, please."

"Tease." Dex grabbed his socks, grinned at him. "You'll be glad that I helped Huck when he broke his arms. I know how to put on someone else's socks. On the bed, please, sir."

Sir. He wasn't going to argue with that. No way. He sat, feeling indulgent and pampered. Breakfast, blowjob, and now he had a dresser? He was living the life.

He'd couldn't wait to tell Les he was finally a real boy.

"I don't know about the strappy thing, and I'll help with your boots, but it's more important they aren't bothering you. Blisters suck."

"They're not even close to new, you'll see where the buckles close, the straps are worn." He loved these boots. He didn't even wear them out of the apartment anymore because he was trying to make them last. He only wore them for scenes. "I'll show you how the harness works."

Dex got his socks on him easily, careful to smooth any wrinkles away. This was... He was going to make his boy so happy. The boots went on, and then Dex stood. "You've got five minutes, now. Show me how this thing works."

Damn. Dex even had one eye on the clock.

He showed Dex not only how it worked but how to position it right the first time so it wouldn't pull on his chest hair because...ouch. He was overdue for some spa time. Maybe he'd have his boy schedule that for him.

Jesus, he was a lucky bastard.

"All good?" Cyrus moved his shoulders, testing the fit. "The client coming in today goes by Steven. He knows you're here, and I've given him rules—he won't look you in the eye, he won't speak to you unless you speak to him directly and first or if I tell him to. If you're comfortable with all of that, I just need to know whether you want to be introduced, or not."

Dex shook his head. "I'm going to go take a shower and start unloading the truck. I won't be a bother, I promise. You won't know I'm here."

"Dex." He took both of his boy's hands and caught those hazel eyes. "The room we're in is soundproof. You could run a jackhammer in the living room, and you wouldn't disturb us. And I will tell you again, this is your home. I want you here. Do what you like, play music, bake, whatever you have on your agenda. I'll move my office before I inconvenience you." He held those eyes for a quiet moment. "You are my priority." It was worth saying again. He'd say it over and over again until Dex believed him.

Dex's hands shook in his, and Dex blushed dark. "I—I don't have a jackhammer in the truck, but I'll keep that in mind. You're fixin' to be late, honey."

Cyrus lifted both hands and kissed them. He understood. It was probably terrifying to think about trusting that someone would put you first when no one had. He could see it in Dex's eyes. He kissed his boy's lips as well, gently. "Thank you for your help, pet."

He squeezed Dex's fingers, scooped up his sunglasses and hat, and left the room just in time to hear the buzzer ring.

"Send him up," he said into the speaker. He took a

breath, pulled on the sunglasses, tucked the hat on his head and reached for the doorknob.

Showtime.

17

Dex made sure the bedroom door was closed, then slipped into the Master bath and closed and locked the door before he slid his hand in his shorts and jacked off with quick, hard strokes. It was dark and quiet, and it didn't take a whole minute before he shot.

Oh.

Better.

He slipped out of his shorts and into the shower. This whole tankless water heater was amazing. No bitter cold showers unless you needed them.

Jesus. He was so confused. There was a part of him that was happy, a part that was worried, a huge part that was totally satisfied, and a part that needed to believe he was going to have a nap soon.

"After you unload the truck," he promised himself.

He figured that would take him at least until lunch, at most until three or so. He'd taken the table top off the pedestal, so really, he could do it all. Get it in the guest room. Nap. Order pizza for supper. There was no way Cyr would be raring to go this evening—he'd had an orgasm last night, one this morning, and he was...working today.

That was a lot of hours to be revved up.

Cyr was right, he and his client might as well have not been there. Dex didn't hear a damn thing from that room. Not one damn thing.

Dex got quite a bit done, hauling things in from the truck and piling them in the guest room before Cyr appeared again. At a few minutes before one o'clock, looking exactly as he had when he went behind closed doors except for a little sweat, Cyr strode out of the room alone.

"I am starving." Cyr pulled the water pitcher from the fridge.

"Hi, starving." Dex pushed over a smoothie with a grin. That hat was...wow. Just wow. "Drink this. Your sandwich has two minutes left in the oven."

He'd had the leftovers and it tasted amazing—strawberry, pineapple, chickpeas, and kale.

Cyr dropped the hat and the sunglasses on the counter. "Oh. So much better. I have a sandwich in the oven?" Cyr looked delighted as he picked up the smoothie and took a big sip. "Oh. Oh wow. That's yummy."

"You do. Turkey, bacon, and cheddar." He beamed over, tickled shitless. "I made coleslaw, but I couldn't remember ever seeing you eat it."

"If it's not too mayonnaisey, I'm in. Mayonnaised? Mayonnaiseish?" Cyr chuckled. "Anyway, the sandwich sounds great."

"Mayo-tastic?" Dex started laughing, too tired to worry about being quiet. "It's vinegar and yogurt. I figured you didn't need a lot of ook on your belly."

Ook—that was a technical culinary term.

"The last thing I need is ook. Thanks for looking out for me." Cyr huffed out a laugh. "I'll try some. How is your day going?"

"Busy. I've been up and down so much I don't even have to press the button no more. The elevator and me are having a wild love affair, and she just opens right up." Honestly, he had four more loads and then he was going to wash up and have a nap.

Cyr glanced over sharply, grinning, then started to laugh. "Opens right up...oh, man. Cheating on me with the elevator."

"Totally. She gives it up. She goes down..." The oven dinged and he grabbed Cyr's sandwich, plopping it on a plate. "Ta-da."

"Oh, pet. That smells like heaven." Cyr smooched him quickly, leaving him blinking, and took a seat at the kitchen table. "Thank you."

"You're more than welcome." He brought the coleslaw, a fork, and a bottle of water. He stood behind Cyr, rubbing, not sure whether he should ask how work was going. How did you bring that up, exactly? His buddy, Marco, was dating a topless dancer in Austin. Maybe he ought to call and ask.

Did you keep your tassels untangled all night?

How many sequins did you lose?

With Cyrus it would be more like, '*does spunk stain leather real bad?* And *don't you worry about chafing your dick?*'.

Not that Cyr smelled like sex. That would smell, right? He'd know. He'd had to crack a window and change the sheets in Cyr's bedroom that very morning after all. Wow.

"That feels good." Cyr was taking big bites of the sandwich and obviously enjoying it.

"Good." He figured he'd get tired of touching Cyrus, but

not today. Probably not tomorrow either. "Should I put out a granola bar for you later?"

"Oh good boy. Thank you for thinking about me. I'll be back out around three. I won't get another break before then." Cyr hummed over a bite of coleslaw.

"How do you feel about ordering pizza for supper? Something easy and yummy?" Because he was going to finish unloading, take a shower, and crash for an hour.

"New York pizza always makes me happy. There's a magnet on the side of the fridge for delivery. I like veggies and lots of cheese." He could swear he just saw Cyr do a happy food dance after the last bite of the sandwich.

"Good deal. I'll call about five thirty." He kissed the top of Cyr's head. "Feel better?"

Cyr nodded. "So much better. I never eat that well on a workday." Cyr leaned away from him and reached back, hooking fingers around his neck and pulling him into a kiss. A real one this time, not a cute peck. Real enough to give him goosebumps.

You'd think he hadn't jacked himself off this morning. Cyrus did it for him. All the way to the bone.

"Mmm." Cyr let him go and stood up. "I better get back to it. Thank you again for my lunch." He got a pat on the shoulder and then Cyr was off again after trading off for sunglasses and that hat again.

He got the kitchen cleaned up, a granola bar and a bottle of water on the table waiting, and he sighed. Four more loads. Four and the truck was empty.

He could do it.

He could.

There was a bed waiting.

18

Cyrus watched as Steven's friend, Tom, escorted the still glassy-eyed and floating sub out of his apartment. It had been a good session; Steven worked hard and left with a few lovely marks as a souvenir.

Out of sheer habit, he locked the door and got in the shower, not even thinking he should have checked on Dex first until he was getting out. He'd been on a high himself. Steven had depth and was so responsive that he'd been able to find the headspace he craved as well.

A good day's work, and more rewarding than most, but he hadn't thought of Dex. Not until he started to come down.

This had never been an issue for him before. He lived alone and had always had plenty of time to recover from a session without having to think of anyone but himself. He wasn't sure that was going to change, but at least he was aware of it now.

He toweled off and dressed in jeans and a T-shirt, then went to the kitchen where he found water and a granola bar, but no Dex. The granola bar hit the spot though, they were so good, and he swallowed down half the water before heading for the guest room and tapping lightly on the door.

"I'm all done, pet."

He waited and didn't get a response, so he knocked more purposefully the second time.

No response. Everything was quiet. His stomach cramped in panic so immediately his rational mind didn't stand a chance of stopping it.

"Don't be a fool, Cyrus," he said out loud, chastising himself.

Dex had just made him a lovely lunch, the boy was happy, everything was fine. Dex had probably run down to the truck to get something and would be right back.

Cyrus decided to have a peek in the guest room assuming that's where Dex had put his things and opened the door gingerly. Just a peek, that was all, and then he'd wait for Dex in the kitchen. He wasn't snooping exactly, but this was technically Dex's room.

The room was full now of totes and trash bags, mandolin, guitar, the tabletop was propped against the wall, its pedestal next to it. In the cleared bit in the middle of the bed was a naked, sleeping boy wrapped around a body pillow.

Sleeping.

Cyrus watched the boy for half a minute, then closed the door gently and went back to the kitchen to sort out how he felt about all of that.

He grabbed an apple off the counter—*huh, how long had there been a fruit bowl on the counter?*—and took a huge bite, chewing thoughtfully. Sure, he'd just had that granola bar, but this wasn't a moment to be thinking and hangry.

Okay. Sleeping was good. That was the first thing he

thought, which was fortunate for Dex because the rest of what Cyrus was mulling over was less positive.

Dex had to have worked like a dog to get all of that stuff upstairs single-handedly in half a day. Hadn't he made it clear he would help? He was sure he'd said to wait on the big things, he didn't want his boy worn out. More than that, if Dex had slept the night through in his arms it would be far more excusable for the boy to be curled around a body pillow at four in the afternoon.

Not every damn thing the boy owned needed to squeeze into that one little room. Hadn't he said, twice at least, that this was Dex's home now too? Wasn't he clear?

He polished off the apple in a few more big bites and tossed the core in the compost.

He'd been clear. Dex just hadn't heard him. Or hadn't understood him.

Or hadn't believed him.

He had work to do.

So. His boy was sleeping, and right or wrong, was quite pretty doing it. Reasoning aside, Dex obviously needed the rest. Cyrus was sorely tempted to crawl into bed with the boy, but he had no intention of rewarding the behavior. What he really wanted to do was give that lovely pale ass a couple of good swats and turn it pink.

Instead he went into the living room, turned on the TV, and ordered pizza.

An alarm sounded at ten of five, and he heard Dex stumbling around, talking to himself, digging through bags. Finally the door opened. "...gotta unpack all these damn bags. Okay, order pizza—lots of veggies and cheese, check your damn emails, make sure you start a grocery list. Ask Cyr if he's got aspirin and... Hey! You're done. Let me order pizza."

Dex was rumpled, the marks of the pillow still on his cheek. Board shorts and a Lucky Charms T-shirt made his boy look young and sweet.

"Come here, pet." He beckoned with one hand out, smiling at his lovely boy.

Dex came right to him, eyes warm. "Good day?"

"Yes, as a matter of fact. It was a worthwhile session." He pulled Dex onto the couch beside him. "I don't have aspirin, but I have Tylenol. And you're welcome to use the computer in the kitchen to check your email."

"Thanks. I brought my laptop and printer and stuff. It's in the tote marked books. It'll take me a few days to dig it out."

"Oh, sure. You mean in all that stuff you brought up by yourself?" Cyrus pinned Dex with a look. "The stuff I specifically instructed you to let me help with after work?"

"You said to wait for the stuff that was too heavy, and you worked all day. It seemed mean when I was so close to done."

Dex didn't get it. At all.

"You wore yourself out, and I assume you're feeling sore since you're looking for Tylenol?"

"Well, yeah. I had a few insane days." Dex pulled away from him. "I need to order your supper, man."

He looked down at the hand his boy had let go of, shocked at how suddenly Dex had retreated, and puzzled as to why he felt stung by it. When he looked back up, he spoke gently. "I called it in. I wasn't sure how long you'd be sleeping."

"I set an alarm on my phone. I found it on the floorboard of the truck. I just left it there last night." Dex sighed softly, shook his head.

"You were exhausted. I ought to have just put you to bed,

but..." Cyrus reached for the boy's hand again. "You're quite a temptation."

Dex nodded and leaned in, cheeks hot, red. "I needed you more than anything. I needed you to let me come home."

"I understand that." He didn't understand much right now but that, however. He combed his fingers through Dex's hair. "I need you too."

Dex moved onto his lap, warm and heavy. "That feels good."

Better. At least with his arms around Dex the boy couldn't simply pull away again. He spun his point another way. "Feeling needed is important isn't it? I like to feel that way too."

Dex nodded, then rested their foreheads together. "I don't want you to decide I'm too much trouble already. I want to fit in your life."

Already. As if Dex thought it was inevitable.

"Trouble?" He needed just the right words. "Your presence here, your energy, your help is already making everything better for me. You're no trouble at all."

Look at those eyes light up. "Thank you, sir. That's... fucking great to hear."

"Dex. I tried to tell you before, and I know it will take time for you to believe it, but this is your home. You're not visiting, you're not borrowing some piece of my apartment, it's yours. Your things don't have to hide in the guest room, they're not an inconvenience. If you want to take a nap, fine. Take it in our bed. If you need help—ask. Just ask."

"I just...it's so ugly in boxes and stuff." Dex grinned at him, kisses dropping on his face. "I got out of the shower, and I went to find clothes and just boom. I was out."

"Okay, that's fair. But listen, you have to work at getting

rest. How would you feel about taking something at night for a couple of weeks until you get into a rhythm?" Dex had so much going on it was no wonder the boy couldn't sleep. He woke up muttering a to-do list to himself.

"I just—I've been busy, you know? Worried. And if I sleep too hard, I might mess up, miss something. I mean…"

"Nothing in the world is going to fall apart while you're getting a good night's sleep, boy."

True or not, he cringed inwardly as soon as he said it. He hadn't exactly been subtle in his tone. "I don't mean to snap, but I need you to start thinking like you're mine. Like you know I will take care of you. You can't mess up if you're pleasing me."

That sweet confusion made him want to wrap around his boy and growl—and the urges that Dex made him feel were uncomfortable and new.

"I'm here to take care of you, honey."

"Is that why you're here?" He leaned back a little to look at Dex. "I mean, is that the main reason?"

Dex frowned, lips twisting. "I want to make sure I say what I mean. I'm here because of lots of reasons. You want me here. I want to help. You've seen me at the bottom and didn't treat me like shit. But the main reason is that I love you, and I want to be with you."

Strangely, Cyrus didn't know what he'd been fishing for when he asked that question, but he knew the answer when he heard it. He gave Dex a deep nod, letting the weight of those words sit with him a second.

That was what had him knotted up worrying last night waiting for Dex to get there. He'd been wrestling with it, and now that his boy had said it directly, things were…clearer.

"I love you, and I want you here. I want you to stay. I

want you to feel welcome. At home. Safe. We will take care of each other."

"Yes, sir."

So simple, so complex.

Yes, sir.

They had done some groundwork, and that was a relief because at least he felt like that had something to fall back on when Dex got overwhelmed, or he couldn't get his head straight.

God, lately he didn't know his head from his tail.

"We'll have to—" The door buzzed and he laughed. "Get the door, pet."

"Time to feed your hunger!" Dex stood up and stretched, back popping and creaking. "I'm on it. This is sorta fun."

It's not a slumber party, pet. Pizza was fun though. "I'll meet you in the kitchen."

What he needed was some advice. He picked up his phone off the kitchen counter and texted Les.

CYRUS

Hey. Got time to talk tomorrow? Not an emergency. I'm fine.

He needed to say that because...well. Because.

It took about a minute for the

LES

Sure. 6? Your boy get in?

to show up.

CYRUS

He did. 6 works. I'm just off my game.

Way off.

LES

cu then. You need me to have M here for him to meet?

Oh. Good old Les, always thinking. Sitting Dex with an experienced sub could be helpful.

CYRUS

that would be great

LES

np. Have a good one

Dex brought the pizza box in. “Did you want me to get you a plate? Do you need tea?”

“Yes to both please.” He put his phone down and took a seat to watch Dex move. The boy was busy but crazy efficient. No wasted movement at all.

Soon he had a plate, the pizza, a kiss, and then Dex was back in the kitchen making two glasses of tea. “Do you have a pitcher? I think I brought my granny’s if you don’t. That way you have tea whenever you want.”

“You know, I don’t think I do.” And even if he did, Dex should use his grandmother’s if he wanted to.

“I’ll dig it out tomorrow. I have lots of kitchen stuff.” Dex brought him his tea.

“You’ll be using this kitchen far more than I ever did, so feel free to move things around to suit you and make some room for what you need for your cookies and everything.”

Dex nodded. “Thank you. I’ll have to make some samples for my store. Take some pictures. We need to talk about bills too.”

His boy wandered to the kitchen, grabbing his notebook and scribbling.

"Well, I wouldn't worry about pitching in for the pizza since you're not eating again." He let the sarcasm be what it was. The boy needed to know he noticed, and that he wasn't pleased.

"Oh." Dex frowned, and then grabbed a plate and his glass, coming to sit with him. "You can just say you'd like company. I got distracted; I'm totally not avoiding you."

"No, you're just avoiding food, pet. And that's not good. If you're going to take care of me, you have to take care of yourself. Of your body as well as your mind." He didn't have high hopes that would sink in, but he had to keep trying. Sooner or later he'd say the right thing. Something Dex would hear.

"I'm not avoiding. I just forgot how to be hungry. I know you don't know about that." Dex winked at him, stroked his leg. Then he took a piece of pizza. "But I do. I go and don't eat for a while, and I stop being hungry."

"Well, you won't do that anymore." He looked at Dex seriously. "Once you...remember how to eat this time, you're going to make sure you don't miss a meal. That's not a request, it's an order. You'll get used to those, it's part of this Dom/sub arrangement we still have to discuss."

So there. The longer he let Dex skate, the harder it would be to change habits.

"An order." There was a long, long pause, and then Dex reached for his hand. "Then you'll have to help me remember, huh?"

"I will." He wasn't sure what that long pause did for Dex except that he got no argument. He took his boy's fingers and squeezed them. "I will remind you, and I will reinforce the order with appropriate demerits and rewards. New habits are difficult to work into a routine. Also, I don't expect you to eat a three-course meal tomorrow. I'll be fair."

Dex looked at him, then he got a quick, rotten little grin. "Those were a lot of words for okay, honey."

"Brat." He picked up his iced tea, giving his boy a sly grin. "You'll get used to that too. Or you'll get a spanking."

Dex went bright red, and his breath caught before he managed to shoot back. "Now, now. I don't feed you cookies for lunch; you don't get to do that."

He raised an eyebrow, looking as confident as he could manage. "Yes, pet. I do."

Dex grabbed his fingers, holding on tight for a second. "Be nice now. We're supposed to be eating."

"Mm. Yes." He pulled Dex's fingers to his lips and kissed them before letting go. "Be a good boy then, and have a bite."

Dex chuckled softly, the sound husky as hell. "Yes, sir. I'm on it."

He dug into the two slices Dex put on his plate, already knowing he was going back for a third. "So what are you looking forward to unpacking the most?"

"Oh Lord. It'll be good to have my kitchen stuff—then I can work. I can get crazy busy before the holidays..."

"I have a new client coming in for an interview tomorrow, and the session will be short. I'll be done by lunch if you'd like some help—only if you want help." He was trying to fill what had been Huck's spot. That was just awkward enough he decided not to mention it to Dex.

"I'd love help." Dex ate a bite of his pizza and hummed. "The pizza here is so good. Honestly, I feel so bad about my stuff making your classy house feel weird to you. I'd love your help putting things where they go."

"That's enough of that nonsense, pet. Feeling bad about being right where I want you to be—with your things—is just...it's...ugh. Well, it's silly." He hated it when he couldn't find the right word. "We'll redecorate together. It'll be fun."

"Yeah?" Oh, look at that smile. "Cool. Thank you. Where do you want me to put my clothes? I can do that in the morning, because it's no fun and it's fast."

"Well, good question. I was thinking of moving my work wardrobe to the guest room so you could have that closet in the bedroom, but then we talked about making the guest room your office so you might want that closet. Unless you want one of the pantries in the kitchen, they're both half empty...that's a lot of words for I have no idea." He laughed and hopped up to get another slice.

"Those pantries aren't going to be empty long, I bet, but I've got three pairs of jeans, a couple nice shirts, and my T-shirts and shorts. Oh, and a hoodie in the truck."

Oh. Well, then. "Let's move Mom's little dresser from the guest room into our room for you, and you can hang your good shirts up with mine." He wasn't a peacock, but he had quite a bit more than that. He'd have to add to his boy's wardrobe subtly.

"That works for me." Dex winked at him. "My shirts would like to snuggle with yours. Oh! Oh, I was going to ask. I never dealt with leather stuff that you wear on your skin. I used to have a pretty vest a while ago, but I traded it. Anyways, how do you take care of it? Or should I just leave it when I do laundry..."

Cyrus appreciated that Dex assumed he was doing laundry and didn't argue with him—didn't even miss a beat.

"Since you're the one who will be doing it, why don't we talk about it? Right now because of my schedule, I wash all my leather once a month. Everything in that closet is actually washable on delicate or by hand and then it gets laid flat to dry."

He had a bunch of drying racks in the laundry room, but that room was way too small to dry everything at once. He would spread the racks out all over the living room on washing day; it was the craziest looking thing. "I'll show you everything."

He had to find more meaningful work for Dex as well. It couldn't be all cooking, cleaning, and laundry if his boy was going to feel truly submissive. Chores had their place, and he understood that Dex got more satisfaction than most from being useful, but he wanted Dex to feel needed—deeply needed—so the boy would understand the meaning in their arrangement.

He didn't need a maid, he needed a sub. He needed a lover. Dex deserved more.

"Oh. My boots get done more often because I wear several pairs of them outside. I often have my clients clean and polish them, but if you prefer that I leave them for you, I will."

Boots were a matter of pride for both Dom and sub. Out in the world, well looked after boots were one of the ways a sub could show how well he took care of his Master. Cyrus doubted Dex understood the significance on that level, but the boy had remarkably strong intuition and instincts so far.

Dex nodded, eyes on his pizza bones, on his plate, and Cy wasn't sure what that nod meant, if it meant anything at all.

He reached a hand across the table. "Tell me, pet."

"It's just hard, you know? To know what to do. A week ago, I hadn't ever even been here. We hadn't even kissed."

Just a day or so ago, Dex had freaked out when he called this move a big ask. Then, everything else was bigger. Cyrus saw the progress, but he could understand how maybe Dex couldn't.

"It's been an insane week. We've moved very quickly, it's true, and we jumped over a lot of steps people usually take to get to this point. If you want to slow down, hit the pause button, I can respect that." He had his heading, and he knew where they would eventually end up. "I'm all in, pet. However this plays out."

"I think that I'd really like to sit with you, snuggle. Just be you and me together. I need that." Dex looked up at him, so serious, so worn out. "Is that okay?"

"I love that idea." The words 'I need' should never be followed by 'is that okay', but it seemed counterproductive to have that conversation right now. The win was that Dex was able to tell Cyrus what he needed at all. And a snuggle was never a bad thing.

"Me too." He got a warm, pleased smile. "I feel like I'm trying to unravel. That's always better with a snuggle."

He stood up and offered Dex a hand. He could have more pizza later. Pizza was good cold. "Unravelling is a scary feeling. But it's okay if you do, it really is. I'm here to fix things, right? I've got an eye on you."

Dex came with him, focused on him, and it felt so right. "I'm not scared. I've been doing it for a while."

"Well finish it up already then, so I can knit a sweater out of you." Cyrus was way too amused with himself as he pulled Dex into the bedroom.

Dex obviously agreed, because the merry laughter followed them all the way into the room and then Dex grabbed him, wrapped around him in a bear hug.

"Ah, pet." Cyrus moved slowly, offering calm energy to meet Dex's intensity, and hugged his boy close. He was perfectly content to stand here with his boy in his arms for as long as Dex needed; he took comfort from the contact as well.

It was true that they'd done this all backward, and he had an idea for tomorrow night that might help. All things in time.

"I work okay as your sweater." Dex kissed the hollow of his throat, tongue brushing his throat.

"You do. You keep me warm." He sighed and arched his neck, encouraging his boy to indulge.

"Mmm..." Dex settled in, proving that his boy was infinitely better at focus than even Dex would believe. The touches were gentle, quiet, and constant.

He let his hands roam, one over Dex's back, and the other down to the boy's ass to get a handful. He dug his fingers into the muscle, massaging and pressing their hips together so he was able to rock, just slightly, against his boy. Nice and slow.

Dex melted into him, trusting him to hold them both up. There were no words, just this connection. It was, in an odd way, very much like that long drive to Huck's house, with Dex trusting him with everything.

He'd been confident then, and he was confident now, but for completely different reasons. There were things about their dynamic that he had yet to figure out, but this wasn't one of them. Neither he nor his boy needed direction right now.

It took nothing at all to relieve Dex of his threadbare T-shirt and he bent to kiss his boy's bare shoulder as he smoothed a hand over warm skin.

"You don't have any ink?"

Dex shook his head. "Nope. I went in once with Huck, but he needed to go home right after."

He didn't want to hear about Huck. There was always more to a story, but from where he was sitting Huck had no appreciation for how much Dex loved him, and made no effort to appreciate the boy's efforts, let alone feelings.

"You don't either, and I've looked most everywhere..."

"I hadn't found anything I wanted to remember forever until very recently."

"No? I hear you." Dex nuzzled his jaw, humming, the sound satisfied. "You shaved in the shower."

"I did. And I'm overdue for a spa day." He led Dex over to the bed and pulled the covers down, then picked up the remote from next to the bed and handed it over. "Your pick."

"A spa day?" Dex turned on the TV, waiting for everything to load up.

"Mhm." He dropped his shirt over a chair and climbed in bed. "Yeah. A little manscaping, mani-pedi, haircut, massage, a nice soak in something. You know. A spa day."

"Oh." Dex settled on something mostly music while he was searching, but he lost interest quickly, moving into Cy's arms and cuddling in.

"Oh. I'll take you along next time, you might like it." Cyrus snorted, but quite happily put his arms around his boy. "When are you planning to open up your shop again? Would you like to spend the weekend getting set up?"

"It's a button and change of address on the site, so as soon as I get my laptop charged, I'll turn it back on. It'll be back-to-school cookies for a few weeks, and then Halloween. Then I hit the season of hell."

Season of hell didn't sound like he'd have much of a sub come the holidays. But this was Dex's career, so they'd figure it out. He wasn't going to get huffy about it. "There are back-to-school cookies?"

"Yes. Especially first day of kindergarten with the kids' names. I'll get orders for homecoming and football, too. They're all custom, really. That's why I can charge so much."

"Do you love it?" He wasn't usually a fidgeter, but something about Dex made him want to touch, and his fingers roamed slowly over smooth skin and combed through thick hair.

"It's a job, but a good job. Some cookies are more fun than others. The really super complicated ones are great, but they take more time, so you can't do as many." Dex snuggled into his hands, expression blissful, joyful.

"It's art, you know. What you do. I don't know why you were embarrassed about it. You do amazing work. You're talented." That was the truth. There was no way he could pull off anything like that.

"It's not super-duper macho, I guess. Some folks would tease real bad..."

"That's okay, I got all the macho we need." He laughed, because he had the opposite problem most of the time.

"Yeah. You're the only man I know that says that. It's... relaxing. I don't like being made fun of. I feel like...you'd respect that."

"I respect everybody, honestly. I mean look at me. Who the hell am I to judge?" That was for sure. "But talent is impossible to ignore."

"You know me. I'm just pretty good at lots of stuff. Enough to get by." Dex licked along his collarbone.

"Mmm. You do better than that at some things. Cookies. Iced tea. Sex."

"Sex with you is different." Dex's cheeks went red-hot, burning against his chest.

"Different?" He assumed that was meant to be a compliment, but what a strange thing to say. "How so, pet?"

"There's more than just getting off. There's feeling."

Sweet boy. "Love, pet. That's the part that makes it

special. Even a little overwhelming. That's the thing we make together."

"I know. And we found it somehow, from all those miles away." Dex's sigh was perfectly happy.

"That's how you know it's right. It didn't let us go." He rolled toward Dex and pressed his boy into the pillows. "You were meant to be mine."

"Yes, sir." The satisfaction in his boy's voice fulfilled something deep inside Cyrus. They had barely begun their journey, and Dex found comfort in him.

He pressed a seductive kiss to his boy's lips, letting his desire drive him, glad they'd gotten past that undeniable sense of urgency so he could explore, tease, make his boy burn. Dex opened up, letting him in, tongue slipping along his.

He loved Dex's curiosity. Even in their kiss it was there, Dex's tongue testing him. He slipped a hand into Dex's shorts, around to that perfect ass, and levered his leg between his boy's thighs, giving them both something to move against.

"Uhn." Dex rocked back into his hand and back onto his thigh, testing the sensations his boy could find.

Cyrus rocked into his boy's hip for some friction, still lingering over the kiss, breathing his boy in.

He'd forgotten how enjoyable just fooling around was. Most of his encounters were more heated with men he always knew would be short-term. Sometimes very short-term. He hadn't taken the time to enjoy someone like this in a long while.

"Mmm..." Dex rocked, eyelids heavy, the look on his face pure bliss. "I love the way you snuggle."

"Good because I'm not sorry I can't keep my hands off you. You're irresistible." For now that was okay, while they were more lovers than anything else. He was going to have to get it under control again though. Somehow. He couldn't be a Dom to Dex and lose it every time the boy smiled at him.

He could right now, though, and he planned to.

"You make me feel like that, like I mean something." Dex took one slow kiss after another, and the world went slow, easy.

"You make me feel..." Whoa. He started that statement, and he wasn't sure he knew how to finish it. Dex made him feel so much. Loved, desirable, strong, capable.

Oh. Yes. The answer hit him so suddenly it took his breath for a second and made his chest ache.

"Worthy."

"Oh." Dex met his eyes, and he knew his boy heard him, felt him. Their kiss deepened, and he wasn't sure either of them remembered to breathe.

Lots of little fragments he'd never quite managed to integrate started knitting themselves together as they kissed, leaving him with a stunning sense of relief and...joy.

He was a lucky, lucky guy.

Cyrus smiled into the kiss and rolled them so he could see, watch his boy move.

Dex didn't believe him, but his boy was lovely and danced beneath him like a dream, lean and beautiful. He pushed Dex's shorts down and watched the boy wiggle out of them, baring more skin for his fingers to explore.

He was burning now, everywhere Dex touched felt like an electric current surging over his skin. Once again he was captivated and couldn't even pretend he had control of this moment.

"You too?" Dex tugged at his sweats, fingertips brushing over the tip of his cock. "I need to touch."

He hissed and nodded. "Yes." Cyrus let Dex tug at them and helped kick them off. God, he wasn't even sure he wanted control. He wanted to lose himself in his boy.

"Mmm..." Dex hummed and scooted them together, catching both their cocks in one hand. He stroked, the touch painstakingly slow.

Cyrus took one more hungry kiss and then moved his lips to Dex's jaw, cheek, ear, and took the lobe in between his teeth and tugged. That earned him a happy little gasp, Dex's fingers giving him a squeeze.

He rocked into Dex's hand. "That's a good trick, pet." Dex's stiff prick felt good against his, and he tried to be patient, but he didn't think that was going to last very long.

"You bit. I couldn't help it." On the next upstroke, Dex's thumb slid across his slit.

That forced him to moan and he dropped his mouth to Dex's chest, teeth seeking out a new target, one stiff, pink little nipple.

Dex whimpered as he nibbled, hand pushing harder, dragging on his shaft.

"God...damn." Cyrus grunted and looked up at Dex. "Want you to ride me, pet. I want to watch you move."

"Oh. Yes, sir. I can do that." Dex grinned at him, eyes twinkling. "Would this be snuggling level three?"

Cute. He could play along. "Level three is only for experts. We can downshift to snuggling level one over pillow talk after." He shifted, rolling them again so Dex was half on top of him.

"Nice one." Dex chuckled for him, reaching for the line of condoms and the slick, handing Cy the bottle of lube as Dex tore one of the squares open.

"Oh, thank you. I get the fun stuff." He could joke, but his eyes were glued to Dex, watching his boy's every move.

"You want to get me ready or what?" Dex smoothed the rubber on him, fingers warm and steady. It was a lovely visual, enough to make his mouth dry.

"Brat." He reached for Dex. "Show me that ass then."

"Me? Never. I'm sweet as sugar." Dex rubbed the tip of his cock. "So hard."

That was no lie. And Dex's fingers were hot on him, hot enough to melt right through his skin. "Are you teasing me, pet?" He reached for Dex again, trying to get hold of that hungry little ass.

"Maybe. But I put out." Dex pushed right into his arms, keeping his ass just out of reach. "You make me happy."

"I hope so. I want to." His boy should be happy. His cock should be happy too. He stretched his arms but still couldn't get a good hold. "I want that ass, boy."

Dex snuggled in, giving him access, but teasing him worse by rubbing against his prick, sweet cheeks sliding along his shaft.

"Damn, pet. Want you." He slicked a couple fingers for Dex. It wasn't graceful and he fumbled the lube bottle, but he got the job done and slid his fingers between those cheeks and over that tight pucker, then eased two fingers inside.

Dex hummed and his head fell back, exposing that sensitive throat. "Good."

So lovely. He went after the exposed area with his tongue, tasting as he worked his fingers inside his boy. "Delicious."

The ring of muscles around his fingers tightened, squeezed him until they curled, Dex's gasp so pretty.

"That works for you, hm?" It was his turn to tease a little, and he gave Dex's ass a love tap with his other hand, grinning at the sound and followed that by smoothing a hand over the warm skin.

"Little bit, yeah." Dex moved on his touch like a dream, his boy buzzing with his need.

"Little bit." Cyrus purred, eyes glued to his boy. "I've got a little bit more for you."

"Oh honey..." Dex reached down and squeezed his hungry prick. "That's way more than a little bit."

He gasped even as Dex made him grin. "You want it, take it."

"Every fucking inch." Dex stroked once, then rubbed the tip against his hole, teasing the hell out of both of them.

His ass clenched, and he grabbed Dex's hips with both hands, his patience at an end. Reflexively, Cyrus rolled his hips up and pulled Dex down with a needy, frustrated groan.

Dex gasped, his boy's eyes rolling, and about the time he was going to pull out, make sure Dex was okay, he heard. "Fuck. Love. Again."

He had no desire or will to argue. He thrust up, fingers digging into Dex's narrow hips and holding on, like if he let go he might lose himself.

Dex took him, let him fuck deep and hard, slamming into that tight hole like a madman. Dex's eyes were rolled back, face a study in need.

It was wild and primal but too intense to sustain and finally Cyrus froze, breathing hard, and rocked under his boy, forcing them both to come down, come back to each other.

"You—you okay?" Dex panted hard, wiggling on his lap as Dex worked his prick, muscles rippling around him.

"Fucking incredible. You?" He hauled in a deep breath that cleared his mind and let him focus.

"Buzzing." Dex rolled his hips, trying to distract him.

He tried, but it was going to work. He knew it would; he ached for his boy. His moan seemed otherworldly, somewhere outside of him. "Pet."

"Yeah. Yours." Dex leaned in, rested their foreheads together. "Need you like breathing. You ready to ride?"

"Mine." He shifted a hand to Dex's cock and pumped it. That was all the answer he had.

"Yes, sir."

He watched as Dex started moving, rolling his hips forward as he knelt up, back as he sank down. Dex had it just right, drawing encouragement from him with every stroke. He took a kiss, intending to steal his boy's breath but ended up losing his own and broke it off to gasp. "Fuck, Dex."

"I got this. I need it." Dex bit his bottom lip and pinched his nipple. "Fuck me like you want to."

Lightning shot from his chest to his balls, and he bucked up hard like he wanted to, unleashing his need.

Like Dex wanted him to.

Everything he took, Dex offered, meeting his need, his hunger, and never shying away. In fact, Dex encouraged him on with filthy pleas and hard, slick hands.

Cyrus grabbed him suddenly, pulling them together, and flipped them so he hung over Dex, using his new leverage to drive even harder, push himself even closer.

"Please!" Dex grabbed his knees and pulled wide, and the sight of his cock spearing that tiny ring of muscles made Cyrus want to roar.

"Mine." Everything after that was heat and sweat as Cyrus pushed toward his climax, felt it build and tower over them both. He grunted as he reached the brink, muscles taut and trembling. "Now, pet! Now."

Dex squeezed him, so tight that it almost hurt, and then his boy was shooting, spunk spraying between them.

His vision blurred, and he didn't last another second, chasing Dex, orgasm so powerful it made him shout, leaving him panting, muscles trembling.

Dex hummed, fingers sliding over his shoulders and down his back, petting him with featherlight touches.

He kissed Dex's face, lips, jaw. "Love. My god. You're... glorious."

"You're—thank you. That was so..." Dex moaned, and the sound was satisfied down to the bone.

"Yeah, it was." He needed to lie the hell down before he fell over and he moved slowly, twisting and lying back in the pillows with a groan. "Damn."

Damn. What the hell was that?

"Kind of an aggressive snuggle." He huffed, a grin tugging at his lips.

"We may have reached that third level after all..."

"I have to be careful how I answer that. If I agree, I have a feeling you'll just go looking for level four. That might actually kill me."

Dex's soft laughter filled the air. "Level three was deeply satisfying, man. I shot hard."

And at his word, which was hot as hell.

He was going to put his boy in the tub for a soak later, Dex was going to be sore tomorrow. *He* was probably going to be sore tomorrow.

"We'll see how long we can stay awake for a little level one pillow talk. Hm?" See how long he could keep Dex's attention before the boy got an itch to get up and *do* again.

"Sounds good to me." Dex snuggled in with a hum, fingers brushing along his side.

He pulled Dex against him. "I am meeting with a friend

tomorrow night at the bar. Les, have I told you about him? I want you to come and meet him and his boy, Milo."

"You mentioned him, yes. That's cool. I want to meet your friends." Dex's skin was hot, not feverish, but from exertion.

"Great. I'm glad to hear that. You'll like Milo, he's been in the scene a while and knows all kinds of people. He's actually a former client of mine too."

"Yeah? Cool. You're a busy guy."

He shrugged. That was an odd comment. "I've seen a lot of people for various reasons. Milo was just a couple of months when he was working through something." Did Dex think that was creepy? Being friends with a former client? "It's not a big deal."

Dex nodded. "So, how did y'all become friends, you and Les?"

"We met at a party. Les was coming off a really ugly breakup, bought me a drink, and just started talking." He snorted. "That happens. I guess I look like someone that will listen."

"I can see that. You have kind eyes."

"He says I looked bored and made a good victim." He laughed. Les had been so angry. The real truth was that Les thought he looked like someone who could handle it.

"I thought you were a reporter."

"I know. I tried not to take offense. I mean, how many tall, handsome Yankees do you get at funerals in small-town Texas?" He chuckled, Dex's cheek bouncing on his chest.

"Very few. Never fell asleep in a stranger's car in my whole life, but Huck trusted you."

"I've never seen anyone so worn out. Honestly. I was honored you trusted me that much." Huck had trusted him.

That was one very genuine thing he knew about Huck; the man understood trust and knew what it meant to hand it over.

"Do you miss him?"

He thought about that. "I don't think I knew him well enough to miss him on a personal level, pet. But he worked hard in our sessions and he had such...strength and intensity. I won't soon forget him, for sure." Huck had fought with ghosts, and the sub's needs ran deep.

Dex nodded once, nuzzling into his chest, but that was it.

"Do you want to answer that question?"

"Nope."

"All right. But I'll listen when you do." Dex was angry. That wasn't going to just go away. Eventually, if he thought it would help Dex, he'd push. But not here, not right now. "Are you going to miss Texas?"

"I don't know. I'm sure I will, once...in time." Dex sighed softly. "Do you miss Pennsylvania?"

"Not even a little. I wanted to be where I could be me. Entirely me. That wasn't possible where I grew up. I've been very happy here." Mostly. There were a few rough years, but he was lucky.

Dex squeezed his hand. "Good deal. It's weird how we know a lot about each other and nothing at the same time."

"I was thinking earlier that we'd done this a little backward. But we have time, and lots to share with each other, right? I think we know what matters most about each other, who we are right now. Who we are together."

"That makes sense. I do lots of things the backward way."

"I think I'm pretty simple." He shrugged.

"Good deal. You're the most complex man I know, but I only know cowboys and rednecks."

"I don't know where you fall in those categories, but either way you're quite a puzzle, pet. So many pieces."

"I don't know if I fall in any categories right now, but that's okay. No worries."

No worries. It obviously worried Dex. "Hey." He tucked Dex closer, made sure his boy felt safe. "That's good, right? You can look at all of them and take on only the ones you want. Leave the other ones behind. But I can give you one. You're mine. And there's only one man in that category."

"I am. It's good to have a place, to know what to do."

"It is. We have so much to explore together." Cyrus kissed Dex's forehead. "Now. I can't decide what I want more, a nap or a snack."

Dex chuckled for him. "Did you want me to make you something?"

He hesitated to answer because Dex was just going to laugh harder, but... "Yes?"

"You know what you want, or should I invent something?"

"How about I just follow you and have some leftover pizza?" Dex sat up and he sat up as well, stopping the boy a second with a touch. "Do you still feel like you're unravelling?"

"You fucked that out of me, thank you." Dex grinned and winked at him. "Are you sure you just want pizza? I'll warm it up a little."

"Excellent. I'll remember the remedy the next time you have threads loose. And yes, pizza is fine. I only got a slice, and it was yummy." Cyrus slid out of bed to find his sweats and pulled them back on.

Dex cracked up. "You had three, you know. Or are we calling it one serving?"

"Ha! Did I? Well, I don't usually have leftovers at all. We'll call that firsts." He tossed Dex the shorts that were on the floor.

"Thank you." Dex put them on, moving slow this time. "Do you see my shirt?"

Poor boy. The world was beginning to catch up with him—lack of sleep and food mixed with loads of stress.

"Right here." He walked it over this time and helped Dex pull it on, not that his boy needed the help, he just thought the touch would be a comfort. "I have nothing planned for my evening. After I eat something, I want to do whatever is going to help you breathe better. We can sit and watch a movie, or we can get started on making room in the kitchen for your things, or we can take a walk and get some air...anything you need."

"I don't—I'm real tired and all. I don't think I'm up to a walk." Dex gave him a hug, leaned into him for a minute.

Cyrus returned the gentle hug. The last time Dex admitted he was tired he was losing his shit in the kitchen. This was another great step for the boy. "You don't have to be up to anything at all. Maybe you want to climb back in bed? I can grab a snack and come back. I'm very happy to snuggle the evening away."

Especially if you actually sleep.

He swore there were tears in Dex's eyes when he looked toward the bed, and he only waited for the barest nod before he was moving Dex to climb back in.

"I'll be right back." He could stay; it wasn't crucial he go eat or anything, but he got the feeling Dex could use a minute alone. A second to breathe—or punch a pillow, or cry—without someone watching. "Right back, I promise."

"Good deal." Dex curled into the pillows, hiding his face.

He kissed Dex's hair. "Promise." He closed the bedroom door quietly, giving Dex some privacy. He expected the boy would be asleep before he got back.

19

Dex had woke up feeling ten thousand years old, sore as a boil and creaking, but a little Tylenol and a long, hot bath that Cyrus absolutely insisted on had put him to rights.

He hadn't had a bath since he was five.

By the time Cyrus had knocked on the guest room door, he was done with his clothes and had dug out his printer, plugged in his tablet and his laptop.

"Hey, you. I made you tuna salad. It's in the fridge. There's devilled eggs too."

"Thank you. Can I have a kiss first?" Cyr smiled, but lingered in the doorway and didn't come into the room.

"Of course. Come on in." He headed toward the door, hand sliding over the pattern carved around the edge of the tabletop.

Cyr went right to him and took a light kiss. "You've had a busy morning. It's looking better in here. I was thinking we could move the bed to storage to give you more room. All the tenants have some of the basement, so it's not a big effort. You probably need a real desk too."

"Are you sure? Where will we put your granny's quilt?" Dex wouldn't argue with more space, but he was used to making do. "Come on, let me feed you. You had all the stuff for tuna salad, so I assumed you ate it. And since I was going to boil eggs anyway? I made devilled eggs."

He had found Granny's pitcher—it was full of hibiscus tea—and a bunch of his pretty and silly platters for cookie pictures, his favorite glass, and his three best coffee cups. Those had been important.

"Sounds great to me." Cyr followed him, fingers resting on his back. "I can put a quilt stand in the bedroom and display it there, right near where we moved Mom's dresser. You need some elbow room to work."

He leaned into the touch in thanks before going to fetch the plate he'd put together. "All I need is to put the crackers on."

Cyr looked at the random things on the counter, picked up an old mug with Dexter's Laboratory on it. He'd had it forever, since he was little.

"This is cute. Looks like it has a history." Cyr smiled and turned it over in his fingers.

"I brought three with me. I got that for Christmas from my second-grade teacher. I made the lumpy one, and the purple one changes colors when you pour the coffee in."

"Lumpy." That got a little laugh. "These are great. Is there room where I keep the mugs? If not, the ones in the back I literally never use, go ahead and pull them out."

He sat the crackers out and Cyr dug in, standing right there, leaning against the counter. He was pretty sure he could put anything in front of Cyr, say it was edible, and Cyr would eat it.

He took one of the devilled egg halves and nibbled on it while he washed all the platters and set them to drying.

"Why so many?"

"Work. The cookies need something to be shot on. Shitty pictures make for shitty sales."

"That makes sense. I bet all the light in the living room windows would make for some nice pictures. I bet you're ready to get back to work." Cyr had taken his cookie business seriously from the minute he'd mentioned it, never seemed to think it was strange at all. Cyr reached for a devilled egg and popped it in whole. "Mmm."

"Thanks." He took another bite of his. "They are good. And yeah. This is my fifth year. Last year I made fifteen thousand dollars between Thanksgiving and Christmas."

"That's pretty amazing for cookies. I guess you weren't kidding when you said you'd be busy. Is there tea?" Cyr went for a glass.

"Oh! Yes. I made hibiscus." He pulled out the pretty cut glass pitcher filled with rosy pink iced tea. "Ta-da. And yeah, I just don't sleep, eat, or breathe for a couple weeks and I think my blood is royal icing."

"Hm. Maybe we can get you some assistance." Cyr set a glass down on the counter. "That pitcher is gorgeous. That's the one you were talking about? Your Grandma's?"

"Yes! Isn't it great?" He swirled the tea in the pitcher, the light making everything sparkle. "It's the first time it's been out of Texas in over a hundred years. It came on a covered wagon."

"Wow. That's a great story. It's beautiful. I bet your grandma would roll over in her grave knowing it's in New York now." Cyr took a sip of the tea.

"No, she would have been excited. She wanted to go somewhere—anywhere, but she was always working and raising kids."

Cyr nodded. "Kids like you. Your tea is delicious. Thank you."

"You're welcome. I'm having a ball inventing flavors from your drawer." He needed to talk to Cyr about groceries. He'd love to do that with Cyrus, decide what to make, shop.

"I'm enjoying it myself." Cyrus finished up the tuna salad and the last devilled egg, then swallowed down with a big gulp of tea. "That was perfect. Thank you. What are my marching orders now, boss?"

"The table? That's the big thing. The elephant in the room." Then the totes would be easy. Most of them were kitchen with a few books, some movies, and some junk.

"Great. Let me get my drill, and we'll take that bed apart, make some room for it. You want to go pull the sheets off, maybe put the quilt somewhere safe for now?"

"I have a whole truck toolbox full of tools too. I didn't want to leave them, so..." He headed to the guest room and started folding the quilt up. He thought it would be comfortable on the couch. Something to cuddle up with. Maybe he'd put it there folded, a little hint.

"The hall closet has room if you don't want to leave them down there. It's safe for New York, but it is still New York," Cyr called down the hall to him.

"Maybe you could come down and look at them in a couple days?" He wasn't sure what they needed, but circular saws could be handy.

"Sure." Cyr came back with a Makita and put it next to the bed. "Field trip to your truck. Maybe we should take it for a spin. Get off the island and joy ride in Jersey or something."

"Okay. That sounds fun. We can give it a good wash too." He stripped the bed, put that in the laundry and piled the pillows on their bed.

Cyrus was bringing out his instruments, one by one, putting them on their stands in the front room. "These will be great out here. I like how they look. I played the clarinet in high school. That's as close as I get to musical now."

"I can play them all. I'll show you sometime. If you want." He felt hot and pleased, a little fluttery. "So, I'll pull the mattress out and take it...downstairs?"

"Yeah, that's a double, though. Let me help." Cyr followed him back to the guest room...or his office. It was his office now. Wow. "I definitely want to hear you play. All of them."

Dex stopped them, stealing a quick, hard hug, sucking up a little calm and giving some of his gratitude.

"Mmm." Cyr purred, holding him just right, breathing in slow. "I so enjoy your hugs." A warm hand stroked through his hair.

"Yours feel necessary." Dex rested a second. "Let's get that mattress moved. Is there something to cover it with so it doesn't get dusty?"

Cyr let him go with a light love tap to his ass. "Other than sheets, no I don't think so. Maybe we can pick something up tomorrow. Should we leave it in the living room for now?"

Hrm. Okay. "Do you have two fitted sheets for it? That would do for now."

"Sure. Top shelf of the closet. Good idea." Cyr's long legs took him over and back in just a few strides. They put one on, lifted the mattress and put on the other. "This will be fine. The sheets don't fit our bed anyway. They're too small." Too small for the giant king that commanded most of Cyr's bedroom.

"Yeah. This is nice and we can wash them if we need to." Look at him, figuring shit out.

Together they wrestled the mattress and box springs down, both of them cracking up as they maneuvered through the challenge of the elevator, which wasn't near as fun as the getting out of the elevator.

"Welcome to the basement." It was chilly down there despite it not being cold out, and the lighting was fluorescent and sporadically working. They walked the mattress down to the storage cage, and Cyr unlocked it.

It was nearly empty. The only thing in it was a really nice mahogany sideboard-style bar.

"Wow. Look at that hidden down here. Wild!"

"That's mine. I had to move it out, I couldn't keep it in the apartment. But I wasn't ready to part with it either." Cyr helped him set the mattress against one side of the little room.

"It's lovely. Can I look at it, please?" He loved the lines of it, the vibe.

"Sure." Cyr stepped out of the way and leaned against the mattress. "It was in my living room forever. It's one of the first things I bought when I had enough money for my own place. I love how the top opens. And the glassed-in parts are all lit from inside when you plug it in."

Oh, he could store all sorts of baking supplies in here. Cookie cutters, tips, bags—it would be amazing. Still, bad memories and all, and Cyr said he didn't want it in the apartment, so that was that. "It's gorgeous. Seriously."

"Thank you. Maybe one day we can bring it back up. I've been feeling good. You make it easier. Maybe eventually. It's a nice piece." It seemed like Cyr was sincere about that, but he watched as Cyr back out of the storage space entirely, more stressed than he'd seen his lover yet. "Ready?"

"Totally. I'll bring the frame down. I can handle that on my own." Poor man. How awful. He took Cyr's hand and led him away. He shouldn't have asked to look. That was mean as hell. "You can take a bit to rest. You worked all morning."

The man's balls had to ache.

"I don't need to rest." Cyr locked the storage unit, took his hand and headed for the elevator. "I'm fine. Sorry about that. I haven't seen it since Les and Milo moved it for me. I'd forgotten it was down here, that's all."

"Sure. I'm sorry I looked." Curiosity would always, always be his downfall.

"There's no need to be sorry." Cyrus seemed more relaxed now but was still holding his hand firmly.

They got into the elevator, and he lifted Cyr's hand to his lips, kissing the knuckles, one at a time.

"Pet." Cyr smiled at him and leaned down. "My lips want one of those."

He looked up and took a kiss, slow and sweet, meant to comfort, to ease.

Cyr's fingers rested against his cheek, stroking lightly. They didn't part until the elevator doors opened, and Cyr held his eyes as they stepped off and headed for the apartment. "Thank you."

"Anytime." Maybe he'd made it better, at least a little. He just needed to take the bed rails down and then that bit would be done.

Cyrus let him take the rails down on his own and got started moving things for him, out of the smaller pantry into the bigger one, leaving him a whole empty one for his things.

When it was done, Cyr dragged him over to see.

"Will this work?" There were shelves on each side and drawers at the back with a cabinet above them.

"Wow. That's amazing. All for me? Wow." Dex took a kiss in thanks.

"All yours. I'm hoping you outgrow it." Cyr gave him a quick squeeze. "I'm not going to even try to put things away in here for you. Shall we put the table up?"

"Sure." The sight of the room without the bed was weird, but the table took up a lot of space, the chairs fit just like they should. From there it was easy. Two stand mixers, books, movies—he was distilled into a single truck bed of shit.

Cyr stepped up behind him as they looked at the room and curled around him. "It looks good."

"It does." It was weird. He didn't want to look at it too hard, because he was okay with comfortably numb. He'd worried that he couldn't get it without beer, but he was busy, tired, so he'd take it. He'd got way too close to not numb last night, but he'd kept it. Thank God.

"I love you." Cyr kissed his neck. "I want you to be happy. I want you to do what makes you happy."

"You're good to me." He leaned in, cuddling hard. "You want to go for a walk? I'll buy you an ice cream cone."

"We can walk, and then we can make our way to the bar. Sound good?"

"Yes, sir. That's a great plan. Let me put on a presentable shirt and some smell good."

Cyr gave him a tight hug and then let him go. "Okay, but you already smell good to me. I need some jeans."

"You need them pressed? My good pair are still creased." He could do jeans pretty good. Shirts he took to the cleaners.

"I have never pressed a pair of blue jeans in my life. I hardly need to make more work for you. The leather will keep you busy enough." Cyr laughed and headed for the bedroom. "Fashionably rumpled jeans is how we roll up here."

He nodded like he knew a fucking thing about fashion. He wasn't no Tim McGraw or Garth. He just knew that he had good jeans and work jeans. It wasn't like he had to worry about it. Wasn't no one looking at him. He pulled out his good jeans and a T-shirt that was clean.

Cyr did the same, rumpled jeans making the tight-fitting T-shirt his lover pulled on look even tighter. He'd never seen anyone wear so much black, but it suited Cyr.

"Hmm. Which boots? These, I think tonight, since we're walking." Cyr pulled out a pair of low, lace-up, black boots that looked a little too hipster until they were on.

He put his boots back on, unbuckled himself to tuck in. Once he was presentable, he put his wallet in his pocket, hooked the chain on. "All I need's my gimme cap and I'm good."

"You are definitely good." Cyr looked him over and slowly licked red lips. "Damn good."

He chuckled, both amused and pleased. "Maybe just damned. I'm still working on that part."

Cyr laughed. "Well. It's good to know you're working on it. But you look good to me. Your cap's in the hall I think."

"Yessir. It's on the little hook." It was weird, because he hadn't been sure if going down to the garage would feel like he needed to put his hat on—it didn't. He grabbed it, stuck it in his back pocket. "You ready, honey?"

"Ready." Cyr got the door and followed him out. "We need to make a quick stop while we're out walking if you don't mind. Just a quick errand."

"Whatever you want. I just wanted to get outside in the sunshine, wander around, look at shit." Dex was easy as pie.

"You're good like that. You'll learn your way around soon enough. It's pretty easy once you get your bearings."

It was hot out. The city air was steamy, but the sun was

pretty, and the shadows were long and dark in the street. One second they were squinting to see because it was so bright and the next because it was so dark. The sidewalks seemed to stick to his shoes in places, and he could smell the asphalt baking in the sun.

"Oh, it's a winner out here. That ice cream sounds like a great idea."

"I figured that would work for you." Ice cream was good and easy, and it would feed Cyrus's belly.

"We're ducking in here, real quick." The wide blue awning over the door said 'Locksmith' in huge white block letters, and the store had a ton of doorknobs and deadbolts in the windows. Cyr looked around, then headed for a counter toward the back of the store.

"Cyrus!"

"Hey there, Bill." Cyr pulled out a key ring and took a key off it, sliding it across the counter.

"Someone swallow a handcuff key again?"

"Ha. Not this time." Cyr snorted.

"Oh! Must be a new backup key for the backup key for your cage, then." Bill's grin was full of crooked teeth.

"Nope. Front door."

"Damn. Did you have a break-in?"

Dex stood there, trying his damnedest not to gawk. Who swallowed a handcuff key? Also, cage? Damn. He was never going in that room. Never. God, he wanted to, though. He wanted to ask a thousand questions, but they never found a place to come out, and some led to Huck, and those questions were a little angry, so he couldn't ask those and... He chuckled at himself. And he needed to buy Cyr ice cream.

"Bill, this is Dexter Appleton. Dex, this is an old buddy

of mine, Bill Davies. Bill's dad owned a restaurant supply place downtown and gave me a job when I first got here."

"There's more to that story, but we'll leave it there." Bill laughed and offered him a hand. "Pleased to meet—wait. Are you moving in?"

"Nice to meet you, sir." Dex took Bill's hand and shook, offering the man a happy grin. "And I reckon I already have."

Bill looked at Cyrus, getting started and shouting over the key cutter. "This is a thing, then?"

"It's a thing."

"Well good! It's about damn time you took on a sub, Cy." The shop was loud for a second as Bill finished up the key.

People just said things like that? Just out loud? Huh. He wasn't sure what he was, except he knew that he was Cyr's, and Cyr was his. That was it, really. Oh, and that Cyrus got hangry.

Cyrus's eyes rolled so hard it was a wonder they didn't pop right out. "About time? Is someone counting?"

"What?" Bill stuck a hand to his ear, but the man had clearly heard. The machine stopped and Bill dusted off the new key before holding it out to him. "I assume this is for you, Dexter. Welcome to the neighborhood."

"Wait. Hang on." Cyr plucked it out of Bill's fingers and attached it to a Statue of Liberty keychain before handing it back with a fond smile. "Now it's yours."

"Thank you, sir. I appreciate it." He dared to touch Cyr's wrist in thanks.

Cyr caught his hand and kissed it.

"Aw. I just love love." Bill leaned on the counter watching them.

"What's the damage, Bill?"

"On me. Call it a housewarming present. Go forth and be happy."

Cyrus shook with Bill and said thank you, then steered him back out into the heat.

"Thank you." Dex hadn't even thought to ask yet. He hadn't felt ready to explore before, but he was starting to get there.

"You're welcome. You shouldn't feel like you can't come and go when I'm working. You might need something. And anyway, it's your place too now." Cyr took his hand and didn't seem to care it was a little sticky out for it. "I bought the keychain at one of those tchotchke souvenir places in midtown. I've had it in a drawer forever, but it seemed like you'd appreciate it."

"It was the first thing I asked to see." He loved that Cyrus remembered. "That was a damn fine morning."

"So much fun. I'll show you everything now. We'll make a list. I hardly ever do the touristy stuff anymore. It was a little cooler that day than it is today, though. How do you deliver your cookies in this heat?"

"Mail. I send cold packs with them from May to September, just in case. I always send an extra in case of breakage too." He had one hell of a rating.

"You must pack them up really carefully I guess too?" They turned a corner and headed away from a busy street onto one much quieter.

"Yes, sir. I have a system. I wrap each one in a bag and tie it, and then I pad each one. I mail out on Monday and Thursday only, so I'm not spending my whole life. So, in an ideal world, I bake on Wednesday and Friday, decorate on Tuesday and Thursday." He looked up and grinned. "Exciting, huh? I also do paperwork on Mondays and marketing on Wednesday because I'm organized and shit."

"Listen to you! That's very cool. You love to make it sound like it's just a little hobby, but it's not. It's a real business. I will never listen to you try to play it down again." Cyr reached over and ruffled his hair playfully. "Silly pet."

"Well, it's not riding bulls or...therapy." He winked over. "But, you know, it's good work."

"To hear Huck talk about it, riding bulls wasn't really all that either."

"I'm no good at it. He did fine at it, when he wasn't landing on his fucking head." Huck had done that a lot.

"It's funny you say that. I was starting to wonder. He never cancelled on me but there were a couple of times we had to take it easy. He wasn't the helmet-wearing type I guess."

"No, sir. Said it fucked with his balance. Said it was for pussies." Dex shrugged. "I tried it once, broke my collarbone and wrist, decided I needed to not do that again."

Cyrus laughed. "No. And I can promise you I never will. I'll leave that to the professionals. Cookies are safer. Therapy is too, most of the time. Though not always with Huck. He was a live one."

Not anymore. "I bet."

He knew all about how Huck was in bed. That was something Huck and his fuckbuddies were into—talking about where they dipped their wicks. Sure hadn't said dick all about Cyrus, though. He guessed Huck was ashamed for wanting to be beat on and all, whatever 'and all' was.

"Sorry. I shouldn't have said that. Huck was very private and... I just shouldn't have." Cyr sighed. "Do you like gelato? There's a great place right up here."

"Oh, honey, Huck is dead. He doesn't give a shit anymore. I'm not sure he gave a shit about a lot for a while. Is gelato ice cream?"

"It's like ice cream. An Italian version. The flavors are much more intense, I think. Would you like to try some? This place even has these tiny little cups for people that just want a couple of bites. That's not my style, but..." Cyr bumped him with an elbow.

"Sounds good to me. Let's do it." He liked that idea, actually. Just a couple of bites until you found one you loved.

"It'll be fun." Cyr held the door open and they were blasted with chilly air. "Oh, that's nice too."

A young guy hopped down from a counter where he'd been sitting and reading a book. "Looking to cool off, gentlemen?"

"We are. I'm a regular, but he," Cyr pointed to him with two hands. "Is a newbie."

"Awesome." The kid looked at him with bright blue eyes. "The most popular today is the blood orange. But the coconut is always a hit, and if you like raspberry I recommend that one too."

Cyr pointed into the case. "The pistachio is amazing also."

"Is that what you get?" Because he could steal a bite then. Blood orange sounded intriguing as hell, and he loved the color.

"Often. I hadn't decided today. Should I?" Cyrus was teasing him. "Do you want to share?"

"I do. I'll taste whatever you get, and you can have bites of whatever I get." The temptation to goose Cyrus was huge.

"So get to tasting. Make sure you pick something good."

The kid behind the counter laughed and handed Dex a bite of the blood orange on a little spoon. "Try this one first."

He took the spoon and tasted, the sweet orange flavor

just busting in his mouth. Oh, he liked that. "Do you have a lemon?"

"We do!" The kid bounced around behind the counter and got him a taste. "It's not as sour as you'd think."

"No? I love lemon. It's my favorite flavor." He tasted, and it was good, but not tart enough for him.

"Yeah, I don't know why they sweeten it up so much. You know what's tart is the lime. Hang on." Another spoon was presented to him. "They call it key lime pie, but it just tastes like lime to me."

He tasted it, the pucker making his butthole draw up. "Oh. Oh, that's the ticket. I like that. I'd like a small of that and whatever Mr. Cyrus here wants."

"He wants pistachio. He only ever gets pistachio, even when he tries things first."

He thought he caught Cyr blushing for a second, but it went away fast. "Yeah, yeah. So I'm in here a lot in the summer."

"And the fall, and the winter..." The kid cracked up as he filled cups with gelato for them.

"Ice cream in the winter, huh? I met a guy once that said they ate ice cream in Moscow when it was bitter." He paid for the sweets, handing Cyr his cup.

"Thank you very much." Cyr gave the kid a wave as they left the shop. "There's no such thing as a bad day for ice cream. Thank you, pet. Bite?"

"Yes, sir." He scooped up a spoonful and offered it over.

"Wow. That's...tart. Whoa." Cyr held out the pistachio for him to take a taste. "We'll hang a right up here and head for the bar."

"Thank you." He took the bite, the creamy pistachio sliding down his throat. "Oh, yummy."

"I should try something new next time. I'm such a creature of habit."

"Are you?" he teased. "You just like what you like." Dex floated around, nibbling and tasting and then moving to a new flavor.

"You noticed. You'll just have to make me try new things."

"I cook a lot. You'll get experimented on. I spend hours with the Cooking Channel on."

"While you're baking?" Cyrus tossed an empty cup in a trash can. "We're here."

"Yes, sir. I get...not lonely and not bored, but something like that."

"You need some input. Background noise. That's pretty common." Cyr pushed open the door to the bar. "After you, pet."

"Thank you, sir." There was something easy about this place—warm, comfortable. He was glad—these people were Cyr's friends when he was drinking, and he deserved to keep them.

"Cyrus!" A rail-thin man flew off a barstool and went right into Cyr's arms, nearly disappearing in them.

Cyr returned the hug and kissed the man's temple. "Hello, Milo."

"It's so good to see you." Milo's voice was muffled against Cyr's chest.

Neither of them moved for a long moment, and then finally Cyr slowly pulled away. "Milo, this is Dexter App—"

"Dexter! I love your name." Milo's smile was warm and genuine. "Oh, it's so good to meet you. I'm so happy for Cyrus. Do you hug? I'm kind of a hugger." Milo looked like someone who'd be pretty disappointed if Dex said no.

Cyrus chuckled. "Be still, boy."

Milo answered quickly. "Yes, Sir. Sorry."

"It's real nice to meet you, man." He grinned, because now hugging would seem a little weird.

A little weird.

Ha.

He lived with a man with a person cage. The boundaries of weird had been blown right the fuck out of the water, so he just hugged Milo.

When in Rome and all.

Milo gave good hugs as it turned out, and it wasn't really all that weird. Being dragged by the hand over to the bar was a little odd, but Cyr was right on their heels.

"Master's in his office, he said to get your coffee and then go ahead and knock."

A coffee landed on the bar a second later.

Cyrus laughed. "Got it."

Dex got a kiss on the cheek. "This is a slightly more abrupt parting than I'd expected, pet. Are you good?"

"I'm fine, honey. I'll get me a Coke and sit here with Mr. Milo." He grinned at Cyr, because that was dear as all get out, to worry. Wasn't any call for it, though. He liked chatting, and he had his phone if he couldn't.

"I'll take good care of him, no worries."

"I'm not worried." Cyrus picked up the coffee and headed past the bar toward a hallway Dex couldn't really see well from his barstool. "Have fun, boys."

"He lies." Milo waved the bartender over. "Coke for Dex, please, Kit."

"On it." Kit grabbed a glass.

"Les is looking forward to meeting you too, but I guess he and Cyrus have business first." Milo looked at him. "We're both thrilled for you and Cyrus. He's so...reserved, you know? Quiet. He's not great with dating."

Had they dated? Maybe that one morning at the Statue of Liberty. That counted.

"He's a good man. He's been very good to me."

"He is. The best, you'll see. Ask anyone. He does good things for people."

"One Coke." Kit sat the glass down on the counter but didn't take his fingers off it. "You did mean a literal Coke, right?"

"That's just fine, thank you, sir. What do I owe you? I'll get his coffee too."

Kit laughed. "Thank you. But Cyrus hasn't paid for a coffee here in...well ever."

"Les owns the place, Dex. It's on us. If it's not alcohol, Cyrus doesn't pay."

"Oh, well thank you." He put a twenty in the tip jar.

Milo just nodded and didn't say a word about that. "So you're from Texas? Are you visiting? I think Cyrus was hoping you'd move up."

"I am. I'm from outside Austin, and I drove up with all my stuff, uh, couple nights ago? Three. We started unpacking today." The last few weeks had been the wildest of his whole life.

"Nice. Welcome to New York. Hopefully we don't scare you off." Milo reached for a pretzel.

"Thank you. I haven't been out much since I got here, but I'll figure it." He was easy enough, he thought.

"Are you like a 24/7 sub, or do you work? What do you do when Cyrus is seeing clients?"

"I make cookies and decorate them, and mostly I stay out of the way in the guest room." He wasn't sure he was a sub. Hell, he wasn't sure what that all meant, but he hadn't had time to think about anything. He was praying it didn't happen. There was a meltdown behind that door.

"He has you hiding in the guest room? That doesn't sound like Cyrus."

"He doesn't have me anything. I'm just staying out of the way. I don't want to—" See. Bother. Interrupt. "—get in the way or anything." He was exceptional at staying out of the way. "Are you from here?"

Asking questions was way easier than answering them.

"Yeah. Born and raised. How can you be in the way? I worked with him for a while. Everything happens in his office, and I'm pretty sure it's soundproof. Don't you have chores and stuff?"

"It doesn't take a second to make sure things are nice after he's closed the door. I've been doing that sort of thing a long time." He had a rhythm, and honestly, he had more to do because he had to finish unpacking and take all the empty totes downstairs and find a nice bookshelf for his shit.

"Is that your thing? Domestic stuff? Les knows I hate it so I'm forever dusting as a life lesson or something." Milo laughed, the sound light and tinkly like little chimes.

"Well, he's letting me stay. It's only fair that I take care of things." Not that he minded. He liked to take care, and Cyr didn't like clutter.

"Letting you—?" Milo set his Coke down on the bar and turned to look at him. "Aren't you two a couple? Like, lovers? That's what Les told me."

Oh, that made him smile. "We are." He chuckled softly. "Maybe even more than like lovers."

He winked at Milo, not wanting to offend. He wasn't teasing; he was happy.

"That's what I thought! You made it sound like Cyrus was doing you a favor. Please. You have all the power here, don't forget it."

"What? I think we're talking about two different things, somehow." Because Cyrus was doing him a solid, letting him come, not asking him for money yet, letting him in.

Milo's blue eyes narrowed. "You're not a sub, are you?"

He felt his cheeks get hot, and he took a sip of his Coke. "I'm just an asshole redneck from central Texas, man."

He knew Cyr thought he was, and he thought he was making the man happy, but he was getting that what Milo was talking about was like what Cyrus called clients. At least he thought so.

Milo grabbed Dex's knee and rocked on the barstool, laughing so hard they drew stares. "Oh. My. God. Oh my god, you are too funny. Jesus, you must be very confused. Les talked like you and Cyrus had an arrangement, which means Cyrus forgot to tell Les—or you—something." The giggles went on a bit longer. "Whew! I need to breathe."

He kept focusing on the bubbles climbing the straw in his glass. That was him. Funny. Obviously he'd missed something. Like a lot of somethings. He'd warned Cyr he wasn't none too bright.

Still that wasn't this guy's issue, and he wasn't fixin' to be rude, so he found a smile. "In and out through your nose, man. In and out."

Milo took another breath or two and watched him. "Sorry. I mean it's good that you're happy together however you are. It is. You've obviously got his number. He's never talked about lovers or even considering someone moving in, not around me. And if he did around Les it wasn't anything serious enough to mention to me. He's been alone as long as I've known him."

"I haven't even known anyone like him. Ever. We probably weren't ever even supposed to meet, but we did."

"That's the best. Fast too, was it love at first sight? Lust? Both?" Milo playfully batted long eyelashes at him.

"Ha. We met at my best friend's funeral. I thought he was a reporter, then I thought he was Huck's therapist. I didn't know for a long time that he was Huck's… That Huck had paid for him."

"People pay therapists." Milo raised a fine eyebrow. "Cyrus is pretty much a therapist."

"Sure. Sure, I don't mean no offense." *Remember, this guy had been with Cyrus too. Don't be nasty. You ain't in Texas anymore.* "I just never even knew this was a thing. I thought it was just in books."

And porn. Lots and lots of porn.

Milo looked impressed. "There are books about Dominance and submission as therapy? Who knew?"

"Well, there's a ton of books with black covers out there, for sure." He winked over, but he was getting real tired of swimming in a pool that was way too big for him. "So, you been with your guy a while?"

"Yeah. Going on six years. Cyrus introduced us. You know those books are all porn," Milo said haughtily. "They're just dirty books. It's not like Cyrus is being paid for sex. Oh my god, could you imagine? The man would be exhausted." Milo snickered into his Coke and took a sip.

"So what…" No. He could figure this out without this guy thinking he was an ass. "I'm sorry. Do y'all have a restroom you can point me too?"

"Sure. It's straight back that way." Milo pointed toward the far end of the room, past a bunch of tables and a jukebox.

"Thank you, sir. I appreciate it." He headed back, his belly acidy, and his brain going a million miles an hour. He needed to look this up on his phone again.

20

"Sorry. It's Milo."

Already? How much trouble could their boys get into at the bar?

Cyrus leaned back in one of Lex's overstuffed chairs with his tea, surrounded by pillows and warmth, and put his feet up on an ottoman.

"No worries." He checked his phone though, just to make sure he wasn't missing anything.

Nothing from Dex, so it couldn't be too bad. Hell, he hadn't seen a hint of hesitation from his boy.

Les's fingers were still flying so Cyrus drank his tea—orange pekoe this time—and looked around the office. It was a very comfortable room overall, not just this lovely chair, but also the warm woods and the classic desk. He'd always felt relaxed here.

He wasn't sure how concerned he should be about the look on Les's face, so he finally just asked. "Is everything okay?"

"I'm not sure, to be honest. Tell me about your boy some more?"

Oh. Something was up. "Well you know he bakes. It's really quite a steady business..."

One of Les's eyebrows went up. "Yes?"

"He's also a musician. He plays a number of different stringed instruments...uh, mandolin, guitar. I haven't heard him play yet. We've been busy moving him in. We turned the guest room into his office, and finally that lovely kitchen will get good use."

"Does he know he's your sub?"

What kind of question was that? "He's a natural. He's absolutely mine."

Les stared at him. Just stared like he was growing a second head.

"Seriously. Seriously, you're going to play it like that and leave my boy embarrassed and worried? You led me to believe you two had an arrangement. Your Dexter doesn't seem to understand much of anything."

"Well, we haven't had an in-depth conversation yet. He's challenging, I haven't wanted to push too hard. He's still very fragile—"

Les scrolled up, then showed Cy his phone.

MILO

MASTER! 911 911 911

Dex thinks M. Cy sleeps with his subs

What do I do???

He read it, then read it again, totally unsure how to handle this one. "Oh my." He glanced at Les and then leaned back in the chair again. "Tell him I don't?"

He deserved the daggers Les was shooting at him right then.

"Sorry. Sorry. Look. This is why I'm here, Les. I did ask to talk, didn't I? I know I'm doing this all backward, but I didn't really have an option." He sighed. "I fell for him. Hard."

"Jesus, Cy. I—" Les held up one finger, texted again, and then put his phone on his desk. "All right. First, wow. And congratulations. Second, Jesus Cy. He thinks you're fucking your clients. I don't know whether to be impressed that he loves you so much that's not a problem with him, worried that your love maps are so different, or fascinated by what he must think your libido must be like."

"I don't either." He thought about that and was more than a little horrified. How could Dex possibly think he... It was flattering, but whoa. "I didn't know he was that... He's got a couple of issues I need to work through with him."

"That's a... Okay. You talk. I listen." Les shook his head, started chuckling. "I don't know if Milo's ever going to forgive you."

He started to laugh, but Les leveled him with a stern look and he sobered right up.

"Talk. Right." He sighed. Talk. Where the hell did he start? "He was living in a house that was owned by Huck, the client that hung himself. Well, not in the house, but in a crate behind the house. A bright yellow shipping container. Huck had this big house with lots of room, and Dex was in a shipping crate."

He wasn't sure what that would tell Les in a vacuum, but he had to start this conversation somewhere.

"Were they lovers?" Les leaned back in his chair.

"I thought maybe at first, but no. They weren't. Huck traveled and rode bulls and was rarely home. Dex took care of the house, and Huck's property, and anything else Huck wanted. They were friends in...high school, I guess? Longer probably. Dex didn't have anyone else. It was...weird."

"Weird? Weird how? Was Dex his sub?"

"More like a slave." That wasn't actually true, but that was how it felt. "No. Not really. He wasn't a sub, but he acted like one. Huck didn't worry about a single detail."

"Okay. Go on. How did you two…connect?"

He thought about the car ride after the funeral, the rain, all the texting and phone calls. "He took care of me. He was so tired and grieving, but he fed me and washed my clothes and did everything right. He's so intuitive, and he knows me. I couldn't ignore how much he needs me. I couldn't get him out of my head."

Les nodded. "And I know you said you told him about your work before he moved up."

"I told him—I started out just saying therapist, and then I did tell him, yeah. I explained what a Dom and a sub are, I told him about power exchange and…he didn't ask many questions."

"Maybe he didn't have a basis to ask from? From what you've said, he doesn't seem particularly worldly?" Les chuckled. "I mean, seriously. Have you ever just googled professional Dom? BDSM?"

"He said he got porn. I told him that wasn't accurate." Had he said he didn't fuck his clients? Ever? "I think I may have assumed he…how could he think I… I mean he wears my ass out, Les. He's irresistible. It's bad. I mean it's amazing, but I don't think I really have any control in the bedroom."

"There's not a thing wrong with that. I mean, there are things I do with my boy in the bedroom that would shock the hell out of you. We're allowed to explore things that get us off together, even if it's something I would never do in a public scene."

"Don't give me a heart attack, Les." He grinned, joking, but the permission was nice. Cyrus felt better about that at least. "So… I need to talk to him. I'd planned to kind of gentle him into serving more formally. He's naturally curious, inclined to submission, I don't know that he'll ever be interested in the tools in my office, but I'm okay with that. And I guess you never know."

"Just think about all the tools that you could never have in your office that excite you. The games you and your boy can play." Les's wink was part wicked, part teasing, and part obscene.

"Really, Les. You're a dirty old man." Although if Dex found that drawer on his own, well...he made a mental note to hide the ones with remotes.

"You have no idea, child."

"Child?" He stared at Les a minute and then started to laugh. "Damn, you're going to make me blush." He took a breath and tried to sip his tea without spitting it. "Look, I don't need help in the bedroom. Dex is a quite capable lover. Where would you start with making him understand what I need outside of the bedroom?"

"Honestly? Make sure you have a starting place, and then tell him. Be direct. Demand questions. He's filled with misinformation, obviously."

A starting place. He'd have to make a starting place; everything with Dex went in circles. Or spirals. He never knew where anything started and ended, it was maddening. "Easier said than done. He's...slippery. He changes the subject all the time. He doesn't say what he needs to say, and then he'll say everything with a touch."

"Well, there's your challenge. How do you focus him? Blindfold? Bondage? Chores? You're an inventive Dom, and you can use sex in your bag of tricks."

He had no idea how to focus Dex. "I'll have to experiment with that." Bondage was a really good idea. His mind started putting something together right away. Something that might work. "I have an idea."

Les chuckled, eyes wrinkling at the corners. "I never doubted you would. Are you going to let me meet him? I can occupy him while you apologize to my boy."

"After what you just told me? I'm not sure I trust you around him." He laughed and stood up. "Of course I will talk to Milo."

"Good luck with that." Les stood, straightening his tie. "Come now, introduce me to your Dexter."

"You're going to love him." He set his tea down and headed back out to the bar where Milo and Dex were still chatting. "Boys."

Dex smiled up at him, gaze warm. "Hey, stranger. Good coffee?"

He loved that smile and moved around Milo so he could sit with Dex. "Finished the coffee and moved on to tea. Dex, this is my very best friend, Les. Les, my Dexter."

Dex stood and shook hands. "Pleased to meet you, sir. I've heard a lot about you."

"And you. Your Master speaks very highly of you."

Cheeky, Les. He wondered how that would go over.

Dex blushed but didn't argue or correct Les. He just smiled and sat.

Cyrus liked that. Very much. "Les, did you have dinner plans? We've just come from ice cream, but I could eat."

Dex and Milo both chuckled and shared a knowing glance.

"I heard that. Naughty boys get spankings." He grinned and cast his eyes in Dex's direction, hoping to catch another blush.

Dex turned bright red, and Milo patted his cheek, stage

whispering. "I'll protect you, innocent baby. I got your back."

Somehow he didn't think that was going to make Dex feel better, but that was fine with him. Those rosy cheeks were everything.

"Let's see. Dex has now tried New York pizza, Thai, and burgers. What should we take him to try?" He shot Milo a look. "And don't say Mexican, boy. I know you love it, but Dex is from Texas."

"Damn." Milo looked to Les. "Sorry, Master."

"Mmhmm." Les winked at him. "Greek? There's a happy irony there." Les was on a roll.

"Mmm. Fig leaves. I'm in." He winked at Les. "Wait. Or do I mean grape leaves?"

"Ooh...dolmas and finger foods!" Milo bounced. "Oh please, Master. That sounds like so much fun."

"Greek, pet?" He ran a hand over Dex's back from shoulder to that lovely little ass.

"S-sure." Dex's ass cheek clenched under his hand. "I'd love to try."

"It's settled then." He leaned in and kissed Dex's cheek. "Come on. I love how I can make everyone eat with me."

21

Dex brought so much food home that it was obscene, putting it away so that Cyr could have a snack later.

What a weird fucking day. Not bad, but weird.

Apparently it was a big deal that Cyr didn't have sex with his clients, especially not Milo, because he heard about that sort of extensively. Also, if you looked up no money BDSM you found things that curled your hair.

Googling no sex for money BDSM was worse.

"I'm actually quite full." Cyrus opened the fridge door so he could put the leftovers in.

"Good deal. It was tasty." And it was finger foods, so he didn't have to eat if he didn't want to. "You need anything?"

"That's a loaded question." Cyr smiled at him. "How about we sit and talk for a minute? Wherever you're comfortable."

Damn. "Sure. Couch?"

"Sure. Don't worry, it's not a scary talk." Cyr took his hand and they wandered out to the couch together, neither of them really in a hurry. Cyr sat on his usual side and put an arm out so he could snuggle in.

"I like not scary." Dex settled, snuggling right in. "Did you have a good day?"

"It was a great day. My interview with a potential new client went well, we got lots done in the kitchen and your office, I had a good talk with Les, and dinner knocked it out of the park. Top it off by snuggling with you? I'm a happy guy."

"Good deal." Dex kissed Cyr's jaw, pleased as fuck. "I'm glad. And tomorrow is Saturday. Bonus."

"Major bonus because we're not working, and I have plans for us. But I have to ask you something, and I'm not trying to embarrass you, but it got back to me that you might think I'm screwing around on you at work, and I just want to say for the record that I'm not. I would never." Cyr turned and caught his eyes, dark orbs holding his attention. "You're it for me."

Oh God. Oh God. "I didn't—that's not what I said. Exactly. I didn't know that you didn't...you know, have sex with your clients. I wasn't mean about it, even in my head. Mostly. Except for Huck. Maybe a little about Huck. I just thought it was your job. I have a friend whose fiancée is a titty dancer, and that's skanky."

"You thought people paid me for sex." Cyr blinked at him, looking confused. "Dex. There's not enough cash in New York for me to fuck Huck."

"Me either." Dex grabbed Cy's hand, just mortified. Him and Milo weren't friends. It wasn't nice to tell stories on your friends. "I didn't know. I'm sorry. I really didn't know."

"Don't be sorry. There's no need." Cyr kissed his fingers. "I'm sorry I wasn't clearer. I can't imagine how you think I have enough stamina to do that and then keep up with you, but I guess I'm flattered." Cyr smiled at him. "And please don't be upset. Milo was a little freaked out about what he should say to you and asked Les. Les passed it on to me because he was concerned, and it was in the context of our conversation."

"I was wondering, but I thought maybe I was just that hot." Dex winked, pretending to play, even though he was embarrassed as all get out. He'd hoped that he'd just get to slide on the fact that he was an idiot, but no such luck.

"Well, you are. I'm just not that young." Cyr squeezed his fingers. "I want to talk with you more about my work tomorrow, so you understand what I do, and why I do it. And I'll give you a tour of my office. It shouldn't be a big mystery to you."

"If you want." He took a deep breath, because he didn't know if he wanted to do it. But he sort of wanted to know and see. "I'm nervous. I tried to figure it out on my own, but... You know, I've been a little busy."

"You have been, and up until now that's been fine. We will take tomorrow for us. It's fine to be nervous. You might hate it, it might scare you, you might be curious and want to explore or experiment...all of that is fine." Cyr smiled at him warmly. "Once you have a better understanding, we'll come to an agreement of some kind. It can change and grow as we do, but we have to start somewhere. It's important that you know what I need, and that I make sure you feel safe and are getting what you need too."

Oh, he did love that smile. That smile was the—not the very start, that was how he could let himself rest with Cyr—but it was the reason. It let him believe that things were going to be okay.

Dex leaned hard. "I feel safe with you. From the start."

"Thank you. I feel safe with you, also. Here's a question, which is similar but not the same question; do you trust me? I mean deep down, implicitly trust me? Think about it."

He didn't have to. "I came here. You heard me lose my shit. You seen me cry."

Cyr was petting on him, fingers roaming over his shoulders and chest, combing through his hair, a constant reassuring touch. "True, I have. I know none of that sits well with you, and it's hard. Thank you for that, and I trust you. We're in a very good place, pet."

"Mmm... I love that. I'll be good to you. Take good care."

"You already do." Cyr hummed softly and kissed his forehead. "And I am going to help you grow, Dex. To be sure and proud of yourself. As you should be."

"I just want..." A reason. That's really what he wanted. Somewhere to be where he was making things better.

"You want it to mean something. I remember." He got a real kiss then, slow and sweet.

He reached up, hand holding Cyr's cheek as he sank into the kiss, letting them just be together.

Cyr covered his hand and tangled their fingers, shifting to kiss his palm lightly and then his wrist. "Shall we go to bed and...read?"

Hardly. His lover's look would set a book on fire.

He chuckled, tickled to death. "You gonna tell me a bedtime story?"

"Mhm." Cyr stood and pulled him to his feet. "Once upon a time there was a wart-covered frog from New York who fell in love with a hot, handsome Prince of Texas."

22

One day. One day, Cyrus promised himself, he would wear Dex out enough that the boy would sleep late.

It was good to have a goal.

He could smell the bacon, though, and the coffee, and Dex had to know he'd be along any minute, his growling stomach driving him out of bed.

Fresh out of bed wasn't his best look, so he brushed his teeth and pulled on his robe, going for a stylish sleepy look, and followed his nose toward the kitchen.

You're an idiot. He had to laugh at himself; Dex didn't give a shit if he walked out in boxers or a tuxedo.

The scent of cinnamon hit him before he got to the kitchen, and the sight of his boy with earphones in, dancing and icing homemade cinnamon rolls was the single most adorable thing he'd ever seen.

He settled against the doorjamb to watch, because happy was a good look on his boy. And new. He really didn't think he'd ever get enough of it.

There was a totally unconscious grace to the way Dex moved, a sensuality in the way he shook his ass.

"There. Breakfast for my man. Now to go wake him up." Dex licked the knife clean. "Mmm...nummy."

For my man.

That made his heart jump. He was such a sap.

"Mmm. He's awake. And jealous of that knife." He grinned wondering whether Dex would even hear him with the headphones in.

Dex blinked, then turned to him with a smile, cheeks going pink. "Good morning, you. I made breakfast."

"It smells amazing." He needed a kiss, so he walked around the kitchen island and got himself one. "Did you sleep? Be honest."

"I woke up at six. My stomach needed coffee in it."

He thought about that. Midnight-ish until six? That was real sleep. He wasn't going to jinx anything by remarking on it, but he could silently pat himself on the back, couldn't he?

"I hear you. Can you pour me a cup please?" He didn't even try to make a pot of coffee anymore, Dex was better at it.

"Of course. Do you still want toast with your eggs?" Dex was already moving, pouring his coffee.

"I think I'll stick with those rolls. They smell so good." Really, this breakfast made to order was almost as good as the sex. And something about cinnamon rolls made him feel younger. Or maybe that was the sex too.

He watched Dex some more as he waited for his coffee, thinking about the day he had planned. The goal was to have Dex on board with something formal by dinner time. He wasn't trying to move mountains, just do what Les had suggested and get them to a jumping-off point.

Dex made his eggs, pulled out a plate, and put together his breakfast. "Do you need juice?"

"No, thank you." He took a seat with his coffee and

sipped it happily. No matter what the verdict was tonight, he felt like a Dom today. He had something to teach his boy, questions to ask, orders to give. And he was planning on wearing a little leather, just because he could.

"I gave you a little extra sweet. I didn't think it was worth dirtying a plate for, but I could get a bite or two. Cool?"

Oh. Good.

"That's an excellent idea. Why don't you kneel right here by me?" He pointed to the floor, then picked up his coffee and took a sip, like this was the most normal request in the world.

Dex blinked and his head tilted. "Are you...? Is everything okay? I don't have to have any."

He let Dex spin a little because that was Dex and calmly looked up at him. "Everything is perfect. *Trust* me."

Dex searched his face, a worried frown between his eyes, but he pursed his lips and nodded. "I do. Okay."

Dex sighed softly and knelt down, confusion pouring off his boy.

"That's it, pet. I'm sure it feels awkward, but it's a fairly standard position for subs, and I want you to get a little taste of a lot of things today." He shifted himself, rather than make Dex move, so that they were very close and Dex would be able to lean, if he could get his boy to relax that much. He dropped a hand down and stroked Dex's back with it, calm and reassuring as could be.

He would let Dex settle a bit and see where it took them. He could talk forever, but there was no substitute for real experience.

Dex finally leaned into his hip with a sigh, fingers curling around his ankle. "I should have brought my coffee with me, huh?"

He wanted to laugh. He schooled himself and didn't, but

he really wanted to. Dex actually sounded bored. Not uncomfortable, not confused, bored. He'd given much more consideration to looking for an opportunity for Dex to kneel than he had to the fact that Dex didn't sit still well. His boy didn't do still very well at all.

But Dex was kneeling, and there was a very happy little piece of him that was dying to cheer.

He gave Dex's back a pat and picked up his knife to cut his boy a nice bite of cinnamon roll, then offered it down to Dex. "If there is something you need, pet, you may ask me."

Today he might even say yes.

"Can you talk to me? Please? This is really weird. We always talk during breakfast." Dex took the bite, humming softly. Oh, that was a good sound. A hungry sound.

He'd known many a Dom who fed every bit their sub took to them. That always seemed a little extreme to him, but he could see the value in trying it occasionally. "I can. Do you want to get your coffee? You may and come right back." Cyrus watched Dex hop up. "It is a little weird, I'm sure. But there is something about appreciating that your place is...wherever I put you. And kneeling is a physical reminder of your status as my submissive as well." Dex was right, though. He did love their breakfast talks. Dex was chatty in the morning after some sleep.

"Did you need more coffee while I'm up?"

"Good boy." Thoughtful. Focused on him. He peered into his cup. "Yes, please."

Dex came over, filled Cy up and left the other full cup, and kissed his temple before putting the carafe away. Then Dex came back to him. "So, I don't want to mess up. Do I bring my coffee with me or..."

Asking questions. Wonderful.

"If I don't make it clear, you should ask, as you just have.

It's never wrong to ask a question, unless I specifically say otherwise. Just be respectful." He picked up Dex's coffee and moved to the side of the table where Dex had been kneeling. "Come around where you were, and I'll hand it to you."

"Yes, sir." Dex settled back down, easier this time. "I'm a Texan. We're made to be respectful, right?"

He laughed as he handed Dex the mug. "Indeed." He cut another bite and held it down for Dex. "Really these are amazing."

"Thank you, sir. It's my own recipe, you know. Like really mine." Dex snapped it off the fork.

"Really? I feel special then. Thank you for sharing it with me." The man who'd taught himself to bake after he saw it on TV had his own recipes.

He carded his fingers through Dex's hair as he finished up his breakfast, saving the rest of his cinnamon roll for last.

"Mmm...that feels good." Dex kissed his thigh.

"I'm glad. Tell me about kneeling."

Dex frowned, head tilting again. "Tell you *what* about kneeling?"

"Anything. Is it comfortable? Is it comforting? Humiliating? Why do you think subs kneel? Why do you think I asked you to kneel? Anything that comes to mind."

"I'm not embarrassed. I like that you touch me. You said it was so I was in my place, but when you said it, it didn't sound ugly. When I do, it does." Dex shrugged and a little grin appeared. "And we have *got* to dust under the table, man."

The dusting bit sounded like a deliberate distraction, so he ignored it. "Your place, as in the place that is yours. It's not meant to tear you down, and it sounds like you heard it the way I meant it." He held his fork down with the last bite of cinnamon roll.

He was relieved that Dex trusted his intentions; it would make a difference when he did, inevitably, make a mistake. Thankfully, Dex was quite human too. They'd stumble along together for a bit.

"Thank you." Dex hummed and sipped at his coffee. "Can I ask you a silly favor?"

He smiled down at his boy, curious. "Go ahead."

Dex blushed pink, but he held Cy's eyes. "I want to know what it tastes like, to kiss you after the cinnamon and sweet. Can I?"

"You want to taste your own personal recipe on my lips, do you?" That was a lovely little fetish. He patted his knee. "Come on up."

"Thank you." Dex slipped into his lap like that's where the boy belonged. Then Dex gently held his cheeks and kissed him, tongue sliding over his lips.

Cyrus was curious and allowed Dex to keep control of the moment. It had nothing at all, of course, to do with how much the sensual kiss was turning him on.

Dex moaned into his lips, then eased back, kissing the corner of his lips before they separated. "Oh, yum."

"I'll second that. That was a delicious kiss, pet." It was probably time to change course before his boy managed to distract him. "I'd like you to clean up the kitchen, then meet me in the bedroom, please."

Dex nodded and took another quick kiss. "Don't forget your coffee, hmm? I'll be two shakes of a dead lamb's tail."

"Okay, but that sounds like you may never make it to me." He snickered and headed for the bedroom to regroup for a minute and think.

It was barely after breakfast, and they'd already made

some progress. He was hopeful for the rest of the day. The trip to his office should be very interesting.

He heard Dex humming again, the water running, dishes clinking. Cy thought it was a peaceful noise, and he hoped Dex was making the kitchen more and more his.

Once the water turned off, Dex's hum stopped, and soon his boy was there, stripping off his T-shirt. "I got wet. I zigged and the water in the bowl zagged."

"Leave it off, pet." He knew this was how the day was going to go; he had to take advantage of every opportunity as it came up. "I like looking at you." He had other reasons, but that one would do well on its own.

That blush just made him grin. "Lord, I swear you can make me feel naked while I still got my pajama pants on."

"Do you like feeling naked?" He grinned, not really expecting an answer, and went to his work closet to find pants.

Dex was sitting on the edge of the bed watching him when he turned around, a little smile on his face.

Well that was naughty. "Go pick out a pair of boots for me, pet."

"I like the ones with the buckles in the back." Dex moved around him to grab them.

"Perfect." He set his pants on the bed and watched Dex, waiting for his boy to return. "You can put those down and dress me, please." He didn't make any effort to remove his robe, just waited for Dex.

Dex smiled at him, sliding the robe off his shoulders. Soft chatter filled the air as Dex touched him. It wasn't nervous talk—it was happy and warm, and it only paused when Dex stopped to inhale the scent of him and leather together.

He absolutely allowed Dex to indulge. That was the point of this day, to let Dex discover and learn.

Cyrus felt like if he blinked or got distracted for one second he would miss something. Dex was fascinating him, completely captivating, and he paid close attention, learning everything he could, trying to put all the pieces together.

"Boots, then?"

"They're comfortable, right? You wear them a lot." Sweet boy.

"They are. I like the heel and the buckles, and they make me feel powerful. Confident." He looked Dex over, admiring the rumpled pajama bottoms. "Did you want to put on something other than pajamas?"

"Sure. I can get dressed. Let me help you with your boots, and I'll hunt some clothes." Dex knelt down and grabbed a boot.

He looked down, lifted one foot and let Dex slide the boot on, surprised at how reverent his boy was. Dex got his other boot on and buckled and stood up.

"There you go. Let me get—How dressed do I need to be? My good jeans are dirty, but I got my work jeans."

"Be comfortable. Shorts or sweats are fine." He crossed his arms over his bare chest and grinned at his boy. "I only mention it because we might find the unicorn jammies a little distracting."

"The unicorn jammies are soft against everything. In the early morning, a man deserves soft against his everythings." Wicked boy. Wicked, laughing boy. Dex slipped off his pants and found a pair of soft, soft cotton shorts.

"The softer the better." He could certainly handle Dex's backside in those shorts, no problem.

He debated for a second—shirt, not shirt, shirt—and finally decided against. Cyrus took Dex's hands and looked at his boy meaningfully. "We're going to go to my office. All I need for you to be is honest."

"Okay. I can do that." Dex squeezed his hands. "I love you, huh?"

Hopefully that would still be the case after Dex saw his office. He smiled at his boy and gave him a kiss, tasting coffee and cinnamon. "I love you."

That was enough said, so he took Dex's hand and led him down the hall. "Go ahead in. The door has no lock, inside or out. That's for my client's peace of mind, and mine."

The centerpiece of the room was a bondage table; the hip-height, leather-covered platform was boxed in with tall posts and under the platform was his cage. That piece was custom-built, as were a number of other things in the room—the St. Andrew's Cross against the far wall between the two tall windows, the stockade hanging on chains overhead, and his spanking bench.

It was the largest bedroom of the three with its own, large bath, originally intended to be the Master, but he needed the elbow room in here more than he did for himself. He tried not to hold his breath as Dex walked in and just waited, reminding himself that anything could happen.

Dex looked around, face remarkably void of emotion. Then he wandered, exploring without a single word, without a question. He even took time to stare out the window at the view.

It was maddening, that silence, especially in a space where his subs made noise. If someone was quiet, it was usually him.

Then Dex came right to him and pushed into his arms, hugging him tight.

Cyrus froze for a second, suddenly aware he hadn't been breathing, and now he wasn't sure he remembered how. He did, though, and took in a deep, deep breath, then folded his arms around Dex so he could hold his boy close. He wasn't sure of everything the embrace meant, but he knew what it meant to him.

Dex's quiet acceptance was what he'd been craving, and it touched him in a place he'd guarded so fiercely and for so long it had become effortless habit. He'd been so worried—*Stop. Your boy needs you.*

He knew Dex needed him right now, needed his reassurance and love, and he tried to push his own, strangely fragile emotional state aside for now. His next breath caught in his throat and he swallowed hard, stubbornly forcing himself to focus on his boy.

Dex stroked his back, petting him in long, slow motions, giving and taking comfort at the same time. Sensitive boy, so focused on him.

Cyrus cleared his throat, managed a better breath, and got over himself. He would be fine in a bit. Better than fine. He needed to find out what Dex was feeling. "Let's sit and talk."

He wanted to stay in the space, have their talk here and start associating it with truth and safety. He moved with Dex, still holding on, to the leather couch in the corner by one of the windows and sat, pulling his boy down with him.

Dex stayed close, fingers twined with his. "You okay?"

Cyrus nodded. "You surprised me. In a good way. Thank you." They were in here for Dex, weren't they? And the first thing out of his boy's mouth was to ask whether he was okay. He'd say he had done something wrong, but actually, everything felt right.

"You're welcome. I wanted you to know that I loved you.

It seemed important." Dex looked around at the room again. "Did you build all this?"

It was the most important thing, and it was astounding that Dex felt that.

"I helped. I had a couple of handy people I know do the design of the room and the custom furniture for me based on what I wanted. I do all the maintenance myself, though. And I test everything regularly, all of that." He rubbed his thumb over his boy's hand. "Are you okay? Honest, remember."

"I think so. I'm... Lord, you know when you want to ask a thousand questions, but you can't think of a single one because there's all these levels?"

"I do. Just pick something, and that will get the ball rolling." He expected Dex would be asking questions for days. But he wanted to try to address the most pressing ones or Dex might never sleep again for thinking.

"How did you decide to do this? How do you decide you're good at this?"

That was a good question. "It was entirely by accident. I fell into it. I've known I was a Dom for a long while, and I met people at parties, played in clubs, moved around in the scene. I was a bartender for a long while at a club uptown where I met all kinds of people who talked my ear off as you do with bartenders." He laughed. "I was a bad and lonely bartender, and I started drinking on my shifts. I had a handle on that for a time and then...at some point people noticed that I didn't anymore. People like my boss. And Les."

He'd like to say he remembered that time well, but really it was a blur. He remembered how he'd felt, humiliated and stupid. Helpless.

"I didn't get fired, I got...reassigned, I guess. I dried out, and then I started shadowing a couple of the professional Doms at the club."

It had been Les's suggestion. They'd wanted someone watching him, and they wanted him away from the bar. He didn't blame them.

"I don't know how I'm good at it, and I don't know why. But I am." Cyrus shrugged and laughed. "Humble too."

"I'm glad you had friends, and that you are—good and humble." Dex squeezed his hand and kissed his knuckles.

"I can't imagine who I'd be without my friends. And without this." He caught his boy's eyes. "And I don't know how I managed without you."

Dex blushed bright, ducked his head. "You did just fine. Great, in fact. You should be proud."

"I'm...better now." He'd never been proud. He was fine, strong, but pride needed a sub. He looked around his office, eyes passing over the neatly lined up floggers and other tools on the wall. "What else can I tell you?"

"Everything." Dex chuckled. "What is your favorite thing in here? I mean, I know it's a job, but there's always the favorite bit."

"Hm." He looked around again. "That's a hard question because some of it depends on the sub or the situation, but I think I'm partial to the spanking bench." He pointed to it to make sure Dex know what he was talking about. "And...oh, it's covered, and you can't see it. Hang on."

Cyrus hopped up and went to the wall and pulled on a long, thick cord, which opened up a heavy curtain to reveal a large mirror. It was tall and wide, the weighty, wooden frame making it an imposing piece of furniture. "My mirror."

"Wow. That's a big old thing. Is it your magic mirror?"

Dex walked to it, tracing the frame. "It's gorgeous. I can see why you like it."

"It is magic. You can stand in front of it and see just about anything." He had, and his clients had.

Dex chuckled softly. "I like that."

It didn't escape his attention that Dex didn't look.

Curious. He pretended he didn't notice. "You laugh, but it's true. Come look."

"Sure." Dex came to him, eyes searching the mirror. "You're there. Now I am totally sure you're not a vampire."

"The not drinking blood thing might have been a clue." He only stood beside Dex for a second and then he stepped away, leaving Dex to look at his own reflection alone. "And then I can do this." Cyrus reached for a dimmer on the wall and lit Dex in a soft spotlight, making the room behind his boy disappear. "Just breathe and look, pet."

"Oh, that's weird." Dex looked up, searching for the light.

"Look in the mirror, please, pet. Tell me what you see." He was blessed with a great deal of patience, as Dex would find out if the boy tested him for long.

"A skinny redneck in shorts." So practical, so straightforward.

"All right." He was good at this game. "Does he have a name?"

"I do." Dex looked over at him. "Dexter Isaiah Appleton, but I'm really just a Dex."

"It's tempting to look at me because it's polite, but I'd like you to just look in the mirror, pet. I didn't know your middle name was Isaiah." He paced behind Dex, just outside of the light. "What makes you just a Dex? What's the difference between Dex and Dexter Isaiah Appleton? And don't tell me fewer letters."

"It just is. I've always just been a Dex." Dex wrapped his arms around his middle. "This is sort of weird. I know what I look like."

They weren't working, this wasn't a scene or a session, and Dex wasn't prepared—nor had his boy consented—to either. Stress wasn't called for, or fair. He stepped up behind his boy and wrapped his arms around Dex's. "Now what do you look like?"

"Mmm… Warm." Dex smiled at him in the mirror. "And I don't think we've ever seen us together."

"No, I don't think we have. We look good, don't we?" Cyrus kissed the boy's shoulder, his neck, his cheek. "I see a very happy Dom."

Dex looked them over, eyes critical, and then his boy smiled. "We do look like we fit together, hand in glove. I approve."

He laughed, amused and pleased. "Good. I accept your approval." Cyrus let Dex go, turned the spot off and pulled the curtain closed. There was much more they could learn here, but he would do it right next time. "More questions?"

He took two waters out of his mini-fridge and handed one to Dex, then sank back down into the couch.

"Thank you." Dex wandered a little, then lit close. "So is anything just for show? For effect?"

"If you mean intimidating things that I would never actually use, yes. Top row." He pointed to a row of things hanging on the wall opposite the mirror. There he'd hung a couple of branding irons, a hammer on a leather strap, and a handful of sharp knives in various sizes. "All the furniture is meant for use, however."

"Branding smells terrible. Good choice." Dex sounded utterly non-ironic. "So people pay you to put them in a dog crate?"

"Let's be respectful, please. Nobody pays me to put them in a dog crate. They pay me to help them work through an issue, or several issues. Fears, PTSD, trauma, intimacy issues—" He looked at Dex. "Intimacy not culminating in sex, of course. Some pros will do that. I'm not one of them. So yes, they may end up in the big cage under the bondage table or the small one." He pointed over his head to a cage hanging on chains operated by pulleys.

"Wow. That's not terrifying beyond all reason." Dex shook his head, eyes widening for a second before looking back at him. "I'm glad you help folks. It's a calling."

"I hope so. Or I'm deluding myself. I can't make things better for everyone I see, obviously." Huck was much more deeply troubled than he knew. It was also quite possible that Huck had suffered enough injury that he was beyond help. They'd never know, now.

He wasn't sure what the emotions that crossed Dex's face meant because they disappeared in a flash, hidden in a gentle kiss. "That's not on you, honey."

"No. I don't think it is. It's just a truth." He caught Dex's face in his hands. "It's not on either of us."

Dex kissed his palm. "No. Not anymore."

"Not at all, Dex. It's never been on you. Huck was a grown man."

"I—He was that. So what do you want me to know most about this room?"

"I want you to know that you are welcome to be in here any time I don't have a client, with or without me. Look all you like, just don't touch anything that's been put away out of easy sight. It's probably there for a reason." All the locks are secured so no one could accidentally get stuck in anything.

"Thank you. I promise not to touch. You have my word. This is your work, and I get that."

"Thank you. Though it's as much for your safety." He smiled at Dex. "So, what most intrigues you in here?"

That earned him an uncomfortable shrug. "I don't know. It's all new, and I don't want to be tacky on accident. Give me a few days to look things up, and I'll be able to say."

"It's not a test, pet." He let Dex have that for now, though, and changed the subject, moving it away from Huck and the boy and onto himself. "My day goes like this. I talk with each client a few days before they are scheduled to come in and we discuss what they need. We talk about the progress they have made, the things they are struggling with, and then I come up with a plan for their next session."

Cyrus took a sip of his water, leaned back on the couch, and encouraged his boy to join him. "Then we meet, and we spend most of the day in session. We take several breaks, so no one gets too tired, and we end about lunchtime. My client has a chance to clean up, shower, whatever they like. And then I spend some time with them in aftercare, tending to any broken skin and talking with them about the session. I'm done at three, and they can stay as late as five. Sometimes they nap, or just float, some of them leave as soon as we're done talking. That's it."

"Wow, I can't imagine. Busy days. At least you have someone that can help with food and stuff now, huh?"

"I am fortunate to have a lover and a sub who works from home and can make me lunch, yes." Cyrus chose those words carefully. Dex wasn't just someone; he wasn't just Dex. He was important, and visible, and had value.

"I'm glad I can do that for you. You deserve someone that wants to take care." Dex squeezed his hand and gave him a smile. "I'm fairly good at it too, which is handy."

"Quite." Cyrus got up and walked to the armoire, pulled out a pair of thickly padded cuffs and a very heavy, short chain. "Do you know what a safe word is, pet?"

"I do. It's like a code word that some people use."

"It's a code word, I suppose. It's a very out of context word that someone can use to put the brakes on a scene, when something like 'no' or 'stop' might not accurately convey what they want to happen. Does that make sense? It's a word that always means slow down, or stop, in any context."

Dex frowned at him, then Cy swore he could see the connection being made. "You mean like 'listen to me right now I'm serious' in one word."

"Yes. Exactly." He sat with Dex again and lay the heavy chain on his knees while he unbuckled the cuffs. "Safe words are sacred and never to be ignored. I want to start talking about our agreement. And the first thing I want to discuss are your safe words." He lifted one of Dex's wrists and set it inside the cuff.

"Okay..." Dex looked fascinated, watching him with bright eyes, so focused.

"I prefer subs have two. One for a pause, and one for a hard stop. The pause allows time to breathe. Maybe you just need a minute, but you don't want to end whatever we're doing. Maybe something is uncomfortable, and you need me to fix it before moving on. Maybe you have a question. Yes? And the other one means no, I'm done, this needs to be over now."

He closed the cuff snuggly around Dex's wrist, then started undoing the buckle on the other, calm and casual. "Plenty of people use traffic lights—yellow and red. I have clients who use all kinds of things. Fruit, nonsense words, one of my clients uses past presidents. They need to be words that don't easily come up in conversation. Would you pick two words for me, please?"

"If you need me to..." Dex turned his wrist over, the chain going taut. "Like angel and demon? Like that?"

"Sure. Let's try those and see how they work. Be careful, this chain is really heavy." This time he opened the cuff and waited for Dex.

"Yeah? Why is it heavy?" Dex put his wrist in the cuff, easy as you please. There was electricity in the air between them, a building buzz.

"To help ground and focus. For someone that has difficulty sitting still or whose mind tends to wander easily." He winked at Dex and secured the second cuff. "Like someone I know."

Dex chuckled softly and met his gaze, eyes dancing. "I know you're not talking about me, now..."

"You know I am." Eyes on his boy, Cyrus took Dex's hands and placed them, heavy chain and all in Dex's lap. That buzz between them grew to a steady hum, and he didn't fight it; he leaned in and took a quick kiss.

The kiss created a spark, and Dex gasped, eyes widening for a second before going heavy-lidded. "Oh..."

"The other thing about safe words, pet, is that you can't be afraid to use them." He stayed close and slid a hand into Dex's hair, getting a fistful. "It's a real betrayal of trust not to. I trust you to make sure I know and understand your limits. Just as you should trust me to respect them. Is that clear?"

Dex shrugged, just a tiny little motion. "I think so, yes. Why wouldn't you? I trust you."

"I only say that because it may be all you have to fall back on at some point. If I ask you to do something that scares you or you're not sure you'll like, it's with the understanding that you have the right to stop it at any time." Such a fine point, but he needed his boy to understand the control a sub kept, even when turning everything else over.

Dex leaned into his hand, so fearless. "I know that, honey. I'm free and over twenty-one and here because I want to be. But I get it. If I say demon to you that means you back off me right now. If I say angel to you, then we'd best talk."

"Good. Then that's the last I have to talk about it." Cyrus muscled Dex onto his back on the couch, lifted the chain above Dex's head and fastened the boy's wrists to a ring on the wall.

"There's a ring in the wall." Dex blinked at him. "Do I need to be real careful—like with a towel rack?"

"No, pet. It's made to hold." Cyrus gave one of his boy's nipples a good, hard pinch. He'd seen how the boy enjoyed nipple play, had felt it when his boy had touched him.

Dex arched and jerked, tugging firmly on the cuffs. "Damn..."

"Pretty." He got his fingers in the waistband of Dex's shorts and slid them off, making sure to rub and bump and jostle his boy's cock as much as possible. Dex looked amazing, every curious, adventurous bit of the boy. "Mine."

"All of me." Dex stretched out under him, totally unashamed. "Every inch."

"Don't let your fingers fall asleep." Oh. That was good. Something coherent. He kissed Dex again, harder this time as the heat crept from his belly into his groin, and curled his fingers under his boy's balls.

Dex moaned into their kiss, meeting him halfway, demanding more. His boy drew one leg up, hips rolling up to tempt him.

He gripped Dex's hips and pressed them down into the

couch and moved from a kiss to a hungry exploration of Dex's skin and slid lower letting Dex arch into his belly.

Dex groaned for him, rubbing against him like he was dancing, sweet cock going from interested to wanting.

"That's it, pet. Show me what you want." He kept moving lower, circling Dex's navel with his tongue.

Dex's body clenched, abs rippling under his hands, pushing up into his lips, cock beautifully erect.

He groaned, his own need making itself well known as his cock pushed and stretched his leather. "Stunning." It was a fantasy he hadn't put coherent thought to yet; Dex, locked down and wanting in his...in his playroom. In his dungeon. It wasn't merely an office when his boy was in it.

He kissed the tip of Dex's prick, following that with his tongue, teasing his boy without mercy.

The chain rattled, Dex trying to touch him, trying to reach for him, "Oh damn..." Dex bucked, a touch of salt teasing Cy's tongue, tempting him.

"Mmm. No, pet. You can't touch." Cyrus took the boy behind one knee and rolled Dex up off the couch, wedging a pillow under his hips to lift them higher off the surface.

"Ah. Much better." Cy was able to stretch out then, move lower to lick the sensitive, hidden expanse of skin behind Dex's balls.

Dex stiffened and whimpered. "Oh my God. I never—"

Excitement shot through him like lightning making him feel powerful—and privileged to be Dex's first anything. Never was suddenly his favorite word.

He licked again, dragging his tongue along that hot, wrinkled skin, loving the way Dex's legs trembled against him. He wanted to blow his boy's mind, make sure to leave Dex craving more.

"Never?" God, his own voice was deep and rough. He

was focused on his boy right now, but he was aching. Making himself wait was a turn on though, and he'd get what he needed soon enough.

"N-no, sir. Never."

The sound of 'sir' in his boy's voice, husky and wanton, was luscious.

"And this?" He drew his tongue, slow and hot, around his boy's puckered hole.

Dex's answer was a shattered, wild cry that suited him to the ground.

The boy got one leg over the back of the couch and hauled the other high, giving him plenty of access. Cyrus didn't think he'd ever seen anything so fucking perfect. He took the offer and set about teasing that tight ring in earnest.

Dex moved with him, responding to every lick, hips rolling in tiny, little jerks. There was no question that his boy was right there, focused on him and him alone.

He flattened his tongue and drew a long, wet line from Dex's ass to the base of his boy's ruddy, straining cock. He had a feeling it wasn't going to take more than a touch, so he stopped there and admired Dex's lovely, blissed-out face. "Show me, pet," he whispered, then gripped Dex's shaft and took the head of his boy's lovely erection into his mouth.

Dex screamed for him, cock pulsing, salty seed pouring into his lips. That need, that passion was so freely offered.

He took it for the gift that it was, and offered a calm, protective, touch in return, and soft words to gentle his boy down, back to him, back to the room.

"Mmm...thank you. So good." Dex blinked at him slowly, a dazed little smile on his face. "You're good to me."

"I try." He tugged the pillow away and settled Dex more comfortably, then moved over Dex to share a kiss.

Dex hummed and leaned close, leg wrapping around his hip and holding him. He rocked his hips down and let his leather-covered cock rub into his boy's thigh, making him groan.

Not intending to take the cuffs off for a while yet but worried about his boy's fingers, Cyrus reached up with one hand and tripped the dog-clip so Dex could bring his hands down.

"Mmm... What can I do you for, honey?" Dex pressed up against his cock again, giving him friction.

"Want your mouth, pet. Want you on your knees for me." Fuck, and soon. "So hard."

"Anything." Dex sat up and slid off the sofa, leaning down to nuzzle his prick through the leather.

His boy. "You don't know...so perfect." Cyrus sighed and spread his legs as he eased back on the couch.

"You're a fantasy." Those sweet lips opened against his balls, breath heating the leather.

He spread his arms out across the back of the couch and watched his boy, caught between an insistent need for release and not wanting to rush this moment.

Dex moaned and worked his leathers open, licking the skin around his cock as Dex bared it. It was a tease, but it didn't last long enough for Cy to complain. By the time he took a breath to speak, his cock disappeared into the sweet mouth.

Cyrus gasped and gripped the couch hard, eyes riveted to his boy and the confident way Dex moved on him. He gritted his teeth and tried to hold back but he knew it was hopeless. Dex could play him any way at all, and he'd fold like a cheap fucking suit.

Dex sucked like a dream, lips parted on the way down,

suction fierce on the upstroke. It was like his boy was having a popsicle, and Dex was enjoying every bite.

"You're going to make me come, pet." His thighs started to burn, and his ass clenched, and he was right there but not quite spilling over.

"Mmhmm." Dex groaned softly, deep throating him and holding him in, bobbing on his cock.

"Dex, I—Yes!" He hands flew to Dex's head and held his boy still as he rocked forward and shot hard enough to make him shake and gulp for air. He caught sight of Dex's cuffed hands where they sat passively on the boy's knees, the heavy chain holding them there, and bucked again. "Mine."

Dex cleaned his prick carefully, humming deep in his chest, keeping the aftershocks going on and on.

Cyrus could only take that for so long, and he squeezed Dex's shoulder when he'd had enough. "Come up here and kiss me."

"Mmm...my pleasure." Dex crawled into his lap, kissing him with fuck-swollen lips.

The kiss was wonderful, but really he needed to get his arms around his boy. "So proud of you."

Dex blushed and snuggled into him, bound hands caught between them.

He was happy to pet on Dex, hold him. "Tell me about the cuffs."

"They're heavy and warm. It was best when I was blowing you because I didn't have to think about what to do with my hands. I wanted to touch you when you were loving on me so bad."

That made him smile. "You liked to pull on them though. I was watching you."

"You said it was okay, so I didn't worry. I was focused on you."

"You were. It was hot as hell." He slid his fingers over his boy's chest and played with one tiny nipple as he came across it. "I have several different pairs, so you can have a look and see if there is a pair you'd like to wear more regularly. If not we can go pick out a pair and have them adjusted just for you."

Dex wiggled the slightest bit in his lap, which widened his smile. "Adjusted? Like the chain part?"

"We can get you a custom length if you like, yes, but I meant the cuffs. They can take measurements and make you a pair that fits just right. Not too wide, not too much overlap at the buckle, to make them more comfortable." A pair for play and a light, decorative pair Dex could just wear. All the time. God, he'd love that.

"Oh, that's neat. I didn't know that was a thing."

That easy acceptance from his boy, the curiosity—he was a lucky man.

"It's a thing that is sounding better and better to me the more we talk about it." He kissed Dex's forehead. "We still have a lot to talk about, and we shouldn't do it in here, nor should you be negotiating an agreement while bound."

Cyrus shifted Dex off his lap and settled the heavy chain on his knees as he worked on removing the cuffs.

Dex watched him, quiet and easy. "I bet you're hungry too. I need to feed you."

"I could eat." He grinned and winked at Dex. He was definitely hungry. He removed the second cuff and set both and the chain on the low coffee table. "I'll ask you to clean up in here later."

"Okay. I assume like a bleach cloth?" Dex kissed his

cheek and retrieved his shorts. "Do you want a hot or cold lunch?"

And there went his boy, floating away to do all the things.

"So thoughtful. Cold is fine. Thank you, pet." He should get up, tuck in, straighten things, something. But right now, he was pretty goddamn happy sitting on his couch. "Call me when it's ready."

23

Dex would jack off to this morning for weeks. There had been weirdness, but there had been hotness and shit that was cool and touching and...it had been good.

Lunch had been good. Napping in Cyr's arms had been magic.

He felt a little tipsy, like he was floating about two inches off the ground.

He wasn't sure where the man found the willpower, but Cyrus had them both out of bed again, and he was waiting on the couch where he'd been asked to stay while Cyrus went back to the office for something.

He propped himself against the arm of the couch and drew his legs up, chin on his knees, making lists on his phone. Groceries. Sample cookies. Pay phone bill. Huck's bday. Finish unpacking.

Cyrus walked in with a bound journal in one hand and a pen in the other and sat down next to him, one thigh covering his toes. "You look deep in thought."

"Making lists. Nothing big. What's that?" Dex nodded to

the journal, wiggling his toes and playing. He loved how Cyr touched him so much, so many places.

"It's a notebook I brought so I can take notes while we talk about our agreement. So we don't forget anything, and I can write it up later." Cyrus looked at him more seriously. "I have to start with an important question that I don't want you to answer until we're done."

"Okay." Sometimes Cyr came to the world in the most fascinating ways. Start at the beginning with a question for the end.

"As we're talking, it will become pretty clear that we have this...well, for lack of a better word, romantic piece of our relationship, and then we'll have this other piece. Most people find a way to mesh them and preserve both. I want to know if you feel, when we're done talking, like we can do that. Like you can do that and still get what you want and expect from me. Is that confusing or do you know what I mean?"

Nope. Not even vaguely. "I'll figure it out. Are we okay? I felt like we were."

"We're fine. That's a real question, not a barometer. It will make more sense after we talk. And I think we're...great. Solid. I'm having the best day, aren't you?"

He wiggled his toes and grinned. "I am having a ball, honey. All the way. I love being with you."

"Good. So this shouldn't be horrible then. We do a formal agreement, Doms and subs do, so we understand responsibilities and respect boundaries. You took on a lot of responsibilities without doing this, I know, so it may seem silly, but at some point it may matter. Cleaning, laundry, cooking...what else?"

"Um...I guess we ought to talk about grocery shopping

and how much money you need from me a month." That was important, right?

Cyrus blinked at him. "I've got it. Maybe when your business starts bringing in something significant, we can revisit that but for now we're fine."

"Are you sure?" He leaned forward, holding Cyr's eyes. "I never want you to believe I'm using you. I'm not a mooch." He'd done a lot for Huck to earn the space for his house, and he'd paid for everything. He wasn't nasty. He was a good man.

"No, you're not." Cyrus turned the journal around and showed him the list. "Cooking, cleaning, laundry, grocery shopping...should I add making me ridiculously happy to the list too?"

"No. That's not about money at all. Not even a bit."

Cyrus stared at him over the book and then took it away. "You're right. That was a joke, pet. True, but not something to put on the list. And I won't add sex either because we both know that no one in this house gets paid to have sex." He got a sideways look and a grin.

"Oh shut up." He rolled his eyes, cheeks heating. "I didn't know, and just think, I was trying to be so cool about it. Like icy."

"I know. I don't know whether to be flattered or insulted." Cyrus hooked an arm over his knees. "I'm going with flattered. How about you buy your own baking supplies so you can keep that as a business expense?"

"Yeah. I'm assuming it's cheapest to mail order everything but the fresh stuff. I'll just have to see." He climbed over into Cyrus's lap. "This okay? All talks should happen like this."

Cyrus chuckled. "Should I write that down?"

"Totally. Talks should be together and close. Especially hard ones."

"Okay." Cyrus tried to balance the book and write and ended up laughing and putting it in his lap. "You get to write. My hands are full."

"I can do that." Dex stole a kiss, before writing down, "talks should be together and close."

"You're adorable. Okay. I know what I'm expecting of you. Other than expenses, what are you expecting from me? And that's a real question too. I have some idea, but I want to hear from you first."

"I want..." He stopped to figure the right words, knowing how important this was. "I want to mean something. I want to be important to you. Because I'm taking care of you because you're important to me. I would do it if I had to work three jobs."

Okay. Whoa. That was heavy.

Cyr took his hand and held it tight. "You're important. You're my highest priority. And I would take care of you if we weren't doing this, if you never agreed to those cuffs. Write those expectations down, please. I'm proud of you."

He started writing, shocked as hell to find his hand shaking. The words hadn't been hard to say, but now that they were out, he felt a weird emptiness inside, like he'd told a terrible, huge secret.

"You're doing so well, Dex. Just breathe. One of the things you should expect from me is safety. Feeling safe to speak, to express yourself all kinds of ways, and to know I'll make sure to catch you. I'll keep these talks between us, and I won't judge."

"You too. I'm going to be the place you can be wild and weird and goofy and everything. All of you. I promise."

Cyr kissed his knees and hugged them, laughing. “That’s me, wild and weird and goofy.”

“Yes.” That was easy as pie. “What now?”

“Well, if you’re really agreeing to be mine, I could ask just about anything of you. Can you think of anything that’s just an automatic no? I mean, I’m only so wild, I promise, but maybe there’s something I should know.”

Dex wasn’t sure what exactly Cyr meant. Cyr could ask a lot. “I—I don’t like being made fun of.”

“Good.” Cyr gave his calf a pat. “I wouldn’t, but write that down anyway. Anything else?”

He scribbled that down. “I don’t know. Seriously. Can I add things? I mean, I’m pretty easy.”

Cyr caught his eye and smiled. “Add anything you want.”

“What do you want? I mean, what do you need me to write down.”

Cyr looked at him. “No conversation is off-limits.”

“No? Okay.” That look was intense as hell, making him focus on the book like he’d forgotten how to draw letters.

“And by that, I mean you can ask me anything, and I can ask you anything. You’re okay with that?”

“Yes. I don’t know if I’ll have the right answer, but you can totally ask.” Half the time with Cyr he didn’t know the right thing to say.

“The honest answer is always the right answer.” Cyr reached over and took the book, closed it, and set it on the couch. “All done, I think. Yes?”

If Cyrus was done, he was. He wasn’t completely sure what they’d accomplished, but he was comfortable and happy, so he nodded.

“I want you to think about the question I asked you earlier. Do you think you can be my lover and my sub at the same time? Does that feel fair?”

He would be him, and love Cyr as best he could. The rest he'd make up as he went along. "I think I can. I know I'll try."

Cyr nodded once, looking satisfied with that answer. "Good. Thank you for this. It was important and will make more sense to you over time. You'll see. And now that we have an agreement, we should celebrate, don't you think? We deserve it. What would you like to do? Dinner? Show? Dancing? Sightseeing?"

He wasn't sure they did his sort of dancing here. "Take me to your favorite places. That's what I'd like to do."

"My favorite places." Cyr frowned thoughtfully, but it turned quickly to a smile. "We already had gelato. Let's find a place together."

Oh. Together. That was one hell of a plan.

"I'm all over that. We can explore." He stood up, held out his hand. "Want to share a shower first? I'll soap you up."

"Mmm. That's a great idea." Cyr was all hands all of a sudden, sliding up under his shirt and over his thigh.

"I have my moments." He leaned down and took a kiss. "I like Saturdays with you, honey."

Cyr wrestled him to his feet and got them moving. "Every day with you is a good one."

"Flattery will get you laid, man." He patted that leather-covered ass. "Come on. Let's go play."

24

Cyrus was damn glad he only saw Casey twice a month. Any more than that and he might need a trainer at the gym. Casey was demanding, between the floggers and the emotional aftercare, the sub was almost as difficult as Huck had been. He left the boy sleeping it off on the couch in his office and shut the door quietly behind him, intending to get a snack and a nice hot shower.

There was a plate with cookies on the pass through, decorated like apples and books and an adorable inch worm in glasses. The whole house smelled like lemon, but the kitchen was spotless, quiet, except for the murmur of noise from Dex's room.

He reached for a cookie reflexively but pulled his hand back, not sure whether they were there for him to look at or eat, so he knocked on Dex's door instead figuring he could ask and get a kiss too.

"Come on in, love. Did you get your cookies?"

He opened the door to find Dex at the table, icing cookies.

"I saw them, but they are so cute I wasn't sure I was

supposed to eat them." He went right to his boy. "I'd like a kiss, please. When you can spare a second."

"I can always for you." Dex stood up, brushed their lips together, soft and sweet. "Those are my new samples. I took pictures of them this morning. I had three orders to bake this morning and this one is a rush, which sucks so hard. Spaghetti for supper okay?"

"I am a fan of pasta. Can I help? I just need a quick shower. Casey is napping in my office." He could handle making spaghetti if it meant they could sit and Dex could eat without stress.

"It's three-ish? I'll be done by the time you get out of the shower. These guys have to dry for at least overnight. We can do it together."

The cookies were two dozen little blue baby buggies decorated with yellow rubber ducks.

"Great. Let me grab a cookie and clean up, and I'll meet you in the kitchen. These are adorable, Miss Sugarsparkles." He took another quick kiss. "I'm going to eat the inchworm first."

"I had no doubt. You wait. I'll start making you naughty cookies for your snack. Those are lemon drop flavored, by the way."

"I can smell them. I love lemon." He laughed. "I love cookies. See you in a few."

He ducked back out of the room, and when he couldn't decide which couple to grab, he took the entire plate of cookies into the bedroom with him.

His boy looked happy. A busy Dex was a happy Dex, but it was more than that. Dex had been getting some sleep, and even managing a few real bites at regular mealtimes. He finally could envision a time when Dex might actually enjoy a meal. Or sleep in a little once in a while.

His shower was hot and woke him right up. He pulled on sweats and a T-shirt and made sure Casey was all right before seeing the boy to the door. Then he took the plate of cookies—he'd had four—back to the kitchen.

Dex appeared a few minutes later, stripped to the waist and freshly washed. Chilly hands slipped up his back, under his shirt. "Feel better?"

"Yes. Oh, God. Why are your hands so cold?" He tried to squirm away from them, but his boy followed easily.

"I was covered in icing. I had to get cleaned up." Those icy fingers found his nipples, teasing them.

"Stop that or I'll put those wrists in chains." He might anyway; it sounded like a great idea.

"I can't make supper if you do that, honey." Dex stroked his nips, fingers almost, but not pinching.

"Hm." How hard was it to boil water? Then again, the boy had a point, and it would keep those naughty hands busy. Too much more of this and his boy would be dinner, right there in the kitchen. He slid his hands down Dex's arms and pulled the boy's hands away by the wrists, holding them tight. "I have all night to change my mind."

"Mmm..." Dex stepped right into him, totally unconcerned. "Kiss me?"

Like he could say no. He kept hold of Dex's wrists and pulled them into his chest, then took a kiss, tongue reaching for his boy's tonsils.

Dex cried out, lips parted, kissing him back with an equal passion. Impressive.

Cyrus savored every second of that long, hungry kiss, but broke it off as soon as he felt his control slipping. He wasn't going to let his sweet, seductive boy sideline his evening plans again. Dex was much too good at that. "Pet."

"Mmhmm?" Dex nuzzled his jaw.

"Dinner." He let go of Dex's wrists, and took a breath, realizing he was going to have to put a little room between them. "And a glass of iced tea, please. And don't dawdle, I'm hungry. I had four of those cookies, you know."

"Well, have another so you don't starve, love." Dex patted his ass, totally unfazed. "Do you want meat sauce or olive oil and parm?"

Cyrus used to think that Dex was just sensual by nature, but the boy learned fast and knew damn well what effect he had. "Do we have that chicken sausage? The olive oil would be great if we do."

"Totally. That sounds delicious. Can we have music?" Dex was already pulling out onions and a cutting board.

"Of course. Put on anything you like." He was going to have to get some Bluetooth speakers for the kitchen. Dex could use them all day. "What do you want to do for veggies? You want me to wilt some spinach?"

"Let's have salad. It'll be nice and crunchy. I can make croutons." Dex brought him a glass of iced tea, gave him a kiss, and turned on some music.

"Crunchy. Sounds good. Thank you." He picked up the tea and took a big sip, toes tapping. "Oh, raspberry? Yum."

"Yeah? I like it too. That's the last of that kind. So if you love it, let me know."

"I do. But I also have a ton of tea, so keep experimenting and we can come back to this one." He danced over to the fridge, pulled out salad veggies one by one and set them on the counter. "What are we listening to?"

"It's my supper playlist. Nice and easy music, nothing angry or sad. I like to listen to it when I'm cooking." Sometimes Dex said something utterly surprising.

"It's got my toes tapping. I like it." Speakers for sure.

"Sounds like you got a lot done today. Do you take a lot of rush orders?"

"Not if I can help it. It's awful. Cookies need time to dry. I have to tell people if they get a rush, I can't help breakage, you know? And people yell, and I hate that."

"That doesn't sound like fun." Cyrus pulled out a big bowl. "Last minute just isn't the way to do things. It makes everyone crazy." He was terrible at last-minute things. Spontaneous he had no problem with, but avoidable last-minute decisions made him twitch.

"Yes! Yes, you get it. I don't like it, having to half-ass shit, when there's a right way to do things." Dex threw the chopped onions in a pan and grabbed a pot.

"Just one more reason we get along I guess." He was tossing veggies in the salad bowl and it was starting to look colorful and yummy. "Oh, speaking of right ways, Casey did all the clean up in my office today. He needed chores."

"Good deal."

Cy wasn't sure Dex was willing to go in the office, to be honest, especially not without him.

He was going to keep mentioning it though and try to make it less intimidating. But he didn't need his boy to go in there; he had a number of options Dex would probably like in the bedroom.

"Do you have a lot of orders to fill this week?"

"Just three. I'll send one tomorrow and two at the end of the week. But the store's only been open for three days." Dex gave him a slightly worried look. "They've been waiting for me to reopen, I guess."

"It's all right. You'll get it done. I'll make sure you have the time you need." He knew a couple of Doms who had subs that could be sent to help. He'd been thinking about asking how Dex would feel about that for the holidays. He'd help if Dex got under water catching up.

"I will. I'm a hard worker. I—I'll figure it. It's been a couple months since I was in practice. The cookies tasted good to you, right?"

"I thought they were great. I loved the texture too." He reached over and touched Dex's arm. "I can get you some help during the day if you need it. An extra set of hands."

"Maybe. We'll have to see. I just—I'll have to see whether I figure it out, right? I bet I learn to." Dex leaned toward him. "Thank you for offering, but I'm here to make things easier for you, not harder."

"I know you'll figure this out if you put your mind to it, and you'll be smart enough to ask if you do need a hand." And if Dex wasn't, there was nothing stopping him from making a call anyway. It was sweet of Dex to be thinking of him first, though. Such a good boy, and Dex still barely understood why.

"So, do you like rounds or chopped up small?" Dex fascinated him, that attention to detail, and how it was directed toward him.

"Rounds, I guess. But you know me, I'll eat either way." He grinned. "You want me to start some pasta water?"

Dex blinked. "Yes, please, sir. I even got the pot out and didn't fill it. Lord have mercy. We got to talking, and I forgot."

He laughed and patted his boy's ass as he walked past. "You can make it up to me later, pet." The pot was right there next to the sink and he filled it and put it on the stove.

"I most certainly will. I love this, you know?"

He knew what Dex meant, but he decided to play. "Sex? Yes. Me too."

"Honey, this is cooking, not sex. Maybe a good precursor

for sex on a nice day, but not sex." Dex's grin was utterly full of shit.

"Heh. No, it's not sex. But I love it anyway. Cooking together makes the meal better." He watched the pot despite the old adage, waiting for it to boil.

"Yes. Me too. Hanging out together is just...it's the best."

Soon they were going to have to start going to the bar, meeting people. Dex had lived with the same people his whole life, and now... Cy knew his pet needed friends.

Dex needed friends in the scene too, other subs, people who understood and could answer questions. Maybe Milo could introduce him around.

Baby steps though. Right now it was just good to see his boy smiling. "I haven't cooked with anyone in years. Honestly. I haven't been a total recluse, but I just wasn't seeing anyone. I was all work and the bar." Friends he had. Lovers not so much, and he'd just decided that was okay.

"I get that. I haven't known many people that wanted to cook with me. Huck was a protein drink guy."

He didn't want to ruin a good moment, but Dex brought Huck up, not him, and he had to ask. "What happened to Huck? I mean, he was a friend at one point I assume. I can't believe he was always the self-centered guy that took advantage of someone like you."

Dex gave him a shocked look. "Huck took care of me, so I took care of him. Then..." Dex shook his head and put the sausage in the pan.

Cyrus didn't make Dex finish that statement. Not yet. And he was careful to keep his tone curious and not harsh. "How did he take care of you?"

"He gave me a place to live, stuff to do. It's hard to be the village idiot in a little town. Huck didn't mind."

There was so much wrong with that statement he didn't

even know where to start or what to say. He made himself breathe a second and not say anything yet and tried to put himself in his boy's shoes.

The biggest issue Cyrus had was with the way Dex characterized himself. The boy did it constantly, putting himself down, saying he wasn't smart, thanking Cyrus just for being friendly when that was really what a man should just expect from people.

He knew it wouldn't do any good to say, for the twentieth time, that Dex wasn't an idiot. That was something the boy would have to prove to himself.

"You've become quite the capable businessman, you know. I don't know what it took to get where you are, but I'm impressed. Your artistic skills should be obvious to anyone. I can't imagine thinking of you as an idiot. I have nothing but respect."

Dex smiled at him, cheeks going pink. "Thank you. That's nice to hear. I had to carry a lot of stuff from my people. That stain wasn't going to go away. Huck stood up for me when he didn't have to. He never let anyone say I was shit because of my folks. He was my family."

Well, that explained something. It didn't explain the last handful of years, but at least he understood the friendship.

"Were you ever lovers?"

"We kissed once, when I was fifteen. He'd told me all about blowjobs, and I was just about nuts, thinking about it, but...it was like... I don't know, like kissing someone on a dare. It wasn't *anything*. And anything is something when you're fifteen and talking about sucking off!"

He laughed gently. "I remember." But the bigger question, even if he thought he already knew, needed answering too. "Were you in love with him?"

"No. It was hard to even just love Huck sometimes. I think you'd have to be a little... I don't know. I just... No."

Cyrus kept busy so Dex wouldn't feel so not on the spot and put the pasta in the pot. "Tell me what you mean." He gave the pasta a stir.

Dex shrugged. "I don't know. I'm mad at him. I've met his lovers, and it was always ugly."

"I think I know what you mean. Our sessions were rough too." Dex didn't need the details. But Huck paid him top dollar and took every second of his concentration.

"I think he needed..." Dex shook his head and went to get plates, lips tight.

Cyrus followed his boy, moving in close. "Needed?"

"I don't want to talk about him anymore." But Dex leaned toward him, not away.

"I know. But we're going to anyway." He put his arms around his boy. "Finish your thought. What do you think he needed?"

"He needed to live on the back of a bull, and he wanted everyone to need that too." Dex shook his head. "I need to feed you."

He hugged Dex close and ignore the change of subject for another minute. "So you couldn't ever have been enough for him."

"I know." Somehow that was brutal—quiet, sure, and completely unemotional. Just *I know*.

"I'm sorry, pet." Ironically, he hadn't been enough for Huck either. He always ran out of steam long before the boy had had enough because there was no such thing as enough for Huck. "It was impossible, you know. Huck didn't understand enough."

"Yep." Jesus, once Dex let himself feel that pain, it was going to knock him to his knees.

Soon. It had to be soon. The sooner Dex just let go the better. Cyrus knew he could make it happen, but he felt like it could be reaching that point organically and that would be so much better. A few more days. A week at the most and then he'd have to step in.

"I love you." He kissed his boy, offering Dex gentle reassurance.

"I know. I love you too. Let's have our supper. It smells good enough to eat."

"Good thing because I'm hungry." Cyrus wished he could offer Dex a beer or something, the boy could probably use one. He offered a smile instead. "Can I have more tea, please?"

"Always." Dex kissed him, the touch melting him. "What kind of salad dressing do you like?"

"Just oil and vinegar is fine." Mmm. Oil. What a great idea. He was looking forward to dessert.

He'd already had his fill of back-to-school cookies.

25

Dex thought he'd make it.

Friday morning came and found him awake at five. He'd done his work before he fed and woke Cyr. He'd sat, staring at the wall in his office until ten, but then he had to get out. Move.

Do something. Even if it was wrong.

He made Cyr's lunch, his snack, a fresh jug of tea. Then he left a note.

Cyr, Going out for a wander. Be back by five at the latest. Love you. D.

Then he grabbed his wallet and headed out. Somehow it was Huck's birthday, and he couldn't just sit still. If he did that, they would find him—all the things his brain wanted to think—and he couldn't do it. He couldn't bear to lose the blessed numbness he'd found.

So, first stop? Bar.

He didn't need to be drunk, but he needed enough to make it through to the afternoon. A shot or four.

Dex headed into Les's bar, knowing it was safe and friendly, and slipped up into a barstool, sliding his hands along the leather bar rail, nodding to the bartender. "Morning."

"Morning." The bartender raised an eyebrow. "Coke? Coffee?"

"I'd like a coffee and a shot of Cuervo, please, sir."

"Ugh. That sounds vile. Coming right up." The bartender brought him the shot first. "Rough night? Dex, right? Cy's friend?"

"Yeah. Dex." He held out one hand. "I've forgotten your name, I'm sorry."

The guy shook it with a smile. "Will. Everything okay?"

"No. You know Cy, you said?" He took the shot nice and easy, passing the shot glass over and nodding at it. "The guy whose funeral he went to in Texas? Well, today is his birthday."

And Dex wanted to hit him in the face. A lot. And that wasn't good, so. Booze.

"Cyrus's client, right? He said you took it pretty hard. I'm sorry about your friend." Will topped off his shot glass and poured him a cup of coffee. "You should have cake. I have cake for my mom every year. It's weird I know, but it works for me."

"Thank you. I might go do that. I'm going to have a couple-three shots, a cup of coffee, and go for a walk. Where is a good place to go see? I need to be home around four-ish."

"Uh. Do you like museums? I love the Museum of Natural History. Or if you want to sightsee you could go up to the Cloisters or downtown to the 9-11 memorial and tower. There's a ton of stuff to see."

"Cool. Thanks." He took shot number two, letting the quiet wave of alcohol dissolve his give a damn. Better. He drank his coffee, just letting himself be quiet and still.

Will hovered the bottle over his empty glass. "Cyrus is never in here this early. He works right? Are you going to meet him somewhere?"

"Hit me. He's working. I want to be home once he's done. I left him a note." He needed to sober up before he got home. He didn't want to be even tipsy in front of Cyr. That was mean. He just needed help to get through today. Cyrus had to work. Dex had to not think too much.

Will poured out and then put the bottle away. "You're new to the city, right? You be careful on your own. Where do you think you'll end up? Anything I suggested sound good to you?"

"I don't know. I may just walk for a few hours and see what I see. Find a bakery and see what they have. I don't know. It's just the walking it off that's important, you know?" He slid over his credit card before he even considered shot three. He wasn't ready.

Will nodded to him but left it on the bar and pulled out a cell phone. "Appleton a common name where you're from?"

"Common enough, I guess. I never thought about it much." He didn't follow, but it didn't matter.

"What did you do in Texas? For work?" Will finished a text and set the phone down on the bar.

"Lots of shit—played mandolin, handyman work, cookies, I just took care of things." Maybe the guy was just friendly. "You like being a bartender?"

"I do. I like people, I like making a decent living, so it works for me. Les is a great boss." Will shrugged. "You play mandolin? Really? That's cool."

"Yeah. I learned a long time ago." Really, he wasn't interesting. He was a guy. Cyr was fascinating, and Huck had told great stories about all the things he'd done and seen.

All those stories were gone. All the memories in the house, almost all the memories from his were gone. It was just...

Stop it.

He sipped this shot, needing to make it last.

"I tried to learn guitar a little while ago but I'm terrible with—"

Will looked up as someone at the other end of the bar waved. "Oh. Excuse me just a second, would you?"

"Sure." He smiled. Sweet man. He didn't need to be babysat, and he was sure Will didn't want to be stuck either. He finished his shot, then sucked back the rest of his coffee. He just needed to pay his tab, that was it.

Will ran his and the other guy's at the same time and set his card and the slip on the bar. "You want a warm-up on your coffee?"

"No thank you. Have a good day, now. I'll remember your name now, I promise." He left a good tip, took a deep breath. Yeah, he was buzzing.

"Be careful out there." He thought he could feel Will watching him all the way out the door.

He would be. Dex checked his watch. Eleven o'clock. He'd walk until half past one, then walk back.

He had his phone, so even if he got lost, he'd find his way back.

He chose a direction and started walking. "Happy

birthday, Huck. You're an asshole. I was good to you, and you were an asshole."

God, maybe three shots wasn't enough.

26

Cyrus left his office, his client kneeling quietly and thinking, and headed to the kitchen, surprised to find the apartment didn't smell like cookies. Maybe Dex was decorating today? He knew immediately though, when he saw the things on the counter with a note leaning against them, that his boy must have run out for something.

Smiling, he picked up the note and read it, but found himself in a weird space between disappointed Dex wasn't there and happy that the boy wanted to get out and get some air. Dex had been working hard, it was good to find time to relax.

Sure was quiet though. He'd always been used to quiet, but then he'd gotten used to company and now the quiet felt lonely.

He found his lunch all made for him and poured himself some tea to go with it, then grabbed his phone and took it all over to the table to sit.

He wondered where Dex was wandering, and whether his pet had walked by that little bakery on 70th. They had cookies too, and these wee little cakes too—petit fours they called them. So yummy.

He started to check his email but he had a couple of texts so he started there. Neither was from Dex, which was disappointing, but there was a string from Will at the bar.

WILL

Dex is here.

You know that right?

I just ask because of the tequila.

You there?

He read them over, and over again, then send a text back.

CYRUS

Is he still there?

Then he quickly fired a text off to Dex.

CYRUS

You okay?

DEX

Hey you! :D Did you find your lunch?

WILL

No sir. :(Left at 11

Dex sounded perky. But you don't start your day with tequila if you're okay. He should know.

CYRUS

I did! Looks great. Is everything all right?

CYRUS

Thanks, Will. Appreciate the heads up.

He was frustrated that he'd missed the text earlier, but he couldn't have his phone on when he was with a client, dammit.

DEX

Can I call? Hard to walk and text

CYRUS

Please do.

Okay good. That was good, right? Dex was fine. He wasn't worried.

The phone rang immediately. "Hey, you. You got my note right?"

"I did. It's good to take a day off. Where have you wandered to?" *Are you coming home soon?*

"I don't know. I stopped at the bar, had a drink, and then started walking. I've seen lots of things. It's hot, though, so I may get another water and turn back a little early. It's not as fun without you."

"Pet?" It was just a question. He wasn't worried, right? Just a question. "Why the bar?"

"I needed to..." Dex sighed. "I needed to just be quiet for a little while. It's Huck's birthday, you know, and I just needed a little numb. I'm not fucked up. That's why I went early, so it would be gone before I came home to you. I've been walking my ass off."

Huck's birthday? Why hadn't Dex told him before now? "I appreciate your honesty, pet. I'm a little concerned about you out there alone and being...upset. Or...just off, even. It would help me if you'd come home soon."

He took a breath.

Cyrus was pretty proud of himself for not simply ordering the boy home and telling him to kneel and think about his choice to worry his Master as soon as Dex got there. Because that's what he wanted to do.

"Okay." The easy acceptance felt amazing. "I'll turn around now. I've been going for...almost two hours, so I should be home by the time you have your snack at the latest. I'm glad it's the weekend, huh? Almost?"

"Almost." He struggled with the urge to remind Dex there was probably a subway that would get the boy home in twenty minutes.

They were going to have a talk. This was unacceptable.

He sighed. What the hell was the matter with him? Dex was just taking a walk.

Jesus Christ.

The last thing he wanted to do was debate himself. But that's exactly what he needed apparently, because the Dom was ready to have serious words with Dex's lover.

"Be safe. I love you."

That sounded somewhat sane.

"I love you too. I have my phone. It'll help me get home."

"See you soon—uh. Pet? Could you...you're not in any trouble and I'm not upset with you at all but if I—"

Just tell him. It'll be okay.

"I need you to come in and...just kneel in the living room and wait for me, please."

Cyrus tried to pretend that he wasn't holding his breath, but that was only going to work until he turned blue. The pause seemed endless.

"I'm pretty sweaty. Is that okay?"

He exhaled loudly enough Dex had to have heard him and his hands were actually trembling a bit. "Yes. Yes, that's fine. Thank you, pet."

All good. Breathe. He heard you.

"I love you. It's muggy today. I think it might rain

tonight." Dex sighed. "Okay. I'm going to grab another water and book it home. Don't forget your snack, and don't work too hard."

"You're good to me. I'm on it." One of them was going to have to hang up first and he was the Dom here, so he did it.

He put his phone down and sat up a little straighter.

God, he was hungry.

27

Dex got into the apartment, the air conditioner making him shiver, and he felt almost sick, it felt so good. Lord have mercy, he'd been hot before, but all these buildings didn't give the heat anyway to go and it was so fixin' to rain.

He wiped his face and his hands at the kitchen sink and took off his boots and socks because they may be toxic. Then he settled right in the way of the vent in the front room.

Then he closed his eyes and just rested, letting himself cool off and—how had Cyr put it? Be where Cyrus needed him.

"Have a good evening, boy. I'll see you next week." Cyr's voice was strong and clear, and echoing a little in the entryway.

"Yes, Sir. Thank you, Sir." That wasn't a voice Dex recognized, but that wasn't so unusual. He knew it was a client anyway.

The front door closed quietly, and Cyr turned the lock,

he heard it slide into place with a soft click, then those heavy booted heels headed his way.

Cyr stopped a foot or so away from him and stood there quietly, looking down at him. “Hello, pet,” Cyr said finally. “I’m glad you’re home.”

“Me too.” He took a deep breath and opened his eyes. Cyr had said he wasn’t mad, and Dex had left a note, so... “Good day?”

“Yes. And also...surprisingly difficult.” Cyr bent and kissed his forehead, then took a seat on the couch. “I was pulled in several different directions, you know? Ever had a day like that?”

“God yes. Lots. I feel like that a lot.” God, Cyr was lovely in his leather and boots. Sexual, yes, but more than that, he was simply lovely.

“Move a little closer, pet. So I can reach you.”

“Yes, sir.” All requests should be so easy to do. He scooted close, drawn right to Cyr, to the only person that seemed to make things better anyway.

“There we go. Much better.” Cyr reached for him and gentle fingers slid through his hair. “I didn’t know today was Huck’s birthday. I wish you had told me.”

“I wanted to, but...” He leaned, letting his cheek rest on Cyr’s thigh. “Is this okay?”

“I like that, yes.” Cyr shifted just a bit, getting comfortable. “I ought to have known, don’t you think?”

“You had to work. I thought about it, but—I don’t want to think about him. I don’t want to feel too many things.” He didn’t know if he was making sense, but it was all the truth. Every word.

“Hm.” Cyr’s fingers slid over his neck to his shoulder and a strong thumb worked into the muscle. “Is that working for you? Deciding you don't want to so you're just not going to? Does that...feel better?"

"Mostly? Eventually it'll just fade, right? If I just leave it alone?" Surely all this hurt and anger and loss and guilt couldn't just stay.

"No. No, it won't. The longer we ignore things, emotional things like anger or hurt or grief, the bigger they get. Until eventually we can't hold onto them anymore at all. Then those emotions win, and there's no alternative but to deal with them. It so much worse than if we just confront the issues head-on and deal with them before they become monsters."

Well shit. He sighed and leaned into those hard fingers, letting them ease him. "I just needed to be numb. Not drunk, but numb, you know? I've been good, but today was...special? Hard? You have to think I'm so stupid, but I don't want to mess up your working anymore than I did already, and this seemed the best way."

Cyr was silent for a long while, just rubbing his shoulders, present and still. He wasn't worried; Cyr was just calm, thinking probably, not speaking until he knew just what to say. Cyr was careful like that.

"The wonderful thing about having a lover and a partner is that you have someone you can talk to, someone that can help you through scary or hard things like this. And that's even better when you have a Dom because you don't have to make choices. You should already know the answer —you have to tell me. That's how this works. I know you're not used to having anyone, and I know we haven't discussed this before so it's not a problem at all, but you'll know for next time, right?"

That touch didn't stop the whole time Cyr was talking, affectionate and reassuring.

All Dex could do was nod and lean harder. "I missed you bad today."

He didn't regret going. He couldn't have just sat and felt all day. No way. But now that he was here, he felt like he could breathe.

"I would have liked to be with you. I feel a little disappointed that I wasn't. But we're here now, and I think it's time to talk to me about what you're not letting go, pet."

"I don't think I can." He wasn't even being a bitch. He didn't think that he could open the lid of that awful jar. No one needed to see any of that. Including him.

"You can." Cyr leaned lower. "Don't we have a rule about hard talks happening in my arms? Why don't you come sit up here with me?"

He moved up into Cyr's arms, holding his lover tight. "I love you."

That was the important part.

"I know. And you're mine, pet." Cyr took one of his hands and looked at it, turning it over and back again before squeezing it tight. "What do you wish you could say to Huck right now?"

So many thoughts slammed through him—I hate you and I miss you and you asshole and you fuck and—"Why."

He nodded. "I have the same question. We'll never get an answer to questions, sadly. We can guess at answers maybe but that's it. Do you think you know?"

"No." Maybe it was just boredom. How the hell would he know? He was just the guy Huck fucked over.

Cyr just held him, that contact constant. "Since you can't ask questions, what do you want to say to him? If you could. Tell me what you'd want him to hear."'

He shook his head. "I'm too mad."

He was scared if he started being mad, he'd never stop.

And then you might end up like your father.

Cyr nodded slowly, more of a thoughtful move than an agreement. “Okay. Stand up.” Cyr took him by the hand and led him to the office. “Trust me.”

“You’ve worked all day...” He followed, confused as hell. “Did you even get your snack?”

Cyr looked at him and opened the door. “Thank you for thinking about me, pet. I have a protein bar in the armoire. And this isn’t work.”

“I love you.” Thinking about Cyrus was what he did.

“You keep saying that. I think you want me to believe it.” Cyr grinned at him, but there was no more procrastinating after that, his lover muscled him right through the door and into the office.

“I know you believe it. It’s just the answer to a lot of questions.”

“I like it. You can say it all you like. I love you too.” Cyrus shuffled along behind him, walking him all the way across the room to the big, black leather-clad ‘X’ between the two tall windows. “How mad are you? What is too mad?”

“I don’t want to be angry at all. Period. Not at all.” He was good at not being pissed off.

“You’re angry at a dead man, pet. He can’t hurt you. You can’t hurt him. Step up close to the cross, please.” Cyr was right behind him, so close he could smell the leather.

“Okay... It’s big.” He stepped up with a sigh, and he wasn’t sure if he was just talking about one thing or a lot of them.

“It is. And strong. It’s anchored down by bolts all over.” Cyr took his elbow and lifted his arm, stretching it out along one side of the X and adjusting a cuff at the top to his height before buckling in his wrist. “Tell me your safe words again, please. I haven’t forgotten. I just like to hear them. I’ll do this every time you're restrained so you know we're clear on them."

"Angel and demon." He felt really confused and worried and tired. "I really need a shower."

"Me too. We'll take one when we're done here." Cyr did the same on his other side, then started on his ankles too. "Angel and demon. Got it. Why are you so afraid of being angry?"

"I don't know. Being angry sucks." What kind of question was that?

"Why? I get angry all the time. Anger is completely human." Cyr straightened again and stood right at his back. "Why are you afraid of it?"

"I don't know." He closed his eyes, then opened them up. "I don't want to be angry."

"Why not?" Cyr was a solid presence at his back, pestering him. "What are you afraid of?"

"Aren't you? Don't you worry? Because you could hurt someone—really hurt them."

"No, I couldn't. Not in anger. Because that's not who I am." Cyr leaned close to his ear. "You can't hurt anyone either. You can't hurt me."

His entire body went stiff, and suddenly he couldn't breathe. He shook, eyes wide as he fought to calm down.

Cyr leaned back, just a little. Just enough. "What have you got to be angry about, Dex?"

"He left me with all this shit. He gives up and doesn't cope, and I have to. I gave him everything, and he fucked me over. Isn't that enough?"

"Is it?" Cyr's fingers pressed between his shoulder blades and gave him a little shove. "Is that all?"

He shook his head. "I'm trying to be good."

"I don't need you to be good right now." Cyr gave him

another shove, harder this time. "He fucked you over? Is that all?"

"Isn't it enough? He was so mean at the end, and then this? I had to see his bloated ugly picture. I had to bury him. That was my home too. I had to sell everything. I had to find homes for the horses, the dogs. He could have warned me, not just deserted me. He knew how hard it would be to lose everything again." And Dex hadn't been important enough to even warn.

"He was mean here too. I really only knew him mean, honestly." Cyr rested heavy hands on his waist, holding tight. "I need more, pet. I need to know what you're hiding from me."

"Why? Why can't you just let me take care of you?" He was good at that. "I didn't make him mean! I was good to him. I never fussed at him, even when I wanted to!"

"It's not your fault," Cyr whispered.

Liar. Liar, how do you know? How many times had he heard that he'd earned whatever he got? "You don't know that. Maybe it was. It happened twice. Maybe it's me. Maybe you should be scared of me too."

"There's nothing for me to be afraid of, pet." Cyr kept hold of his waist, the contact steady no matter what he said. "None of it is your fault. Not your father, not what he did to your mother, and not Huck."

"You're just saying that because you want it to be true. You don't know. How can you possibly know?" He hit the wood, trying to breathe. "You don't know. I could be like him. I could get so angry and never be okay again."

Was he yelling? He thought he might be yelling.

"Dex, remember when I said you can't bottle it up? That's the kind of angry Huck was. Maybe your father too, who knows? You can't hurt me," Cyr insisted, again. "You're not like either of those men."

"Don't say that. You don't know! What if I start being mad and it never stops? What if I just become a monster? What if I hurt you now that you've said it?"

He saw himself like he was standing outside, watching this strange man scream and shake.

"Do you really think you could hurt me?" Cyrus's voice was loud, cutting through his emotion and commanding his attention. "Honestly. I know you love me. Do you believe, can you fathom any circumstance where you could physically hurt me?"

He shook his head with a swallowed sob, because no matter how macho a man was supposed to be, how tough, he wasn't. "I just want to make things good. Let's go shower and stop this."

"It's not your fault, pet. I want you to say it until you believe it."

He shook his head. "Please. My heart is tired."

Strong arms wrapped around his middle, holding him tight. "It's not your fault. Tell me."

He gasped and closed his eyes, the touch wrapping around him, and he sagged, Cyrus catching him. It cracked him, the fact that he'd expected the cuffs to tug his wrists and they didn't. His cheeks were hot and wet, but he focused on his Cyr, on them. "I don't want it to be my fault. I don't."

"It's not, pet. How could it possibly be?" Cyr kissed his cheek, holding his weight easily. They fit together so well. "You want to make people comfortable, happy. You can't fix people. It's not your fault."

"I'm sorry. I was good to him. I promise, but he was broken. He was different. Mean. He wanted things to hurt."

"You're absolutely right, pet. You're right. It's sad, and I'm sorry, but that's the man I knew." Cyrus made sure he had his feet, quickly freed his feet and hands and somehow caught him again, like his lover had expected him to fall. They ended up on the couch where he could lean hard into strong arms.

Cyrus brushed tears off his cheek with one thumb. "Tears are good. Tears are cleansing and healing. They're honest."

"Just don't tease. I can't stop." He hid in Cyr's chest, trusting that he belonged here. "He should have said something. I was his friend."

"Maybe he didn't know." Cyrus dropped that at his feet, sad and heavy.

"Maybe not. It doesn't mean I have to forgive him." He wasn't ready. He wasn't sure he'd ever be ready.

"You'll make your peace eventually. Whatever that turns out to be. I just want you to stop taking it out on yourself."

Cyrus reached behind him and grabbed a box of tissues. "I promised I wouldn't make fun of you. You asked me specifically. I would never."

"Thank you." He took a deep breath. "I'm sorry about... all of this. You worked all day, and then had to deal with me."

"It was the best part of my day, sending my client home and finding you kneeling for me. It was just what I needed." Cyr kissed him and smiled. "That's just work. This is love."

"Do you want your snack before the shower? I made spring rolls. They're a little ugly, but they'll taste good."

"That's love too." Cyr nodded. "I think I better. I'm running on empty."

"Oh, honey." He stood up and held out one hand. Silly wonderful man, worrying about him instead of eating. "Come on. I made a peanut sauce. It'll hold you."

Cyrus took his hand, then stood and followed. "Sounds yummy. You're good to me."

"I try." He pulled out the plate with the rolls, the dipping sauce. "Tea?"

Dex felt...empty? Maybe scoured out. He wasn't sure, but a long shower would help, he knew.

"Yes, please." Cyrus didn't even sit down, just leaned on the counter eyeballing the spring rolls. "I'll be quick. And then we'll make the rest of our night just about us."

"That sounds amazing. Eat." He got them both a big glass of tea. "I'll start the water and get towels."

Then they could rinse the day down the drain.

28

Dex cleaned up like a dream.

As soon as they got the dinner invitation from Les, Cyrus had given Dex some cash and sent his boy out shopping for an outfit, including new boots. They'd had a... well, not an argument, but a little back and forth about the boots until he'd finally called them a gift. Dex made a face but reluctantly agreed.

The boy wanted to contribute and had become rather stubborn about it. When Cyrus refused to take the first bit of profit from the cookie sales—that had been a little back and forth too—Dex bought that week's groceries with it instead.

Sure, he could come up with an appropriate punishment, he could put his foot down, win every argument if he wanted to, and Dex knew it. But the look in Dex's eyes when Cyrus discovered his grocery money still sitting on the counter right where he'd left it, that amazing look—a little defiant, a little proud, a complete absence of worry—was well worth gracefully losing the battle.

In the end they'd agreed he'd leave cash in an envelope

in the kitchen, and Dex would use it when he needed to, no questions asked.

He hadn't said a word about all the effort Dex had gone to breaking in the new boots, he'd just enjoyed how much Dex seemed to enjoy it. And now they were on his boy's feet, Dex looked like a million bucks on his arm, and they were going out. He'd have paid any amount of money for this.

Dex chattered at him—random things that meant nothing and everything all at once. They weren't important, but they were the minutiae that made up their lives.

He smiled at Dex and squeezed the hand that held his arm. "I think you should know that I have never had a dinner invitation to which I was able to bring anyone I was serious about. I'm excited about this."

It seemed important to mention. He used every chance he could find to make sure his boy knew how happy he was, how much he wanted Dex with him. Part of him still felt like Dex might pick up and run any minute, grab the truck keys and head back to Texas. That idea was becoming less rational, but it was there all the same and gnawed at him every time he asked for more or tried something new.

"Yeah? I'm glad. I feel all fancy in my new kit and boots." Dex squeezed his arm.

"You look great. I mean…really. Hot. I can't wait to show you off."

"Silly man. Who would see me with you here?" Dex winked at him.

He laughed, pleased by the compliment. "Flatterer. I guess we're just going to distract everyone then."

It wasn't a long walk to Les's place at all, just past the bar a couple of blocks. "We're going to need jackets soon, at least in the evening."

"I brought a hoodie from home. It's living in the coat closet."

"You're going to need more than a hoodie. It snows here. The wind here can be evilly cold." Dex was going to need a hat and gloves and boots too. "You're not used to cold, I know."

"Nope. It freezes once a year or so, but that's about it. It really snows?" Dex looked like a kid, bright-eyed and bushy-tailed.

"It really snows. Sometimes it snows a lot. Have you not been in a snowstorm before?" Cyrus usually thought of snow as a nuisance, but this year it could be more fun.

"Nope. A couple of ice storms and some flurries every five or six years. My place didn't even have a heater."

"Oh wow. You'll appreciate the heat here. The radiators in the building are marvelous. We'll get you boots and everything. Sweaters. Gloves. You're going to freeze." He laughed. "We can snuggle a lot."

"I like snuggling."

That was the understatement of the century. His boy loved to touch.

"Really? I had no idea." They headed into Les's building and stopped at the security desk, where the guard called upstairs to get permission to buzz them up. The elevator in Les's building was super slow, but everything else about the place had great character.

"Neat building. It's weird to me, how insides and outsides of buildings here don't match."

"That's common in New York. They can't do much to the outside even when they renovate the inside." He put a hand on Dex's back and escorted his boy down the hall to Les's door, where Milo was already waiting for them.

"You guys! You look so good! Oh my god. Come in." Milo was all smiles.

He leaned in and gave Milo a kiss on the cheek. "Hello, boy."

"Welcome, Sir. Dex! Really. You're hot."

Dex rolled his eyes and ducked his head. "Thanks, buddy. How goes?"

Milo gave Dex a hug. "Great. I'm so glad you are here."

"You'll be even happier when Dex shows you the cookies he made for you."

"Cookies?" Goodness. Milo was energetic this evening.

"Where's your Master, boy?" Cyrus pointed toward the living room.

"Yes. In the living room, Sir. Did you say cookies?"

"They're iced lemon." Dex handed Milo the box. "I hope y'all like them."

"What's not to like about cookies?" Milo trailed along after Cyrus, opening the box. "Oh my god, how pretty! Master look. Dex made these." Milo jumped ahead of him and showed them to Les. Cyrus hung back a step and slid an arm around Dex's shoulders.

"Those are lovely." Les lifted one of the suns, the rays decorated with intricate filigree. "And they smell like heaven."

"Thank you, sir." Dex beamed, blushing bright pink.

"You should be in the apartment when he is baking. I'm a hungry man. It's torture." He laughed because it wasn't really, but it was a constant temptation. It's a good thing Dex made those cookies to sell so he had incentive not to touch them.

"Oh, that can't be good, Sir." Milo grinned at him. "You're already a big eater. You're going to be as big as a house!"

"I feed him good food, no worries." Dex patted his arm. "He only gets cookies as a snack."

Cyrus rolled his eyes, then looked at Les. "You hear how he's talking about me? I'm only allowed cookies as a snack. You have to wonder who the Dom is."

"He takes care of you. I approve." Les smiled at him, eyes twinkling. "Maybe he can teach you some manners."

Manners? Uh-oh. He looked at Milo, back toward the door, then at Les again. "What did I forget? Was I supposed to take my shoes off or something?"

"I'm just giving you shit, friend. Come have a seat, and let the boys get our drinks." Les winked at him.

"We'll put the cookies in the kitchen before the big, bad Doms eat them all." Milo closed the box smugly, then smiled at Les. "What are you drinking, Sir?"

"I'll take a sparkling water with lime, boy."

"Do y'all happen to have iced tea?" Dex asked Milo so softly. "That's Cyr's favorite."

Milo winked at Dex. "Come on, honey."

Cyrus couldn't help the fond smile and watched them go, eyes on Dex until his boy disappeared from view. "He does take care of me."

"He adores you. That's beautiful to see. He glows with it."

"We're happy. Things are going well. Milo seems excited about company."

"He's losing his mind wanting to impress Dexter. He's been planning where to order from for days." Les rolled his eyes. "He had to go buy new flatware."

He sat with Les, laughing. "It's his chance to show off a little. Good for him; he needs that. And it reflects on you well, which I'm sure isn't lost on him. Things are still going well between you?" He knew there would be plenty of questions about Dex coming, but he wanted to focus on his friend for a bit.

"Exceptional. Genuinely. He's been reorganizing the entire house. I may kill him if he doesn't put my clothes back where they go."

"Oh my." Cyrus rubbed his forehead. "He needs to get out of the house, hm? Can you teach him to tend bar? Or will he rearrange the beer?"

"Can you imagine Will's face? He would... Oh, dear Lord. That young man would terrorize my Milo."

He laughed, probably harder than he should have. He really didn't have any manners. "Okay. So not bartending. Um. Dog walking?" Okay, no, that made him laugh harder. "Sorry. I adore him. You know I do."

"I'll keep him occupied. Honestly. Once he's organized the closets, he can do the bathroom cabinets. Then I'll send him to work on your house."

"Ha. Sorry, position's been filled. Dex doesn't even like it when I order my clients to clean." He hadn't done that in a while. Dex had hidden in the kitchen and hadn't come out even to pee. Poor pet's eyeballs were floating.

"Oh Lord." Les's lips twitched. "That's his domain, is it?"

"Cleaning? I don't know. Probably. But I think he was trying not to interfere, to make himself invisible. He's very wary of interrupting my work, of being in the way. He has the kitchen, and I helped him turn the guest room into a workspace for him." That space needed some more work, but Dex seemed so at ease he didn't want to rock the boat too much. "I keep wondering if I should move my office space elsewhere, but we have this lovely routine, and lunch together...it's just very comfortable for me. I wish it were more comfortable for him."

He raised an eyebrow. So much for wanting to talk about someone else for a while.

"Does he not approve, then? Or is he nervous?" Les was always so curious, so interested in everyone under his umbrella.

"He doesn't judge. He wants to be supportive. I know that much. Nervous? Possibly. Intimidated seems more likely. But I make such a point of telling him it's his home. I don't know what else to do. I'm not even sure I'm reading him right, honestly. And he's so good at reading me."

"Fascinating. How is your work together going? That's where that confidence comes, at least in my experience." Les looked up as Dex brought two glasses.

"Do you mind if I help Milo in the kitchen?" Dex asked, a fond look in his boy's eyes.

"Thank you, pet." He took his tea and then Dex's fingers to kiss them. "Of course not. I'm sure Milo could use the help."

Dex pinked, the look sweet as fuck. "You holler if you need me, okay?"

"I will holler." He let Dex's hand go and watched, again, as his boy ducked into the kitchen. He looked at Les. "Sorry, what were you asking?"

"I was asking about your work together." Les grabbed his drink. "He's lovely with that blush. So charming."

"He is. Our work...well. It's slow, but it's...he's responsive to the things I ask for." Work. There hadn't been a lot of work, if he was honest. He'd capitalized on some of Dex's natural instincts, yes. Kneeling was a good thing. He'd managed to get Dex to open up about Huck, that was good. Was that work?

Les tilted his head. "That sounded very hesitant, especially for you, friend."

"I'm just being careful. I don't want to overwhelm him. Sometimes it feels like it would take nothing for that scale to tip."

"I understand that. But—and forgive if I'm overstepping —maybe he's reading your care to mean something else? They have to know we believe in them, in their strength."

Cyrus frowned. "You think?" Dex was his first full-time, live-in sub and lover and he was obviously missing something. "Tell me what you mean."

"Well, as far as I'm concerned we have to build our subs up—we offer order, discipline, but we also prove that we know our boys can take what we give, what we ask. If one of your clients balked at something, how would you respond—and I mean at the most basic level, not how would you correct him. Would you correct him? Push him?"

"Unless I hear a safe word, of course. That's what they pay me to do."

"That's what we do. We spend our energy giving them what they need." Les waggled his eyebrows. "Of course, sometimes I spank his plugged ass because I love to see him sleep with his pretty butt up in the air..."

He snorted. "Perv. I like how you think. I don't think I've figured out what Dex needs. I'm very sure he doesn't know either." He supposed that meant he could try pretty much anything and wait for Dex to call out angel. "I should start finding out. At least he's curious. He's like you that way. He's a sponge."

"Then you two can have fun finding out. You two should go through a contract together. Just to see his responses. Milo came close to stroking out...but he was an extremely aroused boy."

"We made a really tentative agreement... I guess I could

find a sample contract for him to look at." Cyrus looked at Les and shrugged, grinning. "I feel so green."

"This is a whole new ballgame. You know...he's not your client. He's your boy. It's not therapeutic. It's everything. It's the difference between the bar and Milo. The bar defines who I am in a lot of ways, but Milo is my life."

He smiled at that because it was good to hear. Milo needed someone who was that dedicated, and so did Les. "Not therapeutic. That's true." He needed to do some of that defining. He liked the sample contract idea; at least they could go through it together and have it be less threatening than a laundry list of the things he really wanted. "Dex just hasn't been a sub before. Everything is totally new. You had to see him when I showed him my office. He didn't say one word, he just hugged me."

"Oh. That's...that's amazing." Les got it.

"It is." That was what he meant when he said Dex made him feel worthy. "There's been a lot of progress, just not work. But it's time, you're right. Before we get in the habit of not."

"You're going to have so much fun. Milo says he should start giving your Dexter toys..." Butter wouldn't melt in Les's mouth.

"The potential for very embarrassed curiosity is high." He looked at Les as their laughter died down. "You know I haven't needed to be at your bar at night in...a long time."

"We could arrange a country and Western night, just for you." Now Les was pulling his chain.

"Ha. Let's not make him more homesick than he already is." He shook his head. Someday he would tell Dex how he was going days at a time without thinking about a drink.

"I should send Milo to visit him—take him to breakfast

or afternoon coffee. Something so he can meet more people. You know Milo's never met a stranger."

"That would be so great, Les. He needs some people, you know? Peers, people to ask questions and scheme with. Friends. Someone that's...not me." A reality check. Someone to measure himself against realistically.

"Sure. I'll drop the bug in Milo's ear. He'll start introducing Dex around."

"Thank you. I think he'd appreciate that too. I'm not sure he's ever had real friends."

"Sirs, are you ready to eat?" Milo asked, poking his head out of the kitchen. Milo was grinning, ear-to-ear. "It all looks so good. Dex is amazing at this! He's coming to all our dinner parties until the end of time."

Les glanced to him. "I'm ready. You?"

"I'm ready." He got up. "All your dinner parties? I didn't know I missed so many."

Milo laughed. "You haven't. I've had to convince Master that we should have people over. You're our first victims. I mean guests." Milo popped back into the kitchen again.

"Oh look, new flatware." He winked at Les. "The table looks great, Milo."

"Thank you!" Milo bounced out with a bowl of chips and salsa. "We're having fajitas! Dex doctored all the bits, and he made salsa from scratch."

"Nice work, pet," Cyrus said loud enough to be heard in the kitchen. That was his Dex. Helpful, resourceful, damn good with food.

"It was amazing. So much help. Seriously." Milo lowered his voice. "He's so sweet. I'm going to have to up his naughty quotient."

"Don't you dare, boy. I'll take you over my knee." Wouldn't be the first time.

"Been there, done that, Sir." Milo kissed his cheek happily.

"You're a good boy."

Les took a seat at the table and gestured for Cyrus to join him. He wondered how long Dex was going to last at the table with all the food that would be going around. Hopefully his boy would get a few bites in him.

"Chips and salsa. Impressive." Les chuckled and took a chip. "They are going to come eat with us, right?"

"I hope. Dex is a little funny about meals, sometimes." He helped himself as well, recognizing the fresh taste of his boy's homemade salsa.

"I'll make sure not to notice."

Milo brought in lovely platters of cheese and sour cream, pico, tortillas, and guacamole. "Dex is following with the sizzling goodness."

"Dex is sizzling. I approve." He turned to watch his boy but had to shoo Milo out of the way. "Sit, boy."

"My goodness. Yes, Sir." Milo laughed and pulled out a chair to sit.

Dex carefully brought a huge skillet of meat and veg over, his boy's arms shaking with the weight. "Where do y'all want this?"

He stood up and quickly cleared a spot, and Les dragged a trivet off the sideboard and set it in the center of the table.

"There you go, pet." He stepped out of the way.

Les cleared his throat. "Forget something important, my boy?"

"Master?" Milo went wide-eyed, then looked at the table.

"Trivet next time. Hm? For the hot things."

Cyrus helped Dex reach and set the hot skillet down. "This smells amazing. I'm starving."

"It does. It looks great, Milo. You did great." Dex grinned at Milo, then offered Cy a smile. "Dig in while it's hot, y'all."

He reached for a tortilla. "This was a good plan, Milo. I know how much your Master likes stuff like this. And anything serve yourself works for me."

He had one eye on Dex, who was still hovering over the table. He knew Dex was waiting for everyone to get settled in case they needed something; that was his boy all over, so he didn't comment. Yet.

"Thank you, Sir. Dex made it amazing." Milo grinned at Dex. "Come sit? You made it nice, so you should enjoy it."

"Everyone's okay?" Dex came and stood right next to him.

He took Dex's hand. "We're all great. Hungry. Have a seat, pet." He nodded to the empty chair between him and Les. "Grab a tortilla."

Dex nodded and took a tortilla, carefully making a fajita heavy on the veg.

"Forgive me for not asking before we sat, pet. Would you prefer to kneel here, with me?" Cyrus watched Dex carefully. "Whatever is comfortable for you is fine."

Dex's eyes went wide, expression going totally panicked, moving quickly into ashamed.

Thank goodness for Milo, who was a genuinely good man—observant and kind. "Oh. Oh, you don't mind, Dex? That's the best. We'll kneel together down here. It's so rare to be able to share with another sub. Let me get a long cushion."

Cyrus glanced at Les and shook his head. He'd fucked that up royally and was grateful to Milo for saving his ass. He didn't dare thank the boy now, but he would later when Dex wasn't in earshot.

Milo came back quickly with the perfect cushion to share and set it down on the long side of the table so each sub could be close to their Master. Milo gave Dex a conspiratorial grin as he knelt. "Come sit with me? Having your Master feed you is so erotic, and I can whisper secrets with you while they're all Master-tastic."

Dex actually chuckled. "Milo!"

"What? It's so true. Sitting with them is like sitting at the grown-up's table. We can lick our fingers."

Master-tastic. That was a new one.

Cyrus went back to making his second fajita, because one on his plate wasn't anywhere near enough. "So Dex will teach your boy to cook, and Milo will teach mine to be naughty. Seems completely fair." He snorted.

Milo ignored him. "It's like a blanket fort. Did you ever make a blanket fort?"

"I did. I used to all the time." Dex leaned against him. "I've never gone to supper and sat on the floor before."

"Subs do it all the time at parties. It's hard to sit up there and be all polite, say the right thing all the time, keep your eyes low. Too much to think about. Down here you can just think about your Master, and what he needs."

He reached down and ran his fingers through Dex's curls, noting Dex hadn't taken a bite of dinner yet. He forked up a bite of chicken and held it down for his boy.

Dex took it, snapped it up. "Th-thank you."

Milo whispered, "Try thank you, Master. It'll make him ache. I promise."

"Milo!" Dex was giggling, and Les just looked at him over the top of the table.

He shrugged at Les. "I'm so glad we came. We'll have to do this more often. Dinner is excellent."

"It's lovely." Les fed Milo a bite, the soft 'yes, Master' earning a caress. "I'm so glad you're both here."

"See?" Milo whispered to Dex, and Cyrus caught him leaning into Les's touch.

It was all he could to pretend he didn't know what was going on at knee-level. He took another bite of his fajita, which was so good he could eat several, and might, and then offered Dex a bite of veggies. "Milo should give Dex a tour of your playroom while we're here. Or are you still renovating?"

"Oh, it's lovely. We've spent hours getting everything to be just as we want it. I'd love for him to show it off."

Dex ate the bite, lips brushing his fingertips. "Thank you, Master."

He caught Milo's thumbs up in his peripheral vision.

"Mm." Milo was right. "I like that, pet." Cyrus liked it a lot.

Like, a lot, a lot.

It gave him a little buzz, made him feel even more that Dex was his. He touched his boy's cheek, warming it with his fingers, and then went back to his dinner.

"So what else do you want to know?" Milo asked.

"Everything. Everything I look up online is wrong."

"No problem. I'll make you a list." Milo leaned toward Dex. "A long one. My favorite part? Have you ever seen a plug?"

Dex was going to have a stroke.

"There are several in the playroom," Les offered helpfully.

Cyrus shot Les a look, but Les just grinned at him.

He lowered a hand to Dex's shoulder and gave it a squeeze but was looking at Les. "Do you still get invited to the parties? I haven't been in ages. I think they want pairs."

"Sure. If you two would like to come, just let me know. Everyone would love to meet your boy."

Dex stroked his ankle, tracing his skin with gentle fingers, the touch sending shivers up his leg.

"Let me know when the next one is happening. Maybe we'll be ready." If it were up to Dex, they likely would never be ready. It was going to be a leap for the boy no matter when they went. But after some real work, and a discussion of higher expectations, his boy would be as ready as any first-time sub would be.

He dug into his dinner in earnest, too hungry not to, and kept offering a bite to Dex for every three of four that he took.

He worried about the day that his metabolism slowed down, he was going to blow up like a balloon. It was a good thing he liked food. A better thing that he now had a sub that liked to make food.

A sub that had just called him 'Master' for the first time.

A sub that was kneeling and laughing with another sub, kissing his fingertips, leaning against his leg.

He knew Les was right, that he and Dex should work more, needed to work more. But honestly, seeing Dex smile, knowing his boy was safe and comfortable was so much of a reward he could have been happy with it.

That was love, though, not service. It wasn't the power exchange he craved. Love was essential, but he had other needs as well, and he had to make sure Dex understood them if they were going to work long-term. He had to respect himself that much; he knew where the road led if he didn't take care of himself too.

Everything in his boy screamed that Dex would discover what he craved, a place and a focus and that quiet that Dex was so desperate to find.

"I think I might be full." Cyrus leaned back in his chair with a sigh. "That was delicious. Would you get me some more tea, pet?"

"Yes, sir. Mr. Les, you need more drink?" Dex unfolded himself and took his glass.

"Thank you, boy." Les passed Dex his glass, and his boy headed to the kitchen.

Cyrus looked down at Milo. "You're an exceptional sub, and an exceptional friend. Thank you."

"You're welcome, Sir. He's so sweet, but he wants to learn." Milo smiled at him, the praise obviously welcome.

"He's very curious. Possibly to a fault." He winked at Milo.

"I don't know about you, boy, but I would like to try one of Dex's cookies. And then, assuming Master Cyrus really is finished, I think you boys may clear the table."

He eyed Lex. "Funny. I'm finished, boy."

"Yes, Sir." Milo hopped up, stealing a kiss from his Master before hurrying off. "Dex, sweetie? They're ready for cookies."

"So ready for cookies. Wait until you try them. Dex is really gifted." He studied Les for a long moment and then smiled. "This has been a good night."

"It has. I'm glad you both came. It's been—fascinating." Les winked at him, the dark eyes lit up. "Worth having to buy new flatware, even."

"It'll be even more interesting after the tour of your playroom." He couldn't wait to hear about what Dex learned in there. He wanted to see it too, but he wondered if Dex would get more out of a tour alone with Milo.

"God, what I'd give to be a fly on the wall for that. I'm almost scared."

"I'm kind of excited. Think of the things he'll learn that I won't have to teach him?" And then he could ask Milo to tell him what Dex was most intrigued by, which the boy would likely tell him all too happily.

"Cookies!" Milo shooed Dex into the room. "I don't know why he's so shy all of a sudden, Sir. They smell amazing."

"Because they are amazing." He smiled at his boy. "Serve the plate to Master Lex first, pet. He's the host."

"Yes, Sir. They're lemon with a hint of blood orange in the icing."

Les took two. "They're stunning. Absolutely. Almost too pretty to eat."

Well, well, well.

Cyrus looked at his boy more closely. That 'yes, sir' wasn't a Texan affirmative, that sounded every bit like a response to a superior. Like a sub to a Dom. That was a 'yes, Sir', he was sure of it.

He stared for so long that Dex caught him, and he gave the boy an approving nod, though he doubted Dex actually knew why.

Dex grinned at him, eyes curious, and brought him a little plate so he could choose cookies for himself. "I'll leave the rest in here. I'm going to help Milo clean up, okay?"

"Of course. I'd like a kiss first, though." He didn't wait for Dex to agree but curled his fingers into his boy's shirt and took the kiss he wanted.

Well, the kiss he'd settle for. The kiss he wanted was on the menu for later.

Dex's eyes went wide, and Cyrus could feel the heat pouring from those pink cheeks. His pet opened up on a gasp, inhaling him in deep.

Oh, how wonderful. He ran his tongue along Dex's

quickly to give his boy a taste, then let Dex go and leaned back. "Good boy." He grinned, so pleased. "Dishes now."

Dex nodded and scrambled, and Cyrus leaned back into the chair. "Damn."

"You think? That was lovely to see." Les broke off another arm of cookie. "These are *good.*"

"He's talented, I'm telling you." He reached for one and bit off a hunk like the heathen he might as well be. He wasn't even a sweets guy usually. "Mmhm."

"I'll have to hire him for the bar's birthday. Can you imagine the hit these would be?"

"That's a great idea." The bar's birthday was a fun idea, and Les usually put on quite a party. "He could maybe make the logo? Or beer mugs? I'm sure he'd come up with something cool. He's creative. You should have seen his back-to-school cookies. So cute."

Hell, the high school mum cookies were stunning—and schools were buying them at two-hundred-fifty a pop all over the south.

Dex might never sleep again.

"You know if Milo is bored…" Cyrus wondered if Milo would drive Dex crazy. Some help wasn't helpful. Would the boy drive *him* crazy?

"Milo is not a baker, but I bet he'd love to help with packaging, mailing, that sort of thing. We'll see how they do, but I wouldn't tell Milo no if he asked to help out."

"I'll mention it to Dex later and let him ask if he wants to." Cyrus wasn't going to tell Dex how to run things, but he could see a storm coming even if Dex couldn't.

"Good deal. It would be nice if they could be friends." Les nodded thoughtfully. "It would be good for Milo I think. It gives him someone to teach the ropes to."

"I think they're well on their way." Cyrus agreed,

breaking off a bite of cookie for himself. "Dex doesn't trust easily, but he trusts Milo. He's made several leaps since we got here. I'm very pleased. I think we'll have plenty to talk about over the next few days."

Plenty. And a couple of things he might not talk about and just do.

"So tell me about your new playroom. I need to know what questions to expect."

29

Dex woke up at four so he could get a little work done and think about...things.

God, yesterday had been fun and crazy and panicky and hilarious, all at once. He'd wanted to be mad at Milo for telling on him before, but it was impossible to stay mad, especially since Milo was just so...open.

The playroom though.

God.

That was not like Cyr's office. Not at all.

It was...a room to have lots of sex.

Lots of messy sex he figured because even the floor was rubber.

Did people really have that much sex?

He started giggling. Who was he kidding? He'd thought Cyr was doing it all day long, and he still had a twice a day tug-off habit.

Milo was pretty damn bouncy.

They had lots of toys, and the strange part was that they were displayed like multicolored art on little shelves all along the walls.

It was a penis wall.

Then there was the 'not a penis' wall.

The giggles got worse.

The not a penis wall made him a little nervous. He kind of wanted to touch things to figure them out because just looking at them was not quite enough information. Were they squishy? Hard? Did they bend or move? Not that he'd dared. He didn't even dare ask.

And what was that thing that looked like a wand of bubbles?

One of those things had to be the size of a basketball!

Maybe not a real basketball, but it would totally feel like a basketball.

No. He knew about sex. He didn't need basketballs to have sex. He didn't need a wall of penises either; he and Cyr had two between them and that was plenty.

Hell, he wasn't a virgin. He had a dildo in his office. It wasn't the size of a basketball or even Cyr, for that matter, but it was nice. He hadn't used it since he'd come up.

He tried to imagine Milo dusting that wall of penises all the time. What a chore. If he had a wall of penises, he'd at least put it behind glass doors. Yeah, that would work, a cabinet with lighting and maybe glass shelving too.

Some of them would even be pretty with lights shining through.

He glanced at the clock. Six thirty. Time to make a pot of coffee. He wandered into the kitchen, washed the icing off his hands, and started fixing the coffee. Banana muffins today? Cyr liked his banana bread...

Dex got the coffee brewing and grabbed his guitar, playing softly, letting his soul wake up. Distracting himself from all his thoughts, from all the bullshit that occupied his head.

This was a good way to welcome the light as it poured into the apartment. He didn't get to play as much as he used to. He was busy these days.

"Good morning." Cyr stepped into the front room looking sleepy, dark hair every which way, all wrinkled pajamas, morning stubble, and bare feet. Warm hands wrapped right around him. Cyr couldn't have been awake long. "I love that sound. It's very peaceful."

"You're up early, love." He snuggled right in with a sigh. "Good morning. I haven't even started your breakfast yet."

"I keep hoping I'll beat you getting out of bed, but I can't seem to wake up early enough. I know we're busy during the week, but I don't want to wake up alone on the weekends."

"It's hard to have your breakfast ready if I do that." How did he know what was most important?

"True, but maybe we can make breakfast together on the weekends. Stay in bed." Oh. That was how. Cyr kissed his forehead and left it at that.

"You want your coffee in bed? I haven't started anything else. We could snuggle." Let Cyr wake up slow.

"Thank you, pet. I'm up now. I'll take a cup to the shower with me though. What's your breakfast plan?" Cyr went to the kitchen and pulled a box of Apple Jacks out of the cabinet and started eating them right out of the box.

He put the guitar on its stand and went to beg an 'o', crunching away. "Banana bread? Banana muffins? Banana something? I just got my hands washed and the coffee started."

"Sounds great. I love banana something." Cyr grinned and tossed a bite of cereal in the air, catching it in his teeth.

He applauded, laughing hard. "You have a preference to type? Bread will take an hour and a half-ish. Muffins closer to forty-five minutes."

"Definite preference for muffins. Oh, man. Warm muffins, a little melting butter, mmm." Cyr pushed off the counter and peered at the coffee pot. "Is that done?"

"Silly man. How did you survive mornings?" He cupped Cyr's ass, loving on the broad shoulders. "It's done." He closed his eyes, hoping he was doing right. "Master."

Cyr caught him behind the neck and kissed him hard enough and long enough he had to suck in a big breath when…when his Master let him go.

"Good boy. I do appreciate that." Cyr smoothed a hand through his hair. "That word is important."

He leaned into the touch, his belly fluttering. He intended to figure this out. He wanted to.

"I'd like a cup of coffee, pet. And then I'm going to take a shower before breakfast. We have work to do today, you and I. What do you need to get done with your cookies first?"

He poured out the coffee and added the tiniest bit of coconut oil in and stirred it up. "I'm all decorated on that awful order. Black and purple double homecoming mum with lights. I don't have to go to the room until Monday now."

"Goth mums. That sounds hideous. So we get our day. That's wonderful." Cyr smiled at him, then sipped the coffee. "Oh. That's yummy. Thank you. I'll want you to dress me after my shower so come on back to the bedroom once you've got the muffins in the oven. Don't dress, I have something for you to try on." He got a wink as Cyr left the kitchen.

Dex started the muffins, finding himself whistling as he mashed the bananas and chopped pecans. There was the oddest electricity in the air, a little buzz. He wanted to run around, get that excess energy off, but there just wasn't room.

So he popped the muffins in the oven, ear out for the sound of Cyr's shower turning off.

It was a long shower, but eventually the water went quiet. He wandered back to find Cyr dry but still in a towel.

"Ah. Pet. Pick something out for me, would you? From the leather closet. Something you like."

"Yes, Sir." He knew exactly what he wanted—the buttery soft ones that moved with Cyr, that smelled like heaven, and that seemed comfortable. They were right where they belonged, and he pulled them out. "Did you have a good shower?"

"I did. I'll need you to make me a spa appointment for this week. I think I can give you access to my calendar and my contacts, right? They'll know what I need when you call. You're welcome to make one for yourself if you like at the same time." Cyr came out of the bathroom without the towel. "I know the powdery look isn't sexy, but putting leather on after a shower is hell otherwise."

"I just need to find me a six-dollar haircut place. Just let me know who to call and all. I guess you'll go after work?" He didn't mind the powder; it smelled good.

Cyr laughed. "Six dollars? Not in New York, pet. The no-appointment places are fifteen. You might like a massage. It's on me." Cyr didn't wear anything under his leather as a rule. They'd done this a lot and it was easy as anything now.

"Wow." He ought to just buy him one of those clippers and shave it pretty short. Lots of guys did that nowadays, and he always wore a hat out. He got Cyr's pants up and leaned, resting against his love for a second.

"Mm." Cyr hugged him. "I can smell your muffins. How long before they're ready? Do we have a minute?"

"We have fifteen or so. The batter tasted nice." He leaned in resting into Cyr's broad chest. "I set the alarm."

"That should be enough." Cyr let him go and went to the closet. "Lace-up or zipper. Hm. The lace-ups are a little longer, maybe better for the first time." Cyr came back holding up a pair of leather shorts. "See if these fit."

He felt like his eyes were wide as saucers. "Those are... wow."

Shorts. Leather shorts. Christ on a cracker.

Cyr raised an eyebrow at him and held them out steadily. "I'd like to try you in a harness too, but those are hanging in my office."

He won't make fun of you. He promised. Dex believed that too. It was written down between them, so he took them and switched out the pajama pants he had on. "I feel like I'm in a Halloween costume."

Cyr looked like he belonged in leather; Dex looked like a dork.

"Hm." Cyr touched him, smoothing the leather over his thigh and around to his ass where it warmed and didn't feel unpleasant. "Well, it is a costume of sorts, just not for Halloween. And these don't fit you. Let me get the other pair. Take those off."

He skinned them off.

"I'm skinny." He knew it. Hell, he was smaller now than he'd been when Huck had died. He'd never been a big man, but— "Do you think I'm too little?"

Cyr handed him a different pair of shorts. "You're too thin. But you're not as thin as you were when you got here. A little more weight, and you'll be fine. Being little isn't bad. I'm not sure how you could be anything else." Cyr smiled at him. "And being thin hasn't stopped me from finding you beautiful."

His cheeks went hot, and he had to smile. "Thank you, Sir. I love you, too."

He pulled on the other pair, this pair tighter, almost clinging to him.

"Ah. Better. These will work for today." Cyr smoothed the leather over his skin again. "Have a look in the mirror."

"You and mirrors." He looked and the shorts made his backside look obvious, like he was trying to make Cyr look at it.

"I like mirrors. They tell the truth." Cyr smoothed a hand over one butt cheek.

He hummed. Oh, that felt so good. Hot. "Looking in the mirror makes me a little wigged."

"Why?" Cyr looked at him in the mirror, talking to his reflection. "All you're seeing is yourself."

He shrugged. "It's uncomfortable? Makes me feel vain, I guess. You're supposed to look at other people."

Cyr smiled and slid a hand over his chest, eyes still on the mirror. "If you say so."

He let his eyes close as he leaned back, his back warm against Cyr's chest. "Oh..."

"See that? Nothing but the truth." He felt those words as hot breath on his neck as Cyr's fingers circled a nipple.

He hummed soft and low, his nip drawing up, when the alarm for the muffins went off, making him groan. "Your breakfast needs me."

Cyr chuckled darkly and stepped away. "You look damn good in leather, pet. Grab my mug? I need more coffee too."

"You're a tease. You know that, right?" Butthead man. He grabbed the coffee cup, finished the last swallow, and took it in with him to rescue the muffins.

"I am not. You're just irresistible." Cyr followed behind him and he could feel those eyes on his backside sure as a touch. "Harness after we eat. And then I have something for you to read."

"Yeah? A book?" He pulled out the muffins, before he poured two more cups of coffee and doctored them. "Do you want anything else or is this good?"

"This is fine, as long as I'm allowed to have two." Cyr sat at the table and waited.

"You can have three. Shit, I made them for you. You can have all of them." Okay. Plate. Knife. Butter. Coffees. Muffins.

"They smell amazing." Cyr looked everything over, then picked up Dex's coffee and pointed to the floor.

He blushed hard, but went, pleased as all get out to find a little cushion there, waiting for him. "Oh. Thank you, Sir."

"My pleasure, pet." Cyr handed him his coffee. The kitchen went quiet while Cyr buttered the muffin and took a couple of bites. "Outstanding."

A second later he was offered a bite of muffin off Cyr's fingers.

He took the bite, daring to lick at Cyr's fingertips. "Thank you, Master."

He was becoming a little addicted to the reaction that response was getting.

He got a little hum from Cyr every time he said it and wondered if it was conscious or not. This time was no different, and Cyr caressed his cheek briefly before going back to breakfast.

"It's not a book I want you to read, it's a sample contract. Les gave me one he thought we could work with. I want you to read it over and think about it for a bit."

He nodded, then looked up. "A contract? What for?"

Cyr finished chewing before answering. "We have something informal in writing between us, but it's time for us to make it formal. To set expectations and boundaries. Discuss needs and limits."

"Oh." Boundaries? What sort of boundaries? What a weird thing to talk about. Did people talk about that? Was that 'don't touch my sheet pans'? He didn't know if it wasn't easier to say, "Please don't touch my *sheet*."

Damn, he was funny.

Cyr snorted as if he'd said that out loud and offered him another bite of muffin. He'd had quite a few now and was happy with how they came out. "It will make more sense to you when you see it."

"I trust you." He kissed Cyr's thigh. "Can you tell me about the harness? I mean, the way about it?"

"I have a couple that I think would work on you. I'll let you try them. Of course it means you'll have to look in the mirror again." Did Cyr just purr?

"What are they *for*, though? Just to make lines?"

"No, not 'just' anything. Lots of reasons. Fashion sometimes. Sometimes to make a certain impression. Today, because I like them and want you to wear one. And also for restraint. Maybe even a leash. We'll see."

There wasn't a hint of sarcasm in Cyr's tone. The man was dead serious.

Because I like them—that was a good enough reason for him. He loved how Cyr liked to see him. Of course, how he'd ended up with a man that thought about fashion... "Thank you. I was crazy curious."

"I like that about you. Ask all the questions you like. Your muffins were great." Cyr rested a hand on his shoulder. "Clean up, and then meet me in my...my office. I need a better name for it when we use it." Cyr pushed back and got to his feet.

Dex grabbed his coffee, finished it, and put the rest of the muffins away, and washed up, and if he wasn't wearing leather shorts he might have just straightened things up and gone to nap on the sofa. It felt a lot like a weekday, somehow.

It wasn't though, because no one would be ringing the bell at nine, and he wouldn't be hiding in his room.

Cyr had left the office door ajar and he went right in, but Cyr wasn't there. The curtain was pulled back from the mirror though and there were three leather harnesses sitting out on the table in the center of the room.

Okay. Okay, damn. He picked up one of them, studying it. It made sense in a weird sort of...who was he kidding? He was supposed to pick one and get it on? There was no way.

Except that he'd helped Cyr do it, hadn't he? A bunch.

He had. So he set himself to figuring it out—finding the smallest set first, then he sat on the floor and worked out what had to be unbuckled.

He didn't realize that Cyr was watching him from the doorway until he stood up to get it on.

"Hi. It seemed like you wanted me to start, right?"

"I didn't say not to, but I can't say I'm not surprised. I just went to get this from the bedroom." Cyr flashed one of those things he'd seen on the non-penis shelf at Milo's and set it down on the table. It was purple and sat flat on its own base. "Would you like a hand?"

He blinked, and his real-penis self gave a jerk. "Yes, Sir. Please."

Cyr's hands moved confidently, helping him get it on and buckled, then Cyr stood back and looked him over, nodding slowly. "What do you think?"

"It feels so odd, but not bad odd, just new odd." He wasn't used to paying attention to clothes. They were what you wore to not be naked. This all demanded attention.

"Do you like the weight? This one is pretty light. You

might like the feel of something more substantial." Cyr brought a second one over to show him. "Feel this one?"

He lifted it. "I thought the difference was size."

"To some extent it's size, but they're all adjustable. This one has more weight, and that last one has more hardware."

"So which one do you like?"

"Let's go with that one for today. It fits well and you'll be able to move in it for a while. It looks good on you." Cyr hung the other two up in the armoire, then came back and curled his fingers under the leather at his chest and gave the harness a tug. "I like it."

"Do you?" He liked the way he felt Cyr's touch everywhere the leather pulled.

"I do. I like the whole look. It's a turn on seeing you like this. I wasn't sure it would happen."

"No?" He stepped close, feeling off-center and needing something to balance on.

"No." One hand gripped his ass and pulled him even closer, and he could feel every finger through the leather. He could also feel Cyr's stiff cock against his hip. "I'm looking forward to many more surprises."

That heavy prick was a great compliment and made him rub against it. It seemed rude not to.

"Mm. That's very nice, pet." Cyr took a breath, kissed his forehead and stepped away. Again. "The contract I'd like you to read over is on the couch. It's just an example, we can add and delete, change wording, anything, but Les suggested it as a starting point and I think it was a good idea."

"Okay. I totally remember how to read." Dex winked over and headed for the couch, finding a comfortable way to sit and grabbed the papers.

"It's a lot of information," Cyr said, joining him on the

couch. "It's—take your time and we can talk about it." He wasn't sure, but he thought maybe Cyr sounded a little anxious. "Don't...it's nothing in stone."

He frowned before just following his instincts and pushing into Cyr's lap. If this was anxiety-inducing, then his lover needed him. "So, let's do this."

The first bit was all about how they were both signing this because they were legal and sane and willing. Fair enough.

"It says six months there, but I think we should make it shorter. Maybe three? So we have to revisit it while things are still developing." Cyr pointed to the paragraph in question.

"Developing? What does that mean for you? Or for us. You know."

"Learning each other. Discovering things. Maybe changing our minds about something. Growing. We can't know everything in this moment." Their relationship would always be developing. Without growth, they wouldn't be human.

"Fair enough." He looked up into Cyr's face. "I'm not here for the short-term, though. I'm a long-term kind of man." He didn't want Cyr worrying on that front.

Cyr smiled. "Love is its own contract, pet."

Oh, that deserved a kiss, so he gave it, holding Cyr close with a sigh. Then he sat up, telling himself to hold Cyr's eyes, no blushing. "Thank you, Master."

"You're welcome, my love." Cyr returned his look. "Contracts aside, you're a gift to me already, I hope you know that."

"You make me feel like...like I could do anything." Which he couldn't, but it felt good to feel it. "Now, three months works, if you want. I'm easy."

"You can do anything. As long as I tell you to do it." Cyr winked. "Three months then. You can move on to my responsibilities to you."

Dex read it through, tilting his head. "I take care of you, love. I'll take care of both of us."

"You take excellent care of me." Cyr looked at the contract. "And you are under my care when you're under my order."

"Okay...when is that?" He needed to make sure he understood. "Are we like Milo and Les? Or is it when I'm in here?"

He thought they were way more like Milo and Les, that it was their life, how they loved each other, but he could be wrong. He knew how.

"We're like Milo and Les. Yes. So, the answer to your question is always." Cyr tapped his harness. "Like right now. I asked you to wear that harness. I helped you put it on. If I strapped you in so tight it was hurting you and you made sure I knew that, then it becomes up to me what to do about it. Maybe I fix it so it's more comfortable. Or maybe I want it tight. Maybe discomfort is the point, and I think it's something you need. It's up to me what to do about it. Unless you use a safe word of course."

Okay. Okay, that sort of made sense. "And if I needed to make sure you knew it was hurting, I'd say angels, right?"

"Yes. Exactly. And if my decision not to do anything about really wasn't okay with you, you'd say demon. At which point it would immediately come off entirely."

"But we could still talk after?" Somehow that seemed important, because getting each other was the point, right?

Cyr nodded emphatically. "Any time you use a safe word we'll talk. Especially a hard stop, because that means I've missed or misunderstood something very important, and I need to listen."

"Good. Good, that's what I thought." He grinned and relaxed because maybe he was getting this. He kept reading the contract, looking at the other parts. "Two questions—why doesn't this say I have to take care of you? What kind of punishments? And is this why you were so worried when I didn't tell you about Huck's birthday."

"Well." Cyr nodded. "Okay. This particular contract says you're to serve me, which is in effect taking care of me, but if you prefer specific language we can put something that works for you in. Punishments could be anything, really, and are subject to your safe words like everything else. I don't... I'm not a believer in punishments outside of a specific scene though. I prefer incentives. Either you earn something, or you don't. And...what was the last one?"

He started to answer, but Cyr waved a hand.

"Huck. Right. And yes. I have to know everything or I can't make good decisions, and I can't make sure you are safe and whole. Leaving the apartment without my permission, drinking at the bar, wandering off into the city... I have no control in any of that."

"But I didn't... Okay, so let's say I want to go out, and you're working?" He wasn't being a dick, but details were important.

"Want to, or need to? It makes a difference." Cyr put a hand on his knee and gave it a light squeeze. "If you want to, you may ask my permission either in the morning or when I'm taking a break for lunch. If you need to—maybe you need something for your cookies, or you must run a work-related errand right away—then you can leave a note or a text I'll see when I'm free again, and go. And I want to know exactly where you're going and why. Planned errands like groceries and dry cleaning...those things you can clear with me in the morning before work. Oh. I want to turn on that thing on your phone that shows me where you are. It's cool. Les told me about it."

"Don't you trust me too?" What was he going to go do? He took care of everything—*everything*—and if he needed to just clear his head and take a break, he would. "I mean, as long as I'm doing what I'm supposed to, what do you care?"

"If you're doing what you're supposed to then there's no issue, is there?" Cyr sighed. "It's not a question of trust. I want to know where you are. Maybe you don't understand... if you're not working, which I respect and will give you room to do without me interfering, then you're mine. Your time is mine. Your thoughts are mine."

Wow. That sounded exhausting. "I'm pretty sure you don't want them when you're working."

Cyr snorted. "You need to change the way you think. If you need something, ask me. If you want something, ask me as well. You'll get everything I think you should have. What reason would you have to go out...just to go out?"

"Sometimes I need to just—don't you just get tired? Overwhelmed? Just have to take a long walk and lose yourself?" Surely Cyr did that. He did good for a long time, but sometimes he needed to run away for an hour and hide.

"Oh I see." Cyr cupped his chin and held his eyes. "And how well have those long walks been working for you? To reduce your stress, make you feel less overwhelmed? Because from where I'm sitting, they don't seem to do a damn thing for you."

"How would you know?" The question just popped out of his mouth. "You've never known me for a second when I wasn't having to worry. You never knew me when I wasn't on shaky ground. I'm only just starting to get in a rhythm and know I am where I am. Shit, I wouldn't know what to do if I wasn't running on stress and caffeine."

"How often have you not been on shaky ground?"

"That's a trick question. After I left home, I thought I was with Huck, but... Maybe that's a lie they tell on TV." He wouldn't be surprised if it was. "And that's not the point. I try real hard not to let my random day shit weigh on you."

Cyr took the contract out of his fingers and set it down. "Don't do that anymore. That's what I mean. That's mine too. All of it. You have to let me have everything. So I can give you what you need. I can help you lose yourself in a way that will actually help you."

"But I love you. I'm trying to take care of you, not weigh you down, you know?" He couldn't afford to drive Cyr away with his bullshit.

"I love you, pet." Cyr frowned and stood up. "How can I...hm." Cyr paced away a few steps. "It's a balance. An exchange. I have things I need and if...if you don't need me in return, then what's the point? I need to know you need me too."

"How can you not know that? No one has ever, ever loved me like you. I could be addicted to you, I need you so bad. I think about you all the time. I talk to you in my head when I'm alone. I dream about you at night." He shook his head. He needed more than was reasonable.

"Well, that's all very good to know." Cyr sat again and pulled him close. "I think about you all the time too. I want so much for you. I will be able to show you more concretely what I mean one day soon, I promise. But for now, can I ask you just to accept that I need to know everything that weighs on you? I think once you see how that works in practice it will make sense to you. The concept is obviously difficult for me to explain. It's a little like knowing I have answers waiting for you for questions you don't know you need to ask yet."

"Yes." He leaned in, soaking up Cyr's strength. It felt good to be here, back in Cyr's arms. It felt better to know that Cyr remembered—this is where they could talk. Touching, holding each other. "I can do that. You promise to say before you get bored with me?"

"I can't even imagine. There is nothing boring about you." Cyr pressed warm lips to his temple. "Promise to tell me before I scare you off?"

"I'm not scared. I don't understand sometimes, but I'm not scared." He met Cyr's eyes. "I told Milo last night. I want to learn everything. But..." He couldn't learn it alone, because what he needed to learn was how to be Cyrus's. He wasn't in this all by himself. "I need your help. I can't learn this on the internet."

"No. No, that's why I think you need to trust me and accept things for a while until the opportunity comes up for you to learn—for me to teach you, show you—what you need to know. I'll... I'll plan some things for us, but I can't plan for everything." Cyr picked up the contract again. "Why don't we move on to the submissive's section?"

"I can do that." He read and, basically, he got it. To be honest, he got this part way better. Be faithful and decent, respectful, pay attention, try to follow the rules. Even the part with the letting Cyr know where he was made sense worded as 'don't make your Dom feel ignored'.

The only hard parts were "tell everything," but they'd already talked about that.

"Look good? Questions? You're awfully quiet."

"I do have a question. Is it stupid that this section makes way more sense? I feel like I'm being dumb."

Cyr smiled and took his hand, fingers warm and holding

tight. "No. Knowing you as I do, it's absolutely right. But I will tell you that it's validating for me, so thank you for saying that. It tells me that I'm…that we are on the right path. Your submission is instinctive, it's your…it's how you love."

"Yes. That's okay with you, right?" He thought it was. He thought that part was absolutely okay with Cyrus.

"It's the ideal, pet. I wouldn't have dragged you away from Texas and asked you to be here with me if I didn't think you were everything I need…that I could be everything you need. It's a journey we're on together now."

"I like being together. A lot." When they were together, he had a reason, something to do. Someone to be.

"I have a job for you this week. You are going to type up this contract using your words, so that it's what we've talked about. And when you're done, we'll talk about it again and then sign it." Cyr must have seen his concern and quickly added, "As you have time. I know the cookie mums are out of control this week. A little each night, or in the morning while you have some coffee. It'll be done when it's done."

"I think I hate the cookie mums." He grinned sheepishly and nodded. "I'll type it up."

He would just carve out time.

"Is this where I remind you that they were your brainchild? Or is that tacky?"

"Shut up. They made a lot of money. I thought I'd sell one or two sets. Not fifteen."

Cyr laughed. "Okay, pet. We're going to work. Get some water, and use the bathroom, you won't be able to for a while." The office had its own nice bathroom and a little fridge that held water and sports drinks.

"Did you need a water too? Hey, am I supposed to… I mean, Milo says Sir a lot. A lot a lot. Is that right or weird?"

Because he said sir a lot, but not like that, and he was thinking that he might ought to say Master when he'd normally say Sir and Sir when he'd normally say honey.

"That's a complicated question, but the best answer is when in doubt, say Sir. Or Master. So, Milo is right. Which isn't to say using my name or being informal isn't perfectly acceptable sometimes, but I think you'll know when those times are, as generally they are quite…intimate moments."

Cyrus stood with him and smoothed the leather of his shorts. "And yes, pet. I would like a water too."

"I'm on it." Dex pushed up and kissed the corner of Cyr's mouth. "I love you, Master. Be right back."

He got that sexy, satisfied hum again as he moved away. Cyr didn't hide when he was pleased.

He did his business and washed up, washing his face while he was in here and smoothing his hair down before heading back out to fetch two bottles of water. He needed to put a couple of juices back here, something to soothe the savage hunger.

Cyr was moving around the platform table in the center of the room. It was flat and padded on top, and framed in. That long cage was underneath, and the frame had tons of eye hooks and bars and crazy things all over it. On the table was a pair of cuffs, different than the ones he'd worn that other time, and a few other things laid out next to that… purple thing.

Lord have mercy. "Where do you want the waters?"

"I'll take mine. You should have a few sips before we get started." Cyr opened his bottle and drank slowly. Looked thoughtful for a second, then went to the armoire and came back with a protein bar. "Could be a long morning."

He shook his head. "Let me get you a couple more muffins? That thing is a crime against humanity."

Cyr didn't argue and handed him the bar. "Thank you. And that would have been a good time for a 'Sir'."

Dex chuckled softly. "That thing is *nasty*, Sir. Nas-Tee. I always have better for you. Gimme two shakes."

He went and put together a little plate—two muffins, a couple of wrapped pieces of cheese, and some grapes. That wasn't hell in a foil wrapper.

Protein bars. Gag.

Real food did not come with a perfect foil wrapper.

Except for chocolate.

Mmm. Chocolate.

"You are good to me. Thank you." Cyr took the plate and set it down, but dug right in. "Have a look at those cuffs. They're wider but lighter than the last set. No chain this time, I'll be tying them with rope."

"So, does that mean something or is it just 'I like this' and 'I like that one'? I mean, is there a purpose beyond the obvious?" He picked them up and looked. They were lighter—more supple but he'd bet the edges could dig like the difference in a bull rope and a piggin string.

"Cuffs I usually choose for function. That heavy chain we used last time needed sturdy cuffs. This time I need you to be a little more...nimble. I always have a plan, unless I tell you otherwise, but you usually won't know what that is. I do that on purpose. If I tell you what's coming, it will be for a specific reason." Cyr was making quick work of the snack. "Also on the table are a blindfold, which I will use today, a plug, which I will also use, and a couple of different tie-downs."

"I like the word nimble." It was true, but it was really to say something when his belly sank—not in a bad way, but in that crazy sensation like someone eased your balls deeper in their sac and your whole body felt like you were fixin' to jump your four-wheeler over the ditch.

"I'm just going to wash my hands." Cyr stepped away, left the almost empty plate on a table by the door and ducked into the bathroom, leaving him alone with all the...things. Thankfully he wasn't there long. "All right, we'll get started. As much as I like those shorts, take them off, please."

He fumbled with the laces, his fingers stupid and silly, but he managed, feeling more than naked standing there in the harness.

"Very nice." Cyr reached for the shorts and set them aside, then walked a very slow circle around him and then opened the armoire again. "I want something...ah. This." Cyr produced a small, black contraption that looked like it was made of rubber.

He blinked and stepped forward. "Can I see?"

"Of course." Cyr handed it to him. "Do you know what it is?"

He snapped it closed. Yeah, he had a fairly good idea. "Is it a cock ring? I've never seen one that snapped. Only solid metal ones."

"It snaps so it will come off quickly if I need it to. Or if you do." Cyr smiled and reached for his prick, gently gliding knowing fingers along his length. "You never know."

"W-with you, I know." Cyrus made him dizzy. "I fantasize about you all the time. You make showers good, Sir."

"Oh. I like that, pet." Cyr looked down between them, both hands on him now, stroking and petting.

His breath got deeper as Cyr touched him, and his hips moved nice and slow, following that sweet touch.

Cyr took the ring back from him and smoothly put it on him, snapping it into place. "This one is purely decorative. If you're wondering, you're wearing it because I wanted to see it on you, and no other reason."

"Decorating me, are you?" He loved that, that Cyrus thought he was worth seeing. Decorating.

"I am. The harness has a purpose as well as being decorative, but I do like to look at that too. Now." Cyr reached for the blindfold on the table. "Speaking of sight. You're going to lose yours. Close your eyes."

He closed his eyes, letting himself feel this—all the way to the bone. Letting himself be right here with Cyrus.

"Give me your safe words, please." Cyr tied the blindfold on. "And it's important to me that you truly can't see, so let me know if this one doesn't work for you."

"Angel and demon, Sir. Angel means I need you to hear me and demon means stop." He lifted his head back and down, turned it side to side. "Wow." Dex grinned, fascinated, reaching up to explore the cloth. "Nope. I can't see. It's so soft."

"It's a nice one. Angel and demon. I'm listening. You're going to have to let me move you now." Cyr took him by the shoulders and moved him to the table, encouraging him to climb up on it. "Get your knees under you please. I'll spot you. You have plenty of room. More than you think."

He followed along, as best he could. Cyrus was way better at giving directions than Huck was when they decided to try driving blindfolded. He got his knees settled, trusting that Cyr wouldn't drop him.

"Good." Cyr rested a hand on his chest. "Bend toward my hand, all the way over, forehead on the table."

He put one hand over Cyr's, and the other searched for the table as he leaned, his heart pounding for a second.

"That's it." Cyr guided his hand onto the table. "There. All the way over now."

He let a long breath out, and Cyr eased him down. His forehead met the leather, and he relaxed, balancing on his one arm.

"That's good, pet." Cyr lay a hand on his back and pulled the one on his chest away, then started touching and adjusting him, his hips, his feet, tapping his knees until they were spread widely apart. "I want you like that, but you may shift a little until it's comfortable for you. Make sure, please. You'll be there a while."

It was odd, because he was open and exposed, but he couldn't see it, so it didn't feel embarrassing. "Master? Can I talk to you, or do you want me to be quiet?"

"Talk all you like. You're always welcome to speak, ask me anything, unless I specifically say otherwise. You know I enjoy your curiosity." Cyr stretched his arms out over his head until they were straight, and his fingers lay flat. "Cuffs now."

"Cuffs now." He bobbed his head and stretched his fingers before relaxing. "This feels like praying. Not like 'o please God', but like soul praying."

"Is that a good thing?" The way Cyr handled him was so careful and deliberate, fingers gentle and unhurried as the cuffs went on.

"I think so. That emptiness feeling where you can be filled up is amazing." He didn't get there hardly ever, but he'd been there once or twice. "Am I being silly?"

"Not at all. I'm very interested in what you just said. Could you tell me more?" Cyr tugged on each wrist, and he found that he could no longer move them. He could pull, though.

"I can try." He settled in. There was something so amazing about knowing he could talk, and that Cyrus wouldn't tease. "I mean, there's always so much—the world fills you up in a million ways. Emails and news and noise and things to make right and things you've done wrong. And you fill and fill and fill until you want to scream. And sometimes you have to make it empty and pray that good stuff starts to grow. Sometimes you just have to be...like a vessel for good stuff, and I know that's stupid, but...It's how I feel."

"Why do you say that? I think it's brilliant. And correct." Cyr kept touching him, hand sliding over his backside this time and down one thigh.

He arched into the touch, humming softly. "Thank you. You hear me so good."

"What I hope to do—what I will do for you—is exactly what you're talking about. I hope to be able to take you to that place of emptiness any time I want. Any time you need it. We'll plant that seed you're talking about, and we'll visit it, and make it grow, and turn it into a place you love to be." Cyr traced the line of the ring that held his balls, the light pressure of his Master's fingers so intimate.

He hummed softly, partially at the touch, but mostly at the promise that Cyr was making. "Do you think we can? Like really?"

"I know we can. I can't promise it will be today, but we'll get there. We'll enjoy each other along the way. There's no such thing as failure, just levels of success. I'm happy if you're trying." Cyr felt up his thigh. "This is bondage rope. It's very soft, I'll wrap it numerous times so it doesn't pinch. I assume you're comfortable?"

"Yes, Sir. This is a good place." Happy if he was trying? God, trying was his superpower. "Sometimes I'm afraid I'm going to wake up and be standing in the rain at the cemetery and you never came."

Cyr laughed softly. “I think in a few minutes you’ll be very clear that this isn’t a dream.”

It was quiet while Cyr worked. Not silent, but Cyr didn’t speak while winding thick rope snuggly around both of his thighs. Cyr tucked fingers in against his skin in places, made sure he was settled before tying them off somewhere tight enough to tug on him.

“I sometimes feel like there could be no other reality. That I was destined to be at that funeral.”

“You were. You had my back even then.” Dex groaned softly, sinking deeper into the leather. “Never…never had any rope on me like this.”

“Do you like it?” Cyr gripped his ankles and pressed them into the table. “Mm. Yes.” The touch and the pressure were replaced by what felt like a wide strap. He felt it tighten, holding his feet down.

“Oh. That’s new.” His heart sped, and he panted softly, his cock jumping. It wasn’t even hot, but his body didn’t care. His body said this was right.

“Take a deep breath.” Cyr’s steady hand pressed against his spine. “And let it out slow. Ready? With me. Breathe in… and out.”

The world began to spin, swinging in sparkly circles, and the only thing holding him down was Cyr’s hand. “Stay with me? Please?”

“I’m right here, pet. I will never leave the room unless you are also free and able to get up and leave it after me. I’ll keep contact for a bit so you know I’m here.” Cyr’s hand slid lower, fingers resting on his tail bone and thumb dipping lower, moving over his hole.

He groaned and, when he tensed to squeeze Cyr’s wandering thumb, he could feel the ropes all around his thighs.

"You look incredible, pet. All the black leather and rope against your skin is beautiful." Cyr's thumb was suddenly slick and gliding freely, the lube only briefly cold against his sensitive skin.

He laughed softly, the slide of Cyr's touch sending a jolt of electricity through him. "Mmm...thank you, Sir."

He knew by now that Cyr's hum meant his Master was pleased, but the gentle, "Good boy," was unexpected and felt like high praise.

He felt himself flush, felt his entire body heat, and he knew he was turning pink.

"Have you ever worn a plug before, pet?"

"No, Master. Only a dildo when I needed some help."

"Some help?" The plug was smooth, and the very tip slipped inside him easily, but Cyr didn't stop there, very slowly encouraging the toy to go deeper, stretching him as it went.

"Mmhmm... I like..." The stretch distracted him, and his eyes opened, his lips parting. Oh, that made his abs clench in pleasure, his hole tighten.

Cyr flattened a hand across his lower back. "Relax, pet. There's a little more to go yet. Just breathe and let it happen."

He wasn't scared. He rocked back and forth in tiny motions that were driven by his breath, by that solid hand.

The burn was sweet, just enough to make him moan until the toy suddenly seated itself inside him and everything relaxed. "Lovely." Cyr jiggled it and gave it another light push. "Perfect."

The last word was punctuated by a light slap to one ass cheek.

He tightened, rocking everything inside him, and there went those sparks again. "Oh!"

"There you go." Cyr chuckled and slipped something small and oval into his fingers. "Play with that, I think you'll figure it out quickly."

"Figure it out?" Button. Three little, clicky buttons. The first button didn't seem to do anything, but that second button started vibrations all inside him. So he dropped it, and had to find it again. "So mean!"

He couldn't stop laughing.

Cyr laughed as well. "I don't know, something about telling you seemed so...boring. I'll let you keep that for a bit. Don't drop it. I won't be retrieving it for you."

Cyr's heavy boots echoed on the floor first on one side, then the other, then behind him again, and he got another smack. Other side this time.

He swallowed, almost able to see the smacks like lights, and the third swat had him clenching the remote and turning the plug on again.

"Doesn't take much to get a little pink in your skin, pet." He heard Cyr's boots again. Thud—Thud—Thud. This time his Master was tucking fingers into his cuffs, under the ropes, between his back and the harness. "Everything feel all right? Make sure to tell me if you're not comfortable, or if your fingers or toes get numb."

Thud—Thud—Thud, and another, harder, smack to his ass. But that wasn't Cyr's hand anymore.

"I—" He stilled, curious, less floating now than sharp, awake, watching in the darkness.

The strokes became solid and rhythmic, no single one particularly painful but piled on top of one another created an ache deep in the muscle.

"Feel that focus, pet? That's the path to follow. My voice, your body, there's no need to think about anything else.

You're tied to my table, you can feel my paddle, you're entirely mine. I will look after the rest."

Cyr's voice was deep and hypnotic, words rolling over him, touching him in waves.

Your voice, my body.

On each exhalation a soft sound escaped him, quiet, raw thing that he couldn't deny.

The paddling went on, and so did Cyr's words. Words like 'beautiful', 'so good', and 'mine.'

His world fell out beneath him, and for a second he was lost, flying, and if not for the ropes, he could have run.

When he came back to himself, the paddling had stopped and Cyr's hands were on him, running on long strokes over his back and sides and his Master was speaking to him gently but continually. "That's it, come back now pet. Listen to my voice. You've done so well."

He sucked in a hard breath, clinging to Cyr's words, fighting the urge to apologize. What he did say was, "Master."

"Oh, pet. You're fine. Just wonderful." Cyr kissed the back of his neck, then loosened and removed the ropes and massaged the places where they'd been wrapped around his thighs.

He felt dizzy, a bit like a new foal, sweaty and trembling and unsure of its place in the world.

"I took the strap off your feet after I took the plug out. You can move everything but your hands now, I'll loosen those next." He knew immediately when the straps holding his wrists were loose because the pressure, that constant tugging was gone, but the cuffs stayed on. "You should move, pet. Stretch out those legs. I'm going to help you roll over."

He nodded and pushed himself up on shaky arms. *Come*

on, Dex. Focus. Get your shit together. You look like an idiot. Sit up.

"Easy. Easy, pet. Just roll, don't try to sit up yet." Cyr was helping, taking his weight, getting him over on his side. "Don't worry, you're fine. There's nothing wrong, I promise. Just breathe and let everything come back. I'm right here."

Once he was on his side, Cyr gave him a pillow for his head and stroked fingers through his hair. "Good boy. So lovely."

"I'm okay?" Was he okay? He felt like if Cyr left him right now, he wouldn't be.

"You're just fine. You and I both were very surprised by your orgasm, and otherwise you're just floating. We'll talk in a bit, but you're fine. I'm right here."

He nodded. "Right here. I'm glad."

Because he felt a little lost. Thank God Cyr was here.

30

Dex was out. It hadn't taken much, a little love, a little aftercare, and Cyrus's boy had fallen asleep right there on his bondage table.

He understood that; it had taken him a while to come down too. He'd used those same restraints, and his same muscles many times before with his clients, he'd tied many men down and spanked them, but it hadn't ever been like this.

Even with lovers from the past, most of whom had been in the scene, he'd never allowed himself to be so self-indulgent, or to get so turned on. He'd never felt so supported in his needs or been so focused that he could simply take everything he wanted.

He'd never felt closer to anyone.

He'd never delivered a blow with so much love.

Once he was sure Dex was sound asleep, Cyrus had puttered around, straightening up. He put a pile of things for Dex to clean up later on the bathroom sink, including that marvelous plug that they'd both enjoyed—though he'd made a note to keep hold of the remote next time.

Finally, he'd carried Dex to their bed and tucked the boy in. Dex had hardly stirred.

He changed and quickly made himself a late lunch with one ear out for his boy. The last thing he wanted was for Dex to wake up alone, but at the same time, he knew he wouldn't be any good to his boy if he didn't get some food in him.

More than that though, he didn't want to leave his boy's side. He felt so protective and possessive that he brought his sandwich to bed and ate it there where he could listen to Dex breathe and be assured his boy was whole.

He was propped up in the pillows now, supposedly reading, though he hadn't actually finished an entire paragraph in all the time he'd been sitting there.

His mind was on his boy.

He was grateful that Dex was sleeping and the apartment was quiet. He'd learned so much this morning he needed to be in his own head for a while and make sure he understood it all. But even after thinking and mulling and going over their morning, he still wasn't sure that he did.

Dex's natural curiosity and the gift of his boy's complete trust made it much simpler than he'd expected to try things. His plan had been the blindfold and simple bondage, that was all. He'd hoped to discuss the plug but hadn't held out a lot of hope. He most certainly hadn't expected to be able to pull out a paddle. The fact was, he probably could have gone much farther if he hadn't been paying close attention. Thankfully, he discovered in plenty of time that Dex was too far gone to know to use a safe word.

Dex, it seemed, had two spaces. What he would consider subspace, where the boy was compliant and floating but coherent and able to concentrate. Between the blindfold and the bondage, the boy had fallen into that space much more easily and naturally than Cyrus could have hoped for.

The plug and the paddle had pushed the boy well beyond that space. Not in a bad or a dangerous way, not at all, but Cyrus knew now that he would have to continue to watch closely, ask more questions, and possibly pull back sooner next time. Dex had definitely needed and enjoyed that release—God, it had been something to see—but Cyrus was thinking now that the feeling of total safety and freedom that came with it was what had overwhelmed the boy. Dex didn't have the reserves to cope.

He worried—he was concerned that he hadn't prepared himself well enough to help Dex deal with the unfamiliar notion that it was absolutely safe to fall. Cyrus didn't know if his boy's disorientation was caused by the cocktail of endorphins, hormones and adrenaline—Dex was just so tired and those could be heavy—or if some deep defense mechanism had kicked in. At this moment, both seemed equally plausible, and one certainly didn't rule out the other.

He was sitting close with his boy tight against his leg, but he reached for Dex anyway and combed his fingers through Dex's hair. He didn't know, and he knew Dex wasn't going to be able to tell him, so he was just going to have to be vigilant.

Dex sighed softly, humming, one hand sliding along his leg. "Love. You okay?"

"I didn't know you were awake." He put down the book he'd been not-reading and hunkered down in bed with his boy. "How are you? You took a long nap. The sun is going down."

"Oh God. Did you eat?" That was his boy—his first worry was Cy's needs.

"I did. I had a turkey sandwich. I had to draw on my base survival skills from before you moved in." He kissed Dex's temple. "Thank you for thinking about me."

"It's my pleasure. I'm sorry for crashing on you, hmm?" Dex cuddled in, warm and snuggly.

"Don't be. It's more of a compliment than you know." It was about damn time he was able to wear his boy out. "Are you sore? Stiff? Does anything hurt?"

Dex stretched, a soft groan brushing his skin. "A little stiff, but not hurting. It almost feels like someone tied me up."

The tease was tentative, testing them out.

He laughed softly. "Dammit. Gotta keep a better eye on those deviants you hang out with."

"Right? Lord have mercy. Damn freaky-deaky folks." Dex kissed the corner of his lips. "Love you."

"I love you. You were magnificent this morning, though I can see that I overwhelmed you a bit." He wasn't sorry. They both learned something.

"I'm sorry. Did I do something wrong? I wasn't really worrying about things…"

Oh, Dex. So quick to apologize, to worry. "Pet, I just said you were magnificent. Not worrying is exactly what I asked of you. I only meant that it was a lot, and it was all so new." He ran a hand down Dex's side, soothing his boy.

"It was. It was big." Dex hugged him tight. "I guess I need to make supper instead of just snuggling like I want to."

There was a dilemma. Should he let his boy cook? Or keep Dex here and talk?

"I'd like to stay here and snuggle too. I think we have a lot to talk about. But you might need some time to think about our morning first. I know I did. So, you tell me. Stay here and talk and order food, or go make dinner together and come back around to this later?"

They were going to have to debrief a little either way.

Dex met his gaze, so serious. "All thinking is going to do is make me worry about what you want to talk about. Can we order, please?"

"We will order." Cyrus was fairly sure that look wasn't meant to turn him on, but it was so Dex. Or maybe it was because his boy got an orgasm this morning and he didn't. He planned to make up for that later. "But I wish you wouldn't worry, pet. We'll always talk after a scene, about what went well and what didn't, about what we liked and what didn't really work for us. I don't have an agenda, honestly. I just want to know your impressions, and to find out what you want to try more of."

"Okay. I felt like I was flying, like my body disappeared for a second. Your eyes are beautiful, did you know?"

Flirt.

"Thank you." He smiled; the compliment felt good. "I suspect that what you thought was a second was a great deal longer than that. We worked for well over an hour."

"So long? I would have said half that, honestly." Dex reached up and cupped his jaw.

"That's what happens when you clear your mind." He turned his head and kissed his boy's fingers. He had a feeling he was going to have a hard time keeping this conversation on track. "Did anything feel particularly right? Anything uncomfortable?"

"I remember your voice the most. It was everywhere, like a song." Dex hummed and leaned down to nuzzle his jaw.

He started to nod but ended up arching into Dex. "That's good. That means you were focused on me, tuning everything else out."

"You were the whole world." Dex licked down his throat. "I didn't even know I'd come. I was just lost in us."

"Mmm. There's nothing wrong with that. Plenty of scenes are set up with that result in mind. I'd like to help you stay more aware next time and figure out where that line is so I know." So he could decide to send Dex there on purpose or to pull back. "How do you feel now?" When he asked that question, he was always listening for the way a sub answered. Hesitant, confident...whether the sub could explain it or not, all of that told him something about a sub's state of mind.

"Tender, snuggly, horny, like I want to stay close to you. Way less freaked than I was."

"You were only anxious because it wasn't familiar. Next time you'll know." Staying close was fine with him, and he understood because he felt the same way.

"I've never floated away like that. Is that okay? You're not disappointed, I don't think."

"It's just fine. It's not ideal if I've got a goal in mind, but for an indulgence, it's just lovely. For today, it was wonderful. But the real answer to that question is what has it done for you? If you feel good, then it's definitely okay. If it helps you rest the way you did this afternoon, it's fine. If it serves you in any way at all, I'm happy."

"I feel like I could relax for the first time since Huck died, maybe longer. I didn't have to do anything—not even be decent. I could just relax."

Cyrus didn't try to hold back the pride he felt at his boy's words. What Dex had just said was everything. He'd done that for Dex, helped his boy find a space to relax.

He didn't try to hide his grin either, or his joy, and didn't much mind if it made sense to Dex or not. He rolled, pressing Dex into the pillows with a kiss, letting his happiness spill over his boy.

Dex opened right up, tongue sliding into his lips, a deep moan filling the air. Oh yes.

Maybe his boy would like an orgasm he could remember.

They were supposed to be talking, but who was the Dom here? He wanted his boy, and he could have what he wanted. How much more was there left to say after that?

He angled his hips so he could rub against his boy. Dex was still naked but he had on sweats he was going to do something about in short order.

"Yes." Dex shoved at his sweats—pushy, needy boy.

He had a fond appreciation for both of those traits.

He let Dex work his sweats over his hips, and he managed to get them low enough that Dex's foot could catch the waistband. They disappeared into the bottom of the bed somewhere.

"Impatient," Cy hissed, well aware that he had none either.

"I can tell you want me, Master, and we can touch and talk." Dex grabbed his ass and pulled him in, fingers digging in hard.

Maybe, but he didn't think he could fuck and talk. Speak, yes. Talk? Doubtful. Dex's well-placed use of his title was just the talk he wanted to hear. "Next time I tie you up I'm going to fuck you, pet." He bucked against Dex, loving the grip his boy had on him.

"Yes, Master." Dex leaned up, groaning low. "I love when you fill me up."

Cy ducked his head, and sucked a small nipple up between his teeth, then let it go with a growl. "Find me a rubber."

"Bitey bitey." That wasn't a complaint. His boy lit up, eyes dancing with a naughty hunger. Dex arched under him, then flipped under him to dig out a rubber, ass rubbing his cock the whole time.

Seriously? An afternoon's hard rest did this? Gave him a joyous, wicked pet?

He might just have planned out every Saturday forever.

He reached between them and gave that sensitive ass a light love tap, just to rattle Dex a little.

Dex rippled underneath him. "Goddamn that is tender. I feel that everywhere."

Dex hid that sweet ass against his lower belly.

"Everywhere. Mmm." He reached around those narrow hips and gave his boy's pretty cock a tug. "Hurry it up."

"I have it. Aren't you supposed to be all patient and all?" Dex wiggled under him, teasing him mercilessly.

"If I'm not, it's your fault. That makes you a naughty boy." He reached for the arm that was holding the condom and pulled up behind Dex's back, pinning his boy down.

"So mean!" Dex didn't fight Cy, but relaxed his shoulders down, rocking his ass up hard. God, Cy needed inside that still-hot, needy little hole. Now.

He snatched the foil package from Dex's fingers and tore it open, watching Dex move as rolled it on and lined up. "You wanted to talk? Make sure I hear you."

Betting that his boy was still plenty slick from earlier he dove right in and tugged his boy's hips back until their bodies fit tightly together.

"Master!" Dex's cry filled the air, and he heard that, loud and clear.

"Fuck, you feel good." He held still another torturous second and then had to move, gliding out slowly and slamming back into his boy.

"Yes. This is—Oh, please. Do that again." He did love to hear begging.

Right before he lost the rational bit of his mind, it occurred to him how completely he'd just been seduced by his sub. And how lucky he was.

Cyrus set the pace his boy was asking for, slowly pulling back and then plunging in again, crashing into Dex and battering the boy's sore ass.

Dex took it, took him, and begged for more. His boy was wild underneath him, burning around his prick. It wasn't going to take either of them long to get what they wanted.

Cy pinned Dex down again, this time with a heavy hand at the base of his boy's neck as his control faded. He hammered into Dex, following the lightning behind his eyes.

Dex's body tightened, the grip like a fist, and Cy roared, the pleasure almost pain as Dex bucked and cried out in need under him.

"Dex...pet..." That was all the warning he could manage. He squeezed his eyes closed to stop the world from spinning as he fought for breath underneath a crushing release.

Dex's body held him tight, random ripples of the muscles keeping his aftershocks going on and on.

He hung over Dex as he finally found air, breathing deep and dropping kisses on his boy's shoulders. "Damn, pet. You all right? That was worth the wait."

"Good. So good." Dex hummed deep in his chest.

He shifted off his boy and rolled over, trying not to groan like an old man. "Come here. I want a kiss."

"Yes, Sir." Dex snuggled right in, lips clinging to his. "That was amazing."

"You're amazing. I needed you." Cyrus got his arms

around Dex and held him tight, wishing they could just share skin. "Mmm. Much better."

"Mmhmm." Dex melted into him, going boneless.

"You're a naughty boy, pet. You distracted me. We were supposed to be talking about something weren't we?" He grinned into their lazy kiss. "I'll have to come up with a suitable punishment for you."

"Mmm...not naughty at all. I'm so good." Dex leaned their foreheads together, eyes twinkling. "Good as gold."

"As gold? Oh good idea. I have a nice, fat, gold plug you can wear tomorrow. Lucky you, it doesn't buzz." He thought about that. "Yes. And cuffs, and those shorts you wore for five minutes today, because naked in the kitchen isn't appetizing. That's for tomorrow."

Dex's cheeks went pink, and he licked his lips. "Mmm... listen to you, Master."

"Exactly right. Listen to me." He did enjoy that blush. Natural curiosity was one of Dex's best traits. It made his boy ready to play, to try something new, and so far, it seemed to be working for them both. "Do you think if we order pizza from bed they'll deliver it to bed?" Maybe he should come up with something more interesting than pizza... Vietnamese or Indian or Tapas or something.

"I doubt it. Delivery drivers are so weird that way..." Dex started chuckling. "Although you know those guys have seen some shit."

"Oh! I could send you to the door in your harness!" Cy grinned.

"Oh, you know that they've seen that. That's probably passe."

Clever boy. "Oh. Well, hm. Nipple clamps then. And a ball gag. And his tip could be in your thong." He actually kept as straight face.

"Oh I would not like that at all. I'm not a thong guy." Dex chuckled softly, nuzzling at his jaw.

"Yeah, me neither. I'm more of a naked guy." He sighed, so satisfied. He was basking a little in the attention and he wasn't sorry. "I feel great. What about you?"

"I feel like I'm right where I belong." Dex smoothed Cy's hair, fingers so careful, gentle. "So yes, great."

"Maybe a nap before pizza." He already had his arms securely around his boy, but he picked up one leg and wound it around one of Dex's to make his point. "Stay."

"Mmm...Yes, Sir." Dex kissed the corner of his mouth, exhaling with a long sigh and cuddling into his arms. "Don't let us sleep too long. You'll be starving."

"No, no. Just a wink. I can't sleep when I'm hungry." He said that, but those little pecks of Dex's relaxed him, reassured him. He was dozing before the words were completely out of his mouth.

31

Dex was fixin' to hit something with a hammer. Seriously.

So he texted Cyr and left a note.

So frustrated. Taking a quick walk down to get a Dr Pepper and a Snickers. Love you

Everything he'd fucking touched had fallen or burned or broken or smeared, and he was pissed. So he ran all the way down all the stairs and went to one of the little stores.

He needed caffeine and chocolate.

Bad.

Cyr would be done working in a few, and this would help burn off some growls.

He bought three Dr Peppers and a Snickers bar, plus a Payday for Cyr, and he had the Dr Pepper down before he headed home.

By the time he got back, he could hear the shower running. He headed for the kitchen to put the Dr Peppers in the fridge and found the empty charging cable for Cyr's phone hanging over the edge of the counter.

He made a glass of tea and took that and the Payday bar into the bedroom, waiting for the water to stop. Then he grinned. "Hey, you! I brought you a Payday. I never see you drink Coke, so I didn't bother, but I have a glass of tea for you. I was so frustrated. I burned a batch of cookies and that one set I iced yesterday? I dropped two! And that's after I broke your egg yolks and uber-toasted your sandwich. I ran the stairs down. I would have run up, but I would have barfed."

Cyr didn't open the bathroom door, instead answering back through it. "You may put everything down on the dresser, and then kneel at the foot of the bed and wait for me."

"Are you okay?" Did the dresser even have a coaster?

"I'm fine." Cyr came out of the bathroom in a towel—hair neatly combed, face shaved—and headed for his regular closet.

"Good deal." He picked the coaster off the nightstand and put it and the tea on the dresser, along with the candy bar. "I wasn't sure what your favorite candy was, but you like peanuts, and this one doesn't have chocolate." He settled on his knees by the end of the bed. "I'm thinking I'll make noodles for supper maybe. I don't know. I may set them on fire."

"I was very disappointed when I left my office to find you weren't home." Cyr pulled jeans out of the closet and then found a T-shirt in the dresser.

"I'm sorry. I was fixin' to throw something. I told you where I was going, and that I'd be right back." He'd brought Cyr a treat, even.

"We agreed that you would ask my permission before

leaving the apartment, pet." Cyr's tone wasn't angry, but it wasn't friendly either. More like a little annoyed.

"I promised not to worry you and to tell you where I was going and when I'd be back. I did that. I texted and left a note. You were busy." This was reasonable. He wasn't going to be kept a prisoner in here because Cyrus was at work and couldn't be contacted.

Cyr stood over him for a minute quietly, then walked away to dress. "That was for important errands. A temper isn't an important errand. A soda and a candy bar are not the cure for your bad day. I am."

Oh no. No, he was not going to get bitched out for being decent. That wasn't nice. "I beg to differ. Walking off a snit so that you don't have to put up with me being evil right when you get out of work is pretty damn important. I needed to walk it off, right then. Not in twenty minutes when you were done working. I was being decent to you, and how often do I go get a Coke and a candy? Not once since I came here. I just needed a change of scenery for a few minutes, so I could come talk to you and tell you how grr I was without just running around in circles and slapping myself in the head."

"You forgot to say 'Sir.'" Cyr turned around and walked out of the room.

Dex told himself not to take the iced tea glass and throw it at Cyr and scream, "You forgot your tea, Sir!" because that would be an asshole thing to do.

He wasn't an asshole.

He just stood up and went to his office. Cyrus could decide that he was glad in the same panties he got mad in, but Dex wasn't going to waste time sitting in there doing nothing. He'd never been very good at that whole 'you're in time out, think about what you've done wrong' thing.

If he did it, then he wasn't sorry.

It was quiet for a while, to the point that he started to wonder if Cy had gone out. But then he smelled the bacon, and maybe five minutes after that, he heard Eric Clapton playing in the kitchen.

He peeked out of the office. Maybe Cyr was in a better mood. Maybe they'd both just had shitty days. "Can we make up yet?"

Cyr gave the black apron around his middle a tug and reached for the music to turn it down. "We're not fighting. I'm just waiting for my sub, who broke a rule, to come apologize so we can have a discussion about it. And making BLTs, I'm starving."

Oh for fuck's sake. Sometimes living with Cyrus was like playing a game with someone that had played a bunch and had house rules and special bonus scores and he was still looking at the rule book every time. "I'm really sorry you think I broke a rule. I honestly don't believe I did, but I know we need to talk so we're on the same page. And I wasn't not saying Sir because I didn't mean to. I was focusing on trying to *talk* to you. Uh, Sir." He rolled his eyes at himself. "Do you want some help?"

"For future reference, 'I'm sorry you thought I did something I didn't do' isn't really an apology."

Cyr shook that head of dark hair and checked on the bacon in the oven, then leaned against the counter and looked him square in the eye. "You were on your knees, pet. You can't argue with me from your knees. It's...confusing. A sub doesn't argue unless they are prepared to be punished—which, by the way, I had planned to do until you weren't there when I got back with your cuffs. That was confusing too. You can't just...get up. Either you're submitting or you're not. We're either 24/7 or we're not. We have a contract." Cyr rubbed his forehead, obviously as perturbed as he looked. "I understand you're new at this. That's why I didn't raise my voice or react the way I wanted to. I was ready to take you over my knee for insubordination."

Of course he could argue and get up; that's what he'd done. Cyr didn't want him to. Those were two entirely different things. "I think you and me need to talk. Like really talk. I'm not sure whether you want me to say angel or demon, but I want to talk, man to man, and figure this out."

"That would be demon, and I agree." Cyr pulled the bacon out of the oven and set it on the stove, then moved in close. "Can we start with a hug?"

"God yes." He wrapped around Cyr and held on, just letting his lover know that he was still right there.

"I love you." Cyr took a deep breath and sighed, seeming pretty rattled. "Okay, that's better."

"Yes." Dex wasn't sure what the fuck was so messed up, but they'd talk and figure it, right? "Do you need your sandwich first, before we sit?"

"Yeah. I think that's a good idea. Would you mind refilling my tea? Did you want one? I made plenty." Cyr let him go and went for the bread.

"Can I just have a piece of bacon, please?" He refilled Cyr's tea and pulled out the head of lettuce, the mayo, and the plate of tomato slices that were in the fridge.

"Of course." Cyr waited for him to put everything down and then held out the bacon for him. "Nice and crispy."

"Thank you." He took it. "I love you."

Dex thought maybe Cyr needed to hear that right now.

He got a quick kiss so he must have been right.

"I think I want to listen first, if that's all right," Cyr said, settling at the table.

"Okay." God, he was just going to make it worse. Still, he had to try. "I wasn't being a bitch. I was—am—having a terrible day. Seriously. So I was losing my mind. I ran down to get a Coke. I left a note and a text. I brought you a candy bar too. I wasn't trying to piss anyone off. I was trying to step away from the ledge. And I wasn't being petty. It was important. How I feel is important."

"How you feel is very important." Cyr agreed quickly, chewing a bite of his sandwich. "How we deal with how you feel is also important." Cyr sipped his tea and leaned back in his chair. "Judging by what you just said, and how you said it, the first thing I think we should talk about it the basic disconnect between how you envision this relationship and how I do."

Well that sounded ominous as fuck. "Okay. What is it you want from me that you're not getting?"

"I don't think that's quite the right question. I'm getting what I need, today was just...inconsistent. That was unexpected, and more disorienting for me than you might realize. Let me...hm." Cyr looked at him, reached for his hand. "Relax. We're fine. I'll explain, we'll talk about it and figure it out."

"Can we go sit on the sofa, after you finish your sandwich?" He held on, squeezing Cyr's fingers.

"We should, right? Good idea." Cyr smiled as he sat up to dig into the last few bites of his BLT. "Everything tastes better when you make it for me."

"That's because I care. It matters." He stood and refilled Cyr's tea and got himself a glass too.

"I know. You care about everything you do, pe—uh. Dex. Sorry."

He frowned over on his way to the front room. "Why are you sorry?"

"Just letting things blur. I'm not used to thinking about it...it's...well, it's part of everything. Let's sit." Cyr sat on the couch in what had become the usual spot for a good snuggle.

He sat close-close, making sure they were touching, his knee on Cyr's hip. "Talk to me."

It was crazy that him trying to defuse a shit day should make everything worse.

"Working on it." Cyr smiled and winked. "Okay. In my mind we've been in a 24/7 Dom-sub relationship, which means that there's no daylight between any piece of who we are. We're Dom and sub, we're lovers, we're friends all at the same time, all the time. This works for me because I'm a pretty black and white guy, right? We're either Dom and sub, or we're not. And if we are, then you're mine. And if you're mine...then everything about you and your day is at my discretion." Cyr squeezed his hand. "I know you're going to argue that it shouldn't be that way and it doesn't necessarily have to be, but that's where my mind has been. That's what I understood we talked about the other day when we discussed our contract. And, for what it's worth, this is exactly why we need one."

Cyr put a hand up, stopping him from responding yet. "So, I come out for lunch and I expect you to be there, to have my lunch ready, partly because I asked, but partly because that's what you've been doing and it's a reasonable expectation. The same thing with the end of my workday. So when you weren't there when I expected you to be...and it's not that what you were doing was unreasonable. It's just that I was thrown by that, and I saw it as not following the rules."

"I'm sorry you were disappointed. I was trying to get back in time, but you have to trust that I can go outside, and I'll come back. You're not available when you're working, and it's not right to act like I can't run and get a fancy coffee for us or a Coke." He'd been out to lunch with Milo. Milo called Les a lot, but Les was available by phone. Cyr wasn't.

"It's not that I don't trust you. It's really not about you at all." Cyr's forehead wrinkled and he rubbed the bridge of his nose. "Okay. Tell me how your day goes. After I go into my office."

"I clean up, have coffee, run laundry, then I get to work doing my thing. Clean up the kitchen so it doesn't look like I've been working." Baking, decorating, packing, designing —work stuff. "Then I make your lunch and snack, check emails, plan supper, work a little more, or if it was a day like today, work a lot more..."

"Will there be a lot of days like today?"

"God, I hope not. It'll be hard at the holidays. Right before Halloween, then all of November and the first part of December is busy to death. But if I keep having days like today, I'll have to hang it up." He laughed, but it wasn't funny. "Today was a stone-cold bitch."

"I haven't been very sensitive to that fact yet, I guess. I'm sorry you had a shit day." Cyr kissed his fingers, his forehead, combed fingers through his hair.

"Thank you, Sir. I am too." He let himself lean down on Cyr's shoulder. "I swear, I wasn't being ugly. And no one's ever said I couldn't speak my mind no matter where I am."

In fact, Cyrus said he could say whatever he needed.

"You definitely did today." Cyr snorted. "You haven't though. That's part of it. My context for you is—different. You were a mess when I met you, you were a mess until recently. Stressed, tired, not eating, not sleeping...capable, sure. Independent only in the sense that you seemed forced to be. So, this is kind of a new side of you. You said you were thinking of me; I believe that. I never said going out was a bad idea, or that I would have said no, just that you'd gone without my permission. I think we should clarify and separate your career from your responsibility to me."

A career. Him. That was funny. He made cookies for money. Still. "We need to do something, because I can't talk to you when you're working. It's setting me up for failure and that sucks." He leaned back and looked at Cyrus. "Do you still like me? Not love me, but if I'm all different, do you still *like* me?"

Those dark eyes held his, like Cyr was making sure he saw right inside. "I do. I might even like you better. How could I not be proud of the way you're standing up for yourself? It's wonderful to know that you will when you need to."

"I'll take my lumps when I fuck up, but I didn't fuck up on purpose." Dex rolled his eyes and sighed, the relief of Cyr's words just a little crushing. He hated being at odds. "And I'm a little crunchy."

"You had a bad day. It's allowed. I hope you understand where I'm coming from too."

"I'm trying to. I feel like I'm breaking rules I don't know." He settled back in again, and God, his head hurt. "You know how bad fucking days just build and build? I was fighting hard to stop the cycle before you got off work."

"I'm sure all of this was very helpful." Cyr rolled his eyes. "What do you need from me right now?"

"I just want to sit for a second and not have anything bad happen, you know?" He was going to have to go take a handful of Tylenol.

"Nothing bad is going to happen. Every time we have a talk like this, things get better. We know more about each other, things are more clear. We're dealing with details now not the big picture. These kinds of issues—when someone means well but it doesn't work for the other person—are actually good. You really can't fault a mistake made with love."

Now they were making up. Better.

He would just sit here a minute and close his eyes and breathe.

32

The longer Cyrus lived with Dex, the more he was convinced that everything happened for a reason.

In a perfect world, yes, he did want complete obedience. Not blind, definitely not that, but complete. But complete obedience one hundred percent of the time required that he be responsible and available one hundred percent of the time, and he wasn't.

He just wasn't.

Moreover, Dex had a business, and clients who were counting on him, and Cy didn't actually want to interfere with that, even if he could.

So something had to give, and he thought, now that they'd had a good night's sleep and a rather routine day under their belt, he was ready to make Dex what he thought was a fair proposal.

As soon as he'd finished his shower he headed for the kitchen looking for his boy.

Dex was sitting with a sketch pad on the kitchen counter, a deep frown on his face. There were a perfect trio of oatmeal sandwich cookies waiting for him.

"Mmm. Yummy." He picked up a cookie, hooked an arm around his boy and kissed Dex's neck. "I bet the cookies are good too."

"Hey, love. How was work?" Dex leaned into him. His boy's sketchbook was covered in drawings—monsters and pumpkins and dragons and paddles and floggers and him.

"It was an easy day. Karen is a sweet girl. How about you?" He traced a drawing of a flogger with his finger. "Busy?"

"Not bad. I've been hunting new designs for Halloween and stuff. I'm better at cookies, but the designs need to be drawn so I can make the cutters."

"You make your own cutters?" He took a bite of his cookie and hummed. "Oh. Mmm. Cookiegasm."

"Yep. Somebody has to do it. Might as well be me." Dex beamed at him. "Good, huh? Oatmeal with cinnamon buttercream."

"So good. Wow." He tapped the notebook and grinned. "Are you going to make a cookie cutter of me?"

Dex went bright pink. "No. I was just thinking about you. Figured I'd put you down here so I could draw dragons."

"I love this dragon. And that odd little monster is adorable." He reached for another cookie. "I think I need a glass of milk."

"Okay. Two seconds." Dex eased himself off the counter and grabbed a glass and poured him some milk. He left the sketchbook on the counter, and Cy flipped a few pages. His boy had a whole series of tools and toys sketched out—everything from ball gags to St. Andrews crosses.

"Huh. Most ball gags I've seen aren't edible," he teased and flipped another page.

"I'm just playing around for an order for Milo." Dex blushed even darker. "These are just tests. Doodles."

"You're a decent artist, Mr. Doodler." He took a sip of his milk. "Are you ready for a break, by any chance?"

"Totally. I try to save my after-work time for you."

"Great. I'd like to continue our talk from yesterday—just for a few minutes." He took Dex's hand. "Come sit with me?"

Dex nodded and followed along, the energy coming off Dex quieter today, less frantic.

He set the milk down next to the last cookie, planning to eat it later, and pulled Dex down with him onto the couch. "I thought a lot about what you said your day was like, and how you have some crazy times of year." He made sure to look at Dex and stay focused on the positive; his boy had had enough bullshit yesterday.

"This business of yours is really quite an operation. You're good at it, you seem to enjoy it. It's important that I acknowledge that it's a priority for you. But my biggest takeaway was what you said about me not being available, and you're right. If I am not at your disposal, I can't expect you to rely on me for everything. You need some autonomy."

Dex nodded and squeezed his fingers. It was so interesting, how Dex spoke so much through those little touches. "It's different than Milo and Les, isn't it?"

"It is, because Milo can expect an answer at any time of day, but you can't interrupt me for hours at a time. Also, though, you have responsibilities of your own that don't have anything to do with me. I have been, and intend to stay, hands off there. So in that sense, you're not available to me when you're working either."

"So what does that mean, practically?" His Dex was trying hard to ask the questions that were important.

"That's what I wanted to talk to you about. If we both

had offices we went to, this would be easy to work out. But we don't. We work and we live here. So this is what I'm proposing. That from nine thirty to maybe four or five, this place is work. You do whatever you need to do, and I'll do the same, and we're just working. Then after that, we're on our time."

He could get his head around that. It was orderly. Purposeful. Meaningful.

"So long as I can make your lunch. It's important to me to make sure you're fed." Dex grinned at him, eyes twinkling. "If I'm still ramped up at four thirty, you'll just have to deal with me."

"I'll take my chances. Four thirty it is." He could look forward to that. Dex's point about lunch was a good one, though, and so sweet of his boy to have taken on his low blood sugar issues that way. "I enjoy eating lunch with you. But, I don't want you to waste your time cleaning up the kitchen like you're not using it anymore. That's your space during the day, as long as I have somewhere to sit, I'm fine."

"Are you sure? I know you told me you liked things neat, and the kitchen can get wild with eighteen colors of royal icing..." Dex climbed right up into his lap. "Thank you for hearing me. Really. Thank you so much."

The appreciation made all the time he'd spent working it out worth it. "You're welcome. I'll always try. I know you do the same. Someday it might be you having to listen."

"I promise. So...do you want to go out and do something fun together? Anything you want. We've never gone to see a movie together, or go to a park, or two-stepped..."

"Yes." He hadn't had any reason to go out until Dex moved in. He went to the bar in the evenings. That's what he did. The only going out he did was to eat, and he and Dex had certainly done their share of that. "I think I told you I used to dance, but I haven't in a long, long time. I don't know the two-step, but I'm sure we could find somewhere in the city that they're doing it."

"It's easy; even I can do it."

Always so self-deprecating, his boy.

"Even you, hm? Even you, Mister Capable of Doing Pretty Much Anything? You think even you could teach me?" He was teasing, and not.

"Maybe. We'd have to learn together. I've never followed, but I bet I can do it with a strong lead."

He hadn't even thought about leading, and Dex's assumption warmed him. Interestingly, he'd assumed Dex would, at least at first. "Well, I'm up for it. Why not? You want to try here first, where we won't be clogging up the flow of traffic?"

"Totally. Let's move the coffee table, Sir." Dex stood up to help, then moved right into Cy's arms and put Cy's right hand on Dex's shoulder. Dex hooked his thumb in Cy's waistband and took his left hand. "This is the position."

"Okay, but...so wait. Who's leading?" He laughed. Something about this felt different.

"You. Here, I'll back off a little." Dex moved the hand at Cy's waist to the crook of his arm. "Better?"

"Not really. I liked closer better." He liked the feel of Dex holding his waistband. He shifted Dex right back where he was and gave his boy a kiss for good measure. "Okay, show me."

"Super simple. Quick quick, slow slow. Start on your left foot." Dex hummed softly, and started, well, topping from below, dance form.

Somehow that felt as right as it did in bed.

"Don't let me crush your toes." He looked down at his feet because he was sure he was going to stomp on Dex's, but he managed not to, mostly. At least barefoot it wouldn't hurt that much. "Quick quick, slow slow…"

"Mmhmm. That's nice." Dex hummed, moving nice and easy.

"You can carry a tune, pet. What are you humming? Whoops." He shouldn't talk and try to be coordinated at the same time.

"I'd hope so. I've been playing and singing backup a long time. I'm not great, but I do okay."

He realized suddenly that Dex hadn't played for him yet and made himself a promise. Dex needed some time to play, and he needed a little time at the bar. He'd make sure to make time for them to share both.

This was fun. He liked listening to Dex hum, he liked being close. Pretty soon he even stopped saying 'quick quick, slow slow' over and over in his head. He firmed up his grip on Dex's shoulder and tried to actually lead. Dex melted into him, and the look on his cowboy's face was blissful, relaxed. Someone loved to dance.

The list he was making of things to find time for was starting to look like maybe he had a life. A life outside work anyway. He could add that to the lengthy list of reasons his boy was good for him.

"Show me how we turn. In a circle, you know? How do I spin you?"

The hand at his waist disappeared and they managed an awkward spin with Dex trying to show him from where he followed.

"Gorgeous." Dex's laughter filled the air. "Try it again?"

"Yeah. I think I can manage that." He was proud of himself getting them back in step, and then he tried it. "The hardest part is just remembering to keep my feet moving."

"You're good though. You're graceful. It's easier in boots." Dex smiled at him, stole a kiss. "This is fun."

"You love this, and I think you like following too. Should we try this at speed? With music?" What was the worst that could happen? They'd trip over each other?

"Let's do it." A few words to Alexa and they were going, Dex helping him the first few steps before they got it settled and the dance began.

At first he didn't talk because he was concentrating—quick quick, slow slow—watching his feet and Dex's and just trying to stay with the beat of the music. Tangling up at this speed would be much more dramatic than Dex's gentle humming pace.

Once his feet got the hang of things, he looked at his boy, watching Dex move with the music, with him. He caught his lover's eyes and smiled, enjoying all of it and not really caring as much if the steps were all right or if he looked like an idiot. He cared more about having fun and taking his boy for a spin.

His pet didn't care. Dex was right here, dancing with him, loving him. Then a slow song came on, and Dex stepped in, bringing them belly to belly.

Dex's lips brushed his ear. "This is called polishing belt buckles."

He laughed and hooked his hand around Dex's back, spreading his fingers wide over his boy's spine. "I think I remember how this one goes." He'd made some very shiny buckles in his time.

"Mmm... Never done this with a man, much less one I love."

Another first. Was he wrong to be smug about this one too? He didn't really care if he was.

"As you are my first and only real love, I can say the

same." This kind of leading he could handle, and he held Dex close, forgetting whatever his feet were doing entirely and just moving with his boy.

Dex hummed softly, lips brushing his jaw, his throat, the hollow of his throat. Seducing him.

"Mm." It took nothing at all for Dex to convince him, just that much was enough. He knew if his boy kept it up, he wasn't going to put the brakes on it. Why the hell would he? But this was his lead.

He reached down, took Dex's hand off his hip and danced his boy under his arm, then pressed their tangled fingers against his boy's chest and pulled them back together, hips swaying against Dex's ass. "One of my better moves."

"Oh. Very nice." Dex moaned softly, moving with him. "I like."

"Oh good." Cyrus got a wicked idea and decided to see if his boy would pick up on it and play along. He pressed his lips behind Dex's ear and whispered, "You must be new in town. I don't think I've seen you in here before."

Dex tilted his head, then he chuckled softly. "Oh, honey, I ain't from here. Not a bit."

Oh, good boy. His cock was happy about it too and he pressed his hips tighter against Dex.

"You've come a long way, haven't you? Are you here alone?"

"I surely could be, for the right man that is." Dex rolled his hips, flirting outrageously. "You think you're the right man?"

"Pretty sure I am." He grazed Dex's nipples with his thumbs. Those little nubs drew up, going hard and tight. "Sensitive."

"Maybe I just caught me a chill."

Cyrus laughed darkly, making sure his breath blew over Dex's ear. "Maybe. Or maybe you like that. Maybe you like this too." He sucked Dex's earlobe in between his teeth and pinched just a little too hard for romance.

Dex arched, that fine tight ass rocking hard into him. "You're awful forward."

That drawl was husky and pronounced, dragging hard along his nerves.

"Gosh, I'm sorry. Should I stop?" Cy slowly pushed a hand down toward Dex's belt line. He loved the way Dex's abs rolled, dancing under his hand.

"Only if you can't handle it, Mister."

He almost laughed. That was a hell of a cue. Cyrus slid his hand over Dex's fly and gripped the bulge there firmly. "I can handle it."

Dex reached up, one hand sliding around the back of his neck, stretching that hard little body out against him. Jesus, that was pretty.

"Don't they teach you about strangers where you're from?" He slid his hands up under Dex's shirt and started walking them toward the bedroom. He made a mental note to have his boy stock every room with protection. Or to get tested. Or both.

The idea of taking his boy with nothing between them, made his balls draw up, and he moved them faster.

"Yessir, but you ain't learned your lesson...yet."

He raised an eyebrow at the confidence in Dex's voice. He loved the surety in it and the husky quality. "Now who's being forward?" He stopped outside the bedroom door.

"That would be me, I reckon." Dex opened the door and pushed it open, bold as brass.

"Uh-huh." He herded Dex inside, closed the door and groaned as he pulled this hot stranger in for a kiss, fingers tangled in Dex's hair. Dex dove into the kiss, pushing him, demanding more from him, kissing him like he was a starving man.

Fuck, yeah. If Dex wanted to drive a little, he could handle that. He let Dex back him against the door, doing his best to keep up with that hungry kiss. Dex pushed one leg in between his, giving him some friction, fanning the fire. Their fingers were twined, clenched, Dex holding on.

He let himself relax and go with it, something Les had said about exploring things together playing back in his mind. He grunted and bucked against Dex's thigh. He wanted to and it fucking felt great. Once that bedroom door was closed, they could be whoever they wanted to be.

"So fucking pretty." Dex bit his bottom lip, tugging nice and slow as that leg kept up the pressure.

"Skin." Cy pushed at Dex's shirt. "Fuck, want you."

"Anything you want." Dex pulled the shirt off, offering him that tight little belly and hard nipples. "I love how you take what you need. How you know how to turn me inside out."

"You make me lose my mind." Cyrus lifted Dex off his feet and hustled them to bed.

"Jesus, you're strong." Dex kissed him behind his ear, tongue dragging along his jaw.

Five days a week with a flogger would do that. He liked that Dex was impressed enough to say something though.

He was focused now, working his clothing off and Dex's, the game he'd been playing almost forgotten except for what it had allowed Dex to do. To be.

Dex moaned, touching and licking every inch of exposed skin. He felt like he was being worshiped, explored, driven a little bit crazy.

He sat back in the pillows and pulled Dex in with him,

taking a hard kiss as his boy straddled his thighs. "This I definitely like," he whispered the words against Dex's lips.

"Mmhmm. This is the best kind of dancing." Dex was right there with him, eyelids heavy, body resting hard against his.

"Let's keep the other in our repertoire too, though." He drew his tongue over a lovely taut nipple.

"Mmhmm... Oh, that's good, love. Sir."

"I like 'Love' too, pet." He moved to the other one, circled and teased it, fingers sliding up his boy's spine.

Dex rippled, humming deep in his chest as he rocked up and back.

He handed Dex a condom and let his boy roll it on, hissing at the touch and the way Dex made it seem so hot and filthy. His boy had quite a little bag of tricks, or just a good imagination. Either way he loved how it was always something new. Dex's ass fit right into his hands and he pulled his boy in close.

"Mmm... Do I got something you want?" Dex took a deep, hard kiss, his boy storming in and taking his lips.

He groaned and rocked under Dex, his need starting to make him wild. "Don't tease, pet," he growled. "Let me have you."

"Everything." Dex grabbed the lube, slicked his fingers, and reached behind him, as he took Cy's mouth again. So mean, not letting Cy watch.

Those kisses though, they made him lightheaded, made him ache, made it hard to focus on anything else. Every time their tongues tangled, all he wanted was more.

He was so focused on the kiss that it was almost a surprise when tight heat surrounded his cock. He gasped, breaking the kiss and his eyes flew open. "Dex!"

Dex chuckled softly, rocking down and taking him deeper. "That's me."

Jesus, Dex was way too coherent if he could still tease.

Cyrus moved one hand to Dex's hip and the other wrapped tightly around his boy's cock.

Dex groaned, ass clenching tight around his prick, stealing his breath. He rolled his hips, eyes on Dex's face, and loosened his grip enough to stroke slowly.

"Tell me how it feels, pet." He couldn't stop the growl in his voice.

"Mmhmm..." That wasn't verbal, but the way Dex rocked between his cock and his hand sure spoke to him.

"Mmm. Good boy." Cyrus could so easily roll them both and have his fill of his boy right now, but he breathed deep and held back. Dex was breathtaking. "So lovely, pet."

"Love..." Dex moaned and moved in the same steady, sure rhythm, taking what he needed from Cy.

"That's right. Love." He kissed Dex between his words, demanding a different energy this time, a slow hunger, a lower flame. "Love watching you."

"Make me blush." Dex held his gaze, blinking slow with their rhythm. And Dex was telling the truth. He flushed a sweet rose.

"It looks good on you, pet. Want to make you come too." He rolled a nipple between his fingers, his other hand still giving Dex all the friction his boy wanted.

Dex's lips parted, and he rocked, moving a little faster, pushing a little harder.

"Fuck, you feel good. So beautiful." It wouldn't be long before Cy's own need was undeniable, he was already struggling to keep control. "So mine."

"Master..." That single honorific spoken with so much need was enough to make him bare his teeth.

"Pet." Cyrus didn't care that his growl sounded animal and he didn't care if he was shameless. He wanted his boy, and he made no secret of it. He shifted both hands to Dex's hips and demanded more.

Dex braced himself on Cy's chest and began to ride, bouncing on his prick, giving him everything.

He leaned hard into the headboard to give them both more leverage and shoved his hips upward, following the building tension and deep and urgent ache in his groin. It was impossible to stay long in that moment just before control slipped through his fingers, when everything felt so right, but he tried all the same until the tether suddenly snapped. "Close. Fuck, pet."

Dex ground hard against him, then his eyes went wide, and his ass clenched. "Love!"

"Love," he answered, feeling it in every nerve. His orgasm was powerful and perfect, and he shuddered with it, pulling his boy into a rough, breathless kiss.

Dex jacked himself hard, two firm strokes, and the feeling of Dex's orgasm around him kept the pleasure going on and on.

"Beautiful. Love you. So good." The words poured out of him between kisses and heavy breaths, and he held on, arms wrapped around his boy.

"Love being with you." Dex stretched and arched on his prick, moaning softly. "Oh fuck that's good."

Cyrus shivered, every nerve in the area firing again. "That's some seriously sweet torture is what that is."

"Sweet works. I love that burn." Dex squeezed him again and again.

"Jesus fuck." Somewhere in the little coherent part of his brain he was thinking he needed to tell Dex to stop, that he was shorting out and he couldn't take any more.

Instead he dropped his forehead against Dex's chest, groaning.

"Mmm…" Dex petted him, the pressure still driving him mad as it eased back.

"Damn, pet." He laughed gently, hands running up his boy's sides. "And it's not even dinner time yet."

"I know. I'll have to make something quick and easy."

He laughed. "I sometimes feel like I should apologize that I'm always so focused on meals."

"I like that I can do something practical and real to make your life better."

It didn't get much more practical than making sure his blood sugar didn't get too low. "You're good to me." He could only hope to be half as thoughtful in their partnership as Dex was.

"I love you." Dex kissed the corner of his lips. "Ten-minute nap?"

Definitely. "Nap. Whether it's ten minutes or an hour." Then maybe he could convince Dex he needed French fries.

"Perfect. Love you." Dex cuddled right in, eyes dropping closed. His boy was learning to nap.

What seemed like victories weren't when it came to Dex, he reminded himself as he tucked his arms around his boy. Suddenly exhausted, his eyes closed too. Mmm. Nap.

Dex had the best ideas.

33

Dex plopped down with his coffee, staring at Milo. "What the hell is up with this cold? It's October!"

It wasn't even seventy goddamn degrees. He was used to eighty-five in the day. Not this sixty-ish. It was unnatural.

"You're joking right? This is warm. Last Halloween I had to wear a winter coat. How the hell are you going to survive February? Hibernate?" Milo grinned at him, sitting cross-legged on the other side of the couch.

"Totally. I'm never going to be naked again. How are you, buddy? Y'all got plans for Halloween?" He cuddled into the sofa. Cyr knew where he was, he had plenty of time to visit, and he loved the coffee here.

"Our Halloween plans are always at the bar. Les has a costume contest and a monster band and spooky drinks and stuff. You guys better be there." Milo broke off a piece of scone and held it out to him. "Bite?"

"Thank you." He took it, nibbled. Oh. Blueberry. Yum. "If that's what Cyr always does, that's what we'll do. I've been making Boo and Eek cookies all week."

"I bet Les would buy some cookies from you for the bar

if you need more work. Like smaller ones, maybe? He's always looking for things to hand out."

"If he needs some, I'll make him some samples, if he'd like." He wasn't sure how many he could make, but he was willing to try.

"I'll let him know. I think it's more about supporting his friends than needing anything. You know how he is." Milo's head tilted. "You look good. Things are going well with you I guess?"

"Yeah, been busy, but it'll be that way 'til right before Christmas." He made the bulk of his pennies over the holidays.

"I'm hella impressed with the cookie business, really." Milo gave him a meaningful look and rested a hand on his knee. "But I meant with Master Cyrus."

"Ah." His cheeks heated and he had to grin—had to. "We've had a couple-three rough spots, but really? It's good."

They'd worked out their leaving the house shit, and they were having a lot of stunning sex. They didn't spend a lot of time in Cyr's office, which he didn't know if that was bad or not, but it was where Cyr *worked*, so why would they spend time there?

"You two have a lot to work out I'm sure..." Milo's eyes twinkled at him. "You think this sub gig is for you?"

"What a question." Did he? He was busy and happy, Cyr seemed about the same, so it stood to reason it was for him. "I'm pretty much just being me and taking care of my man."

"We'll call that a yes, then. For now. Les told me he invited Master Cyrus to the monthly dinner next weekend, so that will probably be enlightening for you too."

"What monthly dinner?" It wasn't on the calendar. He might have to beat Cyr. The calendar was important.

"Oh." Milo looked a little sheepish. "I hope it's okay that

I told you. Les asked like a week ago so I thought...well, whatever, I told you. It's a formal gathering. A dinner party for Doms and subs. We go every month. Cyrus went a few times, but everyone is paired off so if... I mean, alone I guess maybe he felt awkward."

"It's not on the calendar. I'll ask him tonight. He's still learning about things like the calendar." Butthead man.

"I've seen him with his iPad, and he's good with his appointments, but since he only has one a day..." Milo laughed. "How hard can that be?"

"Exactly. My work is way more complicated. Not important, but there's a shit ton of bits to remember."

Milo squinted at him. "Sounds important to me. It's keeping you pretty damn busy."

"It's cookies. No one's life ends because cookies. It's mine, though, and my new spider web pieces are hot this year." He was practical about all this shit.

"If it pays the rent it's important." Milo stuck his tongue out and took a big bite of his scone. "Mm." Milo hummed to get his attention and held a finger up, chewing the scone for what seemed like forever, rolling his eyes and grinning every so often because it was taking so long.

Milo finally swallowed the scone and chased it with a gulp of coffee. "Dry. Wow. Sorry. I keep meaning to ask you what you do when you're not baking cookies? Do you like museums? Have you been to Central Park? You want to try something weird like rock climbing or something? Like, something fun. I want you to meet some people but just sitting here talking gets awkward I think sometimes."

"I haven't gone to do much." He thought that Cyr thought he was delicate or something. Weird, because while he wasn't a rodeo cowboy, he was a guy. He loved to go and do. "I'll try anything once, twice if I like it. Seriously.

You got something you want to try, I'm in." He was good that way.

"All right. Well, I'm dying to try rock climbing. Or maybe an escape room. I'll get back to you." Milo winked at him. "Can't let Master Cyrus keep you all cooped up in that apartment."

"True that. Just let me know when so I can schedule around it." Cyr never fussed when he left anymore. They had worked that shit out. "So do you know what you're going for Halloween as?"

"No, I have no idea. I guess we'll see what Les wants. You?"

Him? All his silly crazy decorations had gone in a garage sale for twenty-five bucks for the lot. He had a string of candy corn lights that he put up in his office, and his T-shirt that said Homicidal Maniac. "I don't know that we're going out. We haven't discussed it one way or the other."

Milo looked at him. "You guys...don't get out much, huh?"

"No. I think...well, he went to the bar and then out to eat. I cook." And they had a lot of pre-supper sex, to be honest. It was a hot sex, nap, late supper, read and snuggle before bed life. Dex was a happy man.

"Les says people miss Master Cyrus around the bar to be honest. They ask for him. But they're all really happy he's happy. What do you cook? It must be pretty amazing." The look on Milo's face made him wonder if his friend was talking about food.

"Whatever Cyrus wants, really. He loves curries, he likes barbecue, steaks, soups, pasta. He really lets me experiment." Dex tilted his head. "I'll let him know that people miss him, if you want."

Somehow he didn't think Cyr was ready to give up a

nice, long blow job or a hard, deep fuck to drink coffee, but he could be wrong.

"Might as well." Milo laughed. "Maybe he can keep his hands off you long enough to show up."

"Maybe." Dex intended to make sure that was a challenging choice. He was loving not having to jack off in the evening. "One day we might slow down, you don't know."

Milo winked at him. "No need to make that a goal. Really you look amazing. I didn't realize you were so hot."

"Ha. You're funny." He was a redneck in need of a haircut. Speaking of… "Do you know a cheap-cheap barbershop?"

Milo made a face. "No. God, no. Master Cyrus deserves better than a sub with a cheap ass haircut. I know a barbershop though."

Good Lord and butter. There was shit to spend good money on—boots, buckles, beer—but a guy's haircut? Fuck that. He was saving for Cyr's Christmas present. "I don't need anything fancy. Just cut it short and be done with it."

"I disapprove for the record. But I do know a place you can get one for fifteen dollars." Milo looked a little like he'd eaten a lemon.

"I'm not like Cyrus, buddy. I don't need time to do my hair. I just wash it and rub it with a towel." He didn't even own a comb until he got here.

"Fine." Milo pulled out his phone and a second later he got a text with a link and a map. "Fifteen is as cheap as it gets in Manhattan. Cyrus is a little weird about his hair." Milo grinned.

"He doesn't give a shit about mine." He winked over, teasing wildly. "You want to cut it for me?"

"You're kidding. I'll send you home looking like

Frankenstein's monster." Milo looked a little horrified and blinked at him. "Wait. You're serious?"

Dex cackled. "You don't want to?"

"No. Master Cyrus might hurt me. I mean...he knows my limits, you know what I mean?"

"Oh now..." He cracked up, Milo just tickling the hell out of him. "He'd never even notice."

"Dex! That man notices everything. I would pay for your haircut before I took scissors to Master Cyrus's boy." Milo laughed as well. "He's fucking scary."

His Cyr? No. Not even a little. He could be a little intense when he needed a cookie, but he was basically a sweetheart.

"He is. Of course, I paid him to be fucking scary so..." Milo shook his head. "Whoa."

Dex chuckled softly. "Man, he obviously has your number. He's a good guy, balls to bones."

"He is. He's a good friend, and I can see he's good to you. I'm glad he has you." Milo squeezed his knee. "He needed somebody."

"Well, he got me. Poor little guy." He winked at Milo, because honestly, it was so easy to tease him.

"You're funny. Poor little—Oh." Milo glanced at his phone. "Time to go home. Master needs me."

"If you change your mind about the haircut, holler. It was good to see you, man. Seriously."

"I am not—not ever—cutting your hair." Milo laughed and gave him a tight hug. "I'm going to call you. We're going to have an adventure, and you're going to make some friends."

"Have a good evening, buddy." He hugged Milo right back, and then went to order two lattes to go. His Cyr would like this with his cookies.

"Hey, you're Dex, right?"

Dex turned to find one of Cyr's clients standing behind him. Short guy, big muscles, military-style haircut. They hadn't been introduced that he could recall, but obviously the guy knew his name.

"Yes, sir." He offered the guy a hand and a smile. "Pleased."

The guy took his hand and shook. "I'm Joseph."

Joseph. Had Cyr mentioned Joseph? He never got any details but sometimes Cyr would make a general comment in talking about the day or mention who he was seeing in the morning.

"You moved in I guess? Or are you just using his kitchen to bake?" Joseph shrugged.

"It would be a little awkward to just haul my ass up and down just to bake, huh?" He snorted, the thought tickling him. "No, I am most definitely moved in."

"Cool, cool." Joseph nodded. Speaking of awkward. "Mr. Hughes says you make a mean sandwich."

Mr. Hughes. Oh, that was dear. "Yeah. Do y'all get to eat ever? Is that a thing?"

Because that seemed like a long damn day. Maybe he ought to talk to Cyr about the care and feeding of his clients.

Joseph's head tilted like that was a weird question. "I bring snacks, but honestly, I don't usually want food. I mean…in that state of mind. You know what I—I mean, I assume you…uh. You two are…aren't you?"

"Honey, look at me. I'm a walking skeleton. I live on coffee and the calories I absorb from frosting." He had to grin though. "And we totally are. He's mine, all the way."

"You mean you're his." Joseph winked at him. "Don't worry. I won't tell on you."

"Nothing to tell, but I appreciate the thought." Cyrus was

his—his to care for, his to love, his to worry about. Cyrus was on his mind a lot.

His phone buzzed, and he grabbed it.

CYRUS

still with M?

DEX

No sir. In line to bring you fancy coffee. See you in 8-10. Love you

CYRUS

You're good to me pet. Love you back.

"Well you want to represent him well, I mean. You want to make sure people know you know your place. That you're his. That he's your...you know." Joseph leaned closer and whispered. "Master."

"He is." Dex grinned at Joseph. Cyr was his Master, and he was fixin' to go home and get laid and have their afternoon nap. Fuck he was lucky. "Pretty fucking cool, isn't it? What are you having? I'll buy your coffee. I'm ordering next."

"Oh. I'm just having a tea." Joseph looked a little uncertain. "I've got it. Thank you though."

"You sure, man?" He got a nod, and Dex ordered him a hazelnut latte and Cyr a caramel mocha. That would go well with the cookies.

"Yep. Have a good night." Joseph ordered the tea, gave him a wave and headed farther back into the shop.

He waited for his coffees, chatting with Libby as she worked. He was ready to head home and see his man.

As she put them up, he texted that he was heading home and then he was off, coffees in hand.

34

You are one spoiled son of a gun, Cyrus told himself as Dex dressed him. Not only did they have a weekday routine, but now they had a Saturday one as well that included pulling out the leather and letting his boy smooth it on.

There were worse ways to spend a Saturday, but he didn't think there were any better.

So far, his boy had done very well during their Saturday scenes. He'd been pushing a little, but not much. Not as much as he thought he should. Not even as much as he wanted to. So, today was going to be a tough day. And, hopefully, in the end, a good one.

He was fairly sure now, at least, that Dex would have a conversation with him before taking the truck and disappearing. Baby steps.

He laughed at that last thought. Dex wasn't going anywhere.

"Careful with the top buckle on the boots, pet. I don't like them too tight."

Dex frowned up at him. “This is the regular hole. Are you swollen?”

Dex ran his hands up along Cy’s leg, exploring.

“What?” He looked down. “Insolent boy, just put them on.” Swollen. Ha. Although, maybe he’d had too many damn cookies?

“Not even, Sir. Loving boy worrying about your leg. You didn’t fuss about the other boot...” Dex futzed and then smoothed out the leather. “Oh. There. Better?”

Dex was very good at that. Contradicting him with some loving comment that made the whole thing seem excusable. It left him completely without recourse. The imp. “Yes, much. What did you do?”

“There was a weird little fold. Just this bubble. The leather’s getting older. I’ll have a closer look tomorrow and see if we need a boot doctor.” Dex kissed his thigh, nuzzled his cock. “Don’t worry, Master. I won’t let your favorite boots let you down.”

“Thank you, pet. I do love these.” He also appreciated that Dex understood the importance of his boots. “Now. What would you like to wear, if I were to let you choose?”

“Anything at all, Sir? I’d wear my soft gray pants. I like how they feel.” The loose-knit pants had been a gift from Cy when the weather got cooler, and his boy loved them, lived in them.

“All right. Pull them on, then.” Oh, he felt good. Dex had made him waffles with berries and bacon for breakfast, and the coffee had been strong and hot. It was dreary outside, drizzling icy rain, but they were going to be warm all day.

“Yeah?” Oh that was a warm, lovely smile. “Thank you, Sir.”

Dex stood and slipped them on, and Cy had to admit, they looked amazing.

"We're going to my playroom. Bring your key." The key wasn't to his office. Cy had asked Dex to stock the room with the fun things they'd been missing—protection, lube, toys—and Dex had a special cabinet now that was only opened when his boy was in the room. It otherwise had a lock on it, and Dex kept the key. While it might help Dex breathe a little easier, the lock wasn't about trust. Cyrus wanted the lock so that they both had a physical reminder that the room was different when Dex was in it.

"Yes, Sir." Dex kept the key on a little chain that he hung on one of the hooks in the bed frame, and he grabbed it and swung it on one finger.

He opened the door and let his boy go in first, then took the key from Dex and hung it on the cabinet for later. "Pull the curtain over the mirror open, please." He didn't supervise, he went to his armoire and pondered the cuffs he wanted to use today.

He heard the soft little, barely there sigh, but Dex didn't hesitate or complain.

Before the hour was out, he expected—he hoped—Dex would be doing more than just sighing at him.

He went with a thick cuff but a lighter chain, the point being to remember the cuffs were there but not put a lot of strain on his boy's arms. Knowing Dex, this could be a long morning.

"Very good. Now please come to me." He took the cuffs with him and stood in front of the mirror.

Dex came right to him, eyes roaming over him, drinking him in. The gaze was almost physical, and it warmed him up from the core. His boy definitely liked him in leather. That was a plus.

Cyrus took his boy by the shoulders, settling them both in front of the mirror, Dex in front, while he stood just behind. After a breath he started putting on the boy's cuffs. The short chain would hold Dex's arms behind his boy's back. "Your words, please."

"Angel and demon, Sir." Dex stayed loose, trusting in his hands.

"Thank you, pet. Angel and demon." He finished with the cuffs and let Dex's hands settle. "I want these to be as comfortable as possible for you. You should feel the cuffs but not the weight of the chain so much. Are they okay?"

Dex rolled his shoulders and nodded. "You don't usually put them behind."

"I haven't yet with you, no. But you know I think about our time on Saturdays. There's a purpose for it." He took a breath and slid his hands over his boy's arms. "Look in the mirror, pet. At yourself. Not me, not the bondage table behind us. Right into your own eyes."

Dex wrinkled his nose. "You're obsessed with this damn mirror. You know that right, Sir?"

Ah. He had no doubt he'd made the right choice for the day. He took hold of the chain, moved Dex's hands slightly and gave his boy's ass a solid swat. "Language, pet. I don't require your opinion. Do as I ask."

Dex glanced at himself, but it didn't last a second before those eyes were moving, lighting on his own gaze for a heartbeat before shifting away, over and over.

He repeated his order, and not gently. "Look into your own eyes, pet."

"I am! I'm trying." Dex was just beginning to sound frustrated.

That was quick.

He didn't offer his boy any help yet. "Try harder."

Dex rolled his eyes and managed a few seconds. Then

he managed a few seconds longer. His boy was trying. He wasn't doing it, but he was trying.

"Good, pet." He made sure to keep contact, fingers touching Dex's shoulders and arms, standing close enough warmth was building between them. "But you can look into my eyes for much longer than that."

"There's something to *see* there, love."

"Pet—"

Cyrus was so stunned by those words he couldn't breathe for a second. He knew Dex lacked self-esteem, but he was stunned to hear it put that way.

As if it were a cold fact that the boy felt there was nothing worth looking at in himself.

He kept hold of Dex's shoulders and thought about what to say because it mattered, maybe even more than he'd realized.

"Surely I'm not that much of a fool to see something where there's nothing to see."

"You love me. You have to see something I can't, right?" Dex looked at him in the mirror. "It would be super creepy otherwise."

The deflection was adorable, but he wasn't going to play along. "What do you see?"

"Just me." Dex searched Cy's eyes like he was trying to suss out what Cy wanted to hear.

"What does that mean? Stop looking at me. Look into your own eyes, please, and tell me what you see." His tone was stern. He needed Dex to understand he was serious, and he wanted a real answer.

"Nothing. Eyes. They're just muddy old eyes. They're for looking out, not in."

"Hm." He took a step forward, forcing Dex that much closer to the mirror. "If that's all you see, who is Dex, then?"

"I've told you. I'm just a redneck. There's a million of us walking around causing trouble. What is it you *want*, Sir?"

"I don't know, but I haven't heard it yet. Whatever it is you don't want to say. Whatever it is you don't want to see." He could direct this more and he would if he had to, but he was hoping for more of a jumping-off point.

He walked away, leaving Dex there on his own in the mirror as he headed for his armoire again.

Dex stayed put, but his boy's frown was deepening, moving from lips to eyebrows.

"Why are you asking me what I want you to say? I want to know what's in your mind." He left Dex there alone and took his time choosing the right distraction for his boy. He finally settled on a pair of weighted alligator clips that had a menacing look but could be adjusted to his liking.

"Because you're looking for something, and I want to give it to you, but I don't understand what it is. I hate when I'm too fucking dumb to get it."

"You're being awfully hard on yourself, pet." He made his way back to his boy. "This is work. If it was easy, I wouldn't call it that. I'm asking for a little soul searching. I want to know why you can't look at yourself in a mirror for more than a few seconds. I want to know who you see."

"I've seen me every day of my life. I'm boring. Everyone is more interesting. I know about me. I see a guy—skinny, simple, pretty fucking happy."

"Okay. So why is that hard to look at?" He placed one of the clips in Dex's fingers and let the boy play with it while he unscrewed the clamp on the other one.

"Isn't it wrong to be all into yourself? Pride and narcissism and all that?"

"That's different than self-examination. Figuring out what makes you tick. Understanding why you are who you are." Cyrus stepped between Dex and the mirror, set the clamp against Dex's skin and rolled a pretty little nipple in his fingers. "You may look in my eyes for now, pet."

Dex stared up into him. "I'm trying to do this right, Master. I promise. I'm not being an asshole."

"I never accused you of any such thing. I know you're trying, and I'm sorry it's frustrating for you. I just have to figure out how to help." Cyrus gave the little nub in his fingers a tug. "I will, have faith. Would you like me to tell you what I see right now?"

"I do have faith in you." Dex's breath slowed, the boy's focus on his nipple now. "I don't know. Yes? I do. I think."

He smiled at that. "I'll take that as a yes. I see..." He looked into his boy's eyes. He knew what he saw, and to an extent Dex was right, it wasn't that complicated. "I see a man that would do anything for me if I needed it and he was able."

And would probably try even he knew he wasn't. That was essentially the definition of a loyal sub, wasn't it?

"I see loyalty and a heart of gold and my love."

Dex blushed dark, beamed, and pushed right into him. "Thank you. I'll take that. That's what I want to be. A good man. Your good man."

He put his arms around Dex, which was kind of adorable considering that his boy wasn't able to hug him back at the moment. "You're a good man, the best, pet. Whatever else you feel or think, believe that. I do. Deeply."

As usual with Dex he'd already had to take his plan and toss it. Or re-engineer it maybe.

Dex kissed his throat. "You make me proud to be yours, you know?"

"Thank you." He took Dex's chin and lifted it, their long, gentle kiss reminding him how good they could be, and how his job today was to make it better. "I am humbled that you chose me, and proud to be worthy of your service." That might sound stuffy, but it was true anyway. Every word. He didn't know how to be what he needed to be without Dex anymore. He didn't know how he'd ever done it.

"That's what I told your client, and he didn't understand!" Dex's eyes lit up, and the smile he got was brilliant.

"My client?" He tried to remember when Dex and any of his clients would have had time for a conversation.

"Uh... Joseph? Joseph. Nervy little guy, drinks tea? I told him you were mine."

If Dex knew about the tea, then they'd run into each other outside at some point. Which was interesting in itself, because it never occurred to him to prepare Dex for that. Joseph and Dex...wow. He'd have liked to have heard that conversation; his boy wasn't trained the way Joseph was. Joseph was quite formal.

"He wouldn't understand that, no. From a formal sub's standpoint you would be mine, not the other way around. Even when intellectually everyone knows it only works if it's mutual."

"Of course I'm yours, all the way. He was sweet and all, just super nervous. I offered to buy his tea, but he wouldn't let me." Dex was relaxed now, chattering at him.

"Do you know why he was nervous?" Cyrus knew exactly. Joseph wanted to be damn sure to impress Cyrus's sub, especially one that had the chutzpah to use possessive language. "You outrank him."

"Outrank him? We're not competing. He's your job. I'm your love. He can't compete with me."

He gave Dex another squeeze, laughing. "Exactly right. Exactly, perfectly right." Wonderful. He was thrilled that

Dex was confident enough to feel superior. To own that. And it was good that Joseph understood it too.

That just made everything easier.

"Mmm… Your laugh makes me happy." Dex rested against him, heavy and quiet. "I can't touch you very good like this."

"No. And we've gotten distracted from my purpose. It's time to concentrate." As loath as he was to let his boy go, he did, and showed Dex the clamp still in his fingers. "Do you know what this is?"

Dex blinked up at him and nodded. Cy loved that, how the electricity between them could ramp up so fast, and a simple question could start a blaze.

He looked down at a little pink nipple and pinched it, rolled it, watched it stiffen in his fingers. "Pretty."

Dex sucked in a deep breath, pushing that little nip into his fingers. "Will it hurt?"

"Do you want it to?" These had rubber covered tips so it would be about pressure not bite.

Dex pinked, but he didn't look away. "I like what you do, Sir. With your fingers, your mouth."

That was a nonanswer, which he took to mean at least that Dex didn't object. "Well, let's just see how you feel about these. They're weighted, they'll pull and squeeze." He stretched Dex's nip and set the clamp in place, then slowly tightened the prongs down at first so they just barely held, then enough to support the weight, watching his boy as he gave the screw one more twist.

Dex groaned, but he didn't move away. Instead he rocked, moving the clamp with his motions.

That was a lovely little show. "Good boy." Cy reached around and took the other one out of his boy's fingers, prepped Dex's other hard little bud and put the clamp in place the same way, gently and then tightening it down.

He loved the little sounds, the way Dex swayed, the need in his boy's face.

"Lovely, pet." Cyrus admired how the clamps looked on his boy, then stepped around behind Dex again. "I'm still—how did you put it? Obsessed? With this mirror. Have a look."

Dex rippled for him, lean abs going tight as he looked. "They're smaller than they feel."

Hopefully that meant he'd made a good choice. "That's interesting. Are they enough? I can make them tighter if you like." He felt Dex's fingers to make sure they weren't cold.

"I think they're enough? They don't seem like they're going anywhere." Dex wiggled his fingers, playing with him.

He snorted and squeezed his boy's fingers. "Okay then." He kissed Dex's nape and then walked away, out of view of the mirror. "There's every reason to like what you see in that mirror. We just agreed you're a good man. Tell me something else that you see. Something positive."

"Like a physical thing? I have a good chin."

Cyrus laughed. "You do. No, not physical. Like...you're creative."

"Oh. I'm flexible." That sounded sure, confident.

He nodded, not that Dex could see it. Dex couldn't see the naughty grin on his lips either. "In every sense of the word. I do appreciate that about you."

"Listen to you." Dex grinned, eyes searching for him, but it wasn't going to work.

"What else? Look in your own eyes, please. You're... capable. Your turn."

"I'm good at loving."

"You are, pet. You care, you look after me, you give me

everything I need. And you don't ask for much, honestly. You're easy to love." He wondered if Dex meant sex more specifically, but he decided he'd throw that in next. "You're intuitive, you read me so well, you know just how to touch me."

Dex beamed at him, actually turned to look at him. "Thank you. I'm glad I give you what all you need."

He had the sweetest, best boy ever. That smile was everything he wanted for them both.

"Look back in the mirror. Tell me that you're proud of the man you see there."

"I feel silly, talking to myself in a mirror."

That was human nature, he knew, not Dex being evasive. "You talk to yourself all the time. I hear you. You talk about your lists and your work and what's for dinner. You can talk to yourself about this too."

"Okay. I'll try. For you, Master." Dex frowned and glared at himself in the mirror. "I'm proud of me."

"Really?" Cyrus snorted. "I wouldn't want you to look at me like that. Have a little compassion for that man in the mirror."

"He's tough. He can take it."

"Pet." That was his best admonishing tone. "Try again. Say it a few times."

"Can't I be proud to be yours? I am." Dex rolled his shoulders, then gasped, belly going tight as a board. "I forgot."

"You did? I should tighten those up for you then." He stepped between Dex and the mirror again and reached for one of the clamps. "Can't have you forgetting."

Dex gasped, staring up into his eyes. "You make me ache."

He rewarded Dex with a quick kiss. "You're stunning."

He finished tightening each clamp, enough that he could see his boy's toes curl and then he stepped out of the way again. "I'm proud of the man, the sub, in that mirror. You should be too. Try again, pet."

Dex's breath came a little faster, cock half-filled in his soft pants. "I'm proud of me, of your sub. Better?"

"Yes, much." Cyrus forced himself to breathe, his eyes glued to his boy, drinking in what he was seeing more eagerly than he ever drank whiskey. "Now say it for you. Tell yourself. Even more important, listen."

Dex met his own eyes in the mirror. "I am proud. I'm happy to be here and yours and helping you."

He smiled and let that statement fill the next minute of silence before stepping up behind his boy again. "Beautiful. I believe you. Do you believe you?"

"I think I do. I know that I'm proud of how I take care of you. I know that."

He curled his fingers around Dex's biceps and held on. "That's the voice I want you to listen to. The one that keeps trying to tell you that you're stupid, that you're too dumb or simple—you've used all of those words—that voice is lying to you. That's not your voice, that's an echo of other people's words. People who didn't really care about you. But I care. And the voice that cares about me is the real one."

"I like the way you made that sound. The voice that cares about you is the real one."

He was getting better at this, he thought. Saying things in a way that Dex could absorb them, in a way Dex understood. "That voice knows who you are. It knows who you are to me. It's the voice that wants to keep you strong, not keep you down."

"Oh love. That's *you*. That's your voice."

"It is...*also* my voice. When it comes from me." Cyrus shook his head and decided not to push it too much farther or they'd both be hearing voices. He reached around and jostled the clamps gently. "You're not someone that learns by talking things to death, you're a do-er, I know. So, I know this talk frustrated you some, but you did very well. Do you have questions?" Cyrus kept on talking like he wasn't trying to make his boy moan for him. He really didn't expect Dex to come back with anything coherent, but he knew better than to count on that.

"No, Sir. But I love the thought of *our* voice. Like we're better together." Dex pushed up into his touch, begging for more, his boy's voice husky and rough.

"So much better together." When was he going to remember that Dex did much better distracted? If he threw in the blindfold it could be even easier but sometimes it was important to see.

He slipped his fingers into Dex's waistband and pushed his boy's pants off, admiring the view in the mirror as they fell to the ground.

"Yes, Master." Dex leaned back into him, bound hands cupping his cock.

Cyrus hummed and leaned into Dex's fingers. Some might argue he shouldn't give into his boy so willingly, but they weren't in the room right now to know, were they? He always seemed to struggle with what he thought he should allow as Dex's Dominant, and what he did allow, and he wondered why.

Dex's needs were being met. They weren't complicated. All Dex really needed was someone to remind him—granted, often—that he was loved, that he was needed. That he mattered. And he needed some quiet in his mind.

Bondage gave his boy quiet. Clamps and cuffs and paddles too. Next time maybe sensory tools or a short, wide crop.

Right now he was going to enjoy his boy's hands. And mouth.

"You're warm." Dex arched to touch him, and that had those clamps moving, and his boy's fingers jerked.

"So are you." He bent to kiss Dex behind the ear. "I love how you look right now. Do you see how beautiful you are?"

"I feel like I'm fixin' to catch on fire, Sir."

"Mmm." Cyrus bent a little more and reached for Dex's lovely, needy cock. "You look a little like it too."

"A little. I look like I need you." Dex leaned his head back, throat working.

"I hope so." He liked the mirror. He liked the look of his hand around his boy's prick, working it slowly, thumb sliding purposefully through the damp slit. He liked the look of his dark leather against his boy's naked skin. He rocked into Dex's fingers and gave one of the clamps some extra pinch with his other hand, watching Dex's reaction with interest.

Dex's lips parted, and that pretty pink tongue flicked out, wetting them and making them shine.

"I want that pretty mouth on me." His hands moved quickly to the chain holding Dex's wrists in place and removed it, leaving the cuffs. It fell to the floor with a heavy metallic thud. He turned his boy around, caught Dex's chin and drew his thumb across those gorgeous lips. "Kneel for me, pet."

"Yes, Master. My pleasure." Dex sucked his thumb in, pulling on it steadily, and he felt it in the pit of his belly, in his balls.

"Good boy." His words cut through the ache, but his voice was rough and dry. "My boy."

Dex slowly knelt down, still working his thumb, hands hot on his fly.

"Pet."

Torn between tearing his fly open himself and forcing himself to be patient, he did nothing at all but watch, and let Dex do as the boy pleased. His cock pressed stubbornly against his fly, stretching the leather, and Dex's touch was threatening to drive him mad.

Dex let his thumb go and focused on freeing his cock. "I'm trying, Master. I swear."

It took another tug, a pull, and then he felt air for about a heartbeat before the cool was replaced by a blazing heat.

He gasped and rocked on his heels, fingers tangling in his boy's hair for balance, ass clenching as fire spread through every nerve. "Oh, fuck." He groaned, catching sight of himself in that state and his boy kneeling in the mirror.

Dex held his hips, cuffed hands dragging him in deeper, head bobbing over his prick. His boy took him, the suction fierce, wild, undeniable.

Jesus. He wasn't going to last long like this, and he didn't care, it felt so fucking good. He planted his feet and held on, encouraging his boy to push him over.

Dex moaned, the sound vibrating deep inside him, and then his boy rolled his balls, pushing him higher.

"Yes!" Cyrus bucked, shoving deep into Dex's throat, pulled back, then started to thrust, trusting that his boy would let him know if he pushed too hard. That sweet heat made him desperate, made him shake until he was just on the edge, so fucking close. "Pet..."

He looked down into Dex's eyes just as two of Dex's

fingers slid back behind his balls, pushing hard against his prostate from the outside.

He stared into those knowing eyes and his mouth dropped open in a silent roar as he came, hips freezing in place. Everything he knew narrowed down to the boy in front of him, and the burning energy between them. When he finally could suck in a breath, he let it out in a long, satisfied groan.

Dex hummed softly around him, holding him gently, tongue cleaning his cock.

He caught his breath another minute, but he wanted to make his boy fly too. Cyrus stepped back and pulled Dex up and right into his arms, carried his boy, and set Dex down roughly on the bondage table.

Dex was hard as a rock, tip wet and leaking, and he squeaked as he landed on the leather. "Master."

"Pet." Cyrus gave Dex a wink and pushed him flat on the table, stretched him out, hands running possessively over every bit of skin in reach.

Except the boy's cock.

Dex stretched under his touch, soft little sounds filling the air. His boy was flushed and needy, and every time he touched those clamped nipples, Dex reached for him, grabbing his wrists.

"Beautiful boy. I'm going to take these off now, and I'll warn you, it'll hurt for a couple of minutes and ache for longer." He slid his fingers around a clamp and gave it a tug, loving his boy's needy moan. "Not to worry, I'll distract you. I'm going to make you see stars."

He didn't wait for a response. He unscrewed each clamp quickly, set them aside, then wrapped his fingers tightly around Dex's straining erection and gave a couple of fast, hard strokes.

"Fuck!" Dex's legs bent and his boy reached for him, curling up toward him beautifully.

The reaction was exactly what he'd hoped and sent a thrill through him. He quickly replaced his hand with his mouth, determined to draw his boy's climax out hard enough to make Dex scream.

"Master!" It took nothing, a few bobs of his head and a single stroke across Dex's hole, and his boy shot, one hand in his hair.

"Mmm." He swallowed the bitter and salty stuff greedily; it was his like every other party of his boy and listened to Dex suck in air and shiver under his hands.

"Love. God, you make me dizzy." Dex groaned for him, licking his lips. "Thank you."

He kissed his way over his boy's abs and chest, stopping to lap at a nipple on the way. "Thank you, love," he said, as soon as he'd made his way up high enough that he could look into Dex's eyes. "I swear you make me come unhinged."

"I love watching you come. It's my favorite thing."

"You work hard for it. I'm glad it's worth it." He had too many favorite things about his boy to mention. "I love how willing you are—to try new things, to do what I ask, to give me what I want."

Dex hummed for him, leaning up for a kiss. "I—I sure do try."

"No one could ask for more." He took that kiss, tongue slowly exploring, fingers sliding around to support his boy's neck. Dex opened easily, a soft moan slipping into his mouth.

They made out for what seemed like forever, lazy and loving, just enjoying each other, until Cyrus pulled away and caught Dex's half-lidded eyes. "We should have a shower. Or a nap. And lunch."

"Mmm... A shower and lunch out? Maybe a walk together? It'll be cold soon." Dex winked at him. "Or so Milo says."

"It will. It's getting chilly now. Do you even own a sweater? A coat?" He started to remove Dex's cuffs with the same slow, gentle movements he had when he put them on.

"I have a hoodie. I'll get me a coat soon." Dex stretched nice and slow, eyelids heavy. "So Milo said we had plans next week and probably for Halloween?"

"Halloween for sure. Les does a big party at the bar, it's fun." Next week... Les had invited them but he had reservations about that dinner, it was so formal and might make Dex anxious. "We'll shop for a coat while we're out today." And more than just one hoodie.

"I can look. I have some money saved that's not earmarked for something else."

"I'll help. After all I dragged your Texan butt up here to frozen Yankee land." Cyrus set the cuffs aside and offered his boy a hand up. "What did Milo say about next week?"

"That it was formal, and they went every month, and we were maybe supposed to come. He also said that they miss you at the bar." Dex didn't look terribly stressed out, so that was good.

He missed the bar too, oddly. He'd planned to do something about that, and he would.

Cyrus helped Dex off the table and made sure he was steady on his feet, then went and grabbed the boy's pants for him. "We have been invited to a formal gathering, yes. Formal means following a certain set of rules than you and I don't typically follow, so I didn't mention it because I was concerned you'd find it more stressful than fun."

They were all good people and none of them would

judge, but unless there was someone new he didn't know about, the subs all understood what was expected of them.

"Well, are you going to get in trouble if I fuck up?"

There was something wonderful about the fact that Dex's first thought was about his welfare.

"No. And neither would you." Not that he expected Dex to make a mistake that could reasonably classified as a fuck up. "Mistakes are allowed; we're only human. But the other subs are very unlikely to make any."

"Well, you should make sure I know what you need. Milo will help me too, I bet. Oh!" Dex got his pants on and came back to cuddle in as they moved toward the bedroom. "Did I tell you he wants to go rock climbing with me?"

"Really? Rock climbing? Is that something you want to do?" It sounded awful to him. Way too much work. He had a feeling it would sound awful to Les too.

"I don't know. I've never tried." Dex's grin was wicked, teasing. "You want to come? I can ask Milo if it's cool."

He steered Dex through the bedroom door and toward the bathroom. "I'll pass, I think. You and Milo should have some time without Doms over your shoulders anyway."

"Fair enough. So, Halloween." Dex started the water in the shower and pulled out towels, before kneeling to help him with his boots.

"Are you interested in the gathering this week, then? Or would you rather wait for next month?"

"November is hell for me, Master. My whole world is work. Halloween is busy, but once the holidays start?" Dex shook his head. "I'll be grouchy."

Well, that was honest. "We'll wait then, until after the holidays when you have less on your plate." The last thing Dex needed was more stress, his boy was doing so well.

He hadn't even had to ask for assistance with his boots.

"If you're sure. Can we go see the people dressed up for Halloween? Lift, love, and I'll pull." Dex tapped his right heel.

He did as he was told, holding onto the door jamb and lifting one foot. "We'll go to the Halloween party. That's more of a neighborhood thing. And lots of the same people will be there but plain clothes. Like at a munch." Oh. Good idea. "We should host a munch. Hm. I'll talk to Les."

"Do you dress up?" Dex got his boot off and started unbuckling his other one, brushing his partially exposed cock with a kiss on the way.

"Mmm. No. Not usually. I've worn wigs and hats and things, but I wouldn't say I dress up. I'm not that creative, I guess. But I enjoy the party." He watched Dex take such care with him. "Do you like to dress up?"

"I'm usually working down in Austin, so whatever the band wants. Halloween is a good time to get laid." Dex's lips curled. Wicked boy. "Maybe I'll get lucky this year. I have my eyes on this hot bastard."

He grinned and shook his head. "Do you? You know, I've been accused of being the jealous type in the past. I better keep a very close eye on you."

"Promises promises. Lift!" And pop, his boots were off.

"Maybe I'll dress you up. Hmm." He offered his boy a hand up and then worked his pants off. "Batman and Robin?" He didn't even try to keep a straight face.

"Ha! I could be the Joker. He's skinny."

"You're less skinny these days and more...lean." He handed his leather pants to Dex as the bathroom fogged up. "I'll see you in there, yes?"

"Yes, Sir. I need a wash." Dex wandered off to put his pants away and to strip off.

Cyrus stepped into the shower and sighed as he stood

under the hot water, feeling one hundred percent fabulous. It seemed impossible that things kept getting better for the two of them, but this had been another perfect Saturday morning. He felt more like himself than ever, more like a Dom than ever, and more in love than he'd ever been before.

35

Dexter had managed not to kill anyone all day. He'd left Cyr his lunch and snack, but he was busy organizing orders and making sure he could do what all he was supposed to and finishing up two orders which had to be mailed out. He still needed to plan Thanksgiving and get Master Les designs for the bar's Christmas party, and if Milo called one more time, Dex was going to kill him.

He may just hand Cyr a peanut butter sandwich and a Coke for supper.

It didn't help that it was cold and gray and every time he needed to run out for something he froze his nuts off. He was trying to love New York but the weather could be downright hostile.

Cyr wandered into the kitchen fifteen minutes early, freshly showered and hungry as always, but thankfully didn't say a word. His lover picked up the plate off the counter, made a mug of hot tea and took a seat at the kitchen table, all without a word, and without getting in his way.

That would have been fine except that he could feel

Cyr's eyes on him, watching him, and he could almost hear Cyr thinking something. The man was always thinking something.

His phone rang again, and he declined the call. He didn't need this shit. He didn't even care what whoever it was wanted. He needed to finish this order of purple furry monster cookies.

Shit, his shoulders hurt.

And he was tired.

And he wanted to have like thirty beers.

Or forty.

In a row.

"Why don't you take a break, pet?" Cyr's voice filled the room, there was no escaping it. "Come have some tea with me."

He looked up, stunned that his vision was a little swimmy with tears. "I want to, but I'm stupid busy."

Cyr got up and moved to him, resting a hand on his shoulder. "Ten minutes won't set you too far back, will it?"

"I guess not." He sighed and poured himself a glass. Assuming he got back up again. Man, he needed to toughen up or he wasn't going to survive the Christmas rush. Had he gotten soft, being in love?

Cyr ushered him to a seat. "You've had a busy week. Does this usually stay this way? Get worse?"

"It'll be—" He shook his head. *It's going to get lots worse. I'm already busier than I've ever been with preorders.* "It's just been a crazy day, you know?"

He watched Cyr take a slow, thoughtful sip of tea, those dark eyes looking him over. "You seem exhausted."

He *was* getting soft. "Do I? I'm missing our naps, I guess."

How had he gotten lazy?

"We'll keep it low-key tomorrow so you can rest."

Tomorrow. Was tomorrow Saturday? Already? Did he have time for a day off?

"Tomorrow's just Friday." Please say tomorrow's just Friday.

Cyr smiled at him. "Did you lose a day somewhere, pet?"

"Yeah. I thought for sure... Jesus." He would work through the night tonight, catch up. He found a grin for Cyr. "How do you feel about peanut butter sandwiches?"

Cyr reached over and took his hand. "I'll order Thai. What can I do to help?"

"I used to do this. No problem. I used to just do it." And it had been busy, but easy.

"You didn't used to have me to take care of too, pet." Cyr stroked that back of his hand with a thumb. "I guess I'm a full-time job."

"No. No, you're my joy. I just need to work harder." He didn't want to lose Cyr because he was lazy. No way.

"I think you're working hard enough. There's no reason to be under this much stress. I support you, you know that, if this is too much you need to say so."

"I'm not lazy. I just—" God. God. He stood up, frustrated and shaky and embarrassed and mad. "I'll catch up. I will."

"What? Dex, I never said you were lazy." Dark eyes were all over him and Cyr looked about ready to jump.

"No. I feel—Just—Fuck!" He needed to calm down. He turned on his heel and headed for the bathroom. He could beat his head against the wall and then chill the fuck out.

"Dex." He could hear Cyr's long stride behind him, steady and sure. "Stop."

"I'm sorry. I need to—" He stopped, fighting to breathe. He couldn't see, he was so frustrated.

Cyr grabbed his shoulder and spun him, then got a tight

hold on both of his wrists. "Look at me and breathe. I'm your Master, and I've got you. Just look at me and breathe." Cyr wasn't mad, there was no sign of that at all. The look on his Master's face was calm, but serious. "Breathe, pet."

"I'm sorry! I don't know what's wrong with me!" He sucked in a deep breath, then another one.

"I think you're panicking, pet. It's all right. I've got you." Cyr led him a few more feet down the hall and pulled him into the playroom. The next thing he knew he was sitting on the leather-covered table. Cyr had just lifted him right off his feet. "It's not a rational thing, pet. You just have to breathe and ride it out. Keep your eyes on me, keep listening to my voice."

Cyr moved to the armoire and came back quickly with familiar cuffs and the short, heavy chain.

"You just worked. You just got out of here." He was fixin' to scream.

"I'm not working now. I'm yours now." The cuffs went on fast, much faster than usual. The chain went on next and hung heavily, pulling on his wrists. "You're mine."

"I don't want you to be ashamed of me. I have to get to work and fix this."

"Not tonight." Cyr actually sounded serious.

"I have to." Not tonight? He didn't—Could Cyr just say that?

"You don't." Cyr reached up and pulled a carabiner on a thick rope down, attached it to his chain, then hauled his arms up above his head, tying them off tight. "You're not going back to work tonight."

"Can you just say that?" He pulled on the chains, and they held. "I didn't feed you! I can't—I—"

What the fuck was going on?

"Can't I? I'm your Master, and I just did. If you don't want me to take care of you, you know the way out of this." Hot hands slid up under his shirt and Cyr kissed him, tongue pushing into his mouth.

He opened up for a second, then he pulled back. He could stop it. Was he selfish if he didn't? He needed Cyr to help him. "I can't think!"

"You don't have to." Cyr tugged his sweatpants over his hips, working them over his backside and off. "Why think? I've got you. You're fine. Everything is fine." Cyr tapped his hip. "Up on your knees."

"I'm not fine!" He was naked, not fine. Naked, aggravated, and mad. Naked, aggravated, mad, and on his knees.

"Good boy." The tether holding his hands was switched to the far end of the table, then Cyr tapped the leather. "Pray for me. I want that ass high."

He blinked. He didn't want to be an asshole. He didn't want to be bad or lazy or selfish. He didn't want to be someone that was using Cyr. "I—Angel. I need to know this doesn't make you think I'm selfish. Please. I need to know."

Cyr cupped his cheek with one hand. "You need my help, pet. And I need you to need me. Tell me which one of us is selfish. It's either both or neither."

"I need help, Master. Please." No one wanted to help him, but if Cyr did...

"Good boy. Forehead right here." Cyr tapped the table again and helped him settle, then gave his butt a hard smack with one hand.

"Pray for you." He sucked in one deep breath after another, eyes burning with tears.

"That's right, boy. Soul prayer. And breathe." He heard a couple of swooping sounds behind him. "I have a crop. Nasty sting, little burn, won't last long." That was all the warning he got before the crop came down with a loud snap against his skin.

He gasped, and the world stopped for a second, his tension ratcheting up. A line of fire crossed his ass, and one of those tears slipped free.

"You have to breathe, pet. Trust me." Cyr smoothed a hand over his backside making his skin burn just a little longer. "Breathe. I'm going to give you one more stripe. If you want any more after that all you have to do is ask me."

There was a brief pause, a soft swoop, and the crop caught him lower this time, the sound a solid crack on electric air.

He rolled his shoulders forward, his body trying to hide from the burn, from everything. But his forehead and his hands kept him still. "I'm tired."

"You've been working so hard." Cyr's big hands felt hot as they smoothed over his ass again.

"I'm trying. I'm trying to do what I'm supposed to." He rocked back into Cyr's hands, stretching out long.

"You always do your best, pet. No one can ask more of you than that." Cyr drew a line over his hole, finger putting pressure on sensitive skin until it stopped behind his balls.

"It didn't used to feel so hard. I used to be… I don't know," Different? Lonely? Bored?

So fucking bored.

"Things have changed, pet. You have changed." Cyr set the crop in his hands and curled his fingers around it. "For the better, but it affects everything. Your time, your thoughts, your focus. Am I right?"

"Uh-huh. I'm—I just—I'm sorry. I'm trying so hard." He held the crop, and it was so little in his hands.

"Why are you apologizing to me? What are you sorry for? I'm not being obtuse I'm genuinely not sure what you mean." Cyr gave him a couple of barehanded swats, the sounds loud and the skin where the crop had landed tingled sharply.

"Ow! I don't know. Not being good enough. Being overwhelmed. Being a fuckup." Those were all good reasons.

"Ow?" Cyr sounded amused. "Pet. You're inventing issues and problems in your head that don't exist. You have plenty of real stress to deal with, you don't need to make things up too. What have I done to make you feel you're not good enough?"

"Nothing. You're good to me. This isn't about you." He felt himself relax into the bench, his upper body stretching tall. "And yes. Ow."

Cyr chuckled again and those warm hands traveled up his back.

"I didn't think so. In which case, there is no call to apologize to me. There's no call for an apology at all. You are enough. The rest is too much. But that doesn't make you a failure, or lazy, or a fuck up. It means there aren't enough hours in the day for anyone to be expected to get it all done. Anyone. You're not falling short. The demands are too high."

"I don't know what to do. How to fix it. I need to figure it out. Loving you is big." Not hard, but big.

"We, pet." Cyrus kept touching him, everywhere, sometimes lightly, like down his spine, and sometimes those strong fingers would dig into tight muscle. "We need to figure it out. You're not alone, anymore. That's one of the things that has changed. I can help. But I only know you need help if you allow me know. If you ask me."

"That's not fair to you, though, and I know it." Cyr didn't need his help; he couldn't weight the man down with his stupid shit.

Cyr's hands disappeared from his skin as his lover started walking a slow circle around the table. There was a long silence, and when finally he turned his head he could see Cyr's frown and the deep lines of thought above those dark eyebrows.

Cyr stopped pacing and braced both hands on the table next to him. "I have been as honest with you as I know how. When I tell you a Dom needs—that I need to feel needed, do you not believe me? Do you not understand how deep that runs with me? I don't know how else to say it. I don't know how to make you hear me."

"I do! I need you all the time." Dex sobbed once, whispering his biggest fear, his huge worry. "I'm scared that you'll get tired of my shit and tell me to go. I'm so happy here, with you, loving you, being with you, and... I'm scared to drive you away."

Cyr released the strap that tethered his hands to the table and climbed up with him. "That can't happen. I understand, I think, why that worries you, but I love you. Your needs, and everything else about you, the things that make you happy, your frustrations, accomplishments, pride...all of it is part of that. I love *you*. Not the perfect you, all of you."

The longer Cyr spoke, the closer they moved together until he was almost in Cyr's lap. The only thing stopping him was his slightly sore backside. "I spent a lot of time worrying I was going to scare you off too, you know. I worried I'd push you too hard, ask too much. That you'd find me overbearing or scary or too...weird. But I decided I just had to trust you when you said you loved me. It was the best decision I've ever made."

"I love you. I want to be perfect for you, but I'm so fucking tired. And this isn't like with Huck—like at all. And

I can't do like I did with him. Loving you is my world—taking care of things so we can have our time together." He sighed softly. "I need help, Master. I'm tired."

"Thank you, pet. I know you are. So tonight you will rest, and I will give you tomorrow. We'll spend our time together getting you caught up a little. We can make it fun, right? A little music, and you get to tell me what to do." Cyr kissed his forehead and held him. "Even fun work feels like work sometimes. But there's no reason to get to this point again."

"I'm scared for Christmas. I'm full now. Like forty hours a week full, and there are weeks left." Dex leaned hard, breathing for his Master, focused on Cyr's breath. "I love you."

"I know, love. If there's anything that puts me at ease when we're working something out it's that I know that, down deep where it counts." Cyr's fingers started working on the cuffs, removing them slowly, moving deliberately. "If you have forty-plus already, then the simple answer is you need to hire help."

"I don't even know how, but... I guess we can talk about it tomorrow? Together?" He almost didn't want the cuffs gone. With them on, it was easier.

"Tomorrow, yes. We'll figure it out together." Cyr must have sensed something because those sure fingers hesitated. "You like the cuffs."

"I do. A lot. They're like having you holding me."

"This pair is heavy and hot. They will get in your way. But I think I may have something you'll like in my closet in the bedroom." Cyr went back to removing the ones he was wearing.

"I need to feed you. You haven't had your supper." And he needed to clean the kitchen.

"You're good to me. Thank you, pet." Cyrus jumped off

the table, then reached for him to help him down. "You know me well. I'm pretty hungry. Do you need help with the kitchen?"

"You don't need another shower?" He picked up his filthy clothes and took them to the washer. God. He needed to clean the kitchen, make Cyr's supper... "I can make you noodles, if you want. Or a sandwich? Uh..."

"Thai. We're ordering Thai, remember?" Cyr followed him, one hand brushing his shoulder. "We'll order, then hop in the shower while we wait for it and scrub the kitchen out of your hair. We'll clean up after that, together. Okay? We've got this, pet. We've got all night."

"All night." He let himself have that. Believe it. Know it. "Thank you, Master."

"You're welcome. Don't let it get this bad again, please. Come to me if you're overwhelmed. Trust me, if I think it's something you should be handling on your own, I'll let you know." He got a wink and then Cyr headed for the bedroom, whistling. "See you in the shower!"

"Uh-huh." He ordered supper, put his laptop away, and then poured Cyr a new glass of tea, cleaning a little as he went. Every so often he touched the marks on his ass, humming softly.

Then he went to join Cyr in the shower.

36

Cyrus ushered Dex into Les's bar and took the borrowed, too-big overcoat off his boy's shoulders. Well, off Watson's shoulders, which seemed out of character for the fabled Sherlock Holmes but not, apparently, for his rendition of the super-sleuth.

The place was busy, with people in costumes everywhere—drinking, dancing, eating. His usual quiet spot at the bar was anything but, and taken too, with three people crowded in where he would normally have been sitting alone.

He hung up his coat and Dex's on the same hanger and zipped and buttoned them up so they wouldn't fall off or easily go home with someone else by mistake.

"Do you see Les and Milo anywhere?" He didn't need to shout to be heard, but he definitely needed to raise his voice over the crowd.

"Are you serious?" Dex looked at him, one eyebrow lifted. Dex pointed unerringly to the bright pink, glittery, rainbow-haired unicorn complete with glowing horn. Dex had gone over to do Milo's makeup this afternoon but hadn't shared what his friend had dressed up as.

"Oh. How silly of me. Why didn't you tell me he was a unicorn? He looks great." Cy laughed and took Dex's hand, heading for the tall man in the white Elton John suit, hat and big rose-colored glasses.

"Elton!" He called out tapping Les on the shoulder.

"Sherlock. Impressive. Who knew you had cheekbones?"

"Ha. Who knew how tall you looked in white?"

"No, no. That's the platform heels." Les showed them off with a bit of an eyeroll. "Everyone loves it. Blame my boy. You look dashing, Watson."

Dex bowed, the costume weirdly dead on. "It's a decent mustache, if I do say so myself, thank you, sir. I may spend the whole winter bearded and shaggy."

"You shall do no such thing, John." He winked at Dex.

"Ooh. I don't remember Sherlock topping Watson, but I can get behind that idea," Les said.

"You have a unicorn to get behind." Cy laughed. "Speaking of—"

"Dex! You look amazing!" Dex got a cheek kiss from Milo and a big grin. "Elementary!"

"Hey! That's my line." Cy had to admire Milo; he looked damn good in spandex.

"Didn't your boy do an amazing job on my makeup? Did you know he could do this?"

Hardly. But he wasn't as surprised as Milo. Dex was resourceful but also creative and artistic, so he really wouldn't put anything past his boy. "I didn't. Not a lot of call for makeup in my house." He grinned at Milo. "But you know how creative he is."

"Hey, he gave you cheekbones for miles. Are you keeping the mustache, Dex? It makes you look older."

"No." He glanced at Dex, realizing suddenly that maybe this was one of those thing Dex would tell him wasn't his decision. "Uh. Or…we can talk about it."

Great. In front of their friends. That wasn't very Domly of him. But it was kind of a partner thing to say so…

"If Cyr doesn't like it, I'll get rid of it. He is the one that looks at me." Dex didn't sound the least bit worried. "I'll even let him watch me shave it off."

Little tease.

"You have a live one, Sherlock." Les winked.

He liked Dex's independent streak because it meant even more when his boy knelt for him. "I do. I wouldn't want it any other way. Not that he'd let me have it any other way even if I did…"

"Oh, Cyrus. That sounds like love."

Dex slid into his arms, just bold as brass. "I would certainly hope so, Master Les."

Milo leaned on Les. "Hear that, Master Les? More flies with honey."

"Mm. I heard. The boy's more polite than you are tonight." Les gave Milo's ass a good swat, loud enough it turned a few heads.

"Ow." Milo pretended to pout. "Fine. I need a drink. Have a tequila with me, Dex."

"No, thank you. I'll come and cheer while I pick up our coffees, though." No pouting, no hesitation, and that warm smile never faltered.

He leaned over Dex's ear. "Have a drink if you want to, pet. It's really okay. Les isn't drinking either. I'm fine. Have some fun."

"I am, love. With you." Dex kissed the corner of his lips. "Save me a dance?"

He thought about protesting, but really, he knew he

should just shut up and appreciate how lucky he was for all the little ways Dex loved him. Some of them were not so little. "They're all yours. Come back and claim one soon."

"Yes, Sir. It'll be my pleasure." Dex wrapped one arm around Milo's waist. "Come on, buddy. Let's go."

Cyrus watched them go and then turned to Les. "Thank you for lending your boy to help Dex. Poor boy was drowning. He's learned that lesson I think, and we'll plan better from now on."

Les nodded. "Milo says he has a problem turning customers down. Milo spends hours just saying no." Les chuckled softly. "I think he likes that part."

"Naughty boy." He gave Les a sidelong, smug look. "Dex hasn't said no to me yet."

"No?" Les arched an eyebrow. "You haven't pushed him to the edge then."

Then Les stuck his tongue out at him.

"No, not yet. We're still looking for the edge." Granted, he was taking it slowly. But his philosophy was to keep his boy curious and hungry and not too attached to any one thing yet. "He's used safe words, but not...like you'd think."

"He adores you. He's good to Milo. That's what I need. I'm looking forward to having my boy back full-time in January, though."

"Nobody there to make a fresh pot of coffee for you, hm? " He grinned. "You miss him. You'll get him back. We're going to—" He stopped himself right there. It was Dex's business, and he wasn't about to take any credit for it. "*Dex* is going to hire someone for the spring."

"Good for him. He's a talented boy. Lacking a little wickedness, but talented."

"I have no doubt that will come. He's still fairly stressed, and very concerned about making sure I'm taken care of."

Les didn't need to know where Dex excelled at that. The wicked side of his boy could stay between them.

Dex's naughty was offered to him like a precious little gift, and that's exactly what it was. Like that sweet peck his boy just gave him. Something just for him.

"He could turn that business into a full-time thing, you know. He might need to find a place with a real kitchen. An office. And he might have to fess up that he's not Miss Sugarsparkles." That just made Cy laugh.

"Miss Sugarsparkles." They both shook their heads.

"I'm thinking about hosting a munch. For Dex. So he can get to know people just as people, you know? Before I bring him to a formal gathering. At my place. Or even here. What do you think?" Low-key, plain clothes...it just seemed less threatening and maybe Dex could finally make some friends. Milo kept trying but his boy had been so busy.

"Oh, that's a hell of an idea. Have a little one around Christmas. A white elephant gift exchange would be hilarious and low-key. We could do it here, if you'd like. Co-host."

"That sounds perfect. Dex will be very ready for a break and some fun around then. Thank you."

It wasn't like he and Dex weren't going to run into some of their friends here tonight, but this was a neighborhood place, and on a night like this everyone stopped in and then moved on or came in late. It would be hard to have a conversation.

Cyrus pointed toward the band. "I think my Watson is leading your unicorn on the dance floor. Are they trying to make us jealous do you suppose?" It was pretty funny watching Dex try to lead when Milo was so much taller.

"It wouldn't surprise me at all. Is Dex two-stepping?"

He opened his mouth to answer when a man in a

cowboy getup came up and tapped Dex's shoulder, cutting in. Instead of taking Milo, though, he grabbed Dex, hooked one arm around Dex's neck and started dancing him around. Dex's eyes were wide, his pet's smile polite but uncomfortable.

"He...is." The little hairs stood up on the back of his neck. He was as uncomfortable as Dex. Probably more. He didn't like this one bit. "Excuse me, Les, will you?"

Cy didn't wait for a response, he just strode over and waded right onto the dance floor. He caught Dex's eyes and tapped the guy on the shoulder. "Cutting in."

"See ya!" Dex moved right into his arms, his pet relaxing immediately. "Master. Hey."

"That was a very forward cowboy." He grinned at Dex, relaxing as well, hooking his own arm around his boy's the way Dex had taught him. He was so focused on Dex he didn't think about his feet, but they seemed to be moving. Hopefully they were moving correctly.

"Yeah. I wasn't sure what the rules about that were here, but... I only want you leading my dances."

He wasn't ashamed to admit he liked hearing that. He felt his shoulders straighten up and he stood a little taller, proud to be leading. "This is just a neighborhood bar. The rules are the same as in any bar." That didn't make Dex any less his, and it didn't mean he wouldn't growl at anyone else that tried to cut in.

"Well, if I was taken back home, my dances would belong to my man, if he wanted them."

"He wants them. All of them." Cyrus smiled and danced Dex in a little circle, pretty damn proud of himself for not stepping on anyone's toes yet. "I forgot how fun this is, Watson."

"Mmm...you get better every time we dance, Sherlock."

"Thank you, pet. It feels easy tonight. Probably because I'm enjoying showing you off." He caught Milo watching them and gave the sub a wink.

"No one sees me with you here. You're the most beautiful man I've ever seen."

He smiled and stepped back, giving his boy a spin under his arm. "You're wrong there, pet. Most of them know me; you're the one they're watching. They know I've been alone a long time and they want to know the man who's special enough to get his hooks in me."

"The one that loves you best. That's how I got the job." Dex looked happier than Cy remembered every seeing him, dancing under the lights.

"It is." He tucked Dex in tighter and kissed his boy, feet stumbling a little, tangling with Dex's until Dex took him by the hips and got them back in step. His boy didn't even have to break the kiss to do it.

Dex blinked at him. "You keep doing that."

"Keep doing what?" This time when Cyrus kissed his boy he didn't think at all about his feet. All he thought about was how he couldn't remember the last time he kissed anyone on a dance floor. It had been way too long because now it was up there in his top five favorite things ever.

"Making my fantasies come true." Dex kissed him again, sweet and hot and wanton.

He accepted that kiss for a moment but broke it off, not anywhere near ready to take the boy behind a kiss like that home yet. Eventually, but they were here to be social for a while. They'd only just walked in the door. "Isn't that kind of the point of falling in love?"

"I sure as shit hope so." Dex grinned at him. "Oh, the bar doesn't have coffee tonight, so I ordered us Cokes."

That made sense; they only had the one little pot. "Works for me. You ready to take a break?"

"Yes, Sir. Everyone wants to see you, I think."

He smiled and danced them off the floor, then took his boy's hand and headed for the bar. "You know, I have no idea if Les dances."

"No? Milo was willing. If not, you could teach him."

"Maybe. I think I said all my dances are for you. Maybe we can teach them both." He waited while Dex grab their Cokes from the bar, marveling again at how crowded it was. It was good for a party night, but he was glad it wasn't like this all the time.

The cowboy came up to Dex again, stopping him, and this time Dex smiled and shook his head, and he saw Dex say, "Taken."

So taken.

Cyrus hesitated before stepping in, he didn't want to come off as a possessive nutjob unless absolutely necessary. He didn't look away for a second though, watching as the cowboy had an indecisive moment and then finally shrugged and backed away.

He's not going to change his mind, slick.

Dex slid into the booth with him, passing over his Coke. "Lord have mercy, if Mr. Fake Cowboy comes back, can you tell him to fuck off, please, Sir?"

"I would be more than glad to. If he hadn't walked off when he did, I would have let him know in no uncertain terms who you belong to." He took his Coke, not realizing how thirsty he'd been until he took a big sip. "Oh. That hits the spot. Thank you, pet."

"You're more than welcome, Sir. Oh! Look! It's a big light up rainbow..." Dex applauded, so happy.

"How does one dance in that?" He liked to see Dex

relaxed and having fun. Happy should be everyone's goal, and Dex was pure joy tonight. "Other than Fake Cowboy, whose costume is obviously the hottest in the room," he rolled his eyes, laughing. "What's your favorite costume so far? I'm kind of a fan of whatever that furry purple thing is over there. What is that? A...bear? Oh. Maybe a panda?"

"I think he's one of my monster cookies." Dex looked around, grinning wide. "I have to say, I love Milo's outfit. He looks so happy."

"Yes, that's something. He wasn't once upon a time. He and Les were...well, kind of like us. A miracle waiting to happen. He's a sweetheart." The one and only time he'd ever dared play matchmaker and look at them now. Something had just whispered to him.

Sort of like Dex had. His boy had been waiting for him, had been the man he needed.

Needed to keep, needed to take care of, needed in his bed. There was no doubt, looking at the smile on his boy's face, that the feeling was mutual.

"Milo was impressed with how you did his makeup. Where did you learn to do that?"

"I watched how on YouTube. Milo showed me what he wanted, and I watched it."

He shook his head. "You're like a sponge, pet. And you're much more talented than you give yourself credit for. He looks amazing, and you just learned that this afternoon on YouTube? You do know that's...most people can't just do that kind of thing."

Dex waved one hand, dismissive. "I'm just making things."

Just.

If he had a nickel for every time Dex said 'just'...

"Okay. Why the dismissive wave though?" He leaned

forward toward his boy to be heard better. "I mean, why isn't that something important to you?"

"It's nice to be able to do things. I like knowing I can. I'm just a mimic, that's all."

"But you're not. If you can do it, then you can do it. It doesn't matter how you learned it. You still have to have the talent to pull it off." He leaned back again and looked at Dex thoughtfully. "If that's what you tell yourself in your head, then you're going to feel like a fake. You're not allowed to use the word 'just' anymore."

The look on Dex's face was almost comical. "What? Can you do that?"

"I believe I just did." His smile stretched out slowly. "If you need a second opinion, ask Les and Milo."

"You can't just say that." Dex blinked. "See?"

He laughed and crossed his arms over his chest. "I can, I did, and that's one strike over my knee tonight. Say it again. I'm looking forward to it. I have the perfect paddle in mind."

He loved the buzz, the electricity that suddenly filled the air. Dex deserved this too—the knowledge that he was worth this, worth his own self-respect.

He watched his boy, held Dex's hazel eyes with his, perfectly happy to let the dare and the promise of consequences vibrate between them. Turn them both on.

"One strike for each time you say it. If you hit five, they double. I expect you to be on your honor as I'm not always around."

"People can't just stop using a whole world, love. I mean..."

He arched an eyebrow. "Of course they can. You can choose not to swear, not to use racial slurs...you are completely in control of your speech. And that's two."

Dex glared at him. "That's not the same. That's like

saying you can't say...is or the or something. That's just mean. God *damn* it!" Dex held up a finger. "Don't you say anything."

He didn't. But he held up three fingers and waggled them at his boy, feeling as smug as he probably looked.

"You are an evil butthead, and I'm going to dance with Milo." Dex stuck his tongue out at him.

He laughed, absolutely delighted. How much fun was this going to be? "Be my guest, pet. The two of you were lovely together." Milo was probably the only man in the bar Cy wasn't going to get riled up about, and he wasn't ashamed to admit it. "Milo will snitch on you if I ask him, you know."

"Yeah, I know. He's your friend first."

He took Dex's hand and held it tight, shocked by those words. "Oh no, pet. I was joking. First of all, I'd never ask. I said you were on your honor. Even if I did, he wouldn't do it. That's not how this works. Milo trusts you, and you can trust him. He's very much your friend."

Dex chuckled softly and kissed the corner of his mouth. "No stress, Sherlock. This is a party." Dex pulled away and gave him a wicked look and a wink. "*Just* a party."

"Imp. That's four." *So there, Les. He's plenty wicked when he wants to be.* He liked it when his boy wanted to be.

"There you are! You can't hide yourselves away in a booth at a party!" Milo the unicorn leaned against their table, grinning at them. "Honestly. The two of you are just so serious all the time."

"Hush, unicorn boy. Come dance with me. Sherlock's in big trouble." Dex winked at Cy, daring him.

"Is that so? We'll see about that." Wonderful, naughty boy. He slid out of the booth pulled his pipe out of his pocket and waved it in the air. "The game is on, as they say."

"Uh-huh. You just wait." Dex grinned at him and took Milo's hand. "You don't want me borrowing Milo's horn…"

Then Dex took Milo and disappeared into the dance floor.

He snorted. No, no he didn't. He scanned the room for Fake Cowboy but didn't see the guy, so he headed for the bar. He managed to find a spot, and now that he was on his own, people he hadn't seen in a long while started coming up to say hello. Some of them just hung out a minute, some of them wanted a longer conversation. All of them were curious about Dex.

He couldn't blame them; he'd spent a long time getting to know the boy and he was still curious himself.

He never did see the cowboy but after a while with Dex out of his sight he was getting twitchy. He excused himself and slid off his barstool, caught sight of Milo's colorful mane, and headed for the dance floor.

He didn't see his Watson with Milo, so he walked up, a questioning look on his face.

"He got hot. He's outside cooling off."

"Hot?" He gave Milo a pat on the arm and a nod, then headed for the door. It was pretty warm on the dance floor. Hopefully his boy wasn't too tired of dancing, he was hoping for another turn or two.

He opened the door, finding Dex sitting and laughing with the smokers. "Lord, y'all. I'm going to have to eat something and find my man."

"Dexy!"

"Dex, stay!"

Dexy? Really? "Your man found you. It was elementary, really."

"Hey! It's Sherlock!"

He tipped his hat to the zombie pointing at him. "You

better watch those cigarettes, my friend. They'll kill you. Again." He grinned and shook hands with the people he recognized, subs mostly.

Dex bumped shoulders with him as they headed back in. "Hey. I got hot in this sweater and scarf. But you found me!"

"Milo said you got hot. I didn't have the heart to tell him you were already hot." Cyrus hooked an arm around his boy and kissed his temple.

"Well, he *is* a unicorn..." Dex's laugh made him grin.

"A very good looking one at that. Here." He stopped Dex and took the scarf and their hats and his coat and stashed them all by the coat rack. "You want to lose the sweater too? We looked great for a while, didn't we?"

"We're amazing. Do you think it would be nasty if I did? I want to dance more, but damn."

"Oh, no T-shirt under there, huh? Well no worries. Half the guys in here will be losing their costumes before too long. Maybe you'll be the trend-setter." If Les had an issue, Milo would be along with a T-shirt before long.

"I have a tank top, but that's all, and it's tight..." Sweet pet.

"That'll work. Hand over the sweater." Did that sound too eager? Was there such a thing as too eager when it came to his boy?

"Yes, Sir." Oh. Oh, skintight tank was almost sexier than naked, the fabric showing off his boy's amazing belly.

He put the sweater with the rest and went right to Dex, drawn there, Dex's body like a magnet. Cy slid a hand around his boy's middle and crowded Dex toward the dance floor, but the music playing at the moment wasn't exactly something he knew how to two-step to.

"Come on." He pulled Dex over to the DJ and let his boy make a couple of requests.

Dex asked for George Strait, Florida Georgia Line, and Nine Inch Nails?

He laughed and let Dex tug him along. "Are you expecting me to dance to NIN?"

"We can dance to anything, and that's a little bumpy and grindy."

While they waited for their song, he took Dex's hands and put them on his shoulders, then tucked an arm around his boy's waist. "I think I like where you're headed with that."

It was an easy walk home; they could sneak out any time.

"I like you, lover. Don't make me hard now. I'll be all showing in my jeans." Dex stepped right into him.

"Well, gosh. I can't help it if I turn you on, love." He held his boy close and rocked to the beat of a song he didn't know.

"You always turn me on." Dex groaned as the crowd pressed them together.

He felt that groan more than heard it, vibrating in his chest. "I'm trying to figure out what fantasy I'm going to make come true next."

"I have faith in you." Dex reached up and wrapped one hand around his neck.

"That checks a box for me." Cyrus grinned and touched his slightly scratchy chin to Dex's cheek, dancing his boy in the little space they'd made for themselves between Han Solo to his left and...whatever the couple on his right were supposed to be. He wasn't sure he wanted to know.

He did give a wave to Elton John though. That was the first time he'd seen Les since they arrived.

Les nodded to him, and then gave a pointed look to his boy, giving him a thumbs up.

"Les approves of your tank top, pet. I have to say I agree with him. You're looking good."

"I'm way cooler. Now I look like a porn star with my pornstache." Dex laughed up at him, so confident and sensual.

"It's fun kissing you with the pornstache. Oh. Our song." There was no elbow room where they were so he maneuvered them off to the edge of the dance floor. It was cooler for one thing, but mostly he needed room to move.

Dex settled right into the dance, relaxed and eager. He loved being the center of his boy's focus.

By halfway through the song they cleared a little spot on the dance floor, people giving them room and watching. There were even a few couples who joined in.

Who knew there were so many two-steppers in here? He was going to start asking Les for one country night a month. Les could bring in a couple to teach even. Could be pretty popular. And his boy would love it.

This was fun. Dex was as happy as he'd ever seen.

"You guys!" Milo ran up to them as soon as the song ended. "You look so good!"

"Isn't he amazing?" Dex asked Milo. "Amazing and all mine."

"I'm still new at this. Dex makes me look good." He smiled at Dex first and then shared it with Milo. "You and Les should try it. Dex taught me, I'm sure he can teach Les."

"I'll ask." Milo looked Dex up and down. "Seriously, Dex. You look so hot."

"Shut up." Dex went bright red.

"Right?" Cyrus covered Dex's abs with one hand. "Shows off his abs, and he's got great shoulders too." Compliments were good for Dex, no matter how embarrassed the boy was. Dex needed to know people saw more than 'just Dex'.

"Y'all! Hush." Dex went red as a beet, and those abs rippled for him.

"You should own it, Dex!" Milo laughed. "I wouldn't be so shy if I looked like him."

"You're a hot little toothpick too, Milo. Don't you worry about that." That wasn't meant as an insult; he'd always called Milo a toothpick. He was a beanpole. Tall and thin. It had become a pet name. Milo had a totally different appeal —looking delicate despite the height. "He's right, pet. You should own it."

"I'm just... Y'all are something else."

He held up a hand and waved all five fingers at his boy, not hiding his satisfied grin.

Dex stomped one foot. "Butthead. You tricked me."

"I did no such thing." He blinked. Had he?

Milo looked back and forth between them. "Ooh. Code. Sexy."

"You be nice." Dex kissed Cy hard, right there at the edge of the dance floor, and he could feel the excitement and frustration and need in his boy.

He caught Dex's eyes, their green and gold shining in the dance floor light. "Mmm. For now."

The thumping beat of Nine Inch Nail's *Closer* started up, and Dex began rocking against him.

"You guys want me to tell Les you said goodnight?" Milo was grinning like a little evil fiend.

"Thanks. I think we'll stay for one more dance." Cyrus tucked two fingers into the waistband of Dex's jeans and pulled his boy back into the middle of the crowd.

The lights went down and Dex pressed against him, lips near his ear. "Mmm...You...Fantasy next, down."

Anyone who still thought he was that nice guy at the bar was about to learn better. He leaned into Dex, got hold of his boy's perfect ass and made damn sure there wasn't a breath of daylight between their hips as they moved together.

It didn't take a heartbeat for Dex to melt into him, their bodies pressed together, both of them hard as diamonds.

The warmth at his back was the only way he knew there were other people around them, his eyes were only interested in his boy. He let the music complete Dex's skillful seduction, glad for the dim lighting.

"Love. Can we go home? I need you." Dex's breath was hot as hell against his ear.

He nodded, not even trying to yell over the music and led Dex over to collect their costumes and coats. He helped Dex pull the sweater back on and found the overcoat, then pulled on his own coat, which handily hid his hard-on. Jesus, it was going to be a long walk home.

And Dex didn't help. His boy touched and stroked, squeezed and teased and played. Someone was begging to be over his knee.

"Come on." Cyrus took him firmly by the hand and hauled him out of the bar, maybe a little more forcefully than he'd intended, but dammit, the boy had him going. The chilly fall air hit him just hard enough, making him blink and slapping a little sense into him. But only a little; home was still blocks away.

Dex hummed under his breath, groping him whenever they hit a shadow, laughing at little pods of costumed people.

"My paddle is going to love that ass, pet." They stepped under a dark stretch of scaffolding and he steered his boy toward the building, pinning Dex up against one of the supports with a hungry kiss.

Dex wrapped one leg around his hip, hooking him close and dragging them together, grinding against him.

Two blocks. Two goddamn blocks.

Cyrus grunted and forced himself to untangle from Dex. "Home. Now." The order didn't hold much weight; it wasn't a minute before they were making out on the sidewalk again, his boy as incorrigible and irresistible as ever.

Somehow, despite Dex's best efforts, he managed to get them home anyway, but the few seconds it was taking him to key into the apartment felt like an hour.

Dex had one hand in his pants, fingers working his prick. The other hand had snaked up his sweater and was working his nipple.

He took a deep breath and turned the key with shaking fingers, slamming the door behind them once they got inside. He dropped his keys and his coat and got hold of Dex's wrists and wrestled himself free, determined to get control of...this. This thing. This situation.

Fuck, he couldn't think.

"Bedroom. Strip." The order was followed by a low growl that felt like he'd dragged it up from the depths of his soul.

"Fuck yes." Dex tugged up his sweater on his way to the bedroom. By the time, Cy was in the room, Dex was skinning out of his pants, leaving his boy in tank and briefs.

He took a few steps into the room, unbuttoning his shirt. "You have sixty seconds to find a pair of cuffs and a chain you like and bring them to me. Ready? Go."

Dex gaped at him for a second before he headed to Cy's office at a bit of a run.

Okay. Good. He had a minute to think.

He got out of his shirt and kicked off his shoes, then went

to his closet, grinning as he pulled out the round, leather-covered spanking paddle that had been on his mind all night.

He set the paddle on the upholstered bench at the end of the bed and checked his watch.

"I still have fifteen seconds, now." Dex slid to a stop in front of him. "Sir."

"Good boy." The addition of his title was amusing considering, but appropriate. He held his hands out for the cuffs, smiling at his boy. "Next time you'll have thirty seconds. Take your tank off."

"Oh ho! That's so cheating." Dex tossed the tank toward the hamper. "God, you make me want you."

Hearing Dex talk that way would never get old. "I think you know what you do to me, pet." He took a wrist and fastened the cuff on. He approved of the choice, but he wondered why Dex made it. "Heavy, hm?"

"I like these best. I'm going to buy some, just for me, that are special."

"That's a lovely idea." His boy. Always so sweet. He kissed Dex gently. "I will buy them for you. It would be my pleasure. We can go together and get you a pair that fits you better." And maybe a tailored harness while they were at it.

"Thank you, Sir. I'd love that." Dex slid one hand behind him, cupping his ass.

Naughty boy. He reached behind him and moved Dex's hand so he could attach the second cuff. "This should help you keep your hands to yourself." He quickly put the chain in place with practiced fingers, then took a seat on the bench. "Briefs off, then come here."

As much as he'd enjoyed all their wild heat, this was better, watching Dex in cuffs, naked. He was looking forward to what came next.

"Want you. I mentioned that, huh? It was so good, dancing with you." Dex stripped off, and then came right to him.

"I loved every second of it. I mean that." He cupped Dex's ass and looked over the lovely, hard prick. "Mm. Beautiful. All right, pet. This will feel awkward since you've never done it before, so we'll take a second to get you comfortable. Lie over my legs, please."

Next time things got heated and wild, he'd just haul his boy right in here. He almost couldn't wait for that.

Dex frowned at him, curious, but he moved without argument, draping over his lap, hard cock caught between their bodies. "Like this?"

He shifted slightly, tucking Dex in closer giving himself a little something to feel as well, then ran a hand over his boy's bare ass, testing the distance with a love tap. "That's right."

"This is..." Dex groaned, shook his head, but continued before he had to encourage. "It's bizarre, weird, hot as fuck. For you too, huh? You're with me?"

He picked up his paddle and held it where Dex could see it. "So with you. How many strikes did I promise you?" He knew damn well, he wanted to hear Dex say it.

"Ten—double five, but I think I should get a recount or something."

He laughed darkly. "I don't think a recount is necessary. But if you'd like to recount for me each instance before we get started, I'll be happy to listen."

"Like I know. You just sprang it on me!" Dex wriggled on his lap, that pretty cock not flagging.

"Oh! That's twelve. This was brilliant. I should have done it sooner." He shifted the paddle into his right hand

and rubbed it over his boy's still-pale skin. "Twelve is quite a lot."

"You're the one that came up with the doubling thing. You could un-come up with it."

Cheeky. He liked that. "I could. I don't think I will, though. You'll *just* have to mind your mouth, pet." He rolled the paddle in his hand, making sure he had the feel of it. "You'll count for me after each one. *Just* so I don't lose count. Ready?"

"You should take off eight for those." Dex wriggled and stretched, but didn't try to get up. "I'm ready, evil man."

No, I don't think you are.

That was the best part.

"Count. And breathe." He lifted his arm and landed the first right on target, hard enough that the sound filled the room.

He felt Dex's belly go immediately tight, Dex bowing as he tucked his tail end.

"Count for me, pet," he reminded Dex patiently, reaching under his boy while there was some room to find that lovely, hard cock and wrap his fingers around it.

"O-one." Dex moaned at his touch, and Cy could feel how his boy needed, how Dex tilted on another edge of understanding how much they could feel.

"Good boy." Cyrus bit back a moan of his own. Watching his boy discover himself, discover who they could be together was a high like no other. "More, now. Faster."

He rubbed the paddle across Dex's ass again to help his boy focus and then dealt out six strikes in a steady rhythm with just enough time for a breath between, not that he expected Dex to breathe and keep up with counting. Not keeping up was part of the fun.

Dex leaked against his palm, leaving wet, slick kisses on his hand, his thighs.

"What number is that, pet?" He pulled his hand away and smoothed it over his boy's back instead. Cyrus arched a little, finding resistance against Dex's ribs. Five more and then he could have that lovely pink ass. His boy would be ready to give him anything.

"Seven? I think seven. I need you. Please. I need you." Dex tried to thrust against his thighs.

The sound of his boy begging made him burn. Cyrus rested one hand on the back of Dex's neck and readied his paddle one more time, finishing off the twelve strokes fast and hard.

Dex arched, almost going over on the floor. The sound of Dex's chain rattling warned him though, and he made the catch.

He dropped the paddle on the bench next to him and settled Dex on his lap, his priority for the moment to make sure his boy was okay. He took a breath, having learned better than to get anxious about these things. If Dex was fine, it would be a waste of his energy, and even more so if his boy wasn't. He swallowed to clear his dry throat. "I didn't hear a safe word, pet."

"Oh, for fuck's sake." Dex raised his head, twisting to stare at him, eyes blown. "Fuck me. You got me all riled up; you fix it."

Damn. That was a look he'd remember. If Dex was that heated, maybe next time he'd keep paddling until his boy lost it.

"Insolent pup. That's 'fuck me, sir' for future reference," he said with a heavy growl. Cyrus stood up while he still had an arm hooked over his boy's back and half tossed Dex at the bed, then dove after supplies. "I want that ass up where I can see it."

Dex went on hands and knees for a second, then lowered his cheek to the sheets, one hand working his cock.

He watched, stroking his own latex-covered prick slowly, taking in one of the hottest pictures he'd ever seen. He shelved all the things he should do, like reminding the boy who that lovely, aching cock the boy was stroking belonged to.

He moved around behind his boy and settled on his knees behind Dex's red-hot ass. "Pretty. Feel good, pet?"

"I feel like I need to come, like fifty times. My balls ache."

Cyrus nodded, eyes narrowing. "Any time, and as many times as you like." He slicked his fingers and gave his boy two, pleased by how easily they slid deep, and tossed the lube away.

"Mmm..." Dex rolled, driving back on his fingers, fucking himself. "God, I love you."

"That's a good thing for both of us." He touched his other hand gently to his boy's red skin, smiling as Dex hissed. That ring of muscles went from tight to stealing his breath as he imagined that pressure around his cock instead of his fingers.

Right. That was enough fooling around. He yanked his fingers back and lined up, leaning his body weight into his boy as he pushed inside that tight heat. "Jesus. Fuck, pet."

"Master." Dex met his thrust, and touch of that burning ass made him want to scream.

They moved together, hard and heavy, Dex taking as much as Cyrus was giving. The room filled with sound, but there just weren't words; they shared the same need, and his boy was as irresistible as ever.

Dex climbed one of the bedposts, slamming back against him, driving down on his cock. He understood then what Dex meant; Cyrus was burning up from the inside but couldn't get enough. He reached and caught Dex's shoulder with one hand, gripping it tight and driving in hard.

"Yes!" Dex looked like a demon writhing on him, like someone magical and wild and lost in his passion.

He'd never had anyone like Dex, seen anyone so beautiful, had anyone's complete need the way he had his boy's. His groan sounded desperate even to his own ears. He felt as if he were leaning over the edge of a cliff, trying to jump, but was caught in the updraft. Dex had him now and was going to keep him right there as long as the boy needed.

Cyrus pressed closer, giving his boy more of his weight and curled an arm around Dex's hips. He found that hot, hard cock and made a fist around it, and after a couple of strokes he pushed his thumb down into the slit, aiming to send them both to the stars.

"Master!" The scream rocked him, and the visual of Dex, arched back, cuffed hands braced on the bedpost, seed spraying from that sweet, needy cock was enough to drive him out of his mind.

Oh, God.

Really.

He thought maybe he ought to pray because for a breathless, sightless, thoughtless moment it felt like maybe this was his last second on earth.

Dex was so tight around him he had to force the boy to let him move so he could come. When he finally did, the room disappeared, and his ears rang. Despite what felt like an enormous gasp, he could only get the thinnest wisp of air, but he didn't really need to breathe anymore, did he? He just needed to hold Dex this tight forever, love the boy this hard forever.

Dex slumped against him, quiet and still, warm and heavy. "Goddamn."

Cyrus nodded and hugged Dex against him. He didn't have words yet. He was pretty sure they'd be back, and his breath too, assuming he hadn't actually left the earth. Hopefully.

Dex got heavier and heavier, dozing against the bedpost. He may actually have worn his boy out.

That made him grin, but he still needed to get his shit together.

He took a deep breath, pleased to find that he could, and shifted them both down flat. "Good boy. So good, pet. Love you."

He spoke softly but wanted Dex to know they were okay, that he was happy, all those things that his boy worried about. He tucked a pillow under Dex's head and reached over to remove the chain so Dex could stretch and move freely but left the cuffs in place.

"Love." Dex almost—almost—got his eyes open to look at Cy but didn't make it.

Yep. Wore his boy's ass out. Finally. He was smug as hell and the wait had been absolutely worth it.

Cyrus got a good look at Dex's backside and decided with a self-satisfied hum that it was fine, it wasn't anything but well warmed up. Then he slid out of bed just long enough to use the head and get the lights. He was ready for a good long night's sleep with his boy.

37

Dex had slept until late, late enough that Cyr was up and moving, muttering about coffee.

He'd managed to make coffee, feed Cyr, and read every bit of news on earth on his phone without saying a single word.

Dex wasn't scared or mad or anything. He was just... wigged. Worried. Worried about what if he said 'just'? What about the whole thing yesterday?

He didn't want to think about it—about how hot he'd been, about how frustrated.

About how freaking wild. About how he was still in those cuffs.

So, he was just never going to speak ever again.

Cyr was... Cyr. It was a little frustrating, bordering on maddening.

Every so often they'd move past each other and fingers would reach out and drag over his shoulders or tap him on the backside and he'd get a smile or a wink. He'd even caught Cyr looking over and grinning at him a handful of times.

His lover seemed to be in a good mood, had eaten a huge breakfast and was sitting in the living room reading and sipping a third cup of coffee.

Dex cleaned up the kitchen and went to curl up in the recliner, dinking around on his mandolin, doodling with little melodies, and markedly ignoring the world. It was tough, but not as hard as worrying about things like 'dude, you draped yourself over Cyr's lap and let him paddle you, and instead of being pissed, you rode him like a wild thing and passed out'.

"I'd ask you for more coffee, but I don't think you want me around under the influence of four doses of caffeine." He could feel Cyr's eyes on him.

He looked over and grinned, choosing words carefully. "Dork. You want tea?"

"No, thank you. I want you to come sit with me. You're very far away over there in that recliner." Cyr patted the couch.

Uh-huh. Right. Still, he went to Cyr, because he loved the son of a bitch, and he wasn't mad. Confused? Sure. Not mad.

Cyr let him sit and didn't question him when he didn't climb right into those arms. Instead Cyr rested a hand on his leg with a warm smile. "I thought last night was something special."

"Yeah?" Okay, he so wanted in Cyr's arms, and if he wasn't mad, why couldn't he be?

Right?

Right.

Dex scooted over and let himself cuddle in, dammit, and fuck anyone who said otherwise.

"Mmm. That's better. Thank you, pet." Cyr combed

fingers through his hair, one arm snug around his middle. "You must have something big on your mind."

The urge to say 'it's just nothing' was huge, so he just—just, just, *just*—shrugged.

Cyr, as usual, was still and patient. "Don't know where to start?"

"Nope." That was safe. Just nope. God, he amused himself.

"Hm." Cyr nodded. "Are you worried you'll say something that will get you another paddling?"

"You think? You know I will, so no more long talks for you." So there. Ha.

"Probably for the best," Cyr agreed like it was perfectly natural. "We wouldn't want a repeat of last night, would we?"

He huffed out a breath. He didn't know. It hadn't been bad. Shit, who was he kidding? He'd been wild after. Wild. Just wild.

"Uh-huh. I know. You have a safe word you know, and you definitely didn't use it. So if it was that good, what are you actually worried about?"

"I don't know. I j—" He glared at Cyr. See? See, he'd almost done it.

"Okay, okay." Cyr rolled his eyes. "Until you get up off this couch you can say whatever you need to, no penalties. Better? I want to hear what you have to say."

"I don't know what to say. I'm not mad. At all." That seemed the most important, right?

"I appreciate that. I didn't think you were, but it's good to hear you say anyway. Tell me...how you feel."

He sighed and rested his head against Cyr's chest. "Confused. Really fucking confused."

"Thank you, pet. I'm sure that's frustrating. If it helps, I would be concerned if you weren't trying to piece things together today. Last night was a big night. A good one, a great one, but I am still processing some of it too."

"It is. What is it for you? What are you thinking?"

Cyr was quiet long enough it made him feel better about not having easy answers either.

"The success with the paddle was a significant step into a part of the lifestyle we've only just touched on until last night. I wasn't experimenting. I was using it full-out, the way it was intended to be used. I think you were ready. I believe it was satisfying for you, but it was a test of my own willpower and I'm not entirely sure I passed. I'm also not entirely sure I needed to. I get tripped up—in my head—when the Dom and the lover cross over."

"Is—I mean, is this because of your work?" Dex thought so. Milo and Les were like them, and they mixed up sex and D/s all the time, but Cyr was different. He did it all the time.

Oh.

What if it got boring? That would suck.

"I don't know. It's possible. I think it's more because I'm too worried about what I'm supposed to do and should really focus more on what feels right for us. Les likes to remind me that no one is in our bedroom but us. He's right, but you're learning and..." Cyr snorted. "See? I think too much. Last night was fantastic because I didn't let myself overthink anything. I just wanted to get you off."

And he had totally gotten off. All over the bed. And the bedpost. Possibly the wall—he'd wiped it down, just to be sure.

"You may have accomplished that," he muttered. "Just fyi."

Cyr's laugh was open and unashamed. "I was pretty sure. You were inspiring."

"I was desperate. I needed you like breathing." He nuzzled into the curve of Cyr's throat and inhaled deep.

"Oh, I know. You shouted at me to make sure I knew it." Cyr's fingers were moving over his back. "I felt the same way. I couldn't get enough of you. Every time you moved I wanted more."

"I would have given it." This was different than last night —last night was all feeling, but this discussion? It was hot.

"You did. You were everything I wanted. It was wild, and it all felt right." Dex could feel the truth of what Cyrus was saying in the satisfied rumble in his lover's chest.

"Oh. Oh, thank you." That was the best gift—even better than last night. He pushed up and met his Master's eyes. "It was a little scary...no. No, you know what? It so wasn't. It is a little scary this morning. I wasn't scared last night."

Cyr smiled and cupped his cheek. "What scares you this morning, pet?"

"I guess... I mean... Even you weren't sure I'd be turned on." God, it was hard to find the right words. "I didn't like it, but—Don't you know what I mean? I was on fire, and you had to help me."

"The paddle was maybe overstimulating at that point. We were already hot when we walked in the door. But I'd promised, and you'd taunted me..."

"I was on fire, and it was fun, to play with you, push you." His cheeks went white-hot. He'd loved pushing it and having Cyr push back. It had made him feel sexual and powerful—even the paddling. That was the hard part, because it had been an over-the-knee paddling and it had hurt, and he'd stayed stiff as a board.

Cyr looked right at him, dark eyes so knowing. "It was fun. I liked that you took chances, understood the stakes. It turned me on. Kept me buzzing. Made me want you."

"All of it, huh? I felt—" Like Cyr couldn't resist. Like Cyr trusted him to take all he needed to give.

"In control?" The words were softer than he would have expected.

"Well…maybe for most of it. In the end, it was all need." Of course, he'd sure told Cyr what he wanted. "Not that I wouldn't have just climbed you and rode."

"Climbed me like you did the bedpost?" Cyr licked his lips, the look pure mischief.

"Shut up. I just…damn." He cracked up, holding on so he wouldn't fall off.

Cyr caught him around the waist, grinning. "No penalty for that one. And don't tell me to shut up, that was the hottest thing ever."

"I was on fire, Master. I swear to God, if you hadn't helped me come…" He waved his still-cuffed hands. "These would have gone on you."

Cyr barked out a laugh, eyes full of joy. "Not likely!" He got a quick, hard, happy kiss. "There are a lot of things I might let you get away with, but that won't be among them."

"No? I like them." They made him feel grounded, settled deep inside.

"Hey. Why don't we go get you fitted for your own today? I think we could both use some air, and I don't think my head is in the right place for our usual Saturday scene."

"Are you okay? I mean, I'd love to. Really really, but is your heart okay?" Dex knew heads were weird, but hearts needed immediate attention.

"Oh, pet." Cyr kissed him again, a slow one with something deep and real inside it. "My heart is fine. You've got it."

"Yes, Sir. With all my heart." Dex kissed the corner of his

lips, then moved to whisper in Cyr's ear. "Just. Just just just. Just justy just just just."

Cyr chuckled darkly. "Got that out of your system now? The word 'just' really shouldn't be a turn on."

"You shouldn't be able to say it either, you know..." He loved that hint of danger, that promise that Cyr had him.

"Really? You're trying to make the rules now? I'm not the one that keeps saying you're 'just' a mimic, or they're 'just' cookies, and that you're 'just' Dex. You keep making yourself small, and you're not."

"I—You think I'm something special that I'm not, Sir." He was going to shatter if Cyr figured that out.

"No. I know you're something special and you are chronically, stubbornly, irrationally refusing to look at yourself in a different light." Cyr shook his head. "I think you're under the impression that anyone can do some of the things you do simply because they come easily to you, and that's not the case."

"I'm glad you do, you know. Think I'm special." He nuzzled in, searching for their earlier mood.

"I'm sure you are. You must think I'm pretty dumb, huh? Seeing something that you insist isn't there." Cyr kept an arm around him and sounded a little resigned.

"Bah. You're the smartest man I know. I love all the things you teach me." He knew that. "Don't be down. I won't say it, okay?" Hell, he was happy not to talk about himself at all.

"I'm not down. I'm...frustrated. Why do you love me?"

"There are a lot of reasons." Dex settled in again, relaxing. "I love how you care, I love the steadiness inside you. I love how you make me smile. I love how you hear me —like really hear me. I love the way we fit. I could go on and on."

Cyr sighed. "How can I really hear you and still not manage to make you feel good about yourself?"

Oh for fuck's sake. Seriously? Sometimes Cyrus got something in his head and wouldn't let it go. "I feel just fine. You make me happy. Seriously happy."

"Okay. Good." Cyr kissed his temple. "How about some lunch?"

And there went his lover, moods swinging like a pendulum. "Sure. Do you want a sandwich? Tuna? Soup?"

"Um. Turkey and cheese?" Cyr shifted and set him on the couch, then got up to stretch. "And then you should probably get a shower."

"Stinky, am I? Sorry." Okay, good bread and tomatoes, lettuce, cheddar, turkey. Mayo. He'd add fruit salad and chips to the plate.

"Not stinky. You smell like sweat and sex and us, which I happen to like but out in the world...?" Cyr grinned at him.

"Yeah. Strange and not very friendly." He delivered lunch complete with iced tea. "I'm going to have a long hot shower. I'll be back."

Maybe after the shower and lunch Cyr would be settled and happy, for the afternoon.

Cyr took his hand and kissed his palm, the gesture surprisingly intimate. "I love you. Thank you for my lunch."

"You're more than welcome, Sir. I love you more than... anything." He held Cyr's cheek a second. "Eat your lunch, hungry man."

"Yes, sir." Cyr winked at him and picked the sandwich right up.

"Good boy," he shot back before running for the shower, laughing all the way.

38

Cyrus ate his sandwich and decided not to think about the conversation he'd had with his boy this morning at all. Even though there were plenty of good parts. He could just think about last night instead, because damn. That had been as perfect as they'd ever been together and yet somehow had left them both more off-balance this morning than ever too.

Wait. He wasn't supposed to be thinking about this morning.

Dex had been captivating. Mesmerizing. It seemed like his boy was a little self-conscious this morning, though it was hard to be sure how much of that was a stubborn resolution not to say words that would get the boy in trouble, and how much was processing and feeling out how Cyrus felt about things before speaking up.

Whatever it was, it was adorable. He loved that little defiant, stubborn streak.

Of course he didn't love it when it kept Dex from understanding—

Shit.

Not. Going. There.

Oh, who was he kidding. Of course he was going to go there.

Maybe he was too obsessed with this. Maybe it didn't matter what Dex thought of himself as long as the boy was happy. Maybe he needed to let it go.

Except that didn't feel good to him.

Not only had it had gotten to the point that it upset Cyrus to hear Dex continue to say he wasn't anything special, but Cyrus had no idea how to go about talking to Dex about it.

He'd just shut it down because he was afraid to send Dex back into that damn turtle shell. One thing that his boy knew how to do well was please people, and if he pushed too hard Dex might decide to tell him what he wanted to hear instead of the truth.

And then he might not ever know the difference for sure again.

There had to be an answer. There was always an answer, he just couldn't see it right now. But he wasn't going to argue with Dex about self-esteem and self-worth again it until he knew what that answer was.

He looked down at his plate, disappointed that he'd eaten his entire sandwich without really tasting it and realized he must have been thinking for quite some time. He put his plate in the sink and decided he'd better go get dressed.

He was going to get his boy some cuffs.

Dex was out of the shower and...talking?

The bedroom door was open, so was the bathroom door, so he wasn't eavesdropping, right?

"...never thought it could be like this, you know? Wild

and all. I love taking care of him, just knowing that he's happy."

That sounded like the words of a sub. But was his boy on the phone? Who would Dex call? He knew he should probably go in, let Dex know he was listening, but he was intrigued now.

"I miss you some, but I'm better here. No one knows I'm trash, not even Cyr."

Cyrus leaned a hand on the door frame, one twitch away from barging into the bedroom. *Don't.*

Don't. You know better. Don't do it.

Yeah, he knew better. But he didn't give a damn. He was done listening to that voice.

He pushed the bedroom door open, storming into the room. "What is your definition of trash, exactly?"

Dex blinked up at him, dressed in nothing but his jeans. "In this case, it's somebody that grew up nasty, that didn't hardly finish school, whose Daddy killed his Momma before turning the gun on hisself. That's what it's called. Trash. And it ain't nice to listen at the door, you know."

He was taken back by the pronounced drawl, which he hadn't really heard from Dex since that last exhausted day in Texas. "I don't think any of that makes you trash. Trash is about how you treat people. You can be born with a silver spoon in your mouth and grow up in a Norman Rockwell painting and still be trash. You, Dexter Appleton, are not trash. You treat everyone who knows you kindly. You treat me like gold. And you're mine."

"I so am. All yours. That's what I was telling Huck. That I got to start from scratch here. That here I'm not Dex with all the bullshit. I'm just Dex. It's so *good*." Dex came to him. "Did you like your lunch?"

Jesus, he couldn't even stay mad around Dex for more

than five minutes. His boy had a way of taking bad energy and turning it to dust. "I was hungry. I ate it fast." He let the 'just' go, because it meant something different this time. Something better. "Why do you talk to Huck?"

Dex stepped away and shrugged, looking a little uncomfortable. "I just do. I used to talk to him when he was gone. It's no different."

"It is different. You have real people to talk to now. You have Milo, you have me." And more soon. He wanted Dex to have a handful of friends to call on.

"Sometimes I need someone that..." Dex shook his head. "You know what, it doesn't matter. I was just talking to myself. What shirt do you want?"

"Finish that thought, pet." He stopped Dex from moving even farther away, fingers wrapping around his boy's wrist as he stepped in close. "Please."

"I just need someone who knew me before I guess. Huck got me. No one knew me longer."

That actually made sense to him. He knew a little about that. "It's hard to have to let go of everything you know. I get it. I hope Huck is kind to you." He hugged his arms around his boy gently.

Dex chuckled softly. "Oh, I know he probably ain't listening. The fucker never listened before; why would he now?"

That was his Dex. All he could do was laugh back. "You're remarkably well adjusted for a nutjob that talks to himself."

"You know it. You should hear me talk to you when you're at work. It's great."

"Do you use that drawl you did a minute ago? I should have recorded that. Wow." He smiled and dropped a quick kiss on Dex's forehead so the boy would know he was teasing.

"Hush you." Dex wrapped one arm around his neck and kissed him back.

He could kiss his boy all day long, but he wanted to buy Dex a gift. "Mmm. That was nice, love. Thank you."

"Let's go play. Maybe I can get into some trouble with you again."

"Shouldn't be too difficult for you. I'm sure you can think of *just* what to say." He winked. "Blue jeans, and that black T-shirt you like, the tight one."

"Mmhmm. Pretty pretty. I'll have to keep all the boys off you with a broom handle."

"Nah, just the fake cowboys." That was his job. Dex could wave it off, but he saw those eyes when they were dancing, his boy in that tank top. He was furniture. People were watching his dance partner.

"All the boys. You're mine." Dex met his eyes, straight-on. "Just mine."

He lifted one finger, holding his boy's eyes. "Jeans, pet."

Dex grinned at him, so wicked, so naughty, and licked his lips. "Yes, Master."

Oh, he was in so much trouble.

He was standing smack in the middle of a long-held fantasy, and all he could think was, *be careful what you wish for*, and that just made him laugh.

Just.

He let Dex dress him and only had to fight off wandering hands a couple of times. Enough to keep his boy right on the edge of trouble but not quite in it. By the time he was in his boots he was ready to take Dex downtown in cuffs to buy new ones.

"Okay. You're all dressed." Dex patted his cock. "You ready to go play?"

He snorted. "You need a shirt and some shoes, and maybe some handcuffs and a muzzle."

"A muzzle? Listen to you. A muzzle." He got a thunderous frown.

God, that was adorable.

"Oh. I don't like that look at all." He kissed his boy, then pulled back and studied Dex's face. "Nope, it's still there." He kissed Dex again, with intent, and when he pulled back this time, his boy's eyes were unfocused, heavy-lidded, and the picture of need. "Better."

"Uh-huh..."

"Find a shirt, pet. I'm going to give them a heads up we're coming." He winked at his boy, went to the dresser and grabbed his phone.

CYRUS

Hey Brandon. It's your favorite recluse. I'm bringing my boy in for some custom cuffs. Possibly a paddle. You there today?

BRANDON

Completely. How exciting! Peter's working with me today, so they can commiserate.

Peter belonged to Brandon, and the tattoo-covered boy looked fierce, wild, but was sweet as sugar.

CYRUS

Perfect. See you shortly.

He put his phone in his pocket and looked Dex over. "Brandon and his boy, Peter, are expecting us."

"Cool. Are they nice?" Dex grabbed his hoodie. "Do you want a jacket?"

"Leather. In the closet. Just pick one you like." He bounced in his boots, feeling damn good. "They're good people."

"*Just* pick one. I'm going to remove one paddling for every time you 'just' me."

He narrowed his eyes and grinned. "No. You're not. And that's three for the day."

"Nope. I'm at a negative one." Someone was feeling his oats—wicked and teasing, but not angry, not mean.

He let Dex help him on with his coat. "Suit yourself. I get to add a punishment for arguing with me."

"Oh, that's cheating. Arguing with you is one of my great joys."

He laughed. "Ah. Understood. I'll be fair, then. I'll save you a step and cuff you to the bedpost myself."

"You liked that visual, did you?" Dex locked the door, and they headed to the elevator.

"You have to ask?" He rested a hand on his boy's ass as they waited for the doors to open.

"No, but it's nice to hear."

He followed Dex onto the elevator and leaned close. "You're beautiful. I like every visual. That one was particularly stunning."

"I wasn't thinking about visuals, to be honest. I was gone."

"I know, that made it even better." It would be a tough night to top, so he resolved not to try. "Oh, gorgeous day."

Chilly, but pretty. He hadn't forgotten that his boy needed a real coat, and he planned to make it an early Christmas gift.

He took Dex's hand as they left the building and headed for the subway. They had a bit of a hike downtown—better than seventy blocks to Canal Street—it made the most sense to take the train.

Dex jabbered at him happily, teasing and playing with him, stealing tiny touches.

He pointed to an older lady with a rolling cart at the end of their subway car. “What do you think? CIA? Alien? Ninja?”

Dex peered, head tilted. “I’m thinking she’s an illusion to distract us from a portal to another dimension.”

“You think?” He raised an eyebrow. “The door at the end of the car?”

“The seat. You are aware and you sit? Man, you’re gone. Zoop!”

He laughed. “Zoop? I dare you to go sit on her.”

“Nope. That’s mean, and she’s not a kid anymore. Too bad.”

He rolled his eyes. “That was a joke, you know. I just wanted to see you ‘zoop’.”

“Dares are serious things, you know,” Dex teased back. “I know from serious things.”

“I thought I was the serious one. At least you like to roll your eyes a lot.” Maybe it wasn’t only him. Maybe they both needed to lighten up. “This is a serious errand we’re on, you know.”

“Is it? I thought it was more important, but fun.”

“Okay, you’re right. It’s an important errand. I like that better. And serious fun.” He winked as they pulled into their stop.

Dex grinned at him as they headed out. “We’re pretty good at serious fun.”

“So far, so good.” He herded Dex out of the subway and across the street while the light was in their favor. “This place is wild. Two stories of leather and kink. He does seminars and classes too."

"Two stories? Really?" Dex blinked and grinned at him. "Impressive."

"Yep. Big spiral staircase right in the middle of the store. Stuff hanging and in cases and all kinds of displays. Very cool place." Cyrus loved that it didn't pretend to be anything but exactly what it was. It was a playground. He'd gotten nearly everything in his office there.

"Huh. That's not something you'd find back home."

He laughed. "No, I suppose not. Basically, if you can dream it up, imagine it, fantasize about it, Brandon can find it or have it made for you. He's a wizard. The shop is on the corner there." The storefront was fairly ordinary aside from the carefully displayed gear in the windows. "Oh, that's Peter working on the window display."

He gave the sub a wave and Peter gave a little salute and climbed out of the window as they entered the store.

"Master Cyrus." Peter ducked his head and lowered his eyes respectfully.

"Peter. It's good to see you, boy." Peter never ceased to intrigue him. Cy was pretty sure the eyebrow piercings were new.

"Excellent to see you, Master. My Master is finishing up with a client. How can I make you and your guest comfortable?" Peter shot Dex a glance, and Dex just beamed.

"Your Ashley is amazing, man. Seriously."

Peter blinked, then bounced a little, wiggling the piercing that ran between the middle of his bottom lip to the corner of his mouth. "You know piercings?"

"Sure I do. That's great work, and it looks magical."

Cy blinked. He'd expected Peter to totally befuddle Dex.

Magical? Did Dex say 'magical'? He'd seen the piercing before, but he didn't know it was an 'Ashley', and he liked it also, but...magical?

"Oh. Oh, thank you. Do you hug?" Wait. Wait, did Peter just offer to hug Dex?

"Always. Hey. I'm Dex, I'm Cyr's, through and through."

And that announcement, just right out there, was unexpected and new. "I've entered the Twilight Zone," he muttered, moving out of the way so the boys could have their hug.

Dex hugged Peter, whispering something in his ear that made the other boy blink and giggle.

Giggle.

"Are we in the right place?" He grinned and hooked his hand around Peter's nape, fingers settling between the piercings there. "You look good. You're finishing your degree soon, right?"

"This spring, yes, Sir. I'm glad Master insisted."

He gave Peter a nod. "Good for you. Left eyebrow thing is new, right?"

"You noticed! Yes, Sir. Do you like it?"

"I do. I like them all. You wear hardware well. I don't know what they're all called, but I like them. The ones I'm allowed to see anyway." He winked at Peter and let the boy go.

Peter beamed at him. "Would you like coffee, Sir? Tea? And does your boy need anything?"

"I'll always say yes to coffee." He smiled at Dex, pleased with their visit so far. "What would you like, pet?"

"Can I just share a sip of yours, please, Sir?"

He nodded and took Dex's hand, giving it a squeeze. "Just the coffee for me, please, Peter."

"Yes, Sir. Be right back with it. Why don't you two have a seat in the lounge, and I'll bring it there?"

"Sounds good." The lounge was an area off to one side of the shop that had a couple of couches and a coffee table. He'd sat there many times talking with Brandon about designs.

Cyrus waited for the boy to head off and then grinned at Dex. "That's four."

"Four? No way. When? I didn't, did I?"

Cyrus sat on the couch and pointed to the floor.

"Kneel, please. You said you'd 'just' have a sip of my coffee. The first was my jeans and the other two were about my jacket. Don't forget, pet, I'm going to ask you later." He didn't think doubling up would be a good idea today though, with Dex still a little pink from the night before. He'd have to think about that.

"Oh for fuck's sake. It's a real, necessary word, love." Dex knelt and leaned, snuggling into him. "I may have to bite you."

He laughed. He knew he shouldn't; he should be giving Dex a good swat for speaking to him that way, especially in a public place. But he couldn't. Dex was right. Although it was meant to be an annoyance, it wasn't serving the purpose. Still, he'd made the rule and they had to stick with it at least until they got home and could talk about the why.

More importantly, though, his boy was kneeling at his feet without protest or question. He decided to dangle a little reward. "If you must bite, pick a good spot. Shoulder, nipple, backside...something like that."

"Mmm... I like how you jump when I bite your nipple." Dex wrapped one hand around his ankle. "I like how excited it makes us, too, the promise of tonight. So, it's okay to call you Master here, yeah?"

He nodded. "It's expected. Are you comfortable with that?"

"I'm proud to be yours, Master." Dex stroked his calf, petting him gently. "I just don't want you to get in trouble ever."

"Well, as far as that goes, I'm out everywhere. The worst you'd do is surprise someone." He laughed. "It's what I do for a living after all, it's not like it's going to hurt me or my livelihood. But I don't tend to wear it on my sleeve."

Dex looked up at him, a curious look crossing his face, and then he nodded, smiled, pulling up from him, leaving his leg chilly.

All this time, and he still couldn't read those looks. He had no idea if he'd said something wrong, or right. "I'm proud to be here with you today, and to introduce you to Brandon and Peter. I told Brandon I was buying you a gift."

Dex smiled and inhaled deep. "Does that mean it's okay to snuggle or no? I'm not sure, really."

"It's okay, pet." He reached for Dex and ran a hand through his boy's hair. "Brandon will want to help us pick out just the right thing for you, so we should be ourselves. Absolutely."

"This part was easy—kneeling, being ourselves."

"Coffee." Peter leaned over the back of the couch and handed a mug to him. "Master asked me to tell you he'll be over in a minute. He's just finishing up."

"Thank you, boy." He took a sip, the bitter heat going down just right, then he offered the mug to Dex. "Mmm. Have some, pet. Good coffee."

"Thank you, Master." Dex drank, humming deep in his chest.

"May I chat with your boy, Sir?" Peter asked him. The

sub was the most interesting mix of trained and formal, and free-spirited.

"Of course."

The boy came around and knelt also, not at his feet but near Dex, waiting on his Master. "I'm sure you're used to this, but we've heard a little about you through the circles. You're from Texas? How do you like New York?"

"It's amazing. So different, but folks have been nice to me. And it was time for a change."

It was time for a change. So few words that said so much more than it seemed.

Peter leaned closer to Dex. "For Master Cyrus too."

"Don't be impudent, boy," he teased, his words not meant to be harsh.

Dex nodded, though, without hesitation. "He needed someone to take care of him, love him. I grabbed the position."

"Not someone, pet. You. I wasn't offering it to anyone else. You fit all the requirements." He grinned and stole back his coffee.

"Lucky!" Peter bounced where he knelt. "So, you know your body mods. What do you have?"

"I don't. I worked at a tattoo parlor in Austin for a while." Cy hadn't heard about that job. Was there anything his boy hadn't done?

"Why not? When you had it right there?"

Dex leaned in close and whispered the answer in Peter's ear.

He'd like to know the answer to that question, but if Dex was whispering there had to be a reason, and he didn't intend to embarrass his boy today. He decided to let it go for now.

"Known each other five minutes and they're already whispering? Really, Cyrus. You're going soft."

"Brandon. I assure you soft isn't the word I'd use."

Brandon laughed and maneuvered his sleek-looking wheelchair right up next to the couch. "You're too much. It's great to see you."

Cyrus stuck out his hand to shake as Peter moved in smoothly alongside Brandon's chair. Brandon reached out and tugged Peter's hair in a slow, casual motion.

"So you've brought your new boy to me today?" Brandon looked at Dex the way that Brandon looked at everyone new, critically but without judgement, with the eye of a man practiced in sizing people up quickly.

"Dex, stand up and say hello to Master Brandon. Let him get a look at you."

Brandon wasn't a mirror, thankfully.

Dex stood up and held out one hand with a smile. "Pleased to meet you, Mr. Brandon."

"Cheeky boy." Brandon winked at Cyrus, then caught Dex's eye and shook hands. "Pleased to meet you too."

"I don't think cheeky was the intention." Surely Brandon knew that.

"You're looking for cuffs, are you?"

Cyrus shrugged. "At least. I thought I'd let Dex look around."

Brandon looked Dex over again. "What are you envisioning, Dex?"

"Something that's mine, something that feels like my… like Master Cyr is holding me."

Cyrus didn't say anything, but he was sure his pride just filled the room.

Brandon smiled at Dex. "I think I can help with that. Do

you want to wear them all the time? Only sometimes? Only in-scene?"

"I'd like to wear them a lot, but I'm a baker, so there's lots of washing."

Brandon's head tilted, and the man got a wicked look in his eyes. "I think I can help with that too."

Cyrus was about to sip his coffee but lowered the cup slowly instead. He couldn't imagine, but he'd seen that look a couple of times before. "Dare I ask?"

"No. No, I think I need to surprise you. Do I have permission to take your boy to the back?"

"You do, as long as he is comfortable with that. I want Dex to have what he wants. What he needs." Cyrus looked at Dex. "I'll be right here. Master Brandon only wants to fit you in cuffs, he won't be restraining you or anything. Are you okay with that, pet?"

"Yes, Sir. I'm interested. Nervous, but interested."

There was nothing wrong with a little nerves.

"He's all yours then." Cyrus stood and offered Dex a hand up, pulling the boy close for a quick kiss before releasing him to Brandon. He appreciated Dex's honesty, well aware it wasn't very long ago that Dex didn't admit to nerves, or really any other emotion. "Have fun."

"Peter, I'll need you. Lock the front door first, hmm? Cy, make yourself at home."

"Yes, Master!" Peter was over the moon, Cy could tell.

Well that was intriguing. Possible unsettling, except that he trusted Brandon, and he knew whatever was swirling in that brain would be something wonderful. Likely wicked, but nonetheless wonderful.

"Lock the doors. My goodness. I'm sorry you're closing shop on our account." He would just have to spend enough money to make up for it.

"Pshaw. Saturdays are for gawkers. Come, boy. We'll find something to show your Master."

He had time to explore, which was a blessing. Just the smell in here was arousing his senses. Cyrus watched the group of them disappear into the back somewhere, and he headed upstairs to have a look at the tools. Paddles and crops, straps and tawse. All the good impact toys were upstairs.

He found a small crop, slapping it on his fingers. He could imagine this on Dex's cock, light slaps that would make his boy's toes curl. He tucked that one under his arm.

He decided he should also look at clamps and chains, they were up here too in one of the corners.

The collars were all kept in cases downstairs. He'd thought about starting there, he knew he was ready, but he wanted to give Dex a little more time.

Though for what he didn't know. Neither of them needed more time. He just...

Just. Ha.

"M-Master?" Dex stood there, wearing a heavy pair of cuffs and—

Jesus.

His pet had on a longline black leather corset, the boning drawing Dex's waist in, bringing attention to that perfect ass, the pretty hard nipples.

"Turn around, boy," Brandon said, showing off the lacing. "It's not too tight, but you have room to play. I thought this might be the way to have you holding your boy when he worked."

He stared for a second, reminding himself that as hot as this was, it wasn't entirely about him at the moment. He took in the whole picture, getting his head around the idea of Dex, his Texan cowboy, in a leather corset. Never in a million years would he have thought of this, or even imagined it. But then, that's why he had Brandon.

"Pet. You look absolutely stunning in that corset. How do you feel in it?"

Dex blinked up at him, his pet's pupil's blown. "I can feel it everywhere, like a hug."

Brandon couldn't have been more smug.

Well, they'd be taking that home. The way Dex looked he wouldn't be at all surprised if the boy just pulled a shirt on over it.

Cyrus took a breath, trying not to let his boy's bedroom eyes get him too far off task. "Good boy. Tell me about the cuffs." He took Dex's wrists in his hands and had a look at the cuffs. They had real weight all their own and he worried a bit about Dex working in them. Surely that wasn't the intention.

"They're heavy. Like I could never forget them, get used to them. Mr. Brandon says you would put them on when I wasn't working."

"Do you want a lighter pair too? Or is the corset enough for when you are? Can you breathe well enough to wear this for a full day while I'm working?" Cyrus could practically feel Brandon's eyebrow climb up to his hairline.

"Really, Cyrus. How long have you known me?"

"That's not a fair question; you've known me long enough to know I'm thorough." He grinned at Brandon. "Excellent choice."

"It can be tightened too. For those times he needs to remember your will." Brandon smiled and moved behind Dex. "Peter."

Peter took Dex's hands. "So, this is weird. Hold onto me and think about your Master and breathe."

Brandon drew him over. "You tighten from the middle. Always."

Then Brandon tugged, Dex's spine getting taller, waist tucking in.

Cyrus replaced Brandon's fingers with his own, feeling the tension for himself so he could remember it. This was all new to him. "So, tighten from here and then work down to secure it?"

"No. The laces come up from the bottom and down from the top. You'll tie here, and tuck in." Brandon smiled at him, conspiratorial. "I'd have a couple—daily, dress, and training. Then you can keep them tied for the most part. His body responded beautifully when we put it on. He relaxed into the pressure like a dream."

He played with the laces, getting the idea of how they worked. "Oh. I got it. Okay." He looked at Brandon. "I assume you have something in mind for the other two?" He loosened the laces a bit, not needing Dex to be anything but comfortable at the moment and tied them again.

"What do you think, pet? Would you like to go pick out the other ones Master Brandon has suggested?"

"I—I think so, yes, Master."

Oh, he loved that husky, confused tone in his boy's voice, and he thought Brandon and Peter understood completely.

"I left a couple out but explore for a few minutes. We'll be out here until you need me."

He took Dex by the hand and led him down the stairs to the back, where Brandon had left a couple of possibilities to look at. Before he did, though, he took a second to check in with his boy, taking Dex's hands in his and catching those bright eyes. "Are you okay? Questions?"

"I don't know. I—" Dex looked around, eyes wide. "I got hard, Sir. Like whoa."

He didn't hide his smile. "So corsets turn you on. Nothing bad there, I had to talk myself down when I saw you upstairs too. It's fun discovering a new kink, isn't it? Does it worry you?"

"A little. Just because it was so fast. So big. My reaction. It's okay?"

God, he wanted to kiss those pretty lips.

"Any honest reaction is okay. It would have been just as okay to hate the whole idea. But you don't, and that's one more thing you've learned about yourself. How could that be wrong? You'll find in this community people get turned on or turned off by all kinds of things, and it's all okay as long as it's honest. I'm sure Brandon and Peter thought nothing of it at all."

That they let on, anyway. Brandon definitely had thoughts. Smug ones.

"I want to know what your thoughts are." Dex put one of Cy's hands on the corset, letting him feel his boy breathe.

"I have many. I already told you it's a turn on. I love it on you." He ran his hands over the leather, feeling the stays and the softer parts warmed by his boy's skin. "I love that you love it so much too. There's something about it that is so... you. You wear it well, like you were meant to. You look completely comfortable in it."

"Thank you, Sir. I guess... I have to take it off, huh?"

His boy's regret at having to take the corset off was possibly the highlight of his day. Could their weekend get any better?

"Only so you can try on others. You ought to know what different styles feel like anyway. You can put it back on after, wear it home if you like."

He moved behind his boy, thinking about lacing Dex

into this beautiful contraption every morning. He wasn't going to argue with that. Not one bit.

"Brandon suggested a formal one. Something, I assume, for wearing out. Have you come across anything you like?"

Dex's cheeks went bright red—Cy swore he could feel the heat. "I have, yes. But I didn't know…"

Dex took him to a corset that looked very much like a Western vest, in brown leather. There was a chest pocket with piping, and under a jacket, no one would know. "This is the dress one. I don't know about the other one. Mr. Brandon said I should show you the two he liked and h-have you choose."

Poor boy. Wonderful didn't always mean easy. He understood intimately how a discovery like this one could be hard to get a handle on. He remembered well his own process of learning who he was and trying to understand how someone with his needs could also be a good man.

He took the corset, but before he took a really good look at it, he set it down and pulled Dex into his arms offering a real hug to replace the corseted one, and held his boy close. "It's all right, pet. I promise you, you're all right."

He was thrilled, in fact. His boy not only discovered a kink of his own, but one that Cyrus had no prior experience with—not in his personal life, and not with any of his clients either. This one hadn't come up. This one was unique to his boy, unique to them.

He might have to send Brandon and Peter a case of scotch as a thank you.

"I love you. It's not too weird?" Dex lifted his face for a kiss.

"I love it. And I love you." He gave his boy that kiss, happily, taking the time Dex needed to feel steady.

Dex relaxed against him, settling. "Thank you, Master. That's better."

"Good. I want you to enjoy this. I think you should feel good about it." Cyrus let Dex go and picked up the dress corset to get a better look. "This is so perfect for you. I love the Western styling. Have you tried it on yet? Does it fit?"

Dex nodded and stepped close. "Want to see?"

Before he could answer, Dex slipped it on, closing the placket. He loved the way Dex stood, the way his boy's arousal was pouring from him, how confident he looked.

He looked Dex over and then walked around behind his boy, taking in the view, the trim silhouette. He shook his head, still astonished that this was his Dex, and let himself buzz along with his boy. "It's perfect."

"Thank you. Do you want to see the others? They're not for public consumption."

"The training ones? Absolutely." The less for public consumption the better as far as he was concerned. Just the idea gave him a high.

There were three hanging on hooks—and they were luscious. One was a heavy rubber corset with locking straps. One was leather, with a leather cock sheath, a strap to keep a plug in. The last one looked like his favorite pairs of boots—tons of straps and buckles, arm and wrist cuffs hooked on, chains with ankle cuffs and a glorious spreader bar.

"Oh my. Well, rubber's not my kink. You?" He disregarded that one fairly quickly. "What do you think of these two?" He knew where he was leaning; he looked the last one over, making sure that all the various bits were removable and adjustable. If he was going to put his boy in a training corset, whose nature was to be uncomfortable, he thought it ought to be as complicated—and kinky—as possible.

"That one looks like your boots, Master." Dex came close, voice low and husky.

"I agree. And it's gorgeous. I believe that's the one I want." He would have to be sure he understood where the safeties were, and exactly how the bodice was to be worn, but Brandon would show him all of that, here, or in the comfort of his playroom if he asked. That would be up to Dex.

"It comes with a matching posture collar, buddy. I'll throw it in." Brandon nodded and beamed as he came in. "Let me give you a demonstration on all the features?"

"That would be perfect. This is a really amazing piece. We both like it. My boy says it reminds him of my favorite boots."

"His eyes lit up when he saw it. Boy, help Dex out of his formalwear, please. And we'll need him out of his boots and jeans, please." Brandon repeated himself so Dex could hear. "The door is locked. It's just the four of us."

Dex let Peter lead him into a little dressing room, while Brandon grinned. "He's lovely, Cy. You must be so pleased."

"Proud. Pleased and proud. You have no idea how withdrawn he was when I met him. How little he thought he deserved. This is...it's everything I've wished for him. To find himself." Not *just* Dex. Dex with needs and desires that were valid and real, who was allowed to be honest, who deserved respect.

"He's amazing. I'm going to let you do the touching, so that he equates this with you and you alone. The buckles are straightforward, and I'm here to advise, but you lock him in, collar him. Fair?"

He smiled at Brandon. "You're good at this, you know. I didn't even think of that. Thank you." People in the scene like Brandon reminded him that no matter how much you think you know, there is always more to learn.

"I know how important the headspace is, and this looks to be powerful for your boy."

Cyrus nodded slowly. "It's deep for him. He was shocked at his own response to the corset, worried. He'll be processing it for a bit I think."

"I'll make sure you get it on, no problem, then I'll give you time for him to process. Maybe an hour?" Brandon put the corset in his hands. It was stiff, unyielding, meant to mold someone's body.

He held it, turning it over in his hands, touching every piece of it. He locked down his own response for now and tried to focus on what his boy would need from him right now. "I expected it to be heavier."

"The boning is unforgiving, so the weight needed to be pulled back. The posture collar attaches to the corset through these D rings in the back."

He laughed. "Dex will hate that collar." Which would make it a perfect tool. Maybe a better choice than not using words that degrade. "Hate it."

His boy was going to love all these buckles though, and he'd put money on the addition of the spreader bar too.

"That's why it's training, right?" Brandon grinned at him conspiratorially. "There's little I like better than a sub that's caught between 'I hate this' and 'I'm so turned on I can't think'."

"I have to agree with you there." The not thinking bit was really the best part.

Peter brought Dex back out quietly and left Dex standing but knelt next to Brandon. It only took Cyrus a couple of steps to move close, to make sure Dex saw him.

"Hello, pet. Master Brandon has said very kind things about you, you make me proud as always. How do you feel?"

"Nervous, weird." Dex swallowed hard, arms wrapped around himself. "Sorta turned on."

"I'm sure Peter already told you that all of that is perfectly appropriate. And also normal. If you weren't nervous, I'd be concerned." He glanced over at Peter. "Am I right, boy?"

"Yes, Sir. This is all new for Dex, but he's doing just what he's supposed to." Peter's expression was a little bit jealous.

"See that? Very good, pet. Would you like to have a closer look at this before Master Brandon talks me through it?"

"No. I trust you, Master. You'll make it fit."

He most certainly would. The corset curled around his pet's body, and he started buckling the corset up, leaving it loose at first.

After he'd set all the major buckles he moved back around front and tugged gently on the narrow buckles over Dex's shoulders. "What about the height of these shoulder straps, Brandon? Lower?"

"You want access to his nipples, Cy, so a little lower."

Dex groaned softly, blinking nice and slow.

That's what he thought. The light groan made him grin. "A little lower, right, pet? So I can add those clamps you liked so much if I want to."

"Master..." Dex's cock jerked, beginning to fill again.

"My own." He kissed Dex lightly and pulled away with a wink. "You look beautiful, and I'm nowhere near done yet."

Cyrus moved back to the buckles. "Brandon. Tighter from the middle and then up? Or the middle and then down first? Does it matter?"

"Totally personal preference. I like middle and down, because I love how it makes a sub's ass look."

"Works for me." He tightened the middle buckle first and realized quickly that Dex was going to need to steady himself if he was going to tug this thing tight. "Hm. May I borrow your boy again, Brandon?" He had bedposts at home, which was handy.

"Absolutely. Boy."

"Yes, Master." Peter hopped up, smiled at Dex. "Hold on."

Dex nodded, a soft moan leaving him as Cy tightened the strap.

"Oh, wonderful. Much better." He was enjoying this far more than he would have expected. Largely, he thought, because Dex was, but that wasn't all of it. He liked all this leather on his boy. He liked fussing with all the bindings and buckles. And Dex looked incredible.

"Take a breath for me, pet, and exhale slowly." Cyrus let Dex breathe, tightening the next set of buckles before Dex had completely exhaled, leaving a little room to breathe but not so much that it would be easy. "Too tight, Brandon? I don't want my boy passing out."

Brandon had Dex breathe for him. "No. No, that's perfect. You don't want it chafing when you bind his arms."

Dex shivered, and Cy began to see what Brandon meant about that gorgeous ass, pushed out and back. Once Brandon and Peter left them, he was taking off the briefs.

"Not to worry, pet. I have your words, angel and demon. I'm listening." He needed to touch so he tugged lightly at the leather, ran his hands over his boy's bare skin. Contact felt important, and it seemed like Dex appreciated it too. "Use them if you're feeling lightheaded or if you're feeling unsteady on your feet."

"Yes, Master." Dex didn't sound breathless as much as he sounded needy. "It's very stiff."

"Mm. Yes." He dared to draw a finger along the outline of Dex's cock. "I can see that."

Dex tried to arch, the boning catching him. "Oh!"

"Oh, very nice. Let me see what I can do with your arms." He looked over the various D rings and straps on the sides of the corset. "Plenty of possibilities here, Brandon. Hm? I can see where I could clip them down straight, use these straps to pull his elbows in... Oh, will this strap let me bend them behind?"

"It most certainly will. There are rings on the collar as well, for the wrist cuffs, should you like."

"I like." He was excluding Dex from this part of the conversation on purpose, letting the corset do its own work on the boy and to give Dex a sense of his place in this company, bound as he was.

Peter hopped up at Brandon's direction and offered him a selection of dog clips and tie-downs. He accepted them with a nod and spent some time playing with different configurations, finally settling for what he'd originally envisioned—Dex's arms turned back, elbows in tight and wrists lashed to a D-ring between the boy's shoulder blades.

He'd try the posture collar next, but he wanted to introduce that piece slowly.

"That's perfect. How do you like it, pet?"

He wasn't expecting the most coherent answer, but it seemed like a good idea to check in with the boy.

"Master." Dex was hard as a rock, a wet spot well-formed on his briefs, nipples tight. Best was the look on Dex's face, lips parted, pupils blown.

And he'd thought Dex was the hottest thing he'd ever

seen last night. The things he could do with his boy right now weren't fit to even think about in company.

Cyrus walked a slow circle around his boy, taking it all in. "I like the contrast of this lovely, smooth front and all the hardware in the back. Beautiful. Just perfect, Brandon."

"Thank you. Your boy is a natural. He's melting into it. Ankles or collar next?" Brandon looked like a proud papa, beaming at them.

He placed a hand on Dex's arm, keeping contact as he spoke with Brandon. "Let's do the collar so he has more balance in case he's not comfortable with it." His sense was that it wouldn't sit well with Dex, and he wouldn't want the boy to get hurt. "This entire scenario is a complete surprise to me, however, so I'm not sure I can guess how the collar will go over."

"Let's try this one first. I think it's the right fit." Brandon handed him the boned collar that would cover from Dex's jaw to shoulder, holding his boy's chin up, stretching his neck the tiniest bit, but to Dex it would feel huge.

He eased the collar on, buckling it in the back. Dex instinctively tried to move away, nostrils flaring, but Cy had him.

"You're all right, pet. Breathe and trust me. It's not meant to be comfortable. It's meant to test your focus." He took hold of Dex by the shoulders, his hands trailing over bare skin as he moved around in front where Dex could see him.

"I trust you have the ankle cuffs, Cy. I'm going to play with my boy. Your Dex has inspired him."

He barely paid attention to Brandon's words; his focus was on his boy. He did manage a nod of thanks before Brandon led Peter from the room.

"Hard to speak in that collar, I imagine." But easy enough to take a kiss when he wanted one, so he did, and tangled his fingers in his boy's hair, holding tight. Dex opened up, tongue fucking his lips desperately, his boy whining softly.

Any hope he'd had of maintaining composure dissolved into that kiss as he fought his boy's tongue with his own, asserting himself, asserting control, demanding that Dex give over.

Dex fought longer than he'd imagined, and the submission in the kiss when it came was sweet.

The victory made him ache with need for his boy. He made very sure Dex was settled before breaking off the kiss, then took a deep breath and yanked those tighty-whities down and off. He raked his eyes over his boy's bound body, head to toe and back to that lovely cock, hard as granite, and decided Dex could stay that way.

He barked his order, reaching out and grasping Dex's elbow to help. "Knees, pet."

"Don't let me fall, please." Dex leaned toward him, trusting his hands. Dex's motion wasn't graceful or lovely, but it did the job.

He made sure Dex was steady and then paced away. Away, then back, then away again, boots rhythmic and heavy on the hardwood floor. As much as he wanted to, it didn't seem safe to fuck his boy's mouth while Dex was in a posture collar, tightly bound and unable to shout a safe word.

But he could still have some fun and make his boy... watch.

As he paced back this time he slowly opened his jeans, then his fly. He pulled out his cock and his aching balls, and stopped just inches from his boy's face, stroking himself firmly, letting himself grunt and moan. "Thinking about your ass, pet."

Surprised eyes flew to his face. "Master!"

The shocked look in those sweet hazel eyes made him grin.

"Eyes on my cock, pet. It's a little show. Just for you."

Just.

He gripped his sac with his other hand and squeezed, indulging in a luscious sigh.

Dex's lips parted, that pretty pink tongue flicked out, tempting the fuck out of him. Naughty pet, trying to distract him.

"Wishful thinking." God, he'd swallowed gravel and lost a whole octave. He watched his boy, swirled his hand over the head of his prick and groaned, leaning just a touch closer. This wasn't going to take long, but he planned to tease Dex with every single stroke.

"Please, Master. I need you." Oh sweet fuck, the passion in Dex's voice made his ass cheeks clench.

"Love." He cupped Dex's cheek and pushed his thumb into his boy's mouth, leaving a wet mark where he rubbed against the stiff collar.

Dex closed his mouth and sucked, pulling on him and sucking him rhythmically.

"Good...boy. Fuck!" Jesus, he was suddenly...he stared hard at Dex as his vision went sparkly, everything about his boy so perfect. "Open. Open, pet. Now."

Dex's lips popped open, his boy yearning toward him.

All it took was a touch of his boy's tongue.

Cyrus pumped his cock and shot hard, spilling into Dex's mouth. He was careful not to thrust and let his boy take what he could, which was easy enough to do with every muscle and every nerve paralyzed by the second shattering orgasm he'd had in as many days.

The smell of leather and his boy, the soft nuzzles and

licks to his cock brought him back to himself. His pet shivered against him, moaning softly.

He blinked to clear his vision and tucked himself neatly back into his jeans as he caught his breath. "Good boy. Thank you, pet. On your feet now. Let me help you up." He didn't take chances. Once Dex got one foot flat he reached down, hugged his arms around the corset and lifted Dex right up. "Hello, my love. You look beautiful, you know."

"Love." Dex panted, moaning for him. "I don't know how —I need—Oh God."

"I know." He ignored that for a moment. "Are you all right? Are your fingers asleep? Does your back hurt? Anything?"

"I'm hot. It's really hot in here." Dex was beginning to relax in his arms, the soft moans easing.

"I'm going to remove the collar." He was able to release the clasps without having to completely let go of the boy, and he only had to reach a bit to set it aside.

"Whoa. Whoa, that's..." Dex closed his eyes, sucked in a few desperate breaths, "Damn."

"Oh. Whoa, okay. Slower next time? More warning?" Dex was fine, but he'd be more mindful in removing the rest. Lesson learned.

"I don't know. I don't know. Just...shh..."

He respected that request and nodded, one arm settling around Dex's middle. No one was in a hurry, least of all their host, who had happily let them be. He stroked the smooth front of the corset and let his boy breathe, doing what he knew he did best, being still and strong.

"Sorry. Sorry, that was..." Dex straightened up. "I'm sorry. I sort of...went away."

"Shh. Stop. I didn't ask for an apology. You're fine. You're amazing." He combed his fingers through Dex's hair. "Where'd you go?"

"I don't know—into you, into me, away. I don't know."

Cyrus knew when aftercare was called for, and Dex was about at his limit. "Are you ready to take this off?"

"Yes. Please. It's not a hug. It's big."

"It is. It's meant to be, and you've done so well, pet. Honestly. I'm so pleased and proud." Cyrus moved around behind Dex and started with his wrists and arms, moving deliberately. "Breathe. In and out. With me."

Cyrus took a deep breath that his boy could hear and exhaled slowly.

Dex breathed, settling in again, letting himself focus and, when Cy let his wrists go, his boy tried to arch again, getting stopped short.

"Soon. Don't fight it, I'm taking it off. I'm going to loosen it first." He worked on all the buckles and straps giving Dex much more room to get a breath, to move. Given the experience with the collar he waited a bit letting Dex settle again before unfastening the corset completely.

Dex stepped away, grabbing his briefs. "I can't believe... God, Master, I need to get dressed."

"Take your time." He watched Dex flutter, not the least bit surprised. It was part of Dex's process. Cyrus hung back and let Dex dress, knowing he'd have to step in and unwind his boy eventually.

Dex dressed quickly, hiding in the too-big hoodie, then began cleaning up the corsets and cuffs, hiding from him.

Like Cy was going to let Dex walk out without his 'hug' corset under those clothes.

"Come here, pet." Cyrus held a hand out to his boy once Dex had managed to run out of things to do.

Dex looked at him, so serious. “I never done anything like this.”

“I think you and I have established that new isn’t bad.” He pulled Dex against him. “I know they are new to you, but Brandon and Peter are family, the way Les and Milo are family. They’re as proud of you as I am, and happy for us both. You’ll leave here with their highest respect, I promise.”

“I hope you’re right.” Dex held him close, face in his neck.

“I haven’t steered you wrong yet, have I?” He stood firm, letting Dex lean against him. “It’s not a world you’re used to, it’s not how you were raised, it’s not a recognizable piece of the man you thought you were. I’ve been through all of that, too.”

“Can we go home soon? Please? I need to wrap my head around this.”

“We can go now. I just need to settle up with Brandon.” He stepped back from Dex and brushed one warm cheek with the back of his hand. “And you need your hug corset. Off with the sweatshirt please.”

“Wh-what?” Oh that wide-eyed expression of want and shock wasn’t going to serve to turn Cy off at all.

“Sweatshirt off, please, pet,” he repeated, as if Dex hadn’t heard him just fine. Poor, adorable, sweet boy. He held the leather corset in both hands and waited, trying to look patient. Maybe bored. Anything but amused and aroused.

Cy stripped off his top, giving him that sweet body—rippled belly, tight nipples. The whole thing.

“Mm.” He hummed approval and circled Dex’s torso with the leather, smoothing it in place before doing up the clasps in front. “Easier the second time. We’ll get good at this soon enough.”

Brandon was right—Dex's face relaxed, expression easing. How lucky that they discovered this.

Cyrus spent a little time fussing with the laces, feeling a little fat-fingered and clumsy even though he knew he'd get used to it. "Too tight? I don't want you restricted at all. You should be comfortable."

"No. It's not bad. It's not." Dex wiggled, going heavy-lidded.

"Not bad..." He grinned, picking up the sweatshirt. "But is it good?"

"Yeah? Yeah, it is." Dex's cheeks flooded, but he didn't look away.

"Yeah. I think so too." He helped Dex put the sweatshirt on. "Gather everything, please, and we'll go find Brandon and his boy."

"You...you want these other two?"

"And the collar, all the cuffs, and the spreader bar." Plus the few things he had already chosen.

"Oh... Thank you." Sweet, overwhelmed pet.

Dex was adorable with his arms full of kinky gear, and Cyrus led him back out into the main room of the shop.

"Oh, Brandon..." he called, unsure where the other couple had gone. "I apologize if I'm interrupting, but I think I need to take my boy home for some rest."

"Peter and I will call you a car." Brandon smiled at both of them. "It's the least we can do."

"Make sure you get that paddle I picked out too, Peter." He ushered Dex over to Peter who started writing down everything they were purchasing. Brandon would bill him, as usual. "Brandon, we can't thank you enough. This has been a very enlightening afternoon, certainly more than I had imagined."

"The paddle and that little crop are in this bag. The chains, cuffs, collar and spreader bar here. The suit bags have the corsets." Brandon smiled at his pet. "Your boy is beautifully polite, and it was amazing, to see his awakening here."

"I love that." He took the garment bags and left the rest for his boy. "Did you hear that, pet? Master Brandon called today your awakening."

"Th-thank you, Sir," Dex murmured, and he could hear how close his boy was to losing it.

"Are you all set, Peter? I think I'll take Dex out for some air while we wait for our car."

"Yes, Sir. It was good to see you. Dex, it was great to meet you. We should have a beer and talk about body mods sometime."

"Please. I'd like that. We could meet for coffee."

"Sure. Coffee. Let's do it."

"I'll talk to your Master, boy. You've definitely made our day. Take good care of Cy, he needs it." Brandon winked at Dex.

"I always do, Sir. Always."

"Always." He tucked an arm around his boy and headed for the door. "Talk soon, Brandon. Thanks again."

Outside was cold, and it reminded him again that Dex didn't have a proper coat. Soon.

Christmas, as they say, is coming.

But Thanksgiving was coming first, and he wasn't sure what their plans were. He'd have to bring that up soon.

Dex stood, arms around himself, thoughts a million miles away.

There was little Cyrus could say that was going to make what Dex was working in his head any simpler. Dex needed to process, to figure out where today, on the heels of last night, sat with him. Where it slotted into his world. The best thing he could do was stay present, stay close, and listen if Dex did have something to say.

There was one thing he could say, though, and he got it in just as their car pulled up. "I love you."

39

Dex stood in the kitchen, pulling banana walnut muffins out of the oven.

He'd stayed in bed all morning, thoughts racing, and then he gotten up to make the coffee and start breakfast. When he'd brought Cyr his coffee in bed, his Master had stopped him and put the corset on him without a word.

Now he was naked with a corset, which was like advanced naked, bonus naked, extra naked.

And he was finishing banana nut muffins.

Cyrus joined him in the kitchen and was not naked, though the soft, gray pajama pants didn't leave much to his imagination. His Master didn't say anything, just left an empty coffee mug in front of him on the counter and kissed his cheek before taking a seat at the small kitchen table.

"Two or three muffins, love?" He fixed Cyr another cup.

"Two, please. I might beg you for scrambled eggs too." Cyrus looked tired this morning. Happy, but like he hadn't gotten enough sleep.

"Scrambled eggs it is." Dex brought the muffins, butter,

and coffee to the table with a smile. His parts dangled under the corset. "You want any meat?"

Cyrus glanced down at his exposed prick and then met his eyes with a wicked grin. "Not right now, thank you."

Dex felt his cheeks heat, but he couldn't fight his grin. "Listen to you."

Still he cleaned up and made Cyr's eggs, bringing them over, along with his coffee and a half a muffin for him. He'd skipped eating last night, and he thought he was hungry.

"These smell so good, pet." Cyr took a sip of coffee and then dug into one of the muffins. "I'm so spoiled."

His cushion waited, and he put his coffee mug and muffin on the table. "Can I borrow your arm, please? I don't know how to get down in this."

"Oh. Yes, of course. We'll have to figure these things out together, won't we? If kneeling is difficult and uncomfortable, we can try something else..."

Cyr helped him down, and once he settled, he felt fine, solid. Held. "Getting to kneeling is new. This is... I'm good, Sir."

"Better with coffee." Cyr handed him his cup with a warm smile. "I'm so proud of you."

"It's weird, huh? All this?" Especially how he felt, right now.

"It can feel that way, yes." Cyr ate breakfast with one hand while the other touched his shoulder and then combed through his hair. "It's different. I understand how it doesn't feel...normal."

"Right? I've never felt so naked as the last couple days." He was used to all the way naked, but not where the clothes pointed to all the naked bits.

Cyr's hum was deep and satisfied. "Nothing wrong with

naked." Cyr reached down, stroked one of his nipples, petting it to hardness. "You have to rearrange your thinking, pet. It feels weird, but it's not, and it is normal. It's not for everyone, but that doesn't make it wrong in any way. Think about how you feel. Two days ago you didn't have this. Now you do. Are you happier because of it? Do you know yourself better? Do you feel even closer to me?"

He hummed softly, doing his damnedest not to be so distracted by that touch. He felt good today, held and happy. Yesterday had scared him—he'd been…somewhere else.

"There are levels and boundaries, there are safe words, there are many ways to help us navigate this and to help you process. I've planned a quiet day, to give you, and us, the time we need."

It felt good, that 'us' and 'we'. It felt real and like all these emotions meant something important. "Thank you. Seriously, Master. This is big."

"You are always my priority, love." Cyr bent down, just folded right over in the chair and kissed him gently. "This is the good work. The important work."

"The good work." He pushed into the kiss with a sigh. This was what he needed. His Cyr.

"My own." Cyr smiled at him and sat up slowly. "The eggs are perfect."

"Thank you, Sir." He sipped his coffee and snapped up the bite of muffin Cyr offered him. "Oh, yum."

He was hungry. He was never hungry in the morning.

"They're really good." Cyr was right there with another bite, as if his Master knew. "There's really nothing as good as fresh warm muffins. Maybe scones. Scones are better right out of the oven too." The next bite he was offered was of Cyr's eggs on the end of a waiting fork.

"I'm never so hungry in the morning. Thank you, Master." Scones, hmm? Saturday. He'd make some Saturday.

Cyr looked thoughtful for a second, but only smiled at him again and offered him another bite of muffin.

He kissed Cyr's fingertips in thanks, groaning as Cyr teased his nipple instead of those fingers disappearing from him.

"I've got some leather for you to clean today, and I thought I might do a little reorganizing in my of—in the playroom. Do you mind working in there?"

"No, Master. Not at all." He wasn't sure he should keep his corset on, because of staining. Maybe he'd put on a T-shirt.

"Wonderful, then that's our day. That, a nap, and take out. Maybe Netflix." Another bite of eggs came into view. "Are you a binge-watcher? Or do you prefer movies?"

"Oh, I'm a binge-watcher. I watch TV all day. I'm in." He took the bite. "Thank you, Master."

"Thank you for making such a stellar breakfast. I do love breakfast, and I didn't always take the time, so I appreciate you that much more." Cyr sipped his coffee. "I'm all finished, pet. Have you had enough? Maybe you should have a slice of cheese or a handful of grapes or something."

"I'm fine, Master. You'll need a snack soon enough." He stood up and took the dishes, popped them in the dishwasher, and put together a plate of berries, crackers, cheese and hummus for later, wrapping it in Saran wrap.

"You're right about that." Cyr got up and added his coffee mug to the dishwasher, then cupped his ass with a warm hand. "You know how much I like it when you call me Master, don't you?"

Oh. His body leaned into that touch as his heart melted. "I think I do."

"You know how you like to talk about fantasies coming true? That's one of mine. So, thank you for making it come true." Cyr smoothed the other hand over his corset, obviously admiring.

"I..." His cock filled, just reaching for Cyr's hand. "You make me ache, huh?"

"Later." Cyr kissed him, hand sliding round to catch the back of his corset. "We'll take our time."

"I should get dressed, huh? To clean your leather?"

"You should be comfortable. I have an apron you can wear of you're worried about your corset, but it's your choice." Cyr's hip pressed against his groin. "You might want pants."

"If it will distract those hands of yours..."

"These hands?" Cyr waggled fingers at him, then tugged gently on his already sensitive nipple. "I can't promise they won't touch."

"I'm going to put on the heaviest clothes I have, now." He leaned into the touch, though, because he had to, it felt so good.

"Good thing you're from Texas, so your clothes aren't that heavy. Which reminds me that we have to do some shopping. Maybe that will be next weekend's errand." Cyr grinned and stepped back. "Assuming I can keep my hands off you long enough."

"Turkey. I can't afford shopping for clothes until after Christmas. I have to get Thanksgiving supper together, plus Christmas presents, plus Christmas goodies and whatever parties you're invited to."

Cyr gave him the eye. "We're going to have to talk about this money thing again, pet. If I want to take you shopping, it's on me. And I want to take you shopping. Also, whatever you're spending on parties is also on me."

"Tomorrow? Our plans for today are more fun than money talks, right?" They were just going to disagree anyway. Cyr spoiled him to death.

"Tomorrow. Or just accept that I'm taking you shopping." Cyr took a quick kiss. "Are you going to dress? Why don't you get comfortable and meet me in the playroom?"

"Yes, Sir. I'll be there in two shakes of a dead lamb's tail." He headed into the bedroom for soft old sweatpants and a t-shirt.

"I'm not sure I approve of that wait time." Cyr laughed and disappeared into the office, or playroom as Cyr called it when it was their space instead of work.

When he went in, Cyr had left a little pile for him. Straps and cuffs, a couple of paddles, a crop and some other random leather items were sitting on the table in front of the sofa. The doors to both of the big cabinets were open and Cyr was studying them, frowning thoughtfully.

Dex sat carefully, the corset keeping his back straight, his body held so well. "What's wrong, Master?"

"I have too much stuff." Cyr shook his head. "There are a lot of things in here I just don't use, but I collected them for a reason, you know what I mean? I don't want to get rid of them. Maybe I need to find space for another cabinet."

"You can use the closet in my office, love. No problem." He started working the saddle soap into the leather.

"That would work for some of these things. You have enough room for all of your baking things in the pantry? I want you to have a place in here just for your things."

"Yeah?" He had to grin. Had to. That was cool as hell. "I have enough room, I promise."

"Okay. I'll figure out what I'm moving out while you start on those things. Oh, set the blindfold aside when you're done, that's the one you like, it's yours." Cyr looked much less frowny now and started carefully choosing things to move and setting them on the desk.

Dex whistled as he worked, happy to be in here with his lover, enjoying their day together. When the alarm on his phone went off, he went to get them both a cup of coffee and Cyr's snack.

By that point Cyr had a stack on the desk and half of one of the armoires was empty. "You have an alarm set for me?" Cyr seemed pleased by that. "And I was just starting to feel draggy too."

"I know you need these little snacks, huh?" He opened as Cyr fed him a bit of cheese. "Thank you, Master."

"I like sharing. It's nice to see you have an appetite, too. Nobody eats like I do, I guess, but you've been so much healthier lately. That's good, since your crazy holiday season is...what? Any day now I guess."

He nodded. It had started, and next week he had six orders a day to get out. The two weeks after turkey day he had twelve orders a day. He couldn't think about that. Tomorrow.

Cyr put a hand on his arm, the touch helping him settle. "How do you usually spend the holidays?"

"I cook Thanksgiving, I work, I play a lot of gigs. If Huck was in town, we played video games. If he wasn't, I went to Mrs. Feezel's house." Simple, easy, busy.

"Do you want to cook this year? If we invited some friends? Or will you be too overwhelmed? You'd have a couple of subs to help you out." Cyr munched away on the snack, looking more energetic already.

"I already figured I'd cook. Who are you going to invite?" He didn't care one way or the other. They would eat well.

"I usually go to Les and Milo's, so I'd love to return the favor, and since you got along so well with Peter, I think Brandon as well. Is there anyone else you'd like to invite? Maybe someone Milo introduced you to? Anyone at all?"

"No. No, we've talked about a few folks, but no one that I've met. Maybe after the holidays…" He wasn't sure that he'd have a ton of time until the summer anyway.

"Okay, then that's the guest list, assuming they're available. Peter is an excellent cook. Milo is…sweet." Cyr laughed.

"He's great at following directions. Great." He had to defend his friend a little.

"He's a sub. Of course he is." Cyr winked. "Milo's come a very long way. I'm proud of him. And he's everything Les needs…a little dependent and a lot adventurous."

"He's wild. He reminds me a lot of Huck, in a weird sort of way."

Cyr shook his head. "Maybe in some ways. As patients they had similar core needs, but I didn't meet them in the same ways at all."

"I don't know them like you do, of course. I just know them how I know them." And he knew them as friends.

"Of course. Milo isn't a patient anymore, he's a friend now. He's in Les's care and very safe there. He hasn't needed me in a long while. Huck and I…would never have been able to be friends."

He didn't know what to say. He felt so goddamn conflicted about Huck, and he didn't want to. He didn't want to feel anyway about Huck right now.

Huck would have laughed at him for the corsets, would have seduced Cyr and not flinched.

Then again it didn't sound like Huck had managed to seduce Cyr while he was a patient, so maybe Cyr would have kicked his ass. It was possible. Maybe.

He looked at Cyr and took a breath, the corset suddenly coming into sharp focus. Huck didn't belong in here with him. In fact, when he was in this room, he was the only man Cyrus was focused on, dammit. He went to Cyr, knowing what he wanted now. "Master, I need a hug."

"I have one for you." Cyr reached for him and pulled him close, sturdy arms wrapping around him. "I've got you."

"Mmm...thank you." He felt himself relax, focus on the way they breathed together.

"Are you okay? Do you want a break? We could put your things in here together. I cleared a space to hang the training corset and there's all kinds of hooks and shelves for the add-on pieces. The dress one I thought we could put in my leather closet in the bedroom."

"I'm good. I just needed you a minute." The idea of his training corset and that collar gave him goosebumps.

Cyr hummed, holding him close. "You have all my minutes if you want them. Except the minutes that have to do with making dinner. Those minutes I need you to get it together." The deep laugh rumbled in Cyr's chest.

"I'm making you pasta and salad. Don't you worry. I take care of you." He grabbed Cyr's ass and squeezed.

"Milo is teaching you to be naughty. I approve." Cyr covered his hand with a larger one. "We have some work to finish up, pet, so we can binge something."

"TaskMaster," he teased. "I'm damn near done, and then I can help you."

"Chop chop, then." Cyr stepped away and sifted through the new things they'd bought, picking out a short little crop.

"I'll put them away, but I am so looking forward to taking them out again."

He shivered and headed back toward the sofa to finish with the last set of cuffs. He didn't want to think about yesterday, about how he'd been so desperate, so turned on, so awkward and uncomfortable and happy.

By the time he was done Cyr had almost everything put away. The training corset—his training corset—was hanging flat in an open space at the top of the armoire, almost like it was a place of honor. The collar and cuffs were on a shelf just below and the bar for his feet was tucked into a clip on the inside of the door along with the crop and a small paddle.

Cyr had a handful of clips and straps and looked like he was puzzling out where to put them.

"Everything okay, Master?" He finished his cleaning and stood to put everything away.

"I need a...something. To put these in. So they're not just everywhere. Do you like how I hung your corset? It framed up nicely right there, looks great I think." Cyr sighed and played with the buckles. "God, you were so beautiful in it yesterday."

"I was...it was big. I felt—" He'd felt like he was Cyr's, all the way to the bone. Like he was there to be seen, to be used.

Cyr looked at him, finally giving him a smile, setting the clips in his fingers down. "I'd like to take this off you for a little while," Cyr said, fingers tucking under the leather corset. "So you can come sit with me. Is that okay?"

"Of course. Sure." He pulled off his sweatshirt, offering the front placket to his Master's fingers.

"Thank you." Cyr moved around behind him and loosened the laces a little, then came back to undo the hooks. "This really is lovely."

"It is. What do you have on your mind, honey?" Cyr's brain went a million miles a minute.

"You. Yesterday. What you mean when you say big. What you stopped yourself from saying just now." Cyr pulled him over to the couch. "Good things. Maybe things that are hard to find words for."

When he sat, he didn't even hesitate. He pushed into Cyr's lap and let the presence of his lover soothe him.

"I want to hear you talk. Tell me how you felt. Tell me what overwhelmed you." His Master settled with him and they fit together so nicely, like he was meant to fit.

"I felt—I don't—It's hard to say. It's a lot to feel inside, you know?" Dex sighed and drew patterns on Cyr's chest.

"I do. I need your words though, pet. I need to understand how you're processing it. Pick a piece of it, start with something simpler. What's the first thing you thought when you saw yourself in it?"

"In the first one? I felt good, you know? Held. Strong." Brandon had told him this was a way to have the peace of the cuffs and work at the same time.

"That one suits you for every day, I can see how comfortable you are in it, even if it is new, even when you're naked. So the training one. Let's talk about that one."

"Okay. What do you want to know?" He had more feelings than he had words for—pleasure, fear, peace, need, discomfort, passion...

Cyr snorted. "Everything. You haven't said anything but 'it's big' since I took it off you. There were a lot of pieces to what we did yesterday, I know. Why don't you tell me the things that felt easy...if there were any?"

"Easy... It wasn't easy. I felt like...like...shit, I don't know. Like you were unavoidable. Like I was more yours than anything else in the world."

"Good." His Master nodded slowly. "Perfect. That's what submission should be. Brandon was right; you've found yourself."

"I don't understand." He'd more lost himself, hadn't he? He wasn't scared—Cyr had him, found him, would find him—but he sure hadn't found himself.

"I'm sorry, pet. You wouldn't, that's on me. We haven't talked about one of the important components of submission yet because we just hadn't gotten to a point that it seemed relevant until this weekend." Dex recognized the thoughtful look on Cyr's face, knew his Master was searching for words that made sense, that he would understand.

"There's a headspace, a kind of ideal state of mind for a sub, in which they are able to let everything go—every thought about themselves, every worry, every desire—and their focus is solely and completely on their Dom, or their Master. It's absolute trust. Absolute surrender. Subs have told me it feels like different things, but they all seem to agree that their only need and desire is their Dom."

Cyr caught his eyes again, the look hard to read. "I'm told it takes some getting used to."

"It's...overwhelming. I would have done anything you asked. I mean, I was in a store with folks I didn't know. I was hard. I was begging for you. That's...outside what I know about me. It was—God, I mean, I didn't like some of it, but it was part of all of it. Does that make sense?"

"That's what you learned about yourself, right? That this practice, our work, can take you there. When it's more familiar, and we've gone to that space together and come back whole or better than whole a few more times, it should turn into something else for you. A release. A way to turn your mind off, to let go." Cyr was so still as they talked, solid and reassuring. "You'll understand better, I think, how light you can be when you don't have to be responsible or make decisions. When you can just...be. And leave it all to me."

"That doesn't seem fair." It sounded like heaven. Like absolutely heaven. And it had been, when it was happening. He'd been Cyr's, and he'd been caught and held and he didn't have to worry.

God.

How fucking selfish was that? How mean and small.

"Oh, pet, it's more than fair. That level of trust is a gift. An honor." His Master kissed his temple. "You'd never been more beautiful."

"I was—out of my mind isn't right, because I wasn't. I was more in my mind than I've ever been. But I didn't..." There wasn't any space for worry or for shame. There was Master and his will, and that was scary out here in the real world.

"Didn't...?" Cyr combed fingers through his hair. "Just try, I'm listening."

"I didn't think about it. Anything. Anything but you." He was suddenly close to tears, his chest tight, and he wasn't sure if he wanted to pull away or press closer. "I was happy. Like stupidly."

He heard Cyr's breath catch, and his Master was quiet for a minute but seemed to be holding him tighter. Finally, Cyr took a breath and said, simply, "I love you."

"Me too." The tears came then, and he ducked his head, trying to keep his breath even, calm.

"That's it. Good boy. Let it go, I've got you." Those arms stayed firm and tight around him.

"I'm sorry. I don't mean to. I'm not sad." He sucked in air, but the tears wouldn't stop, and finally he stopped trying.

"I know, pet. Don't be sorry, it's good. Just go with it, I'm right here."

Dex sucked in a shaky breath, resting against Cyr's chest, the steady rhythm of his Master's heart soothing as hell. He didn't know what to say, but he knew that he was safe here.

Cyr kept up the soft words of comfort and praise, and seemed as relaxed as could be, like this was okay. Normal. Maybe even expected.

Maybe he hadn't fucked up.

He closed his eyes, resting hard for another minute as he tried to put his pride back together.

"Our bodies have a mechanism to get rid of things that are toxic. Tears are how we purge toxins from the soul."

"I wasn't sad. I swear. I don't regret it—yesterday." He hadn't enjoyed it, because that was a little word for small things, but he had no regret.

"Good, because I am looking forward to the next time, which will certainly be next Saturday if not before. I know you weren't sad. I don't think those tears had anything to do with me except that I was able to make you feel safe enough that you could let them out. I think they've been bottled up in there a long, long time."

"Maybe." Figured that he would cry about nothing when he hadn't cried during the worst times of his life. That was incredibly Dex of him.

"Maybe." Cyr nuzzled his hair, breathed in deep. "Brandon and Peter will keep everything to themselves, you know. I can promise you that. Brandon's been doing this a long time, and he understands."

"I hadn't even worried about that. Who's he going to tell? No one knows me."

Cyr laughed softly. "I don't know. I just thought it would make you feel better."

God, that was so fucking sweet. He lifted his face for a kiss. "Thank you. I appreciate it."

"Oh, I'll take that offer." Cyr curled fingers under his chin and kissed him, that familiar little buzz passing between them.

He let himself exhale, fill his lungs with his lover. He wasn't sure if he was spinning or if he was so calm inside that it felt wild, but either way, he'd take it.

"You ramp up faster than anyone I've ever known, pet." Cyr ran a hand over his stomach.

"Is that bad?" Dex stretched, letting himself feel the pull on his abs.

"No. God, no. But you're a constant temptation." He got one of those warm smiles. "And we still have work to finish up. How do you feel? Was this talk helpful?"

"I feel...easy. Like I'm okay." That was probably stupid, but true.

"You are. I shouldn't say this, because I know how you obsess over things sometimes, but the difference between the man sitting here with me and the man who showed up in the rain at night in that packed up truck...sometimes I watch you and I can't believe it. You are okay. You're better than okay, love."

"Yeah. You...I needed someone to love. Someone that loved me back just as hard." And he found it. He found Cyrus.

"Every minute. And I need someone who needs me. So, we're good." Cyr shifted him and stood up. "Let's finish up. Then maybe we can binge watch in bed."

"Sounds like a plan." He stood up, popping and creaking, laughing at himself, at them. "Two blowjobs says you're asleep before the second episode ends."

"Oh ho!" Cyr laughed. "If you fall asleep first I'm adding a paddling."

"Fair. But barehanded?" He was more than willing to negotiate. He was good at staying awake. He could dangle a little carrot though. "*Just* barehanded."

"Just barehanded it is." The look in Cyr's eyes was worth the promise of that swat later.

"You're on, love." He moved into Cyr's arms. "Let's do this."

40

Cyrus moved around the dining room table, trying to remember whether he and Dex had ever used it before. He couldn't recall a single time. They ate in the kitchen, where Dex's cushion was, or in the living room at the coffee table when they did take out.

It looked nice right now, though. He'd hauled out a tablecloth and Dex had bought napkins and some serving things, and it looked very much like a Thanksgiving celebration.

The apartment smelled great, and when the table was done he followed his nose toward the kitchen to see what else he could do to help. He'd been happily taking direction from his boy all day.

Dex was filthy, but the counters were full of pies and salads, casserole dishes heading into the oven, going out.

The turkey was out, covered with foil and resting.

Filthy looked good on Dex, kind of how busy looked good on Dex. "You need a shower, pet. Can things be on hold for a few minutes?"

"Hmm... Let me check my rolls. They're on the first rise.

Everything look okay? Did you get the glasses down? I made tea, and Milo and Les are bringing Cokes."

"The glasses are on the table and it looks great. Thank you for the tea." He kissed Dex's dusty cheek. "I'd almost forgotten we had a dining table."

"It's very classy, that table. It's going to be a great party."

Dex had been busting his ass for two days, only stopping to watch the parade with wide eyes. Cyrus had taken Dex to his favorite spot on Central Park South near 6th to watch. It was a chilly, early morning, but Dex didn't complain at all about that, just got right back to work as soon as they got home.

"It is, thanks to you." He waited for his boy to finish checking on the rising rolls and then pulled Dex from the kitchen. If he hesitated, Dex might never leave.

"You looking forward to hosting?" Dex asked, eyes darting back toward the kitchen.

"I am, are you?" Cyrus ushered his boy right through the bedroom and into the bathroom. He resisted the urge to remind Dex to wash his hair and use soap, but just barely. He didn't hesitate, though, to help his boy undress.

"Once everyone eats and it was good, I'll be able to relax. I just want everyone to be happy."

There was flour *everywhere*. What? Had Dex masturbated with it?

"You know how much we all appreciate the effort, pet. Don't you? We're going to be very happy with dinner. How could anything made with so much love not be delicious?"

He started the water and practically lifted Dex into the shower. "The turkey smells like heaven."

"And I smell like turkey." Dex laughed, and the sound was merry and joyous.

He snorted. "Scrub up, butterball. I'm going to get your

formal corset out. Unless you'd rather not..." But it was Thanksgiving, so was there a better time?

"Can we do it after the cooking? I'd die if I stained it. It's the fanciest thing I've ever worn."

"Of course. And if you'd rather stick with your regular one under something, that's fine too. Honestly, pet. Be comfortable."

"Oh, I want to wear it," Dex called from the shower. "I want to show it off. It's so handsome. I ironed my good jeans and everything."

Ironing jeans still sounded so foreign to him. He did like how they fit Dex's ass, though.

He was going to wear jeans too. And his boots. And whatever else Dex pulled out of the closet. A vest maybe or his black mock-turtleneck. Or both.

One way or the other, all eyes would be on his boy, he had no doubt.

He scooped up Dex's dirty clothes, put down a clean bathmat and left a towel on the counter. It was the least he could do, given that Dex had been preparing a meal for two days. "You're steaming up the place."

"Sorry! Just jacking off! Won't be a sec." Dex's voice was full of laughter.

"You lie." He poked his head around the shower curtain. "I don't hear that adorable grunting."

"Grunting? Seriously?" Dex made dramatic pig noises as he rinsed his hair.

"Hey, I just call it as I see it." He left Dex to the shower and took the dirty laundry to the hamper. "What the hell did you do, by the way? Dump the flour over your head?"

"I'm still looking for a cheap barber! I look like a hippy!" Dex's hair was shaggy, sure, but hippy? No. And he thought the shaggy was adorable.

"There's no such thing as cheap in New York. You want me to cut it? And what does that have to do with the flour that's literally everywhere?" Cheap barber. That was ridiculous. They were a couple. He had enough money for Dex to get a haircut. They were going to have to have another money talk because Dex just didn't get it.

"Sure. Milo freaked out by the thought. And I may have had a wee flour-tastrophe."

"May?" He grabbed the towel as his boy climbed out of the shower and wrapped Dex up in it like a kid.

"Yeah. I cleaned it up. I was opening a bag of flour and poof!" Dex grinned over at him. "Mushroom cloud of flour."

"Poof!" He laughed and rubbed Dex's back through the towel. "I didn't hear you scream or anything. Impressive."

"I figured I was safe. Flour is seldom deadly." Oh, his boy managed that with a straight face.

He nodded sagely. "Such a wise one, pet. Get dressed."

"I'll throw on a T-shirt and an apron. Then I'll put on a nice shirt and my corset once I'm done cooking." Dex tugged on his tighty-whities and socks before pulling out the pressed and starched jeans.

"Brandon and Peter will be here early so Peter can help you. He's a fantastic cook, you'll appreciate him." Peter, Milo, and Dex. That was going to be interesting. Each of them was a challenge on their own, together they could get up to anything.

Well, there were worse things than tying them all together for a while.

"Can I ask you a question?"

That was odd. Dex knew he could ask. "Of course. Anything you like."

"So...is this going to work like at Les and Milo's or more like at the bar?"

"Certainly if you have a preference you should say so, it's your holiday too. But as far as I am concerned it's more like three couples having Thanksgiving dinner together than the way it was that night at Les and Milo's. Informal."

He tried to imagine feeding Dex pumpkin pie with his fingers. What a mess.

"Perfect. I just didn't know what expectations of the other guys were. I asked Milo, and he said—" Dex went pink. "Well, he had lots to say."

Oh, to be a fly on the wall for that conversation. "Anything you'd like to share with me? I'd rather not be surprised." He pointed to his closet. "I need to dress as well, please."

"Am I choosing, or do you know what you want?" Dex found him boxers and socks, straightaway.

"You choose." He shucked his sweats and his T-shirt. "I'm dressing for you after all, love."

"Oh, yum." Jeans and the black sweatshirt that he knew his boy loved came out of the closet. "Milo says things used to get a little interesting when the single men left."

"Anything is possible. Having always been one of those single men who left, I can't say I've participated. But as I understand it, what does or doesn't happen is all spontaneous. Some years have been more interesting—to use Milo's words—than others."

He hadn't even given that possibility any thought. He never had and it didn't occur to him at all. "We're the hosts, pet, so whatever goes on has to be okay with us. Why don't we talk about this a little?"

"That was what I was thinking, Master. That's why I brought it up." Dex knelt before him to help him dress. He didn't think that sight would ever not make his mouth dry.

He reached down and brushed his fingers through his

boy's hair, enjoying the 'shaggy' length. "Smart boy. I've always been single, so it didn't occur to me at all. For what it's worth, as I never have been involved, I'm certainly not missing anything if we decide we'd rather discourage after dinner play."

"So is it okay to just let the evening be what it is? I'm okay with just being if you are." Dex had the strangest expression on his face. "And I can't believe I just said that, but it's just the two of us, no matter what. I learned that at the store. When things happen, it's just us."

"It's just us." Every so often, Dex had a way of making heavy concepts seem so simple. It never failed to leave him breathless. "But let me make sure I understand you. You're saying you're fine with letting the evening be spontaneous—whatever that means? Play? Sex?"

"No one touches me but you. I'm yours. No one touches you but me. You're mine." His boy looked up at him, eyes so sure, so clear. "I'm safe with you—body, heart, and soul. I don't have to stress it."

His boy deserved an answer, but he found himself unable to speak. Cyrus held Dex's gaze, returning all the devotion he saw there, all the trust and love he just couldn't manage words for at the moment. Body, heart and soul was literally everything Dex had to offer and the possessive hard line, that place where they belonged only to each other, was the easiest thing in the world to give his boy in return.

"I'm yours, love," he whispered, knowing Dex would understand.

"Yes, Master." Dex pushed up, kissed him like there was nothing else his boy would ever need more.

He pulled Dex in close and gave his boy everything the kiss demanded. Not just his love, but his attention, his focus.

He always felt a little high when Dex kissed him this way, being needed and desired so intensely at the same time.

His pet was dazed, lips parted and swollen when then they parted. "Damn, Master. You make a man dizzy."

He cupped Dex's cheek and drew a thumb over those gorgeous lips. "You make a man happy. And hungry."

"And we don't have time for fun. It's no fair." Dex stroked his cock, slow and sweet, just keeping them warm and revved.

That made him grin and he stroked one of Dex's nipples through the T-shirt. "We have plenty of time, just not right at the moment. You know as soon as you put that pretty corset on I'll be thinking about you all night anyway."

Dex moaned softly, lips brushing his ear. "Never had a Thanksgiving where I was looking forward to the cooking being done."

He shivered, the promise in those words almost enough to distract him from the meal. "I'm looking forward to all of it." He'd just have to beg off his usual second piece of pie. He took Dex by the hips and physically moved his boy back a step. "I'll finish dressing. You go do what you need to do."

"What I need to do, and what I want to do are totally different things." His boy cupped his cock, giving it a gentle little hug, before Dex backed off with a wicked smile.

"We have time. I don't schedule for the Friday after Thanksgiving. Are you going to have to work this weekend?" He would understand if so, but he had ideas.

"I'll make time for you, love. I promise. I need to go get those rolls in and put the appetizers out." Dex kissed his cheek and left.

Make time for him. He had a bad feeling they were losing their weekends until Christmas, so the time they had needed to be used well. And he knew also that sometimes 'well' might mean resting. If these last two days were any indication, Dex could easily run himself into the ground.

He finished dressing in Dex's chosen outfit, stomping into his boots to finish things off just as the door buzzed. "I've got it!" He called down the hall. Dex didn't need to be bothered.

"Brandon, Peter. Welcome! Come on in." His building was completely accessible, and he was happy about that. Even the Master bathroom was laid out well. He wouldn't have invited Brandon otherwise.

"Thanks for the invite. Boy, go take our dishes to Dex, please."

"Yes, Master." Two covered dishes were handed over to Peter before Brandon took his hand. "Happy Thanksgiving, man. Peter was tickled to be able to spend time with your Dex. He's quite taken."

He shook with Brandon, smiling. "Dex can use the company and the help. I appreciate it. He's been cooking for two days. He loves it, but Peter will be much better help than I have been."

Cyrus led the way into the living room just as Dex and Peter appeared with plates of appetizers.

There were cheeses and meats, vegetables, dips, little cheeseballs, little phyllo tasters, and then there were bowls of chile con queso and salsa, chips and something Dex called grape jelly meatballs.

"I promised I'd try one of the meatballs." He had, even though the concept sounded vile. He grinned widely. "I think we should try them together, Brandon."

"There's nothing you can do to meatballs to make me scared, Cy."

"They're wicked good, Master. Seriously. I had two." Peter licked his lips, so dramatic.

"I'm sure they are, they just sound odd." He stuck a toothpick in one and handed it to Brandon, then speared one for himself. "Cheers," he said before popping the whole thing into his mouth.

"Oh. Mmm." He looked at Dex and nodded, still chewing. "Good." Tangy and savory and remarkably delicious. Not what he'd expected at all.

Dex stood there, eyebrows lifted with a grin. "See? I told you. Cooking is a thing."

"Very creative, Dex. I'm looking forward to your meal even more now." Brandon moved right in close to the coffee table and looked everything over. "I'm glad I came hungry."

He picked up one of the phyllo things and popped that in whole as well. Maybe not the best idea, because it was hot, and he fanned at his face.

Brandon laughed. "I see you haven't managed to cure your Master of his appetite even with your amazing cooking."

"I love cooking for him. It's rewarding. For real." Dex beamed at Brandon. "Can I get you something to drink, sir? I have Cokes, water, iced tea, coffee."

Cyrus loved the way Brandon looked at Dex. It reminded him of a proud uncle. "A Diet Coke, please."

Peter looked at Cyrus. "And you, sir?"

"Iced tea for me, please, boy." Peter looked great tonight, the black utility kilt and boots so good on the boy.

Dex seemed...happy, totally in his element cooking and hosting and serving. He was laughing and chatting with Peter easily, which shouldn't have surprised Cyrus. His boy was social, had been used to having dozens of people to care for.

He was even more glad dinner was casual; Dex would get to be...totally Dex without being nervous.

Cyrus took a seat on the couch. "Dex is going to wear his formal corset in a bit, he wanted to get dinner set first. He just loves his regular one; he wears it every day."

"I knew, when you guys said the cuffs were like being held, that corseting might be his thing. Some subs need that constant touch, that assurance that you're with them." Brandon looked almost smug. "I'm so pleased, man. Seriously."

"That was one of those once in a lifetime things, right? So amazing. Has Peter ever had a moment like that since he's been with you?"

"My Peter's kink is orgasm control. It gives him the high of body mods without the danger of pushing too far."

Oh, that was hot. "Lucky you." Cyrus grinned at Brandon over another meatball.

"You have no idea." Brandon's eyes twinkled like they were lit from within.

"See what I'm telling you, Dex? Never leave the Doms alone. They give each other ideas. Look at those faces." Peter winked at Cyrus and handed him a tall glass of iced tea which had been garnished with an orange slice and mint.

"I'm learning." Dex handed Brandon his Diet Coke. "They can be wicked, can't they? Naughty Doms."

"One of them will make some sly comment, and they'll talk each other up, and the next thing you know you'll be wearing cuffs and have a little red bottom. I know mischief when I see it."

He gave Brandon a sidelong look. "Did you offer Peter amnesty tonight or something?"

"Amnesty, no. But permission to relax with his new friends, yes. It is a holiday after all." Brandon winked at him.

He loved the way Dex crossed his arms, pretending—or

possibly not—to dare Cyrus to disagree with Brandon's suggestion.

"Right. A holiday, after all." He winked at his boy.

"Yes, Sir." Dex kissed his cheek, whispering so that only he could hear. "*Just* a holiday."

He hadn't anticipated that this new rule meant the word 'just' would make his balls ache. He did love his boy's brand of naughty.

"Are you ready to get dressed? Is Peter going to help you?"

"All I have left is the gravy, but Peter's volunteered to do that. Will you please watch the rolls, Master?"

So sweet.

"Absolutely." He gave his boy a confident nod, but secretly felt like the pressure was on not to let them burn.

"Thank you. Peter, can you please give me a hand?" Dex asked, and Peter waggled his eyebrows.

"I'll give you two."

Cyrus laughed. "Good luck with that. Dex has rules."

"I'll bet he does." Brandon glanced at Dex and then at Cyrus.

Cyrus shrugged. "Negotiated rules." Right. Dex's rules that he'd readily agreed to weren't really a negotiation. That worked for him; he appreciated that Dex was firm on the rules but flexible on their execution.

"That's what makes the world go round, yeah?"

Peter elbowed Dex. "Come on, let's get you dressed up."

"Rolls, Master. Please." Dex led Peter off to the bedroom.

"Rolls," he repeated. "Brandon, you better join me in the kitchen. If I let these things burn I'll have to hang my head in shame." He handed Brandon his tea and took the handles on the Dom's chair.

"Thank you, man."

There was something wonderful about having permission to help. Brandon didn't allow it often when the subs were out and about, but when they were alone, he did.

"Can't have you getting lost." He chuckled and parked Brandon near the kitchen table. "Doesn't it smell great in here? Have a look." He lifted the foil that was over the turkey to take a peek.

"Oh, great job. What are you responsible for here? Or are you like me, dependent on your boy or starve?"

"I took direction reasonably well, but I can't claim responsibility for any of it. The way I eat, I barely managed not to starve before he came along. I'm so spoiled now, it's a wonder I haven't gained weight. He even puts together snacks for me." In some ways the snacks were the best part. They'd been completely Dex's idea. He'd have just come into the kitchen and grabbed an apple. Now he had carefully planned plates with protein and carbs and everything.

"He cares for you. You can tell." Brandon chuckled. "Mr. Bachelor Dom got himself caught."

"Owned, I think. I'd be embarrassed, but it's the best damn feeling in the world." Some piece of him had always known it would be like this. That if he ever found the right man, the right sub, the right lover, it would be fast and forever. As he got older he'd started to wonder if it would happen, but he finally gave up worrying about that and decided to be happy and live his life.

Living his life was what had guided him to Dex, and he'd known—the moment his boy fell asleep in his rental car he'd known there was something in Dex worth taking a deeper look at.

"Isn't it? I thought...well, you knew how it was back then,

before Peter found me. It wasn't hell, but it sure as shit wasn't heaven."

He could only imagine how it felt. But Peter fell for Brandon first. It took Brandon a little while to believe it but nobody, including Peter, blamed Brandon for that; the Dom was understandably cautious. Peter was both persistent and patient and, in the end, that was the magic potion.

"God, those rolls smell amazing. You said he's a professional baker? Lucky bastard."

"You too, because you get to eat his dinner." He peered into the oven, feeling like he was hatching them. "I'll be in deep trouble if they burn though."

Naturally, that was when the door buzzed again. "Crap. That'll be Les and Milo." He looked at the oven again, then peered down the hall. "All right, I guess you're in charge."

"Me?"

"Yep. No pressure, just yell for me if they're looking too brown. I'll be right back."

He laughed and hurried down the hall to get the door.

They were bogged down with covered dishes and soda and flowers, both men laughing and leaning on each other. "Little Dom, little Dom, let us come in!"

"Oh my god." He reached for the bag of soda and took the flowers too, trying to be helpful, smiling as somehow in the middle of all of that Milo planted a kiss on his cheek. "Come in, you nuts. Come on, right to the kitchen. Brandon and Peter are here."

"We brought mashed potatoes and an apple pie, Cokes and ice, and Master's weird cranberry salad." Milo kissed his cheek. "Where's the cook?"

"Getting dressed. Peter is helping." Cyrus wondered how much to say. He thought maybe he should let Dex make his own impression. "I've been tasked with keeping the rolls from burning."

"So far so good, man." Brandon gave Les and Milo a nod. "Gentlemen. Happy Thanksgiving."

"Happy Thanksgiving!" Les shook Brandon's hand and Milo stole a kiss on the cheek.

Dex came out of the bedroom with Peter, looking like something out of an Old West fantasy. The long-sleeved button-down was just a bit dressier than a regular one, and the brown leather corset made his boy's figure exaggerated, perfect.

Cyrus set everything down and went right to him. "You look incredible." He had to touch it, slide his hands along that amazing waistline.

"I'll go make gravy," Peter murmured as Dex looked up at him.

"You'll make me hard, Master, looking at me like that."

Aw. Wouldn't that be a shame?

"I can't help it. Look at you."

He didn't want to embarrass Dex though, so he gave his boy a quick kiss and a smile. "Come say hello to Les and Milo."

He kept one arm around Dex, though. That sweet, bound body begged to be touched, and the boning and leather fascinated his fingers.

To his great relief, Peter was taking the rolls out of the oven when they turned around.

"Les, look at what Brandon found for my boy." He moved Dex out in front of him, so proud.

Milo jumped and took a step toward Dex. "Dex! Oh my god!"

Les caught Milo by the shoulder, stopping him. "Easy, boy."

Milo's grabby hands dropped right to his sides as Les stepped forward. "Dex you're making your Master look damn good."

Cyrus stretched tall. "Isn't he?"

Dex was blushing so hard he was almost purple. "Thank you, Sir. It's brand new. Master Brandon found it."

"You look absolutely comfortable, boy. You must like it." Les stepped back and gestured to Milo who was still grinning when he gave Dex a big hug.

"You look amazing. This is amazing."

"Yeah? It's cool?" Dex beamed at Les. "Peter helped me put it on."

"You have a tiny waist! Damn, man!" Milo held Dex out at arm's length. "Wow."

"It's not too tight, is it boy?" Brandon was talking to Peter.

"No, sir. I was careful. Dex just has this beautiful shape."

Brandon nodded approvingly. "He does."

"I think I'm jealous." Milo laughed. "You're *hot*, baby."

"Milo!" Dex hid his face in Cy's chest. "Warm up the potatoes, buddy."

"You shouldn't be so modest." Milo went over to the stove. "If you got it, flaunt it."

Cyrus laughed gently and hugged an arm around his boy. "Peter saved your rolls, pet."

"Thank you, Peter. How do they look?" Dex's need to look at the rolls overrode his embarrassment, and he slipped away.

Les looked at Cy with a wicked smile. "Impressive, my friend. He glows."

Cyrus lowered his voice and leaned closer to Les. "He found his thing. It was amazing. It's been...well you can see for yourself, obviously. He has an everyday one that

Brandon helped him with that he wears most of the day now when I'm working."

"He needed to believe you were holding him, but with his work, cuffs couldn't work." Brandon high-fived Les. "It was immediate, that connection."

"Stunning. It was the most beautiful thing I've ever seen." He'd seen subs have all kinds of wonderful breakthroughs and epiphanies in his line of work, and in the lifestyle, but this was different. It was his sub, his partner. His boy. His lover. It was something else entirely.

He looked over at their boys, all working together to get dinner ready. "Shall we get out of the way, gentlemen?"

"Absolutely. Milo said you didn't need munchies, and he wasn't lying!" Les shook his head. "Your boy should cater. Look at this."

"Don't give him ideas. He's already stressing the holiday rush. I hope Milo is ready to be busy for the next month." He gave Les a wink and headed for the living room. With more company around, he picked up Brandon's soda to bring with them but didn't touch the chair.

They all settled, the munchies on the coffee table delicious. He imagined they would be eating on leftovers for days, even after sending everyone home with goodies.

"You know, this is the first time ever that I haven't been single on a holiday." He grinned and picked up some cheese. "It doesn't suck."

"No. It really, really doesn't." Brandon took another meatball. "Damn, these are like crack, buddy."

"Blame Dex. I just eat here. We're all going to need more gym time this week."

He tried not to eat too much though, and that was good because it wasn't long before their boys started bringing out platters of food.

The turkey looked amazing, and the food kept coming and coming. It was like a cartoon—dish after dish, until the table groaned with it.

Peter helped Brandon get settled at the head of the table, and Cyrus took the other end, ridiculously pleased by how their evening was going. Eventually the parade of food ended, Milo refilled water and soda glasses, and Cyrus stood up for a toast.

"I feel like I should say something to mark the holiday, and because this is my first time having you all here." He picked up his Diet Coke. "I think it's fair to say that every man at this table lives in gratitude pretty much daily. I know I do. It's not easy to articulate, so I'm just going to say thank you to each of you, and especially to Dex, for...literally everything." He had no idea how good it would feel to say that. He gave his boy a smile as he raised his glass.

Dex went pink, but that expression of comfort and wonder was everything.

Everything.

They clinked glasses, and then Dex cleared his throat. "I hope y'all don't mind, but I'd like to say grace, if it's okay."

"Of course." He put his glass down and sat. "Go ahead."

Dex took his hand and Peter's, bowed his head. Cy took Milo's hand, and suddenly they were a circle.

"Lord, I'd like to thank You for all the blessings You've brought me. I never thought that I'd—Lord, I never thought I'd find a home, friends, a soulmate, but I did." Dex looked up, met Cy's eyes. "I'm a lucky son of a bitch, lucky and thankful, and I pray that everyone has as full a heart as me. In Jesus' name. Amen."

"Amen." He squeezed his boy's hand and then leaned over and kissed Dex's forehead too. He didn't know what higher power was out there, but he was sure there was one.

He didn't think it mattered what he called it. "There's a lot of that kind of luck at this table. And a lot of hungry people too."

"Amen to that also." Milo laughed.

"Well, God knows there's enough food for all y'all. Eat!" Dex sat back with a smile like a king surveying his kingdom.

They ate. Plates were passed and platters went around the table. Even Dex had more than four bites on his plate. Nothing like good food to put everyone in a good mood.

"Peter, save some mashed potatoes for the rest of us," Milo teased.

Peter laughed and put another spoonful on his plate. "Potatoes make the world go around, man."

"Your stuffing is so good, Dex." Les took another bite. "Is it a family recipe? Your own?"

"It's my granny's, sort of. It's what I remember my granny's tasting like." Dex chuckled and shrugged. "It's good, no matter what, thank you, sir."

"Really good. Where did you learn to cook?"

Cyrus wondered if all the praise would help Dex understand it was a real talent.

"Watching TV and eating."

They all stared at his boy for a second.

He knew how they felt. "Dex likes to tell me he's a mimic. I can't seem to impress upon him that not everyone can Master a skill they learned on TV or YouTube."

"It's true. He just looks at something and figures it out." Milo nodded to Cy. "It's too cool."

"I'm just handy is all. Y'all eat now and don't worry on me."

"It's remarkable. But you see how he is." He gave Dex a fond smile.

"Talent needs to be appreciated, Dex. I hope you do."

Brandon ate the last bite of turkey off his plate. "I know I do."

"I never doubt that I'm appreciated here, sir. Me and my Cyr, we got it."

Brandon nodded approvingly. "I like your style, Dex."

Cyrus did too.

"When are you coming to get a piercing with me, Dex?" Peter grinned across the table.

"After I save up my pennies from Christmas." Dex's smile was just naughty.

"Oh ho! I don't recall discussing piercings." Not that Cyrus would stop the boy from getting one. Cyrus could argue about facial hair but Dex was Master of his own body.

"No?" Dex winked at him. "Not something you'd love as a surprise?"

"I do like surprises, in fact. You can keep that one on simmer."

"I want to come!" Milo chimed in.

Les snorted. "I don't think so."

"Not into piercings, Les?" Brandon asked, voice teasing.

"Oh, no. I love piercings. Milo tends to forget that he panics about things like that." Les took Milo's hand.

Milo sighed. "Right. It's true, I do."

"Yeah? It's okay, Milo. I worked in a piercing salon for a long time. Lots of people do." Dex dropped that bit of information so easily, like it was common knowledge.

Which, of course, it was not. He had a feeling he'd be learning things like this about his boy for a long time to come.

"Really? Cool." The smile Milo had for Dex was so appreciative. Dex was so good about making people feel comfortable.

"Is there anything you haven't done, Dex?" Les's head tilted like he didn't believe there was.

"Tons of things, but I've done a lot. My 'a lots' are just real different from city 'a lots'."

That got a laugh. "I'll bet."

"What's your favorite job so far?" Peter was asking a real question; the boy could be so serious sometimes.

"Taking care of Cyr. I mean, it's like a calling, more than a job, but it's what I love best. The rest is making pennies."

Peter didn't answer out loud, instead he bumped shoulders with Dex and nodded.

Brandon snorted. "Okay, Cyrus. You win the Dom of the night award."

"Shut up and pass the turkey, turkey."

Brandon's eyes rolled like dice. "Gobble gobble."

There was a few heartbeats of silence, then the entire table cracked up with happy laughter. While everyone was distracted and laughing, he leaned over and gave Dex a quick kiss. "You're my favorite job too."

"Good. I'll work at keeping you busy." Dex's hand found his and held on a second.

The rest of dinner went fast, and everyone helped with dishes before they set all the pies out on the table. His favorite was a traditional pumpkin pie and Dex's was amazing. He also had a few bites of the others—pecan and this rich chocolate one—and after all of that he was glad for the strong cup of coffee he was sipping on one of the couches in the living room, and for the boy snuggled against him.

Dex hummed softly, smiling at the sight of Les and Milo sitting close on the love seat, Peter right in Brandon's lap. "You happy, Master?"

"Never been happier." Cyrus sighed gently. "Looks like everyone enjoyed their dinner. How are you feeling now?"

"Wonderful. I'm so glad. I wish it could just stay here and not be Christmas season tomorrow."

"Shh. We're not worrying about tomorrow yet. We're hanging out in the right now."

"Definitely," Brandon agreed, one hand sliding under Peter's shirt. "All about now, right, boy?"

"Yes, Master. That's all that matters." The need in Peter's voice made him smile, but the fact that Dex didn't tense? That made him proud.

This was about the time he would generally excuse himself and leave the couples to themselves and their evening. He never had to; no one would have asked him to leave but it had been awkward not having someone to share the rest of the evening with, whatever the rest of the evening turned out to be.

But this was his home, and he was with his boy, and he felt absolutely comfortable being just who they were.

The corset that Dex was wearing kept his attention all evening. Every time the boy moved Cyrus noted the way it held him, restrictive and also not, showing off Dex's ass or accenting his shoulders. Now though, this close, he wanted Dex to be able to move.

He slid his hand over Dex's narrow waist. "I think we should take this off now, pet."

"Yes, Master." Dex stretched, lips brushing his cheek. Together they worked the hooks open, and Dex slipped out of the leather.

Cyrus inhaled deeply, the warm, earthy scent of the leather and his boy making him tingle. "I love that smell."

"You and your leather kink." Les chuckled. Milo was lounging in Les's lap like a cat.

"It's a lovely kink to have," Brandon agreed, and Dex chuckled softly.

"Says the leatherworker!" Les shot back, and the laughter moved through the room.

Cyrus grinned. "I do appreciate your talents, Brandon. I'm not ashamed to say so."

"I appreciate them too!" Milo chimed in. "God, you are pretty in that thing, Dex."

"Thank you. I feel...pretty damn wonderful in them." Dex nuzzled in, and his nipples were hard under the button-down where they pressed against Cy, just begging for attention.

Cyrus started working Dex's buttons open slowly, no ultimate intention in mind, just letting the energy in the room guide them.

"I hope you have one he can wear to a party, Cy." Lex brought Milo to a number of different gatherings, some of them formal, some of them kinkier than others. He wasn't sure yet if any of that was really Dex's cup of tea, or his anymore. It had been so long.

"We'll see. I'm still planning on that munch after the holidays. Did I tell you, Brandon? Just a low-key informal thing so Dex can meet people."

"Sounds amazing. Invite us and I'll bring something special for your boy to wear." Brandon chuckled. "Hell, we'd come just for the food. You're amazing, Dex."

He felt his boy flush with heat. "Thank you, sir. I'm tickled shitless you enjoyed supper."

"I told you they would. You didn't need to worry so much. Most of us just appreciate the effort."

"Most," Milo said, voice haughty, playing with Dex. "Personally, I appreciate the food."

He appreciated the food too. But he didn't need to say that for Dex to know it was true.

Dex snorted. "You have a hollow leg, man."

"You wish you could have my leg, buddy!"

"You wish you had his waist." Everyone looked at Peter, who wasn't usually given to that kind of teasing. Even Milo looked surprised. "What? I'm right and you know it."

"Oh, you were serious?" Milo winked at Peter. "Right, of course you were. You're always so serious."

Dex whispered to him. "He totally isn't, you know. He's really funny."

Cyrus nodded agreement. Peter didn't talk as much in groups, but alone the boy was as quick with a joke. He just didn't care much for teasing. Milo was a lot of company.

Once he got Dex's shirt open he pushed it back, encouraging his boy to take it off, and his fingers found one of those lovely pink nubs to tease.

Dex gasped softly, eyes flashing up to meet his for a second, then his pet relaxed, all but that belly, which twitched and rolled with every touch.

"Only me," he mouthed to his boy and followed that with a wink.

"Gentlemen, there's a rollout in the playroom, and the couch you're sitting on, Les, is one as well. Make yourselves at home. The only thing I ask is if you choose to use anything in the playroom, have your boy clean it before you head home. Dex will appreciate assistance from your boys with breakfast in the morning if you stay."

He didn't know whether anyone would or not no one was drinking and it wasn't all that late, but it seemed like good hospitality to put the offer out there. He was happy to have all of them if they felt like crashing.

"Thank you, friend." Brandon smiled over, nodded to him. "We appreciate the offer. You have a lovely playroom."

Les hummed softly, and he thought that was agreement, but there was no way to know with his mouth busy teasing Milo.

"Look at Milo," he whispered to Dex. "He's lovely. Watch them." Milo boy was putty in Les's hands in front of people. They both got off on an audience. "It's okay, you can watch; it's a thing for them."

Milo leaned back into Les's hands, showing off, almost dancing on Les's lap.

Dex's eyes went wide, the shock utterly charming, if Cy was honest.

Guess that was something else the boy hadn't seen in Texas. If he wasn't so sure this lifestyle was deeply necessary for them both he might think he'd been a very bad influence. Everything was good between them though, no matter how Dex had been brought up.

Cyrus shifted and pulled Dex onto his lap so he could more easily taste his boy's pert little nipples and nipped gently at one with his teeth.

One of Dex's hand slid to the back of his head, tangling in his hair, and he bit again, answering that hunger with a bit more of his own.

Someone in the room moaned and someone else gasped, and there wasn't any question where the rest of the night was headed but he knew what he wanted. He wanted his boy, his lover.

Alone.

"Master," Dex whispered, eyes huge in the dim room. "Love."

Cyrus hesitated, torn for a second about whether it would be rude as the host to hustle Dex off to the bedroom, but Brandon moved first, heading for the playroom with Peter, and that made the decision very easy. He gave Dex a little push. "Only me, pet. Let's go."

"Only you, Master." Dex stood and grabbed his hand with one, his corset with the other, then tugged, hauling him up.

He stared into Dex's eyes as he got to his feet, his boy's self-assurance making his heart race and intensifying his need.

Despite losing their audience, Cyrus was pretty sure Les and Milo didn't notice any of them leave.

"Do you know what it does to me when you look at me like that?" Cyrus let himself be pulled into the bedroom and kept his eyes glued to Dex as his boy stepped around him to close the door.

"Show me." Dex was hard as a rock, belly tight, nipples stiff and eager.

Jesus.

The heat in those words went right to his balls.

"I can do that." Cyrus crowded Dex against the door and took in those lovely eyes for another second before kissing him and pushing the boy's open shirt off his shoulders.

The cuffs caught Dex's wrists, the bulk of the shirt between Dex's lower back and the door. Dex was trapped between his kiss and his will, and it suited them both to the ground.

Dex's skin was smoldering under his fingers. Cyrus was burning up in all his leather too, but right now he didn't want to slow things down enough to get it all off. He tugged at Dex's belt and opened the boy's jeans with practiced fingers so he could tuck his hands under the denim and get hold of that sweet ass.

Dex rocked back into his hands, that muscled butt rolling against his touch and making heady demands.

He wanted Dex more than he'd wanted anything or anyone in his whole life, but that was too many words to say on so little breath. "Love," he whispered between their kisses and gulps of air, knowing that single heavy word would cover it.

"Yes. Please, Master." Jesus, that need made Cy dizzy, that honest hunger that proved he was not alone.

He let Dex go and made it to the bed in three long strides, where he sat heavily. "Boots, pet." He shucked his shirt and tossed it over the end of the bed, then dropped his hands to his waistband and opened his pants. Dex worked out of his shirt and knelt before Cy, head right where he wanted it as Dex worked his boots open.

Cyrus was impatient but loved this view and forced himself to breathe and watch his boy so carefully, lovingly, dealing with the buckles on his boots. "Thank you, pet."

"It's my pleasure, Sir." Dex nuzzled his knee, inhaling deep. "You make me ache, so good."

He stood up and pushed his pants down over his hips until Dex took over, sliding them down and off. He dropped a hand down offering his boy a hand up. "Come here, love. Kiss me."

Dex stood and pushed into his arms, meeting him, head-on. One arm wrapped around him, holding him tight as their lips crashed together.

That was his boy, hot and hungry and totally his. He took Dex's mouth, tongue sliding along Dex's, tasting, claiming. Their hips rocked in sync, Dex's denim grating against his aching cock. Dex made the best noises—low and heady, pushed into his lips. His pet burned for him, and he took in every cry.

He spun them, lifting Dex just high enough to move them to the bed. As Dex crawled back on it, he grabbed the boy's jeans and peeled them off. "Mmm. So much better." He hummed and crawled up over his boy.

"Better." Dex reached for him, dragging him close. "What do you need?"

His boy was flushed and lovely, wanting, and putting him first anyway. That was everything he needed. "You. Just you." He dropped his mouth to Dex's lovely nipples, teasing one with his tongue, and reached for the boy's dark, heavy cock.

"Oh fuck..." Dex arched and danced underneath him, begging for more. "All yours."

Damn right.

Cyrus was going for another slingshot around the moon.

Dex's hands were hunting, diving into his hair and digging into his shoulders, and all he could think was the boy needed to focus. He took a second and got control of the issue by tucking both of his boy's hands under his own neck and then pinning them there with one hand.

All the chaotic scrambling stopped, and he nodded.

Good.

This time he tugged on Dex's balls and gave one nipple a fast, hard pinch with his teeth.

"Fuck!" Dex's belly went tight so quick he swore he could hear the muscles squeak. "Please. Yes."

Greedy boy. Dex took every sensation and fed from it. So hungry.

He put a little more strength into keeping his boy's hands still, giving Dex something to work against as he tasted more skin, moved to the other nipple. He lapped at it gently, letting Dex anticipate, watching sidelong how it made his boy's toes curl. "That's my boy."

"Yours." There was a quiet wonder in the single word, a fascinating mixture of need and pleasure, hunger and peace. "*Just* yours."

"*Just* so." And a small but problematic word turned into something big and wonderful in an instant.

"I'm going to let go of your hands, but you are to keep them right where they are, pet. Lock your fingers together if you have to, but they're to stay behind your neck. My mind is on them even if my hands aren't. Understood?"

He knew he was, just as he knew he'd be obeyed. He only asked because he liked to hear Dex tell him so, and that was his privilege.

But while Dex took a breath to answer he slid lower, leaving little pressure marks over his boy's abs and wet tongue trails as he dipped below his boy's navel.

"Yes, Sir. I hear you." Dex licked his lips, pulling in his abs and lifting his shoulders to watch him like a hawk. Pretty pretty.

Oh nice. If he had an audience, he was going to put on a show. He shifted lower still and pushed Dex's knees open wider, studied his boy's straining prick for a moment and then bathed it with a wide, flat tongue from root to tip, finishing off with giving the head a good polish and driving his thumb into the slit.

"Master!" Dex pulled himself up to sitting, and Cy doubted he even knew. What impressed him was that those hands didn't move.

He pushed up on his arms and pulled Dex down for a hard kiss, keeping his boy there until they both had to tear away for air. "Beautiful boy," he whispered, and ducked his head again letting Dex's cock slide past his lips.

Dex fell back to the mattress, hips bucking in a few

restless motions before he settled. "God. God, you make me ache."

Then he was doing something right, wasn't he? He didn't just want his boy to ache, Cyrus reminded himself. He wanted to make his boy lose control. Make him come.

Hard.

Dex's scent was strong and heady, and he inhaled deeply, surrounding himself with his boy inside and out as he took Dex down his throat.

He pulled Dex in, pressing one finger against Dex's hole, tapping and teasing. Dex's steady rhythm stuttered, but only for a second before his pet pressed back, rocking between his mouth and his fingers.

Fuck he wanted his boy; he wanted to feel that rhythm from deep inside. He was enjoying the little high of making himself wait though, and he wanted the edge off his boy so he could take his time, let Dex build back up nice and slow. Cyrus let Dex move, encouraged it even, letting his boy take as he gave.

"More, Master. Please." Dex squeezed his finger with that sweet tight ring of muscles.

He had more. He had anything Dex needed.

Cyrus hummed, knowing just how those little vibrations felt, and pinched the skin behind Dex's balls intending it to sting.

Dex gasped for him and spread even wider, cock jumping on his tongue. "Is that where I should get a ring, Master? Right there?"

His boy had the best ideas.

He pulled up enough to get out a rough, "Yes." Then he dove his tongue deep into his boy's slit and stroked Dex fast, the little tease of bitter and salt making him groan.

Dex offered him a rough groan, something deeper than

a cry, harsher than a moan. That was all the warning he needed before Dex came for him, his boy giving himself over, filling his lips.

"Mmm." He made sure to savor every drop. He didn't do this often enough, he forgot how much he enjoyed just focusing on making another man come. And Dex took even that to a whole new level.

"You can move your arms now, love." He stayed focused on his boy until the high wore off a bit and then went after a rubber and lube. He wanted Dex like this, totally relaxed and focused, he wasn't wasting time.

Dex reached for him, hands ghosting over his skin, loving on him with a clumsy touch.

Cyrus moved over Dex, pinning his boy with his eyes and his bigger frame. "You're beautiful. You're everything I need, and I want you."

He lined up with that hot, hungry little hole, then took a slow, heavy kiss, pushing his tongue into his boy's mouth while he slowly stretched his boy and eased himself inside.

Dex slowly exhaled, fingers wrapped around his head, tangling in his hair. The muscles around his cock fluttered, gripping him and welcoming him in.

He broke the kiss with a soft moan and rolled his head back. "God, you feel so good."

"Good." Dex rolled up, hips rocking, teasing his cock.

That tease was just right. He was loving this buzz, loving being turned on and ready enough that he didn't want to rush; he just wanted to enjoy it. He worked against Dex's hips, pulling back and then sinking deep again. "You made me so proud tonight, pet. Because of how you reflect on me, but more because of how you presented yourself. So special."

Dex blushed dark, but his smile was so pleased, honored. "I was just me, just yours. That's enough."

"Just mine. And I am so proud to be yours." He drove a little harder, making them both moan. "So much more than enough, pet."

"Uh-huh..." Dex arched, a soft cry escaping his boy. "Oh, right there, love."

He nodded. Right there, he could do that. "I've got you." For as long as his boy allowed it, anyway. It was a slow build, but he knew they would both get lost in each other before too long. He braced himself and worked to drive his boy higher.

Dex's face was a portrait of hunger, and each slide in left him shaking all the more, begging Cy for one more thrust.

"Fuck. Oh, fuck, pet." He wasn't sure if he was begging or apologizing or both. He ducked his head, feeling himself start to unravel, the knot that was solid control coming undone. He hooked a shoulder behind one of Dex's knees and surged forward, their bodies making a slapping sound as they came together, as he pushed deeper still.

"Fuck!" God, he loved that—love the wild cry, the utter lack of shame. The way his boy needed him. It made his ass clench and his balls ache, and with a grunt he let go, his body taking over, hips working hard, everything in him seeking more sensation.

Dex grabbed his knees and pulled, offering himself up, wholly. Cy took the offer, slamming into his boy, driving to find their pleasure.

"Dex." God, he was riding that edge, so fucking close. He curled his fingers around his boy's cock, groaning at the feel of smooth, hot skin covering the hard length.

"Love you. Master." Dex's body went tight, gripping his cock like a fist.

A few more shallow thrusts and he started to shake, every muscle coiled tight and focused, every nerve tingling. "Love...pet."

"Love..." Dex's fingers joined his on that needy cock, pushing them a little faster, squeezing them hard.

The push from his boy was all he needed. Cyrus looked down between them, watching how their fingers moved together as his hips thrust wildly. "I'm...oh God. Gonna..."

"Please. Yes. Now." Dex slammed his head back, cock throbbing in his hand as his boy shot again.

He hit that wall and shouted something, he was sure he had, but his ears rang and the only thing he seemed to be able to see was the long, luscious curve of his boy's throat. Dex felt so tight as muscles contracted around him, and he thought he might never get another breath.

When he did suck in air, Dex's hands were there, running along his back, loving on him.

His recovery was slow, and he was still panting as he kissed his boy. Still working on a deep breath as he rolled to one side and pulled Dex into his arms. His heart was racing but his mind was still and calm, a little hormone addled maybe, but grounded in his boy, in their moment.

Dex was boneless and lazy, snuggling into him with soft little sounds. There was something amazing about having his boy, melted and quiet against him.

He had to grin, remembering the moment not so long ago that he'd swore one day he'd figure out a way to wear the boy out. When his biggest concern was just getting Dex to sleep and eat more than two bites at a time. Right now Dex seemed pretty damn relaxed, and he didn't doubt they were both ready for some sleep.

"I love you, pet." He kissed Dex's forehead and sighed, finally feeling like his heart might stay behind his ribcage.

"Best Thanksgiving in history, Master." Dex's smile was sweet as honey.

"Mhm. Best ever." His mind drifted for a second to their friends—to Les and Milo who were probably fucking in the living room and not caring who walked by, and to Brandon and Peter who were up to naughty things in his playroom. "I'm going to bet we have breakfast guests."

"I'll make waffles, and there's little bags of muffins for everyone to take home. I saved some for you too, just in case."

That was his pet—taking care of everyone, especially him.

He tucked Dex tighter against him just to prove to himself he wasn't dreaming. Yet. He yawned, and he knew it wasn't going to be more than a minute before he was.

"Good boy," he whispered. "Goodnight."

"Night, Master. Sleep."

41

"Three dozen trees, eight dozen ornaments, thirteen dozen Santa and Mrs. Claus, and a metric fuckton of snowflakes..." And those broke, so he always put them on galaxy glazed black backings.

He checked Cyr's toast and started the eggs.

He could bake eight trays an hour, so that meant all day today and most of the evening and night, but then he could start decorating.

"Damn. That sounds like a long day. Is Milo coming to help?" Cyr got up for more coffee and stopped him when he tried to help, grabbing his fingers and kissing them. "I've got it, pet."

"Two minutes to your breakfast, love. How are you?" He wasn't sure if Milo was coming over or not. He may just send Milo with money to buy groceries and Christmas stuff that he couldn't order online.

"I am fine. It's funny you have to ask me that, you know. I'm missing you a little already. Is it Christmas yet?" Cyr winked at him, smiling.

"I wish. I'm going to put a pot roast in the slow cooker

for supper." He grabbed the toast and buttered and jellied it before taking Cyr his breakfast.

"Sounds fine to me. You'll be tired by dinnertime." Cyr touched his arm and gave him a pat on the backside. "Thank you. Have you eaten anything?"

"No, Sir. I'm not hungry." Dex leaned down to beg a kiss.

He got one, and then Cyr held up a piece of the toast. "Sit and eat this."

"I only made enough for you, though..." He loved the offer, but Cyr needed that.

"It's a slice of toast. I'm not going to starve. Sit."

"Yes, Sir." Dex sat and shot his lover a look. "You might starve. Hell, you might eat Steven."

"Doubtful. He's skinny. If I get hungry I'll just send him out all trussed up to get me a snack." Cyr shot a smug look right back at him. "You'd love that, I'm sure."

"No naked men in my kitchen, love. I will be grumpy."

"He'd have a harness on. Maybe a ball gag." Cyr laughed, and took a bite of eggs.

"Butthead. Hell, maybe I'd just put him to work. It could be our own little sweatshop."

"Cute. Eat that toast before I add a butt plug to your day."

Lord, that would not help his focus. At all. It was a tingly little thought though, and it made him smile as he took a bite.

Cyr swallowed down the last bite of eggs and toast and chased that with a big sip of coffee. "Okay, pet. I'm off to work. I have to get the room ready."

"Have a good day. I love you." He missed their mornings —from feeding Cyr to dressing him to blowing him.

"Hey." Cyr put an arm around his waist, slid a hand over his corset and kissed him. "Thank you for my breakfast."

Cyr took his chin in warm fingers and smiled as their eyes met. “I love you. I’ll see you at lunch.”

“I love you, Master.” He leaned for half a second, sighed, and then got himself prepared for work. Butter, sugar, eggs, and flour; time for hell week.

42

Cyrus leaned against the door jamb looking into Dex's office. The room looked like a disaster area even though he knew his boy had a system and it was more like organized chaos. There were piles of fancy bakery boxes for the holiday-themed cookies, piles of packing and shipping supplies, the printer had a stack of paper beside it, and there was a stack of boxes ready to ship by the door just to his left.

Dex was in here somewhere too, he was pretty sure, but he couldn't see the boy. He took a couple of steps into the room and looked around again. "Pet?"

"Yeah?" Was Dex crying?

"Where are you?" He headed in the direction he thought he'd heard his boy's voice come from.

"I'm icing." Dex was kneeling on the floor, icing on the seat of one of the chairs.

Oh boy. Someone was having a day.

He stepped up close and knelt as well, carefully resting a hand on his boy's lower back so he didn't jostle Dex's arm. "You...ran out of room?"

"I'm just looking for comfortable positions. My hands

are bitches." Dex held up one hand, and it was a claw, red and curled.

"Jesus, pet." Cyrus shifted to sit flat, took hold of that hand, and gently started to rub, working the fingers in his own. "You need a break."

"Oh God." Dex broke out in a cold sweat, curling toward him. "I—Oh God."

He reached one arm out and pulled Dex in to lean against his chest before returning to those hands, gingerly but stubbornly massaging each finger, the palm, the wrist. "Have you been decorating all day?"

"I have to get things decorated so they can dry. Today and tomorrow, mostly." Dex moaned softly as he hit a sore spot. "Not there!"

Oh, definitely there. "Hush, pet. You've been at this since I saw you at lunch?"

"Yes, Sir. Trying to push this out."

"I understand. How much more do you need to get done tonight?" It was unrealistic to expect Dex to drop everything now, with delivery dates looming and more work to be done, but he could possibly get the boy fed and tucked in early.

"I was hoping to finish them all, but...I don't know." Dex met his eyes, pure exhaustion written in them.

"Fine. That's just fine. Let's eat and think about it; maybe there is something I can do for an hour or so after dinner to help you catch up and then we'll turn in early. Your hands need a rest. They won't do you any good gnarled up and painful, right?" He'd stood while he was talking and coaxed Dex up off the floor as well.

"I'm sorry. I'm just hurting." Dex followed him, blinking slow, his boy beginning to tremble. "I hate Christmas cookies, you know?"

"I can only imagine." There was nothing to be gained by

pointing out that Dex didn't have to do this or that he could take fewer orders…none of that was constructive in this moment, and Dex naturally wanted to contribute. His boy was tired and hurting, having to work hard to keep it together. What Dex needed was his Master to step in and make some decisions for tonight.

He kept them moving, one arm around Dex's waist and pulled the boy into the kitchen, where Dex had a soup of some kind going in the Crock Pot and a lovely crusty bread on the counter. "Have a seat, pet." He steered the boy into a chair. "It smells fantastic in here."

"Beef stew. I've been smelling it all day. So good."

"Yours is the best too." He left Dex sitting and went about serving up some dinner for them both. He didn't kid himself that Dex would eat a whole bowl of stew; he knew better. The more stress, the less his boy ate. But he made sure there was enough in the bowl to be tempting.

The real measure of Dex's stress level was that the boy only protested lightly as Cyrus moved around finding spoons and cutting hunks of bread he was sure Dex would have preferred to have had time to heat. It was all fine, these were tough weeks, and he'd been well warned. He knew what he'd signed on for.

Dex sat there, hands in his lap, head down, and Cy wasn't sure if he was sound asleep, meditating, or just in a fugue state.

He knew himself well enough, though, to know that he needed to eat or he'd be no good to his boy or himself. He set the bowls down and bread down on the table and touched the back of his hand to Dex's cheek. "I'm here, pet. I'd like you to try to eat something."

"I can't." Dex looked up at him, eyes panicked, swimming with tears. "It hurts."

God, that look broke his heart. There was nothing worse than a boy that wanted to do the right thing but just couldn't. "All right, pet. I understand."

Cyrus knelt in front of Dex's chair and started working open the hooks in his boy's corset, and once he'd set that aside, he pulled Dex over to his own chair and into his lap.

"Master." Dex sighed softly, resting heavy against him, no resistance at all.

"That's it. You rest while I eat." Maybe he'd get a bite into his boy. Maybe. But really he just wanted to ease Dex's soul a little.

He tried the stew, and of course it was delicious. Dex might be tired and stressed, but his boy still put so much energy into caring for him.

Dex worked one hand under his shirt, those poor fingers like a brand against his belly. "I miss you."

"You've been working hard. I'm right here, I've been here." He ate quickly, taking bites between words. He didn't have time to really enjoy it tonight; he was just hungry. "I miss you too, but it's not forever right? A couple more weeks? Not even?"

"Not even. About ten more days, and I shouldn't complain. It's good to have business. Good to be busy." Dex tried to sit up, but Cy kept him close, held him until he relaxed again.

"Of course you should. You should complain, and you should make sure I know how stressed you are. You should, because I can't help you if you don't, and you know how I feel about helping." That last bit was meant to be playful, maybe make his boy smile—at least on the inside. "I have plenty of bad days, as you know. Just because it's good work doesn't mean I can't blow off some steam, right? You know that better than anyone."

"I love blowing off your steam, Master."

Oh, his wicked pet.

Teasing was a good sign, at least his boy was still in there. "You're a naughty boy. I like that about you. A lot." He tore some of the softer bread away from the crust that would take more effort to chew and held the bite out for Dex. "Did you make this one or buy it?"

"I bought it. It's good, though. Almost as good as mine." Dex took the bite.

"It's very good. Sops up the yummy stuff just as well as yours does." He winked, relieved that Dex got one bite at least, and also glad to know that trick still worked even under this kind of stress. "The stew is really good. And there's plenty for dinner tomorrow, so that will save time, right? One less thing."

"Yes, Sir. Can I have a bite of soup, please?"

Excellent. He wouldn't make a big deal of it; he'd just play along. "Oh yeah, you should definitely try it." Cyrus scooped up a bite with some of the tender meat on it and held it out for Dex. "The meat is perfect."

Dex ate it, smiling softly, the look oddly sentimental. "That tastes just right."

"It tastes homey." Not like home, because his mother hadn't been the world's best cook. It just tasted like home should. He took another bite and then offered one more to Dex.

Dex took the bite, humming softly. "It tastes like my granny's. It's good."

His boy was relaxing steadily. "I'm so impressed that you can do that. Recreate family recipes? It's nice to be able to have that with you."

"It's good to share with you. And I love that you don't mind eating. It feels...right."

He snorted, grinning. "I never mind eating, and this stew reminds me of home. Of you, because you are my home." Cyrus hummed as he mopped up some of the stew with a hunk of bread. New traditions really could be the best ones.

"I hope I am. I want to be, more than anything. This—you and me—it's the good part."

This was the good part. And his job for the next ten days was to keep reminding Dex that good part was still there, even when it was buried under layers of stress and frosting.

He offered Dex one more bite. "Let's clean up, and then I'll finish that hand rub."

"Did you get enough, love? I can get you more." Dex stood up and reached for his bowl.

"I did. I was eating while we were chatting. See? I even finished my bread, and half of yours." And if he got hungry later, he could come back for a midnight snack. He wanted to love on his boy a little.

He hovered close while Dex did the dishes and cleaned up the Crock-Pot, helping some, but to be honest he was mostly getting in the way trying to keep contact between them.

Dex came to him as soon as the kitchen was mostly to rights with only the barest glance toward the office.

"I know, pet. Maybe you can start your day a little early tomorrow morning." He ushered Dex into the bedroom, feeling the weight of stress and exhaustion heavy in his boy's shoulders.

"Tomorrow morning. Yeah. I'll set my alarm. We're good." Dex smiled at him. "Let me jump in the shower before I come to bed? I'll be right there."

"All right, love. I'll be waiting."

He'd be waiting to tuck his boy in, and tomorrow

morning he'd make sure Dex got something to eat before all the craziness started.

43

Dex stared at the batch of decorated cookies, broken on the floor in their bags.

"I'm sorry, Dex. I tripped and..."

Oh God.

Those were his last *last* orders before he was done. His last one for the bar's Christmas party Saturday night.

He closed his eyes and counted to thirty. He had to remake the batter, bake them, cool them, make icing, ice them, put them in the oven on super low heat for a few minutes to dry them, cool them again, package, and get them ready for someone to pick up in the morning.

"Dex, I'm sorry. Let me... Oh God, you're crying. I'll..."

"Go home."

"What?"

Had he stuttered? "Please go. I'll finish this, but you go home."

"Wait." Milo blinked at him looking hurt and despite the protest, did take a step backward. "You don't want to do this by yourself, and it's my mistake..."

"I love you dearly, but I need you to leave. I'm fixin' to be ugly, and I don't want to in front of you." Dex was fixin' to lose his shit in a massive way. He was supposed to be off work by the time Cyr was done. He was supposed to be done. "I'm fixin' to hurt something, and I wouldn't have it be you for anything."

Milo raised an eyebrow, hesitating, and then turned abruptly and left the kitchen. A moment later, he heard the apartment door close and a deafening silence was left behind.

"Motherfucker!" he bit out. "Motherfucking shithead bastard asshole fuckmonkey!"

He grabbed the broom, shaking with a wild fury, and for a second he wanted to just get in his truck and drive. But he couldn't. He had cookies to make.

He had to decorate the house. Wrap presents. Mail presents. Survive December.

"I swear to God, Huck. I can't..." He stopped himself and sighed. No. He had to. He had a responsibility to Cyr, to Les, to himself, and that's what Huck would tell him.

Suck it up, Buttercup. You got to work, just like the rest of us.

He knew. He did.

And he knew he was a worthless shit for bitching.

He worked, what? Twelve hours a day for a few weeks, twenty hours a day for the last week? And what?

"Fuck me."

He got the cookies swept up and pulled out his mixer.

He'd give his soul for a fifth of tequila and a beer chaser.

Too bad it was already given up whole to Cyrus.

———

Cyrus paced in a circle around his client, Luke, who was folded over the spanking bench and tied down tight at the wrists, ankles, thighs, biceps, and neck, pondering his next move when he heard a familiar but worrisome ringing coming from his desk.

Very few people had the number for that phone, which he kept charged and in the drawer so he could be reached in the case of a real emergency. In fact, at the moment it was only two. His boy, and Les.

"Apologies, boy. Breathe, please." He covered the space between the bench and his desk in four long strides and pulled the drawer open, the ring growing louder as he pulled the phone out and looked at the display.

It was Les.

Damn.

Milo was with Dex today, he was sure of it, so what in the world could this possibly be about?

He answered it before it stopped ringing. "Les? What's the matter, where are you?"

"Your boy is in crisis. He fired Milo for dropping the bar's cookies. He was in tears and suggesting that he might hurt himself. Milo tried calling him once he left, and when Dex didn't answer, he came back to the apartment and could hear Dex sobbing and breaking things. Those cookies aren't important, Cy, but Dex is."

"Fired? Fuck. I...dammit." He had a client in bondage that he couldn't leave alone and... "I'll take care of it. I'll—Thank you for calling. I better go." His heart was pounding. This soundproof room had its disadvantages.

"Do you want me to come over check on him? I have a key, and I'm capable of dealing with him, if you need. I wanted your leave to do it first."

"Yes. Would you? Quickly? I'd appreciate some eyes on

him at least, just until I can resolve my session with my client." If he knew his boy, Les wasn't going to get much farther than the kitchen door, but at least the boy wouldn't hurt himself with someone watching.

"Already on the way. I've got this."

He didn't know about that. Dex was as hard-headed and prideful as they came and was on the very edge of his control.

Ironic that they'd made it to what was meant to be the last day of this holiday baking business without this kind of crisis.

He turned his attention back to his client, the sub who also had very real needs and was currently deep in subspace and restrained. He had a responsibility here, too.

"Luke, boy. Listen to my voice and breathe, it's time to come back now."

44

When the front door opened, it scared Dex so bad that he dropped a bowl of icing, the whole thing shattering on the floor, covering him with sugar, egg whites, green food coloring and glass.

"What the fuck are you doing!" he screamed, hoping to scare the intruder away before he found his gun.

Heavy, steady footsteps came down the hall toward the kitchen. "Relax, Dexter. It's Master Les. Cyrus asked me to come look after you until he can get...free..."

Dex could see the look in Les's eyes as the Dom stared. He must look like a freak right now. Like a lunatic.

"What?" Cyrus did what? Like he needed fucking taking care of. He wasn't some asshole to be handed off to Joe Blow because Cy was...what? Too busy to stick his head out the office door but oh-so-terribly worried? Fuck that shit. He was fucking busy, and Les could fuck right off. Cy too, for that matter. With bonus fucks. "I'm fine, thanks. Busy. Real busy."

Go away.

Les crossed slim arms over his narrow chest and stayed

put. "I see that. And Milo told me as much as well. Perhaps I can help?"

"I wasn't mean to him. I just needed him to go. Now, I have to clean this up and make more icing." *Go away, man. I'm tired and friggin' hysterical and I don't need this shit.* "The cookies will be delivered in time."

"Suppose I let you off the hook?" Les didn't look like he was going anywhere, damn him. "Cookies aren't important; your well-being is."

"Work is important, and I promised." He wasn't going to cry. "I have to clean up."

He was covered in icing, surrounded with glass, and his feet were bare and sticky and green.

"Is that your cushion over by the table? Is that your Master's chair?"

The question threw him completely off track, his thoughts just stopping for a second. "I'm sorry?" Les repeated the question, calm as all get out, and Dex nodded, totally confused. "Yes, sir."

"Thank you. Good boy. Go and kneel while we wait for him, please." Les's words were calm, but the authority in them was both clear and confusing.

"I can't. There's glass, I'm covered in emerald green goo, and my feet are bare." *Please go away so I can figure out how to fix this. Please.*

Les didn't even twitch. "Unless you're bleeding badly enough to be dangerous to your health, do as I say, please, boy."

God, he wanted to scream, but he also wanted to listen; he wanted someone to help. He wanted to trust that this wasn't where he cracked down the middle in front of his Master's best fucking friend on earth.

He stood there, frozen and shaking, tears heavy on his eyelashes.

"I'm just coming over to help you, Dex," Les said in a quiet voice as the Dom moved closer to him. "It's all right. You're overwhelmed. I see that. I promise your Master is coming—he has a client in bondage and can't just walk out on that. He'll be here very soon."

Gentle hands took him by the shoulders and moved him slowly toward his cushion.

"I'm only here to help you feel safe until Cyrus can join you."

"I'm—" *So stupid*. The first tear dropped on his cheek.

If Les noticed the Dom didn't say a thing about it. Les did keep talking to him, though; soft, slow words offered like a lifebuoy. Words for him to hold on to. "That's it, right here next to your Master's chair. That's your place. Just kneel and know you're safe, know you're loved. Your Master will be along soon."

He did know. He was safe and loved and overwhelmed and tired and wigged, and he was broken a little. Maybe a lot. Right down the middle.

Les went quiet and the hands on his shoulders slipped away. He knew, though, that the Dom was still there somewhere, even if out of his line of sight. It wasn't long before he heard soft voices behind him, one of them Cyrus. He couldn't make out the words, but he knew they were talking about him, about the goo in the kitchen, about Milo—about this mess.

Fuck. This was not how today was supposed to go. This was all wrong.

Get up, Dex. Get up and apologize and clean up your mess. Move.

But he didn't have time. Cyrus was kneeling at his side before he could find the energy to move.

"Hey, pet. I'm so sorry I made you wait for me. I think you should come get in the shower and then we should talk, okay? Les and Milo are going to help us out in here, so don't worry."

"I dropped the bowl. It broke, and the food coloring..." Don't worry? That wasn't in his DNA.

"Yes, I see it's a bit of a wreck. It's not a big deal, and bowls can be replaced. Let's get you up, love." He intended to help, but it seemed like Cyrus just lifted him right off the floor.

Dex just didn't know what to do. He felt...like he was wrapped in cotton, like there was this explosion so close and, shit, didn't that scare him?

He let Cyrus move him, and they were suddenly in the bedroom, and then the bathroom where Cyr started undressing him. "You're okay, pet. I'm here now. I know just what you need. But first we need to get you clean. Do you want me to get in with you?"

"I'm sorry. I wasn't mean to Milo. I didn't scream." The words bubbled out of him without his permission, and none of them were the answer to Cyr's question.

"Milo is fine. No one is upset with you." Apparently Cyr had his answer because his Master started to undress as well, and then opened the shower door. "Our friends were only worried about you. Get in, pet."

He stepped into the water, letting the shower rain down on him, hiding his hysteria, his tears. What the fuck was wrong with him? Had he lost his mind? Maybe so. Maybe that was just it. He'd been really happy, and now he was going to be insane.

Cyr didn't talk, just started gently working shampoo into

his hair, fingers massaging his scalp. Calm, steady Cyrus, always so still, always so grounded. It was so natural it almost wasn't fair.

He wasn't sure what was going on—he knew he was in the shower, he knew he was with his Master, and he knew he was home, sure, but...still.

"Talk to me, pet. What happened?" Cyr scrubbed him with a washcloth, and the floor of the shower turned green from the food coloring that had dried on his skin.

"The cookies fell on the floor and broke, all of them, and I have to make them again. All the ones for the party. So I told Milo to go, and I started them." He sighed, swallowing hard. "And I have to ice them still before the party."

"Les isn't concerned about it, pet. If they're not done, they're not done. Don't worry." Cyr took a second and washed up, scrubbing shampoo in and rinsing it out.

"But I was hired to do them. And I wanted to be done with the fucking cookies. I have so much to do with the Christmas party and all the pieces-parts." He didn't have time for this. He was supposed to be Cyr's until after the first of the year, dammit.

Cyrus didn't reply to that, just shut the water off and climbed out, wrapping up in a towel before grabbing another and offering him a hand. "Come on out, pet."

"There's no glass in the shower, right? Master Les scared the fire out of me when he came in. I screamed and dropped our bowl."

"I didn't feel any under my feet. We can have a look at it later." Cyr wrapped him in a warm towel and then pulled him close, one arm circling around his back. "Mmm. That's better."

He closed his eyes, trying to figure out what the actual fuck was going on with him, with his day. "Love you."

"I love you." Cyr rubbed his back, keeping him close. "But you can't push yourself this hard again; you have limits. You have to accept them."

He shook his head. "There's something wrong with me, that I can't even work a part-time job without fucking it up. I can do this. I can."

Surely he could figure that out.

"Part-time job?" Cyrus moved them out of the bathroom and back to the bedroom. "This hasn't been a part-time job since... God. Since before Halloween. Maybe in as long as I've known you."

"I did it, though. I took care of Huck and the ranch and did gigs and made cookies and I did it then, but..." But now he wanted to be a spoiled ass and take care of Cyr and do cookies when he had the time. *Lazy ass.*

Cyr handed him his soft sweats to pull on. "But you weren't taking care of yourself. You didn't eat, you didn't sleep, you were unhappy. And you do so much more for me on a daily basis than you ever did for Huck. You can't compare, pet. That was a different lifetime."

It so was, but he wanted to be perfect for Cyr. He wanted to be right. He wanted to be everything.

Cyr cupped his cheek and looked at him silently, then went to the closet and pulled out leather jeans. "Grab our clothes off the floor, please, pet. In here and in the bathroom."

"Yes, Sir. I'm sorry." *Come on, asshole. Focus*. "How was work?"

He wasn't sure what Cyr's look meant, it seemed worried and thoughtful, but it flashed across his Master's face quickly and disappeared.

"Fine. I would rather have been spending time with you.

No apology required, pet." Cyrus was powdering and pulling on the leather jeans as he started cleaning up.

"As soon as the cookies are done, we can start our holiday, though? Our first one?" God, he felt like he was fixin' to shake apart.

Cyr waved him over but also moved toward him, meeting him halfway. Those steady, big hands curled under his jaw and Cyr's dark eyes held his. "Are you really dead set on finishing those cookies? Even though Les said it will be fine if you don't?"

"I—" The tears threatened again, and he stretched his eyes open wide so they'd stop. "I need... Oh God, please. Help me. I'm so fucked up right now."

"Good boy." Cyr's nod was immediate and decisive, and his Master turned him around, curling an arm behind his back to support him. "To my playroom, please."

He held onto those words—that sure 'Good boy' that meant that his Master had him, heard what he wasn't sure how to say, and would help him put things back together. Because Jesus Christ, he needed help. He needed Cyr.

It was the easiest thing in the world to let his Master lead him through that door at the end of the hall.

The silence in the playroom after the door closed was different than anywhere else in the apartment. The room itself was quiet but other things seemed louder, like his own breathing and the sound of Cyr's bare feet on the dark floor.

"Take your sweats off, please, and set your training corset out on the bondage table." Cyr left him near the armoire that held his things and went to the table to wait for him.

Oh, that was...big. He didn't know if he wanted to do this today. He looked at Cyr, and those pretty, warm eyes were calm and sure, no worry, no stress.

Okay.

If Cyr trusted this was right, he could.

He had to.

Dex stripped easily before he reached for the corset. "Master?"

"Yes, pet?"

"Do you want all the bits, or just the corset part?"

Cyr smiled at him. "Good question, thank you. All of it, please, except the collar, it won't be safe with what I have in mind."

That smile was everything.

It took him two trips, and on the second he went to Cyr. "Please. I need a hug."

"That's the plan, pet." Cyr pulled him in tight and held him, no questions and no hesitation.

He let himself breathe deep, inhale that scent that proved that he was home. "Love you."

"I love you. You are always my priority, my biggest worry, my greatest joy, and my dearest friend." Cyr kissed his forehead. "I know what you need. What we need."

"I believe in you, Master."

Cyr swallowed, then cleared his throat and let him go to reach for his corset. "Thank you, pet. Arms, please."

"Yes, Sir." He had a love-hate relationship with this corset, but today he moved without thinking.

His Master fitted it over his arms, tucked it down on his shoulders, and smoothed down the front. Cyr's expression changed, evened out into something more pleased, and hungry.

Wordlessly, Cyr moved around behind him and began working on the buckles, the steel boning and leather going tight. Cyr did them up once, let him breathe for a moment while his body adjusted, then tightened each one a bit more.

He groaned softly, letting himself feel the pressure, the push, the weight all around him, pressing at him.

"That's it, pet. Relax." Cyr dropped a hand to his ass and gave it a solid slap followed quickly by a warm caress. "Cuffs next. Bring them to me."

Moving in this corset was so different, stiff, holding him so close, and he felt like every step was different, special.

He held out the cuffs and Cyr took them one by one and put them on with care. "These were such a good choice, pet. I love the weight of them, the look. So you. A little tradition, and a little something naughty. Something more personal."

He nodded. They were a good choice. He loved the sensation of being held, of knowing that Cyr was with him. Holding him. Touching his soul.

Cyr walked around him once, then reached for his nipples, both at the same time. He pulled them, making Dex's eyes cross, pinching and tugging until he was breathing hard, totally focused on Cy's touch.

"All right. Spanking bench, please." Cyr's voice had settled into that rough tone and his Master punctuated the order by pointing at the bench. "Make sure you feel secure without your hands so I can bind them."

"Yes, Sir." He settled in, the scent of leather a comfort as he rested, letting corset and bench support him.

"Good boy. Let me see." Cyr started touching and testing, fingers finding pressure points and checking the corset, finally taking one arm and turning up behind his back to bind it to the corset. "Can you get a good breath?"

Dex sucked in air, finding all the places things got tight, and nodded. "Yes, Sir. I can feel the breath, but it's good."

"Thank you, pet." Cyr took his other arm and did the same so his wrists were bound together and then held fast to his corset. Between that and the incline of the bench he was dependent on Cyr to make sure he didn't lose his balance.

But Cyr seemed to have that covered too. The next thing was the spreader bar, which he felt Cyr setting in place but couldn't actually manage to turn and see. The bar was just the perfect length so that his legs stayed firmly on the rungs of the bench but were now locked together behind it steadying him in place.

"Oh, pet. You look stunning. And I'm not even done yet. Stunning." The heated growl in Cyr's voice betrayed his Master's arousal.

He shivered, that tone, that promise suiting him to the bone. How did this soothe him? How could it?

Cyr laid a wide leather strap across his shoulders and anchored them down, then added more straps around his thighs, securing them to the bench so he was well and truly unable to move. "How do you feel, pet? Test those bonds for me."

"You got me. All the way." He tried to wiggle, but there wasn't a lot of give.

"Perfect." Both of Cyr's hands landed on his ass, the touch searing hot and the pressure just right. "I have your words, angel and demon. I'm listening." Strong fingers dug into the muscle and spread his cheeks enough that he could feel cool air move across his hole.

He groaned, his ass muscles tensing, relaxing, and tensing again.

The dark chuckle as Cyr paced away from the bench seemed to fill the entire room. "I've got your paddle, pet. I'm looking forward to using it."

He didn't know what to say, really. He wanted to beg for it, beg for Cyr to stop, scream and kick, have a good, hard cry.

It didn't matter though because Cyr was going to use it, and a second later, the tapping started. Light pats to his ass, alternating one side and then the other, over and over and over again until he knew the rhythm, anticipated the contact. His eyes fell closed, he let himself float, the awful day letting him go a bit.

"You're mine, pet. Breathe, and tell me you're mine." The light blows continued, the rhythm steady.

"I am. You have to know. All yours." Cyr had to know that.

"I do. I just wanted to hear you say it. You are mine." The paddle came down harder but not faster. "That means I'm every answer you need, pet. Am I right?"

He nodded, swallowing hard. "I need you, so much."

"Good boy. You do, and it's so important that you tell me so. When you have a dilemma, I'm the answer. When you start to feel off-balance, I'm the answer. When you feel out of control, I am the answer. I am your Master. Breathe."

Cyr's next set of blows were solid, strong, and loud in his ears.

He gasped for air, his ass hot, the brush of air before the paddle hit unbearable.

"Tell me, pet. Who am I?" The intensity of the blows backed off again, but not that relentless rhythm.

"My Master." He tugged at the cuffs, sweat pouring from him. "You're my love."

"Good boy. And who are you?" The paddle was suddenly gone, replaced by light, rhythmic pats of Cyr's hand.

"Yours. I'm yours, Master. Your boy." *Your good boy.*

"Just mine." The blows stopped entirely and became strokes and caresses, hot hands on heated skin, and a thick thumb gliding over his hole. "Love."

"Just yours. Your good boy. So hot, Master."

"So good. Everything I need." All the touching stopped as Cyr moved away. "I'm right here, pet. Remember, I promised I will never leave you alone and bound."

He nodded, his body throbbing, tears stuck on his cheeks. His soul was—not quiet, not yet—but focused. Every breath his Master took, every step, every heartbeat—Dex felt it.

He even felt Cyr was back at his side before he heard it. His Master made instant contact, checking the buckles on the back of his corset and sliding fingers under his bonds. "How are your fingers?"

Dex wiggled and rolled his shoulders, testing them out. "Good. Good, Master."

"It's a good fit. Brandon does such amazing work." Cyr moved into Dex's line of sight and stopped so the prodigious bulge in his soft, leather pants was just inches from Dex's face. "You see this, pet?" Cyr rubbed himself through the leather. "You did this to me."

"Good." And it was. He wanted to be the one that made Cyr burn.

Cyr's laughter was both happy and dark and cut off abruptly as Cyr started to rub himself through the leather. "You can be a naughty boy, pet."

He watched his Master open the jeans and ease a heavy cock out from behind the zipper.

"You're going to take care of this for me."

"Yes. God yes. Please, Master. I need you." Dex groaned as his words made a single drop of clear liquid form at the slit of Cyr's cock. "Master!"

Cyr stepped closer and slid that hard prick across his cheek, stopping just at the corner of his lips, and growled out, "Show me."

He opened up, tongue dragging over the mushroom

head, his entire body straining to get more. He needed this—to suck, to give Cyr pleasure, to have Cyr take him. He was his Master's boy.

Cyr gasped and leaned closer, pushing farther into his mouth and rocked in and out gently. "Yes, pet. God, your mouth." Cyr's sigh of pleasure was almost better than an orgasm. Almost.

He closed his eyes, focusing on nothing but his Master. The act of sucking, of giving himself to Cyr, it soothed him to the bone.

"That's it, pet. Just slow." He knew this was build up; Cyr didn't do slow for long. His Master liked to take as much as he needed to give. Cyr bent slightly and hot fingers explored the edge of his corset where it left his shoulders bare, tracing the hard line of the edge from one shoulder to the other, and working into the leather where it met the steel boning.

The whole world was Cyr—all of Dex's senses were overwhelmed, and he melted into it, allowing himself to be here. Right here, right now, and nowhere else.

"Fuck." Cyr pulled back with a grunt and crouched next to him, taking his lips with a hard, needy kiss and sweeping a commanding tongue through his mouth.

His eyes popped open, meeting Cyr's dark, hungry gaze, his world spinning around them.

"Good boy. Love you." Cyr stood and left his line of vision, but he heard the foil open, and he definitely felt Cyr's thumb press hard across his ass and then push inside him.

"Oh love. Master." He squeezed hard, not fighting, but welcoming the touch.

"I wish you could see yourself. You...oh. Oh, pet." Cyr moved away again, and he watched as his Master reached for the heavy pull cord and opened the curtains covering the big mirror. The bench was right in front of it. “Look at how beautiful you are.”

He looked, seeing his own need, his hunger painted on his skin, on his kiss-swollen lips, on his tear-streaked cheeks. “Master, please...”

He saw. He did. He was the picture of desire.

Cyr nodded, moved behind him and shoved the leather jeans down low on strong hips. “I’m here. I’m yours, love.” A second later his Master’s cock sank deep inside him, stretching and filling him just right.

“Mine. God, I needed you.” He watched Cyr move as long as he could, but his eyelids kept getting heavy. Long enough to notice that Cyr wasn’t watching in the mirror at all, Cyr was looking at him.

Watching him.

Needing him.

“Fuck, pet.” Cyr’s thrusts were deep and heavy, but the bench was solid and took their weight without complaining. He could hear Cyr’s climax building with every thrust, every breath. His Master’s sounds growing more and more urgent.

“Yours. Your own. I promise, Master.” He moaned, so fucking happy, relaxed, settled.

“Mine.” Cyr’s hips went wild, thrusts quick and shallow, and his Master’s breathing dissolved into harsh pants and deep grunts. It felt good knowing he was exactly what Cyr needed.

Cyr’s fingers dug hard into the leather at his waist and electricity shot down his thighs every time Cyr’s thighs slammed into his burning, paddled skin.

“Pet, I...” That was all Cyr managed to get out before freezing up as that cock jerked and swelled inside him.

Dex groaned, holding Cyr close, squeezing him tight. “Got you, Master.”

Cyr sucked in a shaky breath and bent over, resting against his back. "Got me. So good, love."

They breathed together until Cyr hauled himself back up and they both moaned as they separated. His body wanted to roll, wanted to rock back, but he was caught. Held there for his Master's will.

Dex caught a glimpse in the mirror of Cyr carefully tucking back into his leather pants. "I'm going to start on these straps, pet. You'll want to, but please don't move until you're completely free of the bench."

"Yes, Master." He kept his eyes closed, resting deep in the leather, refusing to come back to the world.

"Every time I think you couldn't be more beautiful, more perfect..." Cyr removed the strap across his shoulders first and the ones around his thighs, setting them aside neatly, taking time. "You dig just a little deeper and find something more for me."

"Everything I have. Anything, Master. I love you." He would give his soul, if he hadn't already.

Cyr crouched beside him so they could look at each other, dark eyes soft and smiling. "And for you, love. Anything you need. Always." Gentle fingers lifted the hair off his forehead and smoothed it back.

"Oh..." That was good. He needed that.

He got a quick kiss and then Cyr moved a bit faster, freeing his feet from the spreader bar, and finally releasing his wrists, which his Master helped him lower carefully to the armrests on the bench. "You can move now, wiggle your fingers, let me know when you feel ready to get back on your feet."

Dex wiggled, stretching out nice and slow, groaning as he found himself coming back into the here and now.

Cyr fussed over him checking his toes and hands, sliding

knowing fingers over muscle and under the edges of his corset, smoothing a hand over his ass. "Excellent, pet. You've done so well. I'm proud of you."

"I don't know if I'm supposed to apologize or just hug you. I needed you. So bad." He wasn't sorry for the needing, just the psycho bit.

"There's no reason to apologize for truth, however raw. Truth in all its forms just brings us closer. In *truth*, I needed you too. I'd been feeling a little disconnected." Cyr cupped a palm under his chin. "Are you ready to sit up?"

"You mean I can't just float here forever?" He had to tease. Had to. He nuzzled into Cyr's touch. "You'll have to help me. This corset asks a lot."

"You absolutely could. But I'd prefer you come to bed and float with me. I want to hold you." Cyr moved around to his side. "And get you off. Ready?"

"Yes, Sir." He stood with Cyr's help, and his knees tried to buckle. He grabbed for his Master, knowing that he'd be right there.

"I've got you." Cyr was solid as a stone, catching him and holding on. Cyr took a few steps, moving him backward so he could lean against the bondage table. "There you go. Better?"

"Whoa. Wow, huh? Rubber band legs." He grinned at Cyr, breathing deep.

"And a red ass. And this." Cyr kissed him, and hand wrapped solidly around his cock.

He gasped, eyes going wide. He had been so fucking focused on his Cyr that he hadn't known he needed.

Dex fucking knew now.

"So mine." Cyr drew a hot tongue over his throat, then bent to one nipple and it drew up hard and fast at the touch.

He arched to give Cyr everything, to take all the pleasure

his lover was offering. The corset held him, making him aware of every breath, every motion.

Cyr straightened up and caught his eye, still stroking him firmly. "Tell me how you want it, love."

"Touch me. Fuck me with your fingers, please. I want you to make me come." Jesus, he felt so fucking fierce, so wild so free.

"That's my boy." Cyr spun him and bent him right over the table, and he barely had time to get a grip on it before Cyr's fingers breached him. "I wish you could see yourself like this—red ass, tiny waist, tight hole gripping my fingers."

"Master!" Fuck, he spread a little wider, arching as best he could.

Cyr was jacking him steadily, those fingers having learned him so well they were better than his own. "Better than any fantasy, pet. You're wilder than my dreams."

He groaned, his calves clenching as he went up on tiptoe.

"I love making you fly, love watching you come. Are you riding that line, love?" Cy's thumb burrowed through his slit and the thick fingers inside him twisted and curled.

"Oh fuck!" He started to shake because he was right there, ready to scream, ready to shoot, and it wouldn't take anything to push him over the edge. Cyr found his gland, nudged it hard, and his orgasm washed over him in a rush.

"Fuck, yeah." Cyr was leaning over his back all of a sudden, pumping his cock through it, making it last. "Good boy. Such a good boy."

"Your good boy. Fuck..." He couldn't even hold himself up anymore. "Master."

Cyr let him rest there just as he was, draped over the bondage table and made quick trip to the bathroom, returning with a warm cloth to clean up, then slowly loosened the buckles on the back of his corset a little at a time until the side fell open on the table. It took a while, longer than it seemed like it should, but as he started to breathe more easily, he felt less light-headed and he understood why Cyr had been so careful.

"Our bed, pet. Yes?"

"Yes, Master. Please." He held onto Cyr as they walked, the apartment blessedly quiet.

"I'm going to cancel my client for tomorrow." Cyr undressed while he climbed into bed, and it wasn't until he put his hands down in the sheets that he noticed his Master had left his cuffs on.

He didn't mention it. They grounded him, and his Master wouldn't have left them if he didn't want to. "Thank you, Master."

Dex needed some time, one-on-one, with Cyrus.

Cyr smiled and nodded, climbing in after him and settling in the pillows. "Purely selfish motives." Cyr held an arm out, reaching for him.

"You can help me decorate for Christmas." He curled in close, cuddling into Cyr's arms. "Love you."

"Love you, pet. I hope you feel better. I know I do." Cyr nuzzled his ear.

"I do. Thank you. I needed this." He let himself relax. "You. I needed your hand."

"You asked me for help. I know you were hurting and desperate, but you asked me. That was a gift, love. I don't know if you understand what that meant, what it said to me, and that's okay. But it was important, and what we both needed."

He brought Cyr's hand up to his kiss his knuckles. "I think I need help, Master. I think I need to..." He closed his eyes. “I want to be able to focus on loving you first, and cookies second. Even at Christmas.”

Please. Please get me.

He felt Cyr smile against his forehead. “Is it selfish of me to say I would love that?”

“Yeah?” He leaned back, met Cyr’s warm, happy gaze. “It’s okay to need that?”

“Nothing would make me happier. Or you, I think.” Cyr slipped a thumb along his jaw. “There are many ways to contribute to a household, and not all of them have to bring in money to be considered important. I want you to find your music again and get out with friends. I want you to feed your mind and your soul as well as you feed me.”

He didn’t have the words to say what he wanted to, so he took a kiss instead, thanking his lover for hearing him.

“Mmm.” Cyr hummed as they parted and yawned widely. “That was very nice, pet. Thank you.”

“Did you need a snack, Master?” He hoped not, but he’d get up and make one if Cyr needed it.

“I think I have a late-night fridge raid in my future but I’m fine right now. Sleepy, hm?” Cyr seemed to sink deeper into the pillows after he said that.

“Yes, Master. You wore my ass out.” He got the covers over them and closed his eyes, his soul quiet, ready to rest.

45

Cyrus and Dex did nothing but eat, sleep and fuck for two solid days and Cyrus didn't feel the least bit guilty about it. He and his boy had some lost time to make up for. Actual time, and quality time. The good news was that Dex was crashing hard when the boy slept and had a little bit of an appetite back again. The bad news was that Cyrus was going to have to wake him up to go to Lex's holiday party at the bar.

Yes, their days and nights were a little mixed up at the moment—or more accurately they just hadn't paid any attention to the time since they'd done that corset scene in the middle of the day. Dex had made him dinner at two o'clock in the morning, and things got a little crazy after that.

He grinned, feeling smug, feeling high, loving that they'd been able to tell the world to back off for two whole days.

Maybe he'd plan a vacation for New Years.

He leaned over Dex in bed and kissed his boy lightly, all over that sweet face until Dex started to stir.

"Mmm...Master..." Dex reached up, holding him, drawing him into the blankets.

Dammit, that was the most tempting thing ever. But he'd been up for an hour and was already showered, and they had a party to go to.

Cyrus slid a hand over Dex's belly. "Mm. No. Time to wake up, pet. We're going out."

"Out?" Dex arched for him, wiggling happily. "You could come in."

Oh, the shameless little devil. "You're being naughty again. Save that for after the party."

"Again? I'm innocent as all get out." One hand slid up to cup his cock.

He could stay right here, he really could. He could stay here and let the party come and go, even Christmas come and go. Everything he really needed had a hand on his prick right now.

But.

"Pet. I need you to get me dressed and Master Les is expecting us." The party was going to be fun. Les liked to play Santa and Milo had put in time decorating.

"Yeah, and we can't disappoint him. I know." Dex held his hands up so Cy could haul him up off the mattress. "We could be fashionably late, though."

"Oh, we're already flirting with that territory." He got Dex standing up. "I woke up over an hour ago. That's a new one, right?"

"You give me good reasons to stay in bed."

That was a good thing to hear and he intended to keep it up. "I'm beginning to like showing you off, pet."

It was interesting if he thought about it; He was finally able to keep Dex in bed longer, and at the same time, Dex was making him want to go out more often. Just another way they were taking care of each other.

"What does a gorgeous Dom wear to a Christmas party? Do you have a sweater hidden in there with Santa spanking a reindeer?"

"That would be something, wouldn't it?" Cyrus laughed and gave Dex a kiss on the cheek. "I don't know what a gorgeous Dom wears, but I have a candy cane striped shirt and a red leather vest in the closet. And there's something hanging next to it—the hanger with the fabric drape over it —that's for you to wear."

"Me?" Oh, that was a pleased expression on his boy's face. "Thank you, Master."

"You're welcome. Merry Christmas to me." Cy didn't think he deserved to be this happy, but too damn bad.

Dex kissed him and bounced over to the closet, pulling out his vest and shirt, plus the draped hanger.

"Let's dress you, Master."

"Thank you, pet. Should I wear leather or jeans do you think?" He'd lost the battle over ironed jeans, and Dex had managed to convince him that if they were well taken care of, jeans were appropriate for many occasions.

Dex looked him up and down, then smiled. "Jeans. I love your ass in jeans."

His Texan.

"That's a compliment. You pick them, then." He let Dex lay everything out on the bed and didn't uncover the gift just yet. He'd let that wait until after he was dressed.

Dex chose his jeans, and knelt at his feet, sneaking a nuzzle to his cock. Cheeky.

"Going to be one of those nights, is it? I approve." Keeping a little buzz made Dex feel that much more his. He stepped into the jeans but didn't help at all otherwise, Dex had this down, and it was one of the rituals they both enjoyed and had been missing with Dex getting up early to bake. He could tell Dex had missed it with the extra care and all the lingering touches. "It's good to have this back, pet."

"Yes, Master. It's Heaven. I love this. It's what I'm made for."

He nodded. "I believe that. I felt it the day I met you. I'd never even considered enticing a man into my lifestyle before. But something about you called to me, made me feel like it was right."

"You soothe my soul." Dex stood to help him with his shirt. "You do wicked things to my body, though."

He couldn't help his grin. "I do. And I think you like it." He shrugged into the shirt and let Dex do up the buttons.

"You think?" Dex laughed and tucked him in, fastening his belt. "Which boots, love?"

"Oh, my stompy ones with the buckles. They really are my favorite, and I can dance in them." He adjusted the jeans a little so they sat more comfortable on his hips.

Dex groped his ass on the way to the closet. "Stompy boots it is."

He wanted to see Dex wearing his gift. He did his best to be patient as his boy got him into the boots but didn't let Dex waste a minute finding jeans for himself. "Let's try your light gray button-down, pet. Or a white one if you prefer. Either will work."

"I like the gray one. It's safer at a bar, and it matches my winter felt." Dex dressed quickly, jeans, boots, shirt, and hat.

"Oh, let me look at you." Cyrus took a step back and took his boy in, eyes roaming from the tip of the boots to the top of the hat. How did that little mouse in Texas turn into this amazingly handsome man? "Love. You look amazing."

And Dex didn't even have the best part yet.

Dex blushed and the smile he received was blinding. "Thank you, Sir. I clean up okay."

"Have a look at what I found you." He inclined his head toward the bed.

Dex picked the hanger up, uncovering a deep emerald green satin corset, made for his exact measurements. "Oh. Oh, look..."

"Brandon worked with me to make it. I chose the fabric." He stepped behind Dex and rested his hands on Dex's hips. "What do you think?"

"It's beautiful. Honest. Can you put it on me, Master? Please?" That honest eagerness suited him to the bone.

"With pleasure, pet." He took the corset and lay it flat to loosen the lacing in the back before opening the hooks in to front, then put it around his boy and fasted all the hooks again. "Let's see how well Brandon taught me, shall we?" Brandon taught him just fine; it was more about how well he remembered how to fit it correctly.

Dex grabbed the bedpost, holding on so Cy could tighten the laces. "It looks perfect, Master. So fine."

He ran his hands down Dex's sides and over that narrow waist, fascinated by the feel of the satin and the curve of his boy's body. "Beautiful. And classic. Just what I was hoping."

Tonight he could put his boy over his knee, warm that gorgeous ass, and fuck Dex hard, his boy caught in his corset, his will.

"Master. Thank you." Dex's voice was husky, rough.

"You're welcome. It's my pleasure, love." He pulled his boy back against him, pressing his half-hard prick against Dex's ass, letting the boy feel him. "Absolutely my pleasure."

"Oh... Parties are dumb. I want you."

He laughed. "You'll have me. But I'm going to make you

wait. Make us both wait." He stepped back and pulled his boy over to the dressing mirror hanging on the inside door of his closet. "Have a look at yourself and then we better run."

Dex looked himself up and down, his boy all smiles. "Yeah, I dare any stranger to dance with me in this outfit. You'll eat them."

"You know me so well." He growled for Dex's benefit and grinned. "Fake cowboy better keep his goddamn distance."

"Yes, Sir." God, look at his boy glow. The pride and confidence made him hard as a rock.

"Good boy. Come on." He took Dex's hand, planted a very chaste kiss on his boy's cheek and headed for the door. He had one more surprise before they left the apartment, an early Christmas gift hanging on the coat rack by the front door, unwrapped except for a big red bow tied around the collar.

It was a shearling coat, brown leather on the exterior, soft wool on the inside. Heavy. Solid. Warm.

Dex gasped. "Master? For me?"

That gasp meant Dex liked it, and that made him happy. "For you. It's supposed to be a Christmas gift, but it's fifteen degrees out. I felt like you should have it early. So... Merry Christmas."

"Oh. Oh, wow. That's...thank you. Oh, Cyr, it's the finest thing ever."

"It was a bit of a splurge but keeping my boy warm is worth it." He pulled it off the hanger and held it for Dex to slide his arms in. "I hope it fits."

Dex slipped in, eyelids going heavy with pleasure. It fit perfectly, wrapping his pet in warmth.

"See? I told you we should go out." He shrugged into his

leather coat, the winter one that had wool and quilting on the inside. "Ready?"

"Yes, Sir. Let's do this." Dex squeezed his hand. "I can't wait to show you off."

"I'm all yours, pet."

It was damn cold out, but the walk was fun with all the festivities going on in the days leading up to Christmas. This area was usually quiet, but people were out, there was Christmas music coming from cars and restaurants they passed along the way.

The bar was hopping. Festively decorated on the outside, warm and glowing on the inside. Les had a coat check set up and they handed their coats over and collected their tags. "How about this? This is a party, right?"

"It is! How pretty!" Dex was all smiles, curling into his side.

"Dex! You came! Oh my god, Dex, you look amazing. Are you feeling better? I was so afraid you wouldn't come." Milo appeared out of nowhere bouncing and a little over-revved. He started to give Dex an excited hug, but Les reached out and grabbed his shoulder.

"Relax, boy."

"Yes, sir." Milo went still.

"We're glad to see you both." Les shook his hand and then Dex's.

Dex took Les's hand and then hugged the Dom hard. "Thank you, Sir. So much. I needed help, and you were so kind."

Les closed his eyes and returned the hug. "You're welcome, boy. I was glad I could help. You're important to me, and to my boy."

"You're a good friend. Thank you." Then Dex turned to Milo and grabbed him. "Tell me we can go shopping next week, man. Shopping, coffee, a long lunch—I'm so ready to just hang out."

Milo nodded, smiling at Dex. "Yes, please. I'd like that."

He didn't point out that Dex just asked Milo to eat out, but he wanted to. He didn't want to jinx his boy's appetite.

Les was nodding as if everything was just as he wanted it. "Your corset is stunning, boy. You both look so festive. I have nonalcoholic eggnog for you at the bar."

"Oh thank you. Master? Would you like a glass?" Dex leaned close. "It's not as good as mine, but..."

"Naughty boy." He kept his voice low. "I'd love some anyway." He followed, watching Dex, sure he couldn't be more proud or more turned on by his boy's confidence. He should have known he was being ambushed when Milo cut between them and herded Dex away.

Les took his arm. "How is he?"

"Good." He looked at Les and smiled. "He's really fine. And we're even better."

"You two were heading for a breakthrough. I'm so pleased."

"He figured out how to ask for help. Finally. And that he didn't have to prove anything to me." He watched Milo and Dex talk together at the bar. He thought maybe Dex finally understood he was good at something. Made for it.

"Are you able to be excited for your holidays now?" Les asked as the boys headed back toward them.

"We already are. We're going to have a good day, just the two of us. We're going to get the tree out of the storage locker and...whatever Dex wants. He has plans. Doesn't he look great?"

"Happy and healthy. Whole." Les's smile warmed him to the bone.

"Master Les thinks you look awfully happy, pet." He

accepted his cup of eggnog and looped an arm over Dex's shoulders.

"That's because I am, Master. Crazy happy." Dex leaned in with a happy sigh. "You?"

"I believe the term is stupid happy." He held up his cup. "To us."

"Yes, Sir. To us." Dex clinked their glasses together, but his pet was focused somewhere else.

He leaned close to kiss Dex's temple. "Where'd you go?"

"Master, *look*."

He turned to look where Dex pointed, the snow starting to fall outside the bar window.

"Snow." He looked at Dex. "Do you want to...hold on. Milo, will you hold this for me?" He handed Milo his eggnog. "Come on, pet."

He took Dex's drink, put it down, and they stood. Dex didn't even question, simply following him out.

It really was snowing. It had warmed up a little and fat flakes were coming down heavily. They instantly caught on his eyelashes and landed on Dex's hat. "Is this your first snow?"

"I've seen a few, but not this. Not like this. Oh, look at it come down..." Dex was wide-eyed, the joy on his face utterly charming.

"It's pretty isn't it?" He pointed up to where the flakes flew fast through the beams of a streetlight, lit up and sparkling. Then he stuck out his tongue to catch a few, the icy little drops tickling as they fell.

"It's magic. I—It's magic." Awed. Dex was awed.

He nodded. It was magical. All of it.

Cyrus hooked an arm behind Dex's back, ducked under the cowboy's hat and kissed him.

Hide Bound

Les's Bar, Book 2

By Jodi Payne and BA Tortuga

Peter Marshall has had enough of working for Parks and Rec when he comes across an opening for a real carpentry job and decides to give it a go. Building things is his passion, so even though the shop seems a little out there, and the owner seems pretty grumpy, Peter decides to go for it.

Brandon McPhail wishes he didn't have to hire a new carpenter, but his current one is going out on maternity leave. He's especially wary of this kid who can't possibly be old enough to spell BDSM, let alone know what the lifestyle means. But Peter impresses Brandon with both his talent and his tenacity, so Brandon hires him on, reminding himself that he's in a wheelchair due to his MS, he had a terrible experience in his last relationship, and despite how clueless Peter is about the lifestyle, he's not interested in taking on another sub.

The chemistry between them is undeniable, though, and it's not long before they're exploring what they can learn from each other. Peter is a natural at fulfilling Brandon's needs, and Brandon thinks he's teaching Peter everything he's eager to learn, but when danger threatens, they have to help their friends through it while trying to navigate their new relationship. Can they forge bonds strong enough to bind them together for life?

Note to readers: Each book in this series is a true standalone, so don't be confused when you discover that Hide Bound takes place before Just Dex in the "timeline". That was deliberate, and you don't need to have read one to read the other.

Find Hide Bound HERE

WANT MORE BA & JODI?

Interested in learning more about our East Meets Westerns?

Join BA & Jodi's Newsletter
https://lp.constantcontactpages.com/sl/nzvRTTy

Patreon: https://www.patreon.com/BATortuga
There are lots of tiers to chose from, and also free serial stories.
Discord: https://discord.gg/Vba5P5Qv
BA's Discord server has a channel for BA/Jodi related chat and info.

Hey, Y'all!

We want to thank you for giving Just Dex a try. We hope you enjoyed the story.

If you can spare a few minutes to post a review at the retail website where you made your purchase, we'd very much appreciate it!

Don't forget to "like" our Facebook pages and groups to keep up with all the news--new releases, sales announcements, giveaways, sneak peeks-- and of course the rodeo pictures, coffee memes and just general fun. We'd love to have all y'all!

Yeehaw and thanks for reading!

BA & Jodi

ABOUT JODI

JODI takes herself way too seriously and has been known to randomly break out in song. Her queer MCs are imperfect but genuine, stubborn but likable, often kinky, and frequently their own worst enemies. They are characters you can't help but fall in love with while they stumble along the path to their happily ever after. For those looking to get on her good side, Jodi's obsessions include nonfat lattes, basketball (go Celtics!), and tequila any way you pour it.

Website: jodipayne.net

Newsletter: https://readerlinks.com/l/2317334

All Jodi's Social Links: linktr.ee/jodipayne

ABOUT BA

Western to the bone and an unrepentant Daddy's Girl, BA Tortuga spends her days with her hounds and her beloved wife, having mother-daughter dates, and eating Mexican food. When she's not doing that, she's writing. She spends her days off watching rodeo, knitting, and surfing Pinterest in the name of research. Following their own personal joys, BA and Julia heard the call of the high desert and they now live in the New Mexico mountains. BA's personal saviors include her wife, her best friends, and coffee. Lots of coffee. Really good coffee.

Having written everything from fist-fighting cowboys to rural single dads to werewolves, BA does her damnedest to tell the stories of her heart, which is committed to giving everyone their happily ever after. With books ranging from heart-warming stories of found families, to rodeo cowboys that are fighting to make a mark, to fiery passionate love affairs, BA refuses to be pigeon-holed by anyone but the voices in her head.

BA loves to talk to her readers and can be found at http://batortuga.com/ and her newsletter signup link is http://bit.ly/BAJulianews

AVAILABLE FROM JODI & BA

East Meets Westerns

The On the Ranch Series

Tending Tyler

Roped In

Diamonds in the Rough

Outfoxed

The Wrecked Universe

Wrecked

Flying Blind

Special Delivery, A Wrecked Holiday Novel

Seeds and Sunshine

Pickup Man

Cowboy for Sale

The Merry Everything Series

Window Dressing

Cowboy Protection

Cowboys and Cupcakes

Thawed Out

A Present for Parker

The Higher Elevation Series

Heart of a Cowboy

Keeping Promises

Bigger Than Us

Home Free

BDSM/Kink

The Cowboy and the Dom Trilogy

First Rodeo, Book One

Razor's Edge, Book Two

No Ghosts, Book Three

The Soldier and the Angel, a Cowboy and Dom Novel

The Sin Deep Series

(set in The Cowboy and the Dom Universe)

Sin Deep

Trouble with Cowboys

Gemini: Ryder

Gemini: Roper

The Triskelion Series

Breaking the Rules

Making a Mark

Making the Rules

Les's Bar Series

Just Dex

Hide Bound

Wholly Trinity

New Tricks

Lost Boy

The Barn Series

Zeke & Wesley

Other Titles

The Collaborations Series

Refraction

Syncopation

Puzzles Series

Cryptic

Single Titles

Temptation Ranch

Land of Enchantment

Summit Springs Sapphic (F/F) Romance

Christmas Bizarre

Honeymoon in the Cards

www.ingramcontent.com/pod-product-compliance
Lightning Source LLC
LaVergne TN
LVHW010049110826
845155LV00028B/261

* 9 7 8 1 9 5 1 0 1 1 3 9 0 *